Nicky and the Night Owls: Part One

A Heats & Hearts Omegaverse

Sierra Cassidy

ISBN 978-1-988931-23-4 (Paperback)

ISBN 978-1-988931-24-1 (Hardcover)

ISBN 978-1-988931-22-7 (eBook)

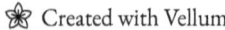 Created with Vellum

Content Notes

Nicky and the Night Owls is a polyamorous omegaverse romance. The polycule that is front and center contains alphas, betas, and omegas, and it is multi-gender, containing men, women, and nonbinary individuals. This book is also part one of a duet.

There will be graphic sexual scenes with our main character and all of the love interests, the love interests with each other, and various combinations in group activities. Consent is established and respected throughout, and the polycule is built on kindness and communication.

The omegaverse staples of knotting, purring, scents, biting, growling, heats, ruts, and bonds are all present in this story.

Some potentially upsetting content includes: slut shaming, stalking, non-fatal harm to an animal, break-and-enter of multiple homes, threat with a deadly weapon, physical violence, and brief scene at a hospital.

Kinks and sexual acts that will appear on page: masturbation, voyeurism, light bondage, overstimulation, fellatio, cunnilingus, PinV intercourse, PinA intercourse, pegging, fingering, group sex/orgy, wax play, ice play, sensation play, primal play. Mpreg and pregnancy is not present in this book, but will be present in part two.

Some notes on how Sierra's Omegaverse functions:

Omegas go into heat once or twice a year depending on the individual. Knotting and bonding only occur within the confines of an omegas heat. All omegas, regardless of sex or gender, can be impregnated. Mpreg is not present in this book, but will be present in part two.

Alphas only go into a rut (similar to an omega's heat) if they are in the presence of their bonded omega. If the alpha isn't bonded, they don't experience rut. All three of the alphas in Nicky and the Night Owls are bonded to their omega, and will experience a rut. All alphas, regardless of their sex or gender, are able to impregnate.

Bonding is a permanent and irrevocable two-way (usually consensual) connection that involves the individuals biting on the scent gland (throat, wrists, and thighs) of the other hard enough to break the skin. Only one bond per scent gland, so biting over an existing bond mark wouldn't trigger a bond so long as the original bondmate is alive. The one-way alternative is a claiming, which is not permanent. Bonding makes the individuals more in tune to the people they are bonded to, and it is functionally the same as a marriage in this omegaverse.

Healthcare and birth control are readily accessible to everyone regardless of dynamic, sex, or gender. Heat leave is provided to omegas and their partners as needed. This world is still learning things about the dynamics, bonds, and other unique things that affect the inhabitants of this omegaverse.

Chapter One
Nicky

"**N**icola," Mom tutted, filling every syllable of my name with her own special brand of disappointment.

It didn't matter that I was thirty-three because apparently the urge to shrink when your mom uses *that* tone never really goes away.

"You're never going to find anyone at this new job of yours," she continued. "You can't just work all night because you dislike people."

I bristled. It wasn't that I disliked people, it was crowds that overwhelmed me. And I damn well *could* be a night librarian for the dual purpose of spending my time with books and avoiding most of the general populace while still helping the library function. This pilot project for the city was *perfect* for me.

"Mom, leave Nick alone," Sidney, my younger brother, piped up. "She can work nights if she wants to."

1

Ah, Sidney. The family's golden boy with his new bride and charm up the wazoo. I both loved and envied him. His recent marriage to Allie had turned mom's spotlight back onto me now that he was settled, and I'd almost forgotten how exhausting that was.

Mom rolled her eyes. "You didn't get your wife because you worked nights." She gestured to the beautiful, dark-haired omega that had officially joined our family not two months earlier.

"I mean, if you want to get *technical* about it, I definitely got with her because I worked nights." Sidney grinned and gave me a cheeky salute.

Allie burst out laughing, and I couldn't help but join her. The two of them had first met while Sidney was working as a Heat Helper and nurse. He'd been Allie's chosen alpha for her first heat, which meant he'd fucked her around the clock—a fact that I did my best to ignore when I saw them. They hadn't properly gotten together until half a decade after that experience, but it had stuck, and I loved the woman who'd snared my brother.

"Mom, you know I've been dreaming of being a spinster since I was little," I said. "You're trying to crush my dreams over here."

Mom rolled her eyes again. "We balance out then because you crush my heart each time you show up alone to a family dinner."

"Luca shows up alone." I crossed my arms over my chest. Mom was always gentler with him than with me, so I didn't feel too much guilt over throwing him under the bus.

Luca shrank in his seat.

"Lulu is my baby boy and if he never finds anyone at all, that suits me fine. He can stay with us forever."

"Ouch." Sidney laughed and slapped a hand to his heart.

"Oh, hush. I always knew you'd leave me," said Mom. "You've been independent since the time you could walk."

I pushed my meatballs around in my pasta. Mom had been poking me about finding someone since I was a teen. And I had. Several someones through my late teens and twenties. Alphonse had been my longest and most recent relationship, but I'd high-

2

tailed it out of my engagement with him when he moved overseas. Mom had been heartbroken.

I hadn't had the masochistic urge to dive back into the dating pool since. I hated modern dating a bit more than I hated Mom harassing me about being single, so I'd given myself a break with it when I'd left Alphonse and adopted my cat, Spud. To her, it had been my first step to becoming a cat lady, but to me it had been the most peaceful stretch of my life thus far.

Sidney's engagement had been a blessed distraction as Mom focused on bridal showers, engagement parties, and wedding planning, but with all that out of the way, she had picked back up on the needling.

I sighed and turned to Dad, who sat quietly at the end of the table ignoring the entire conversation. He was a beta like me and the rest of our immediate family except for Sidney, who was the only alpha. Conflict of any sort had never been Dad's strong suit, and he left all the parental poking and prodding to Mom.

Sometimes I lamented my dynamic when I got to hear about the lives of alphas and omegas, but mostly I found it to be peaceful. Worrying about heats and bonds and all that sounded draining. The two-week heat leave to get fucked silly or take care of your partner did sound appealing, though.

Dad patted my hand and gave me a sympathetic look. "No shame in being a late bloomer or finding contentment in your own company."

"Her own company isn't going to give us any grandkids, Manuel," Mom snapped. "She's going to be so lonely as she gets older if she doesn't snap up someone decent now."

Dad rolled his eyes. "Give our girl what time she needs. We have three children and none of them need to have babies for us."

"*Yes*, but—"

"*Maria*." Dad's stern tone had me smiling around a mouthful of spaghetti. "You didn't like it when your parents bothered you about children, and I suspect Nicola isn't fond of you bothering her."

"I'll give you grandkids," Allie piped up. "But maybe not right this second."

I high-fived my sister-in-law. "Allie taking one for the team."

I wasn't opposed to having kids, but I tried not to think about it too hard since there was no one I wanted to have them with. No sense in getting any hopes up.

"Enough talk of babies." Dad speared a meatball and held it aloft on his fork. "I added roasted garlic to these meatballs instead of fresh, and no one has said a word about it."

I laughed quietly to myself as the conversation shifted and ignored Mom's pointed looks, eating my food while listening to the family chatter.

After dessert was finished, I escaped to the guest room to catch a couple of hours of sleep before my night shift while everyone poked through the plethora of board games my parents kept on hand for visits. I'd slept after my last shift, but I was still adjusting to my new schedule.

When I woke up, there was a heated discussion going on about the rules of Monopoly, so I turned right back around to steel myself for chaos. I loved my family, but they were *a lot* and I was peopled out for the moment, even with a solid nap.

"Patatina?" Mom poked her head into the spare room.

I smiled at the nickname. Mom had been calling me *little potato* for as long as I could remember, and I'd shared that family tradition with the cat I'd adopted by naming him Spud.

"Oh, good, you're awake. You're not hiding in here, are you?"

"Nope. Just checking my emails," I lied.

"Come, come. Your father wants to play teams and we need you to partner with Lulu."

I didn't really want to play, but Luca would get absolutely demolished without me. He was too much of a sweetheart and didn't have that ruthless energy you needed to truly trounce loved ones in friendly competition.

Smoothing down the bedhead of my dark brown hair, the same color I shared with the rest of my family, I added a couple swipes of mascara from my purse to make my equally dark brown eyes look more awake, and ventured out.

I indulged Mom until the clocks hit ten, upon which I promptly excused myself for work with hugs all around and the assurance that I'd be at the next family dinner.

The further away I drove, the more my shoulders relaxed. Family time would be so much better if Mom could filter herself, but alas.

The new community facility they'd built in my neighborhood came into view about forty minutes after I'd left my parents and I slid into the reserved staff parking. There were three other vehicles parked there, but I hadn't actually met everyone that worked the same hours that I did. There were a small handful of other vehicles scattered around the lot as well.

Nighttime had always been my favorite. The quiet of the late hours was often the only peace I'd been able to steal with two younger brothers and an opinionated mother. Now, at least, I didn't have to suffer through school after staying up all night. I'd work until seven in the morning, take myself home for breakfast/dinner, and sleep away the morning.

It was the perfect schedule.

The building was quiet inside when I arrived and made my way to the second floor library where Miranda waited for me at the desk to pass over the keys at the end of her shift. I waved and crossed the short distance to the circulation desk, tossing my purse behind the counter.

"Quiet evening?"

"Mostly. There's a couple of people hanging out on the bean bags and a pile of college students in the study rooms. Wander over every so often to make sure they're not having sex." Miranda laughed at my scrunched nose.

"I'll invest in a water gun to keep the public horniness to a minimum."

Miranda grinned and handed the keys over. "As long as you don't hit the books I'm all for it. Have a good night."

"Night." I waved Miranda off and took up my station in my own little castle.

The to-do list had me cataloging a sizable donation from an estate sale that morning and reordering the romance section after finishing. I'd get set up for that first and then do a quick round to check on the patrons.

There were six massive boxes sitting along the back counter. Upon closer inspection, only one of the boxes seemed to have been gone through, with codes and plastic cover protectors added onto the hardcovers. It was kind of hard to reorganize the section if the books weren't ready, but at least I could chill while preparing them and inputting them into the system. I hauled out an armful from the second box to get started on processing them.

A bright laugh from the back corner of the library drew my attention. I set aside my task in favor of doing a round. I checked on the students first and found them all blessedly clothed and studying. I introduced myself, then left them in peace to slip through the stacks, not seeing any other patrons on my way to the corner where bean bags and comfy chairs were set up in a reading nook.

I paused at the sound of another laugh. The sweet scents of coffee, caramel, and spices wafted toward me. Good god that smelled *delicious*. It made my heart jump and my skin tingle as the sweetness invaded my nose. I wandered closer and caught sight of two people, an alpha and a beta by the scent of them. The beta had black and purple spiral curls spilling over their shoulders, pale skin, and black lipstick, with a massive coffee table book on renaissance art spread open on the table. The alpha had locs down to their mid back, warm dark brown skin, and bright red nail polish, with a laptop in front of them. They both turned at my approach.

Oh, *damn*.

They were both way too pretty for my own good. I gave myself a half second to mentally fan myself before forcing myself to speak.

"Hi there, sorry to interrupt. I just wanted to let you know that I'll be the librarian on duty until morning. My name's Nicky.

If you need anything and I'm not at the circulation desk you can call it out."

The beta's smile was a bit dizzying. "Newbie?"

"Yeah, this is my third shift."

"Where'd Carolyn go?"

I shifted, mildly uncomfortable with the intensity of their stare. "She moved, as far as I'm aware."

The beta laughed sharply. "Good riddance. No offense if you liked her or anything. She hated us hanging out."

I quirked my head. "The entire facility is *designed* for that."

"Try telling that to Carolyn." The beta thrust their hand out. "I'm Billie Gibson. It's nice to meet you. They/them is preferred, but I won't slap you if you use she/her."

I took the offered hand with a smile. Their grip was firm and warm, sending little tingles up my arm. "Noted! And I definitely won't be chasing anyone out as long as you behave."

Billie nodded. "My silent companion is Tony." They shoved the alpha's arm.

"I was letting you talk first." Tony shoved them back with a playful grin. "Nice to meet you, too, Nicky. I'm Tony Agani. He/they for me."

I took his hand too when he offered it.

"She/her for me." I perched on the edge of the table. "You two hang out here a lot?"

"Only a few times, but with you here now, we might be reconsidering that," replied Tony.

I sucked in a little breath. Work. Focus on *work* and not how gorgeous the patrons are. "Is there anything you think the facility still needs? I can pass along suggestions to my supervisor."

Billie's blue-eyed gaze flicked over me with enough heat to make me blush. "Hiring a librarian that's as welcoming as she is pretty is the only suggestion I've got, and they knocked that one out of the park. Tony?"

"No complaints here." He appraised me with the same heat as Billie. His dark brown eyes were deep enough to drown in, and his smile spread easily across his full lips.

God.

That smile was dangerous.

I was not remotely equipped to be around this level of beautiful. I had never been particularly good at being flirted with. It made my brain spark, and then words got hard, and I tended to stare at people with panicky eyes.

Heat prickled up my spine. They were looking at me and expecting some kind of response, but my tongue was a lead weight in my mouth. I hopped up, panic making my heart pinball against my ribs.

"Work!" I blurted out. "I should, I mean...I have to...get back. To work." I spun and trotted away, merely grateful that I didn't trip in my haste and somehow embarrass myself even more.

"Come hang out if you get bored working," Billie called after me.

I tucked myself behind the circulation desk and took a deep breath. I wasn't good around hot people. Now there were two sitting in my library that looked at me like I was a snack.

It was fine.

I could focus on processing the books instead of thinking about the beautiful people...

I'd made it through an hour of half-hearted focusing when Billie appeared at my desk.

"Hey, sorry to bug you. I'm finished with my book. Do you want me to put it back on the shelf or on one of the cart thingies?"

"Oh, cart, please. I'll need to log the use for funding purposes." With Billie this close, I was able to pick out the scent that was theirs specifically. It reminded me of a chai latte or a spice cake. Their scent was warm, inviting, and more delicious than it had any right to be.

"Huh, neat." Billie leaned on the counter. "I sort of assumed it was a dick move to leave stuff for the librarians to deal with. Though, to be fair, I also thought Carolyn asked us to put stuff on the cart because she didn't trust us to put it back properly."

I laughed. "In her defense, a lot of people *don't* put stuff back properly. But it does have a purpose to leave it for us, I promise."

"Good to know." Billie looked at me through thick, dark lashes, tilting their head to the side that drew my eye to the bond mark on their throat. "Sorry if we freaked you out. I'm not great at keeping my eyeballs to myself."

I fussed with my shirt hem. "It's okay, I'm just not used to being eyeballed, I guess?"

Billie raised a manicured eyebrow. "Sounds like a lie to me. Who wouldn't want to look at a cutie like you?" They chuckled softly. "Sorry, sorry, I'm doing it again. My point is that if you want me or Tony to rein it in, we can do that. Don't want you feeling uncomfy working here, you know?"

"I appreciate that. Sorry I ran off. I kinda panicked."

"Our fault entirely." Billie smiled and tapped the stack of books I had next to me. "Whatcha working on?"

"Cataloging, at the moment. Trying to get them cleared away so the day staff has more time for programs."

Billie picked one book up off the stack, eyes scanning the back. "Oooh. These are spicy. Shy, wilting flower omega Katrina dreams of finding her alpha soulmate, but a delicious wanton beta catches her attention and leads her astray into a night of passion she won't soon forget." Billie pressed the back of their hand to their forehead in a faux-swoon. "The scandal!"

I covered my giggling with my hand. "I personally love old school romances, though I'm glad the newer ones are focusing more on betas now. And different pairings instead of only alphas and omegas."

"Oh my god, right? Betas need rep too." Billie thrust a hand into the air. "Beta pride!"

I stared at them for a moment before the hand wiggled and I realized they were waiting for a high five. I obliged with a quick slap and a laugh.

"Beta pride," I echoed.

"Tony's an alpha, but we'll forgive him for that." Billie grinned. "Have you tried out the cafe here yet?"

"Not yet."

"I'm going to head over and grab something. Do you want anything? My treat."

"Oh, no, I can't ask you to buy me something."

"You're not *asking*," Billie chided. "I'm offering. Now, what's your fave?"

"Is it weird if I ask for a chai latte?" Billie's subtle spicy scent had me craving the flavor.

Billie's gaze blazed with heat. "Nope. I have that effect on people. One chai latte coming up."

"Oh, you can't have drinks in the library."

"No worries, Books. I'll stay on the legal side of the line." Billie flashed me a grin and bounded out of the library.

I had just decided to focus back onto work when Tony appeared in my field of vision. I turned to the tall drink of water that glided towards my desk and perched on the edge to watch me."So, what prompted you to become a night librarian?"

"Combo love of libraries and night," I replied. "I couldn't apply fast enough when I saw the job go up in the library systems."

Subtle whiffs of coffee and caramel floated towards me. Damn if these two didn't smell like a gourmet coffee shop together. That gave me pause. Were they *together* together? Or were they platonic friends hanging out? Billie had a bond mark, and this close to Tony I could see one on his throat too, but that didn't mean they were each other's marks.

I couldn't ask, of course. For one, that would be invasive with strangers, and for another, it was none of my business. I hadn't started this job to date anyone. Though, that would be mildly hilarious to rub in Mom's face.

See mom, I can too find someone at my night shift job.

Billie appeared again with a cardboard tray of drinks. "Come on over, Books. You can keep eyeballs on the library from the entryway, right?"

My cheeks warmed. It would be rude to refuse since the drink had already been purchased. "Yeah, I can take a quick break."

Tony looked between the two of us and raised an eyebrow at Billie. "Books?"

"It's what she smells like," said Billie. "Those fancy old ones. Plus, ya know." They gestured to the library.

"Fair point." Tony turned back to me. "You cool with the nickname, or should I be chastising them in private?"

"Uh, I guess it's fine. It's not inaccurate."

Tony nodded. "I'll leave it for them, then. I'll call you by your name, Nicky."

His voice was smooth as melted chocolate, like velvet in my ears, and I swallowed hard. He stepped past the threshold and took his cup from Billie.

I accepted my cup in turn and hovered in the entryway with them. "You don't have to stand here with me. You can sit down somewhere."

"Standing with two beautiful betas isn't exactly a hardship." Tony gave me a mischievous smile, hiding it with a sip of his drink.

I took a nervous gulp. Sweet, spicy cream the temperature of *lava* flooded my mouth and it took every ounce of willpower to not spit it out onto the floor. I swallowed the liquid fire and huffed in some cooler air, my eyes watering. "Burned my tongue."

Billie took the cup from my hands. "Go run some cool water over it for a bit."

Embarrassment was defeated by the searing burn and I dashed off to the bathroom and cupped some cool water into my mouth.

Good job, Nicky.

I rolled my eyes at my reflection. What a great first impression I was making on my patrons. At least I was getting all the embarrassment out of the way. No need for them to think I was suave and put together only to shatter the illusion down the road.

Chapter Two
Billie

I waited impatiently for the return of my pretty librarian. True, I already had four lovers, but I'd never been able to take my eyes off of a beautiful person. Nicky had nerdy librarian written all over her, which ultimately meant I wanted to get *me* all over her, too. She had that sweet, flustered, sexy vibe that hooked me and yanked me in. Jasper had been as equally flustered when I'd met him. I dunno what it is about that whole vibe, but hot damn did it do something for me.

"What do you think?" I asked Tony.

He shrugged. "She's cute. Bit nervous, is all."

Cute.

Uh huh.

I pushed further. "I think Jasper would like her."

Tony sighed. "We've *just* met her. Slow your roll a bit."

My rolls weren't capable of being slowed. They were like a

snowball going down a hill, only getting bigger until I got smushed by them.

I huffed. "I can't help it if I get insta-crushes."

"No, I know." He smiled indulgently. "Let her know you more than an hour before you start laying it on, though."

"*Fine.*" I caught sight of Nicky returning from the bathroom, her cheeks pink and her expression sheepish. I wanted to squeeze those flushed cheeks. I flicked my gaze over her, taking in her dark brown hair that was so tidy I wanted to muss it up, soft curves tucked into chic business casual clothes, and big, brown eyes I could drown in. "You okay, Books? Do we need to amputate?"

Nicky giggled nervously. "I'll survive. Gonna let the drink cool for a bit."

"A wise choice." I handed her cup back to her. "How're you liking the job so far?"

"So far, so good. I like quiet spaces with minimal people and lots of books."

Tony hooked an arm over my shoulders and tapped his cup against Nicky's. "Not to rush out on you, but we've got to head out to pick up our boyfriend for work so he's not late."

Nicky raised an eyebrow. I thought she might ask about the *our boyfriend* portion of the statement, but she latched onto the rest instead.

"In the middle of the night? What does he do?"

"Jasper runs his own bakery," Tony supplied.

"That's so cool! Fresh baked bread is such a dream." Nicky's smile was soft, and it made me want to show up with an armful of loaves fresh out of the oven.

Good thing I was dating a baker.

"You got a favorite bread, Books?"

"Focaccia, hands down. I don't even care what kind, it's all amazing."

I stuffed down the internal surge of excitement. I was totally going to woo her with baking. She wouldn't even know what hit her.

Be calm.

Be cool.

Do *not* let the pretty librarian know you're about to implode.

Tony dropped his arm to my waist, digging his fingers in as a teasing warning. Damn, if he wasn't good at reading me.

I could be casual.

"I guess we'll see you tomorrow night if you're working," I said.

See...casual.

"I'll be here." Nicky smiled sweetly.

"Don't miss us too much." I blew her a kiss, gratified at the flush of her cheeks.

Tony led me out of the building and into the pack minivan. There were other vehicles to choose from, but this one was so convenient when you never knew how many pack members you'd end up carting around. I was always the cartee, rather than the carter. Driving gave me anxiety up the wazoo and the pack was very indulgent about not forcing me to drive when none of them minded the chore.

Tony looked at his watch. "You made it a whole hour without flirting in front of me."

"How am I supposed to *not* flirt when she has a blush like that? It's like a siren song to me."

He laughed and climbed into the driver's side, waiting until I was buckled into the passenger side before gliding out of the parking lot to head back to the house.

"I'm pretty sure it wouldn't take too many asks to get her to go on a date with you."

I grinned. "Oh, I fully intend to bribe her with bread and an invite to breakfast if the rest of the pack is cool with it. You have to tell me your vibes. You wanna go on a date with the sexy librarian?"

He smirked as we pulled up to a stop sign. "I could be persuaded pretty easily."

I pumped a hand in the air. "Fuck yeah!"

"*But* there are three others to consider, and you know how Hana is with change."

14

"Oh, damn. True. I'll cross that bridge when I get to it."

"Why do I feel like this isn't so much a case of crossing bridges as it is throwing yourself into the river regardless of a bridge?"

"Because you know me too well." I leaned across the gap in the seats to press a kiss to his cheek. "And I'm not opposed to you getting to know me even better after we drop off Jaspy at the bakery."

His coffee and caramel scent bloomed, raising goosebumps on my skin, and pulling a moan through my lips. I leaned closer, flicking my tongue over his throat.

"Don't tease me while I'm driving or I'm going to pull over and Jasper will be late to work."

My clit tingled at his words and my breath came shorter. "He's the boss. It's not like he'll get in trouble."

Tony squeezed my chin between his thumb and forefinger after pausing at another stop sign. "You're being a brat."

"I dunno why you'd expect anything else after I've been exposed to a pretty lady. My bits are all needy." I licked the thumb. "I can be fast."

Tony sighed deeply, but the corners of his mouth lifted. "Okay, but you're taking the blame if Jasper's late."

"Hey, I offered *after* the bakery. You're the one succumbing to my wiles early."

The van rolled to a stop in an empty parking lot and Tony hopped out of the driver's seat, circling the vehicle to open my door. He kissed me first, stoking all the little embers floating in my body until I was struggling to pull him closer.

"Off." He tapped my pants.

I gave a delighted squeal, popped my seat belt, and shucked the waistband of my pants to my knees, moving to scoot out to remove the rest.

"That's far enough."

I froze, looking quizzically at Tony, but he only hooked a forearm under my knees and pushed them up against my chest before pulling the seat belt around to clip it into place. He gave a sharp yank to the strap and all of my wiggle room vanished.

"Ooh, spicy Tony tonight." My laugh disappeared into a groan as Tony's palm pressed against my core. "I knew you liked her. She's got you all riled up, too."

Tony silenced me with another kiss and I surrendered as he drew a teasing finger through my slit. "You'll have to make do with some quick attention."

"Less talking, more touching." I yelped at the slap against my cunt that followed.

"*Brat.*" Tony nipped my bottom lip.

I squirmed, panting as Tony obliged me, dipping two fingers inside my already wet pussy, and twisting to rub my clit with his thumb. I let out a high pitched whine and Tony gripped the back of my neck.

"Hush, beta. You want the whole neighbourhood to know you're getting finger-fucked in a parking lot?"

"Maybe. They should know you're doing a good job." I moaned as his fingers curled. "Oh, *fuck.*"

His thumb rubbed smooth, quick circles over my clit and he covered my mouth with his to drown out the needy sounds. I bucked and squirmed, stymied by the taut seat belt that was both a pleasure and an annoyance. Sensation burst under his hand. I tensed, cunt squeezing his fingers as I came. He devoured my cry and eased me down with slowing touches and nipping kisses.

"Better?" he asked, playfully biting my ear, lingering to kiss his way down my throat and over the curve of my neck and shoulder. I turned to nuzzle my cheek on his locs, breathing in the sweet caramel notes of him.

Languid bliss settled over me. It wouldn't last long, but I wouldn't need to have him pull over again.

"For about the next ten seconds." I laughed. "Someone's gonna have to destroy me when I get home."

Tony chuckled and withdrew his fingers, sucking one clean himself and offering the other to me. I curled my tongue around the digit until I'd licked away my lingering flavor on his skin. Tony gave my cunt a light slap again and pleasure zinged through every cell. He smiled mischievously when I jumped.

He unclicked the seat belt and helped me out of the vehicle, standing in the way of potential onlookers catching a glimpse of my ass. His fingertips wandered appreciatively over my skin and I gave into the urge to let my chest rest against the van seat.

Tony growled behind me. "We don't have time for me to fuck you." Ignoring his own words, he squeezed my butt cheek and leaned over me, his hips tucked up against my butt, body enveloping me. "Quit being so tempting."

I wiggled against him, rocking my hips, teasing his already half-awake cock to full attention. His teeth on my throat stilled my movements and I shivered beneath him, fingers curling around the edge of the seat.

"Pants up," Tony whispered huskily in my ear. "Jasper's going to be texting soon if we don't get going. You and I can play more at home after."

I pouted and adjusted my clothing, standing on tiptoe to kiss him. Tony let me distract him for a few more moments with heated kisses that got me all squirmy again. He put me back on track with a smack to my ass.

"Get in the van." He stepped aside to give me space to climb into my seat.

When I'd buckled in, Tony swung my door shut and climbed back into the driver's seat, taking the final ten minutes to home with a touch of reckless speed on the empty roads.

Jasper was waiting in the driveway, half asleep with a to-go coffee cup in his hands, his lean body stuffed into a fuzzy sweater to ward off the early morning chill. His red hair was prime bedhead, but considering he kept it tucked under a hair net for the majority of his shift, he never really bothered with it. His facial hair was bordering on excessive, though I would never say that out loud. Jasper tended to go through phases with his appearance and it didn't matter what the style was, I always smiled and told him he looked gorgeous.

I rolled down the window and stuck my head out. "Jaspy! Get your butt in here."

Jasper was already trotting toward the vehicle and whipped

open the back door, leaping inside and swinging the door shut behind him.

His eyes widened, nostrils flaring.

"Holy fuck." He palmed his crotch. "A little warning next time. I'm gonna have a boner at work."

I laughed maniacally in the front seat. "I can get some traffic law violations and take care of that for you if you want."

"That would be unsafe." He sighed, leaning forward to wrap his arms around my chair and hug me from behind. "Are you late because you were fucking?"

"Seat belts," Tony demanded.

Jasper sighed again and sank back into his seat, pulling his belt on as we rolled out of the driveway to head to the bakery.

"We're late because Billie got all hot and bothered by the new librarian at the community center," Tony said.

"Tell. Me. Everything." Jasper poked my shoulders. "I need the deets."

"She's cute as a fucking button," I said, turning in my seat to face Jasper despite Tony's disapproving tongue click. "Brunette, brown eyes, wee bit taller than me. She smells like old books and nutmeg, and she turns bright red if you get flirty with her."

"Color me intrigued." Jasper toyed with his beard, looking contemplative. "And is Tony smelling like a caramel macchiato because you got spicy or because of the sexy librarian?"

Tony sighed deeply. "You two are going to give me gray hairs."

"I vote both," I said. "There's no way I'd have convinced him to pull over for shenanigans if he didn't get worked up over her first."

Jasper patted Tony's shoulder. "I want to come with you next time. If that's okay?"

Tony laid his hand over our omega's, lifting his fingers for a quick kiss. "You're always welcome, Jasper. Plus, if Billie has their way, the entire pack will be there within the week to eyeball this poor woman."

"I'm very respectful about my eyeballing." Jasper grinned.

"I have it on *very* good authority that you're *not*." Tony reached between the seats and clapped a hand onto Jasper's knee.

"That's because we're already fucking. I'm allowed to be disrespectful when I look at your cock before I put it in my mouth."

Tony choked on his laugh, and I cackled.

The phones all buzzed. I pulled mine out, seeing a notification from Gabe, and let out a huff as I read it. "Boooo. Gabe's gonna be late tonight."

"Trouble at the club?" Jasper asked.

"Probably some drunk people causing a fuss," I replied.

Jasper growled. "If he comes home with another black eye, I'm going to leave some baguettes out to go stale and bludgeon some assholes on his behalf."

"Jasper the Red Knight." I giggled. "Fighting for our honor."

"If people want to fuck with my pack they can find out how vicious this omega can be." Jasper crossed his arms.

"Anyone with half a brain cell would avoid pissing you off," I said. "I'm surprised anyone ever tries to take a swing at Gabe, but I guess that's more to do with the alcohol consumption than any kind of active choice."

Tony pulled to a stop outside of Jasper's little shop—*Go with the Dough Bakery*. It was the cutest thing, with a glowing sign featuring a tiny redhead holding a loaf of bread over his head. Jasper's dream was definitely one of my better investments.

I hopped out of the van and waited for Jasper's exit to pull him into a hug. "Have a good shift, Jaspy. And bring me home some of your rosemary focaccia, okay? I've got a pretty lady to bribe with it."

Jasper kissed me soundly and squeezed me to his chest. "I'll save the very best for you."

Our omega swept around the vehicle to kiss Tony through the open window before heading inside, and I hopped back into the van.

"Would it be weird if we went back to the library?" I asked.

"Yes. Give Nicky some space."

I pouted. "*Fine.* I'll wait until tomorrow."

"You'd think that four lovers would be enough to keep you occupied," said Tony.

"You're all more than enough," I insisted. "I love all of you to the moon and back. I dunno why I get like this."

"You've got a lot of love to give." Tony scooped up my hand as he set off for home again, kissing my knuckles. "You're also a slutty little beta who needs constant attention, and I say that with the most love possible. Besides, you were right."

"About?"

"I do kinda like her. She has good vibes, and I think Jasper will like her, too."

"Yes!" I raised our joined hands and Tony stole his back to put it on the steering wheel. "Pack trip to the library."

"You are not going to descend on that woman with the entire pack. You'll scare her off."

"Dream killer."

"Baby, I'm trying to keep your dream *alive*. I'll teach you some patience when we get home."

I grinned. "Can't wait."

Chapter Three
Nicky

The rest of my shift went by relatively smoothly, and I'd gotten enough work done that the day staff wouldn't be giving me the stink eye. It was weirdly quiet without the ambience of Billie and Tony in the background. The students were astonishingly well mannered in the study rooms, and they vacated the premises around four in the morning, so I turned on some music to compensate for the silence. I buried myself in tasks—cataloging, sorting through the donation boxes, tidying, and setting up for the morning programs—before gratefully heading home when the day staff arrived to take over.

Pushing open my apartment door, I stepped into the dark. A plaintive meow echoed. I flipped on the light and my little gray cat, Spud, trotted down the hall towards me.

"Hello there, my sweetest little baby boy!" I scooped him into my arms and kissed his head in a series of loud smooches. "Who's my prettiest boy? Did you miss mommy?"

Spud meowed and headbutted my face, purring up a storm.

"Should we have some breakfast?" I kicked off my shoes and carried Spud into the kitchen. "Wet food incoming for my very good boy."

I set Spud onto the floor and peeled open the can, scooping half of it onto his plate, nearly dumping it onto his head as he shoved himself in my way to get to it a microsecond faster. He inhaled the food with gusto while I packed up the remainder and took a portion of lasagna leftovers out of the fridge to microwave for myself.

Spud finished his meal and curled up in my lap as I sat on the couch with my own food, turning on the TV for some background noise. He sniffed all over me, curious nose wiggling.

"What's up, Spudster? You smell the people mommy hung out with tonight?"

Spud meowed and whipped his head, trying to steal a bite of lasagna as I lifted it to my mouth. I dodged him and pushed him to sit on the couch next to me.

"You had your food. Don't be greedy."

Spud huffed and sprawled across my lap, looking as cute as possible in hopes I'd change my mind and share.

I didn't.

I did, however, indulge him in some quality cuddle time. Once I'd gotten in my snuggles and finished eating, I stripped out of my work clothes and washed up for bed, making sure the blackout curtains weren't askew before sliding under the sheets. I stared up at the ceiling, willing myself to fall asleep, but my brain remained stubbornly active. With Spud curled up at my side there was only the hum of the appliances to accompany my thoughts.

I would never give Mom the satisfaction of knowing that sometimes my apartment *did* feel too lonely. If I didn't have Spud I'd have probably succumbed to Mom's many requests to set me up. Most of time I was completely fine with being single. I hated modern dating more than I hated coming home to an almost empty apartment and every time I'd tried to test if that were still true, the people I'd been matched on dating apps with went out of their way to remind me *exactly* why I preferred singledom.

Billie's pretty blue eyes and Tony's slow smile filled my head, setting my skin to tingling. I sighed. The two of them already had a boyfriend they shared. There was no reason they might want me, too. I let out a giggle at the thought of turning up to family dinner with three lovers in tow. Mom's head would probably explode.

I could still indulge myself even if I wasn't planning on dating anyone. I might not be falling into bed with the beautiful library patrons, but I could embrace a little mental inspiration. I rolled over and fished out my vibrator—a hot pink one that always got the job done—and a bottle of lube to get myself started. I let my mind wander to the infinite possibilities. The allure of being the filling in a Billie and Tony sandwich was stronger than I was comfortable admitting so soon after meeting them.

The first zing of the vibrations against my clit had me biting my lip. I teased myself slowly, eyes closed, letting my thoughts wander to hot goth betas and sexy alphas. One hand slid over my breast, the other pressing the toy into my pussy with an easy glide that had me arching off the bed with a low moan. Imaginary hands ghosted over my skin and I moved the toy in a steady rhythm, dipping my hand under the blankets to work my clit in time with the thrusts. I rolled my hips, breath panting.

Almost there.

I shivered, touching the bright, fleeting edge of pleasure. Spud tackled my hands and I let out a shriek, panic-flailing, the toy whipping in one direction and Spud sailing through the air as I jolted up. I scrambled out of bed and gathered up my baby boy who was looking at me with betrayal in his eyes.

"Spuddy, I'm so sorry. You scared the shit out of me."

A knock sounded and I hastily tossed on a robe. I peeked through the peephole, swinging open the door a moment later.

"Hey Mrs. Poppadakis. Can I help you?"

"Kiki, dear, I heard you scream." My senior, widowed neighbor stood in the hall, concern pinching her face.

I smiled at the nickname even through my discomfort. She'd misheard my name at our first meeting, and it had become something of an inside joke and endearment between us.

"You're usually so quiet," she continued. "I wanted to make sure you were okay."

"Yeah, sorry." My cheeks warmed. "Tripped over Spud."

"Little troublemaker." Mrs. Poppadakis laughed. "Good thing he's cute."

As if on cue, Spud appeared at my ankles.

"Hello little man." Mrs. Poppadakis leaned down to pat his head. "I'll get out of your hair. Have a lovely day, dear."

I waved and slunk back into my apartment, rolling my eyes at Spud. "You little mood killer."

Spud looked completely unabashed.

I sighed and wandered to my bedroom, finding the vibrator between the wall and bedside table. I gave up on satisfaction for the moment and went to wash the toy, laying it on a washcloth on the sink to dry, and retreated into bed.

Spud headbutted me awake hours later when his hunger got the best of him.

I whined and buried my face in my pillow. Spud meow-screamed to protest his lack of immediate attention. I held a hand up for him to rub his face on and focused on working up enough energy to pry myself off the bed.

"Spuddy, mommy's tired. Evolve some opposable thumbs and feed yourself."

He nipped my hand.

"Jeez, okay. I'm getting up." I groaned and shuffled into the kitchen. Sunlight streamed in through the window. I glanced at the clock on the stove. It was only two in the afternoon which meant I'd had barely six hours of sleep. Not enough for a coherent Nicky.

I dumped the rest of Spud's food onto his plate and slumped back to bed. "Fuck this. More sleep."

I passed out for another two hours and woke to my phone insistently buzzing. I answered it without looking.

"Hey."

"Nicola, I found a date for you."

I groaned. "Mom, no."

"If you found your own dates I wouldn't have to find them for you."

I let out a pitiful sound and sat up, rubbing my eyes. "I'm working on it."

"Oh?" Mom's voice was bright and curious.

Fuck.

"Uh, yeah. I have a date planned with someone already."

"And you didn't tell me?!"

"Well, it was two in the morning and you were asleep, so no."

"When do I get to meet them?"

Shit.

Backtrack!

Run away!

Deflect!

"Let me go on an actual date first."

"When is that happening?"

"Oh nooo, Spud needs me. Gotta go, I love you, byyye!" I hung up and buried my face in my hands. "Fuck me."

I distracted myself with laundry and chores until it was time to get ready for work again. Billie and Tony were going to be there and somehow that made me nervous. I took a few extra minutes on my hair, chose a cap sleeved blouse with a little flounce, and added gold star earrings. It was enough to look a bit more polished, but not so much that it would look like I was actually *trying* to look cuter.

Spud got extra cuddles and a full serving of food to munch while I was at work.

"Be a good boy, okay?"

Spud looked at me, eyes full of innocence, like he'd never done a thing wrong in his whole entire life. We both knew that was lies.

25

I made kissy sounds as I closed the door and rode the elevator to the main floor and zipped off to the library.

Miranda was waiting at the circulation desk when I walked in.

"Three's company tonight at the bean bags," Miranda said. "And the board game tournament down the hall is still going strong so you'll probably see some of them by morning."

"Sounds good. Have a nice night." I waved my coworker off after accepting the keys and dropped my purse behind the desk.

Billie was trotting over when I looked up again. They were as gorgeous as yesterday, dressed this time in black denim shorts over fishnets, combat boots, and a black sequined tank top. I shoved down the little spiral of desire that swirled under my skin.

"You're here!" Billie grinned and leaned onto the desk, crossing their forearms.

Their excitement over *me* made my stomach flip.

"Jasper's here tonight. Do you want to meet him?"

"Yeah, of course. Let me check my task list first so I don't miss anything time sensitive."

I only panicked a teensy tiny bit that they'd brought their boyfriend to meet me. What did that *mean?* It shouldn't mean anything. They were only being friendly.

Oh, god.

Okay.

Focus, Nicky.

Billie tapped their dark purple nails on the desk while they waited. The evening staff had gotten through the rest of the donated books which meant I was on task to get them on the shelves.

"Don't laugh when you see him, okay?" Billie's gaze was soft. "Jaspy is going through a *phase* with his facial hair and we're trying to be supportive."

"That's sweet. Everyone deserves to experiment with their self expression." I wasn't sure what Jasper could possibly look like that would make me laugh at him. I locked my purse in one of the desk drawers and looped the key around my wrist. "Okay, ready."

Billie took my hand the moment I was in range and the easy

affection had my cheeks heating. I followed along to their usual hang out spot, seeing two figures with their heads tucked together and watching something on a phone.

Billie's fingers dug into my arm as we approached, and I reminded myself not to laugh just in case. Jasper turned toward me. I took in his fluffy mop of red hair and the most ostentatious mustache I'd ever seen on someone in real life. He looked like an old timey ringmaster, complete with the ends curled into full circles.

His face brightened, and he stood with a smooth grace, walking over with his hand extended. "You must be the famous Nicky."

I took his warm hand and was instantly caught in a cloud of chocolate, cinnamon, and baking bread. He smelled like a fresh chocolate croissant, and I wanted to bury my face against him. His eyes were a warm brown, like a cup of tea in sunlight.

My tongue tangled, and I swayed towards him before I caught myself. I bit down on a whine as I went to greet him.

"Famous?" I managed.

Jasper lifted my hand and kissed the back of it, lips lingering an extra beat. "Mhmm. Billie hasn't shut up about you."

My heart needed to stop its ridiculous pitter-pattering *right now*. No one had ever kissed me on the hand in a romantic way. Not that this was romantic...I was just meeting the boyfriend of the very pretty library patrons.

I glanced over to the beautiful goth beta that held my other hand. They didn't seem the least bit embarrassed by Jasper's statement.

Billie shrugged. "We've all accepted my obsessive tendencies. I apologize for nothing."

Jasper laughed and released my hand. "I've got a present for you."

"A *present*?" I squeaked.

Tony appeared behind him with a small tote bag in his hands.

"Hey, Nicky." He smiled and it made my stomach flip again.

Damn them all for being so beautiful and smelling delicious. How was I supposed to be a normal person around them?

Tony passed over the bag.

"Billie insisted," said Jasper.

The beta freed up my hand so I could open my gift. Inside was a slab of focaccia wrapped in plastic.

"Oh my god."

"It's fresh too," Jasper said. "I brought the dough from work and made it when I woke up."

"Can I eat some now? Would that be weird? I'm not supposed to eat in the library."

Jasper laughed softly. "I won't tell anyone."

I danced in place and unwrapped one corner of the plastic, biting into it with enthusiasm. My eyes nearly rolled back in my head as the bready perfection filled my mouth.

"Oh my *god*." I hugged the bread to my chest. "I'm in love."

My three companions laughed and Jasper swung his arm over my shoulders. "I like this one. She's good for my ego."

Billie snuggled up to us, making me dizzy from the proximity. Other scents lingered among their group that I couldn't place. Tea, mint, brown sugar. I wasn't sure who they belonged to, but I liked them.

"You two are going to get Nicky in trouble at work. Give her some space." Tony nudged Billie and Jasper away.

"Who would even know?" asked Billie.

"There's security cameras," I said. "I won't get in trouble for talking to the patrons, especially if it's for a specific purpose, but I'd be nervous being so new to the job if they thought I was bringing friends to waste paid time."

"Well, in *that* case," said Jasper, "do you think you could help me find some cookbooks?"

Bless him for giving me a work-related task. *That* I could do.

"Oh, absolutely. Let me just put my focaccia on the desk and we'll find you some good ones."

"We'll be at the bean bags," said Tony, pulling Billie along with him. "You two have fun."

I pushed away the quiet urge to tuck myself back into Jasper's arms to breathe in his scent, and slotted him into a mental box. He was a patron of the library. I could handle that.

Setting my bread out of the way, I turned to Jasper and led him over to nonfiction, winding through the stacks to the cooking section. "Anything in particular you're looking for?"

"Well, I'm mostly here for the company to see what all of Billie's fuss was about. But for the sake of you not getting into trouble, I'd love to see something that highlights recipes I probably haven't tried."

"A tall order when I have no idea how adventurous you are."

Jasper's eyes flashed with mischief. "As adventurous as you'd like."

My mouth went dry. I tucked Jasper back into my mental patron-box. I should have done that with Billie and Tony, but I wasn't always as swift on the uptake as I needed to be. At least I hadn't masturbated over Jasper, yet.

"Oh, actually I saw a couple neat ones when I was poking around the other day." I pulled out one text on Uzbek cuisine and another on Ghanaian. "Are those okay?"

He reached for them. "I see bread on the cover and that's good enough for me."

Relieved, I leaned against one of the shelves. "Billie said that you run a bakery?"

Jasper lit up. "You heard correctly."

I indulged myself in a few minutes of chatting with Jasper about baked goods. I may not know about the finer points of the business, but I was no stranger to delicious treats, and Jasper seemed more than happy to talk about his work.

At a lull in the conversation, I sighed. "I should get to my overnight tasks so my coworkers don't hate me in the morning."

"Understandable." He winked. "Come hang out when you have time, yeah?"

"I'll try to squeak some time," I promised.

The three of them let me work in peace for the first two hours of my shift, but it felt *weird* to know they were there and I wasn't nearby. I hauled the romance section around, making room to slot in the new authors and series we'd acquired. Every so often I'd catch a whiff of spices or chocolate or caramel, and I'd have to forcibly pull my focus away from them. I wasn't usually this pathetic. Though, to be fair, most people didn't smell that delicious.

I'd rearranged half the section by the time Billie wandered over.

"Hey, Books." Billie grinned and leaned against the shelves, purple curls falling over their shoulders. "I dunno how to be any way but how I am, so I'm gonna ask you an awkward question if that's cool?"

"Um, sure?"

"What're the odds you'll let me take you out for breakfast at the end of your shift?"

My heart kicked my ribs so hard I struggled to pull in a breath and my blood hummed with the bucket of adrenaline just dumped into it. "On a..."

"Date, yeah."

My gaze flicked in the direction of where Tony and Jasper were.

"But, what about—"

"They're cool with it. The whole pack knows I've got a giant crush and they're pretty chill about me dating when I have the rare inclination. They all met each other because of me thirsting over everyone, so they've learned to trust my thirsty judgement."

I could hardly think past the roar of my pulse in my ears.

"Did I turn your brain off?" Billie asked.

"A *bit*." I laughed.

"I know the pack thing kinda throws people off sometimes, but Jasper and Tony both like you, and the others will too."

"*Others?*" I choked out. "How many people are involved here?"

"Five, including me. Six if you say yes to a date, though the date is only with me unless you want someone else to join us."

My head swam. "I don't know how any of this works."

Packs weren't uncommon, but I had never personally met anyone in one. That I knew about, at least. It wasn't like people went around carrying signs that announced their relationship set ups.

"Ignore the complexity for a minute." Billie took my hand, and I squeezed the anchor gratefully. "Does breakfast with me sound good?"

I nodded.

"Cool. Then we can go from there. You just focus on aaall this," Billie said, gesturing to their whole body. "I don't know how to be subtle. You're cute as fuck and I'm excited to take you out."

I giggled, every bit of me flushed with warmth. I buried my face in my hands. "Oh god, I'm bad at compliments."

"Don't worry. I'll desensitize you to them in short order." Billie nudged me playfully. "Jaspy is already talking about baking lepyoshka and sugar bread thanks to your books."

"I would turn into a little ball if I had a boyfriend that baked. I have no self control with fresh bread and it goes straight to my butt."

Billie laughed, very unsubtly checking out my posterior. "Just more of you to love."

I grinned. "Honestly, this is kinda opportune timing."

"Oh?"

"I lied to my mom today about having a date so she wouldn't make me go on some godawful setup."

"Someone's naughty. Lying to your mama. Tsk. *But* I suppose since I've negated the lie, it's fine. Nice to have a parent that's interested at least."

I contemplated asking more about that, but Billie was already moving right along and asking for help finding some books on famous beta artists. We found a thick tome with artists separated out by their dynamic and Billie hauled it back to their hangout spot.

Tony hadn't asked for any books, and was sitting at a laptop, typing away when I came over to let them know I was going to be running the vacuum.

"What're you working on?" I asked him.

Tony glanced up. "Copyediting a novella for a client. It's much more fun than my usual work of copyediting political paperwork."

"That's so cool! I definitely want to hear more on my next break."

The floors weren't going to clean themselves. I had a few chores on my list to keep them off the plate of the day and evening staff. Most of the programming was relegated to day and evening, leaving the nights for staying organized, tidying, and setting up programs for the morning. There was something so soothing about making sure everything was in order. Chores at home were less fun, but doing them here felt like much less of a Sisyphean ordeal.

Billie popped up while I was lost in my own thoughts, swishing the vacuum over the carpet. I leapt away, hand to my chest, when I finally noticed them hovering. I flipped the switch on the vacuum and stood it up.

"Sorry, you scared me. What's up?"

"We're taking Jaspy to work now. I'll come back at seven. That's when you get off, right?"

I nodded, feeling a little breathless at the prospect. "Yep."

"Perfect." Billie's wide smile had my stomach flipping. "See you in the morning, Books."

Chapter Four

Jasper

The first few minutes inside *Go with the Dough* were always peaceful. I was too used to chaos so it never lasted for long before I had to disturb it. That usually involved classic rock going full blast. I tucked my hair and beard behind hair nets and got to work sanitizing the workspaces and doing a quick eyeball inventory to make sure everything was organized for the day. Yan and Rita would arrive any minute to help me get started on the absolutely monstrous amount of dough we needed to run the bakery.

It was mostly a consistent menu with our core items being prepared every day, but, for the sake of my enjoyment, we had a mini menu that changed daily so I could mix things up. Today that meant pizza scones and caramel apple cinnamon rolls.

Yan pushed through the back door of the bakery, his white-blond hair neatly slicked back. "Morning, boss."

"Morning, Yan. The croissants are calling your name. We've got that catering order being picked up at eight."

"The croissants can wait two damn minutes." Yan laughed and hung up his coat. I focused back onto my own dough as Yan got washed up and ready, disappearing into the cooler to collect the slabs of butter and dough for the two hundred croissants he needed to make between the order and the bakery's regular sales.

Yan was a pastry wizard and loved all the finicky technical items at the bakery, which was fine by me. I could make them all well enough myself, but I preferred the more rustic items—scones and peasant breads—over the fussy stuff.

"Good mooorning, bakery buddies!" The door swung open again and Rita popped inside, brown curls wrestled into a bun, and hot pink lipstick accenting her mouth.

"Morning, babe." I waved a floury hand at her.

Rita handled the sweeter items at the bakery—muffins, cinnamon rolls, banana loaf, and danishes. It was a good system between the three of us, each having our favorites and being allowed to focus on them. She got straight to work after washing up. I focused on my bread recipes, mixing the ingredients with delicate care and getting each batch into the proofer with a timer set before moving onto the next.

The bakery was a buzzing hive of activity, the three of us moving around one another with practiced ease. Music kept us company through the early hours. We didn't need to talk much to stay on target after a solid four years of working together.

I danced in place at my station, pulling another batch of dough out of the mixer and getting it ready for the proofer. Everything smelled of yeasty dough and butter.

It was my happy place.

Beautiful, delicious chaos.

Rita carried over a massive bowl of scone dough and set it on my station. "All yours, boss."

I divided it up into thirds and got the savory scones going while Rita did the sweet ones. It was a meditation for me, but better than trying to sit and focus because I got to eat the results and make people happy with food. Most people walked into the bakery and left without eating their purchase, so those moments when I got to see people enjoy what I made—like Nicky gushing over my focaccia—were precious and always reinforced why I did this job.

The bell above the front door jingled, and I turned toward the sound, reaching up to turn down the radio. It was still a couple of hours until we opened, which meant it was one of my pack coming to bother me. With love, of course.

I wiped off my hands and went up front. Gabe gave me a tired smile, his hazel eyes exhausted as he held up a cardboard carrier with four to-go cups nestled in it. His leather jacket was undone and his dark stubble was so perfectly sexy I wanted to pull him into my office and lock the door.

"Hey, beautiful." I tugged off my hair nets, pulled off my apron, and slipped around the counter and into his arms. I was a tiny bit taller than him, but it didn't stop me from slouching down to bury my face against his throat, inhaling the scent of fresh steeped black tea and brown sugar. There was a burnt edge to the sugar, and it mellowed with each little kiss I pressed to his skin.

I stepped back to steal one from his lips too and ruffled his already messy brown hair.

"You're going to make me spill the drinks." Gabe wrapped his free arm around my waist and gave me one more kiss.

I indulged him, nudging us toward the counter, and he set down the drinks. "What tea did you bring me today?"

"Jasmine, peach, and mixed berry." Gabe lifted two of the other cups out of the carrier and set them on the counter, leaning over to call into the kitchen space. "Yan, Rita, I've got your coffees."

"Spoiling them," I teased.

"I have to take care of the ones who prevent you from working twenty hour shifts."

Yan and Rita trotted up to the front, discarding their hair nets and moving into the shop area to have their drinks.

"Fifteen minute break," I told them. "I'm taking Gabe to the office to sit down."

I pulled him along with me, and he grabbed his own cup, following after me. I closed the office door behind us and flipped the lock.

"How was work?" I asked him.

"Ugh. A very drunk alpha came from one of the other clubs with his friends and tried to trespass. I'm getting too old for this job."

"Wanna de-stress?" I set my drink down on my desk and turned him to sit on the edge, tucking myself between his knees.

"Please."

I pulled him close and purred, stroking a hand through his hair and down his back as he relaxed against me. My sweet alpha. He worked so hard making sure the omegas and betas at the club he was a bouncer at were safe. There was bruising around one of his eyes from a previous altercation that he'd covered with makeup, but knowing it was there made my blood boil.

Gabe's hands settled on my waist and he sighed deeply. He lifted his head, one eyebrow raised in question. "Why do you smell like books?"

"Billie's new obsession. I saw her tonight."

"Oh, yeah. I forgot about that." Gabe lifted the hem on my shirt and rubbed my hip bones with his thumbs. "You want to get frisky before you go back to work? I bet I can beat my record."

"I should be the one trying to break the record here. You had the shitty shift. You deserve some *special* attention."

"Flip for it?" Gabe laughed. "Heads for you, tails for me."

"To give or receive?"

"Making me think of everything." Gabe pulled me down by the collar of my shirt. "Heads, you get on your knees for me. Tails, we see how quiet you can be so your coworkers don't know you have your dick down my throat."

I swallowed hard, pulling my phone out of my pocket and holding down the button. "Flip a coin."

A computer generated one danced across the screen and came

36

up heads. I set the phone aside and peeled off my shirt, hanging it on the hook behind the door.

"Stripping for me?" Gabe leaned back on the desk, lounging comfortably.

"Avoiding cross-contamination. Just a happy coincidence that it involves stripping." I tugged open his jeans while I devoured his perfect mouth and breathed in the warm caramel notes of his scent. Dropping to my knees, I looked up at him. "Try not to be too loud. I don't need Yan and Rita knowing I use the office to fuck around."

"Heaven forbid."

Gabe's hazel eyes were alight with fire, burning brighter still as I took his cock in my hand and slid my tongue along the underside. His breath hissed, and he bit his lip, threading one hand into my hair. I teased soft licks over the tip, gliding my fist over the shaft.

If I weren't on the clock I'd have taken my time with him until he was cursing and bucking down my throat with reckless abandon. Alas, I had precious few minutes to take away from my tasks. I sank onto his cock, bobbing head and hand to the beat of his sharp breaths. Consistency was the name of the game to get him off quick. I maintained my pace with a ruthless efficiency, his thick cock cutting off my air with each descent. His grip pulled my hair with the perfect tension to make me melt.

"*Jasper.*" Gabe growled my name, low and quiet.

It was the only warning he gave before clapping a hand over his mouth to silence himself and pushing on my head to take him deeper. He poured down my throat, hot and slightly salty sweet. I swallowed each drop and kept up my rhythm until he yanked my hair, lifting my face to slide himself out of my mouth.

My cock was protesting its confinement, pressing against the seam of my pants with a vengeance.

"Against the wall, omega. Facing me."

I obeyed quickly and pressed my bare back against the cool surface.

Gabe dropped to his knees, not even bothering to tuck his cock back into his pants.

"We only have three minutes." I bit down on the whine that tried to climb free. If we were home I wouldn't have to worry about being quiet, but I didn't want to make things weird for my staff.

"You doubt I can get you off in that amount of time?"

I pressed my lips together and shook my head. Omegas were easy to set off. A perk of our biology that had led to me getting extra talented with my mouth and hands so my partners didn't miss out.

"Good." Gabe wrestled my pants out of the way and swallowed back my cock with a practiced ease that obliterated every thought in my head. His hot, wet mouth suctioned on and a hand pressed between my legs, his thumb applying pressure to a spot I'd never been able to replicate on my own. It buckled my knees, but Gabe pressed me harder against the wall. He worked his hands and mouth like fucking magic, unraveling me.

I came without warning after only a few strokes and I bit my arm to keep myself silent. My lover kept up the smooth glide of his tongue, drinking me down as I helplessly bucked against his mouth.

Gabe grinned up at me as he pulled away, licking his lips. "I think we *both* set a new record."

"Coming fast isn't generally something people are proud of," I muttered.

"I can be proud when I made it happen." He stood slowly and pinned me against the door. Gabe kissed me fiercely as he tucked me back into my pants and did them up for me. "And you can be proud you snuck in some satisfaction for both of us on a very short break."

I hummed softly and wrapped my arms around his neck. "You're terrible in the best way possible."

"You love it."

"I do." I kissed him once more.

"I should get breakfast back to everyone," Gabe said. "What are you sending me home with?"

"Definitely the caramel apple cinnamon rolls. They should just be coming out of the oven."

"Sounds perfect." Gabe helped me get dressed again, and led me out back into the kitchen where I checked the timer to confirm. There were only ten seconds left on it, so I turned it off and pulled the steaming pan out of the oven. They would still need time to cool so I got Gabe to rest with his tea while I flipped the cinnamon rolls and let them rest for a few minutes before boxing some up for him.

I sent him home with the steaming buns, kissing him good-bye, and finally settled back into work. That bread wasn't going to bake itself.

Chapter Five
Nicky

B y the end of my shift I was a bundle of nerves. Every time someone new arrived at the library I nearly jumped out of my skin expecting it to be Billie. After the tenth person, it finally was. They showed up at exactly seven, right as the day librarians were pushing me out the door.

"Morning, Books." Billie grinned at me. Their lips had a fresh coat of black lipstick and their purple curls were tied into two braids.

My heart did an excited flip. "Good morning. Where are we going for breakfast?"

"I know this great little bistro a few minutes away. I hope you don't mind driving, Tony dropped me off."

"No, not at all. Lead the way. Do you not like driving?" I asked, curious.

"I hate it, always have. I can do it in a pinch, but the pack never makes me except for refresher lessons each summer."

Billie and I left the library together, heading into the parking lot to where my car waited for us. "I don't blame you for not enjoying it. Driving has never been my favorite, just a necessity."

They directed me through the streets and we parked in front of a tiny little hole in the wall bistro. The sign hanging above it had loopy text and a cartoon chef.

"I know it doesn't look like much, but the food here is incredible."

We were seated quickly since it was still very early, though there were a few tables occupied already. Our server came by and I ordered a cup of mint tea so that the caffeine wouldn't keep me up all hours.

"I usually get eggs Benedict when I go out for breakfast. Should I get that or is there something specific you'd recommend here?" I asked.

"You enjoy your eggs benny. I'm going to get the stuffed French toast and you are more than welcome to steal some bites."

The server took our orders when she returned with our drinks. Billie had gotten a fruit smoothie and took a long, noisy swig of it.

"So, tell me about the pack?" I asked. "I know there's you and Jasper and Tony, and two others, right?"

"Yep. Hana and Gabe, too. Both alphas. Hana's basically a goddess—tall, strong, could definitely bench press you—and she works as a personal trainer running sunrise boot camps and classes. She's kind of intense, not a huge fan of big changes, and super loves her alone time. Hmm, what else? Hana's not *quite* our leader since we're a very egalitarian pack, but she does make sure all the bills are paid on time and keeps us organized."

"I can relate on the loving alone time," I said. "I feel like a sunrise boot camp might end me."

Billie giggled. "You and me, both."

Hana sounded intriguing, if a tiny bit scary. "What about Gabe?"

"Gabe is our chill alpha. He works as a bouncer and is really sweet, very go with the flow kind of energy. Basically the opposite of me for vibes." Billie laughed.

"Do you all work overnight then? Sunrise training, bouncer, baker—those are all off daytime hours."

"Oh, yeah, we're pretty nocturnal. We coordinated our sleep schedules so that we can spend the most amount of awake hours together."

"That's so handy. How long have you all been a pack?"

"Jasper and I met in university when we were taking the same business class. That was almost a decade ago, now. He and I started dating Tony three years after that. A year after that we met Hana and Gabe, then all moved in together. So I guess about six years for all five of us being together."

"Wow! I feel outclassed." I laughed. "My longest relationship was two years."

"No sense wasting time on a relationship that doesn't suit you," Billie said.

"That's fair. So, the pack is all okay with you going out with me? How exactly do I fit into all of this?"

Billie picked up my hand, boldly nuzzling the scent gland on my wrist and pressing a soft kiss there that had a full body shiver rolling through me.

"You fit into it exactly how you want to fit into it. That's the beauty of our situation," Billie said. "If you just want to hang out with me, that's cool. And if you want to include some or all of the others, that's cool, too. Obviously, you'd still have to meet Hana and Gabe, but that's not hard."

My head spun at the idea. "Sorry, this is all kind of new to me. I haven't dated much in general for a while, and I've never dated multiple people."

They rubbed their thumb in circles over my wrist and it took a considerable effort to not squirm in my seat.

Billie took another sip of their smoothie, watching me with a mischievous gleam in their eyes. "Try not to think about it too hard. You approach this one person at a time. Right now you're just on a date with me so you can worry about the others later."

I took my hand back to add a splash of milk into my tea and took a long drink to collect myself. At least this time it wasn't so hot it burned my tongue. "I guess that's fair. Tell me about *you*, then."

"You first," Billie insisted. "You're hoarding all the knowledge and I want to learn about you, too. Tell me fun Books facts! Favorite food, color, animal, and hobby. Go!"

I laughed. "Okay, um, anything Italian is my fave since that's what I grew up with, but specifically I love stuffed shells the most. Favorite color is purple, I love cats, and reading is my biggest hobby, though I'm sure that's not a surprise considering I work in a library."

Billie leaned on their elbows, watching me expectantly. "What else?"

"I'm bad at fun facts. Um, I'm the oldest kid, two younger brothers, ten million cousins scattered over the country and back in Italy. I'm thirty-three, and I've been a librarian for about eight years now. Your turn again."

"What do you want to know? I don't personally think I'm that exciting."

"Everyone's exciting in their own way," I insisted.

"Well, for starters I'm twenty-nine. I don't really have a consistent job, but I do love painting and pottery."

"You never found anything you liked? What did you go to business school for?"

"That was just for fun. At one point I thought I would work at the family business," they wilted a little, shrinking down in their seat, "but...they're not such a fan of me making my own way in the world. They don't like the pack either. I was supposed to marry some hoity-toity asshole for a business deal for them. Spoiler alert, I didn't do that, so now I'm disowned, but sort of in a good way."

My heart squeezed. "There's a *good* way to be disowned?" I reached over automatically and Billie let me take their hand.

"Kinda. I get the benefit of the cash without having to see the people who don't think that I'm worth anything. My grandparents set me up well prior to their passing, and there were some strict stipulations that kept my parents away from my inheritance. I have enough stocks for voting power in my grandparents company so my parents can't get rid of me entirely. I haven't seen them since before the pack moved in together."

"Wow. I couldn't even imagine. They don't deserve you," I said firmly. I was curious what exactly their family did if they were trying to arrange marriages for business deals. That sounded like big money to me, but I didn't feel right asking.

Billie squeezed my hand and gave me a soft smile. "Thanks, Books. Didn't mean to get so heavy for a first date."

"You're absolutely fine. I'm so sorry your family doesn't appreciate you. Mom drives me crazy sometimes, but I know she means well. I'm so used to seeing my parents all the time."

"That's nice, though. I definitely don't begrudge people having good relationships with their parents, it's just not something I have." Billie fussed with their straw. "The pack makes up for it a lot and most of them have decent relationships with their families. Jasper's moms have always liked me."

The server arrived with our food and we took a few minutes to tuck into it. Billie watched me with a pleased expression as I shoved a too-big bit of eggs Benedict into my mouth. It's always been one of my favorite breakfasts, but it's a pain in the ass to make myself so I always leave it for restaurants to handle. Hollandaise sauce is the food of the gods, I swear. This place made it extra buttery.

"I'm in love."

"Right? You want a bite of my French toast, Books?"

"Yeah, I'd love to try some. Do you want some of my benny?"

"Fuck yeah! Bite trade."

Billie assembled the perfect bite onto their fork and held it out for me to eat. Their French toast was stuffed with strawberries and cream cheese topped with yet more strawberries, whipped cream, and syrup. The sweet flavor exploded on my tongue.

"I think I'm going to get a sugar high just from this one bite. It's so good."

"I pretty much live in a state of sugar high." Billie chuckled.

I couldn't help but giggle. They were so cute with their bright smiles and easy laugh.

I gathered up the perfect bite of benny and fed them like they'd fed me, tidying a smear of hollandaise from the corner of their mouth with my thumb. Billie's gaze ignited when I licked the sauce away.

We chatted through the meal, and it was surprisingly a lot easier than I was anticipating. Whenever I struggled to come up with something to say, Billie was right there to fill in the space, or give me a chance to think by focusing on their food.

My stomach regretted my exuberance by the time we were finished eating. I patted my food baby and leaned back contentedly. "I'm not going to have to eat for a week."

"Cannot relate." Billie laughed. "I'm pretty sure I'm always hungry. I eat my three squares, plus snacks, no matter how much food is involved in any of them."

I giggled. "You need all that energy to keep up with socializing. Maybe that's my problem. I just need to eat more."

"More snacks are always a good idea." Billie nodded. "Could I entice you on a walk?"

"I can be enticed into most things when I've been well fed."

Billie winked. "Good to know."

Chapter Six
Billie

I'd lost count of how many times I'd made the cute-ass librarian laugh over breakfast and our walk afterwards. She let me hold her hand the whole time, and her cheeks were perma-pink.

We passed a tiny florist on our way back to the car and I pulled her to a stop, dragging her inside.

"What are we doing?" she asked.

"Pretty girls deserve flowers," I stated. "How do you feel about sunflowers?"

"I love them, but you don't have t—"

I pressed a finger to her lips. "I want to get you a gift that's as bright and beautiful as you."

Nicky sucked in a sharp breath. I slid my hand to the side, cupping her cheek, and she angled towards my wrist, breathing in the subtle mix of Gabe's scents overlaying mine on the bond mark there. "Okay."

I picked her out a bunch of mini sunflowers in a fat purple pot, and she cradled them to her chest as we walked back to her car. We paused next to it when we arrived.

"Do you..." Nicky fidgeted, kicking the ground with her toes, "...want to come over for some tea or coffee?"

A cozy warmth filled my chest. Being invited over seemed like an excellent sign, regardless of what intentions she might have. "You bet your sweet ass I'd love to come over for anything you have in mind."

Her shoulders dropped down from her ears, and she gave me a shy smile. She clicked the auto-locks on her car for us both to get in. I slid into the passenger seat and chattered at her for the short drive to her apartment. The place was a bit older than I'd expected, but it seemed to be in decent repair as we rode the elevator up.

"You don't hate cats, do you?" she asked as we paused outside of her door.

"Heck no. I love kitties."

"Okay, good. I forgot to mention Spud. He's usually not too bad with strangers." She unlocked the door and a ball of gray floof came galloping towards us. He skidded to a stop and looked at me warily.

"Hey there." I crouched down and held out my hand for him to sniff. "Who's a handsome boy?"

He sniffed all over my fingers, eventually deciding I was acceptable when he shoved his face into my palm.

"Oh my goodness! Hello, little prince. It's very nice to make your acquaintance."

Cat acceptance has been a main goal in my life ever since I first learned what a cat was, but Nicky's cat specifically liking me was a definite perk for my wooing goals.

I turned to Nicky. "How does he feel about being picked up?"

Her eyes were all sparkly as she looked down at us. "He's good about it."

"Aww yeah." I scooped him straight into my arms and he relaxed happily, head butting my chin. "I have been blessed."

Nicky giggled and leaned in to pet her cat. "Spuddy, did you make a new friend?"

Spud didn't answer; not that I expected him to.

"Are you going to give me the grand tour?" I asked.

"There's not much to see. It's just a one bedroom apartment."

"Yes, but it's *your* apartment. Show me what makes it special to you."

We removed our shoes, and Nicky got the kettle going so it could warm while she walked me around. She showed me the little knick knacks she'd gotten on trips and framed photos of her family, including pictures of her brother's recent wedding. The whole place was decorated in cool tones with purple seeming like the main theme that tied most of it together, which made sense since she'd told me it was her favorite color.

Nicky was comfortable here, even more so than when I'd gotten her giggling at the restaurant or on our walk. I was pleasantly surprised at how chatty she was once I got her into story-mode, and Spud sat happily in my arms while I listened to his mama tell me about a trip to Italy as a teen to meet some distant relatives.

"I haven't been to Italy since I was little, but I would totally love to go again. Your family sounds cool."

"They are most of the time," she agreed. With the story over, she lapsed back into her sweet shyness, and I was already craving nudging her back into comfort. But first, I needed to pee.

"Do you mind if I use your bathroom?"

"Nope. Go right ahead."

I passed Spud to her and trotted off to the bathroom. I stopped short, seeing the hot pink vibrator sitting out on the sink. Before teasing Nicky about it, I did my business and washed up, wiping off my black lipstick so I wouldn't smear it all over her, and found her staring in horror as I stepped back out.

"Did you...Um. Did you see...?"

"The neon vibe? You bet your ass I did." I laughed at her

48

stricken expression. "Don't worry, Books. You should see *my* collection."

Nicky fidgeted adorably and couldn't quite meet my gaze.

A devilish thought passed through my brain. "Are you embarrassed just because it's a vibe or because I was the reason you used it?"

Nicky let out the cutest squeak. Poor thing looked like she wanted the floor to swallow her whole. Lucky for me, she couldn't manipulate the laws of physics.

"I was partially joking, but now I'm pretty sure it was the latter." I grinned wickedly at her.

"God." Nicky buried her face in her hands.

I slunk towards her and put my hands on her hips. "You know, Books, I'm not really opposed to being fantasy fodder for you. Though I would *much* rather make it your reality."

That gorgeously sweet and spicy smell of her filled my nose—nutmeg and old books. It made me want to bury my face against her throat and breathe her in forever.

She was warm beneath my fingertips.

"What are your thoughts and feelings on making it a reality?" I asked.

Nicky swallowed hard and sat Spud down on the back of her couch. "The anxious part of me wants to hide under a couch cushion."

"And the other parts of you?"

"They might be a little interested."

"Only a little?" A grin broke over my face. "Can I kiss you, Books?"

The poor dear opened and closed her mouth a couple of times, and finally settled on nodding. I walked my fingers around to her back and laced them together, pulling her closer as I rose up on my toes to meet her mouth with mine.

She tasted like tea and spice, and her lips were delightfully soft. Her quiet moan of desire sent lust bolting straight up my spine. I lingered at her mouth until the tension slipped from her shoulders, and lifted my hands to cup her cheeks, letting her acclimate to not only the feel of me, but to the scent of my packmates that clung to my skin like a brand, Gabe at one wrist, Hana at the other. If she shied away from either that would make moving forward rather difficult.

Nicky shuddered and surged toward me, diving fully into the kiss, lips eager, tongue meeting mine in greedy sweeps. She backed me up too far and I tipped over, landing flat on her couch with her standing between my knees, a shocked expression on her face.

"I'm happy to get on my back for you, Books, just wasn't expecting to right this second." I laughed and rolled over to right myself on the cushions.

"I'm sorry, I wasn't thinking, I didn't mean..."

"Don't you worry, I am completely chill with this. Now, sit your cute little butt down on the couch."

Nicky followed the instruction easily, even though her cheeks flamed even brighter. She watched me expectantly.

I put a knee to either side of her hips and sank down on her lap. "You let me know if you ever want to stop, okay? Or slow down. I can be patient when I need to be. Anything you want is fine—stop, red, wait—as long as you let me know, I'll follow your lead."

I dove in again, and she rose up to meet me. Tipping my head to the side, I licked up her throat, sucking at her scent gland until she was writhing. It was my favorite spot to tease because it was like a fucking gold mine of sensation no matter the gender or dynamic of the person. Nicky clung to me, fingers curled into my shirt and face turned toward my throat as she panted, inhaling the lingering scent of Tony on my bondmark there.

"Billie," she huskily whispered my name, fingers flexing, kneading me like a kitten.

I lifted my head and grinned down at her, smoothing her hair back and tugged out all the bobby pins holding it in place, teasing my fingers into the fallen strands. "You are far too beautiful."

Her perfect mouth dropped open at the statement. All that said to me was that she wasn't told she was beautiful often enough. I was going to have to change that for her.

I kissed her slow and smooth, tangling my hands in her hair, and rocking my hips against hers. She held on tight to my waist and slowly melted back into it. I could feel every shift of her body, every increment of her relaxing, and the subsequent tightening as the desire wound her up.

She shivered beneath me.

Not for the first time, I wished that betas could purr and growl the way that alphas and omegas did. She moaned softly. I suppose I would have to settle for that sound, not that it was a hardship.

Nothing felt quite as amazing as her tentative hands cupping my cheeks and sliding into my hair, mindful of my braids. I was going to have the best fucking time digging past her anxiety and insecurity to unleash that trembling, lustful beast I could already tell lurked inside of her.

Desire coiled like a snake in my belly and simmered my blood. I wasn't a patient soul by nature, but I did my best when it came to sexy time. I pulled back and looked into her perfect, dark eyes. "It doesn't have to be today. We can move on your schedule, but I want you to answer the next question based on what you want, because I'm more than happy to move things forward or pump the brakes for you. Got it?"

Nicky nodded.

"Good. How far do you want to go?"

I caught the unsteady flicker of her gaze towards the bedroom. She knew exactly what she wanted, but was afraid to say so.

"It feels so fast for a first date to say it," Nicky mumbled.

"I'm not going to think you're a loose woman for wanting to fuck me on the first date. I jumped on Jasper at the first opportunity. Tony, too. I'm a person who knows what they want, and I want *you* to know what you want, too."

Nicky's cheeks were perfectly flushed, the spice in her scent overwhelming. She went back to her kitten kneading, fingers working up the front of my shirt to pull me back down.

"We could work *towards* the bedroom," she said, pressing a soft kiss to the hollow at the base of my throat.

"I'm a big fan of moving towards the bedroom."

Nicky gave me a shy smile and pulled me back in. For a while, it was just slow sweeping kisses. Then her fingertips snuck under the hem of my shirt. I rewarded her with a groan and nipped her perfect bottom lip. I also took it as an invitation and slid my hands between us, settling them on the soft plains of her stomach. The muscles twitched beneath me. She got squirmier and more adventurous, her fingers pausing at the clasp of my bra.

Nicky pulled away to look at me. "Is that okay?"

"You could strip me down naked in the doorway and it would all be very okay."

She made a choked off sound that had more of her sweet spicy scent puffing out. My clasp was undone by dexterous fingers and she arched into me to allow me to do the same to her. I lifted my arms next and let her peel off my shirt, shucking my titty prison to the floor. Her gaze whipped between my face and my boobs, as if she couldn't quite decide where to lay those hungry eyes.

"My turn!" I worked off her top and popped the clasp of her bra, whisked it off her, and tossed it to join mine. I sucked in a breath. "Damn, Books. You're a hottie with a body. Can I touch?"

She laughed nervously. "If you want to."

"What's this *if*?" I walked my fingertips up the soft squish of her stomach and cupped the overflowing bounty of her boobs in my hands. "Hana and I are both part of the itty bitty titty committee. I never get to play with softness like this."

Nicky arched as I swept my thumbs over her nipples and leaned to press a kiss to the swell of each breast.

"I have a small confession. I haven't been with someone like you before. My sex life has rather unfortunately been exclusively with cis men up to this point."

I could practically feel the gleam in my eyes at those words. I was going to rock her fucking world. "Nervous?"

"Extremely, but that's just regular sex nervousness, not because it's you in particular. I like you."

"Well that's good because I definitely intend to get my tongue on you in very short order."

A strangled sound left her mouth, and I laughed.

"Do you mind if I do so right now?"

Nicky shook her head, and I leaned in to nip her throat, sucking hard on her scent gland and letting my tongue sweep over the delicate skin while she shivered, clinging to me tightly as she made sweet, perfect sounds to encourage me on. I raked my teeth over her and that got her panting, so I did it again, earning a whine that had my clit throbbing. I ground down against her, more eager with each passing moment to get her on her back.

She keened softly as I slid off her lap, but that was only until I got on my knees and lifted her breast, pulling the nipple into my mouth.

The quietest, "oh fuck", fell past her lips.

I closed my teeth as gently as possible around her nipple just to see what she would do. Her head tipped back, and her breast was thrust into my mouth as her back arched. I guess she liked that. I did the same with the other, pinching it slightly between my teeth and laving it with the tip of my tongue until she was squirming and desperate.

Nicky cupped my ribs and lifted me, bringing me towards her own mouth. My fingers dug into the back of the couch as she sucked one of my nipples into her mouth. Her tongue was hot and slick as it danced over my breast. She toyed with the other, eagerly caressing and gently pinching.

Oh, she was going to be fun.

I let her do as she pleased, and my pussy clenched around nothing. I'd had a nipple orgasm in the past, the result of two very determined alphas, and while I knew the odds of Nicky being able to bring me there were pretty low in our first time together, I was perfectly content to let her try.

I cradled her head with one hand and tried not to dig too firmly against her skull. Every sweep of her tongue at my tit only made me more eager for the rest of her. I contemplated slipping my hand between my thighs to hurry things along, but then I would either have to stop touching her or stop keeping my weight balanced.

I whined, my desperation growing.

"Bed?" she asked.

"Lead the way, Books."

I got off her lap entirely and waited for her to rise. She walked on unsteady legs, and I trotted after her into the bedroom. Seeming unsure, she looked back to me with questioning eyes.

"Anything you want, Books. We go with your speed."

"It's just a little bit of a mental war between the speed I usually go and how much I want to get you all the way naked."

I laughed softly. "Nice. Spicy Books is coming out."

Her cheeks turned fuchsia. "It's a rare appearance. Be grateful."

"Oh I am. I'm here for every bit you ever want to show me. Spicy Billie is not a rare occurrence though, so it's not quite as special."

Nicky tugged me all the way into the room, and, before I could blink, she pushed me back onto the bed, climbing on top.

"Hello there," I said with a grin.

"Hi," she whispered.

"Look at you, taking charge."

"Do you like it?" she asked.

"If you finish stripping me down and get one of those hands between my thighs, I think you'll find that I'd rather enjoy it."

"Oh my. I suppose I should speed things up then." Nicky laughed and pulled down my pants. "My previous boyfriends would be so jealous."

"Yeah? Why's that?"

"I always made them work for it. I needed them to show a modicum of patience first."

"You don't want me to work for it?"

"I'm pretty sure you've been trying to woo me since the second we met. And besides, I want you a lot more than I wanted them."

"Well, I *am* irresistible. I think we should balance out the lack of clothing in here. It's very unfair that you still have pants on."

She giggled softly and gestured to the front of her pants. I reached out and undid the button, clip, and zipper, pulling the fabric away to expose the plain black cotton panties she wore.

I kissed her hip just above the waist band. "Perfection. Now hop up and let those hit the floor."

I had always rather enjoyed it when someone followed my instructions in bed. Jasper usually let me run the show, and once in a while the alphas would let me be on top, but I was having a delightful time figuring Nicky out. It would be much easier for her to play with the others if I already had a decent idea of what she liked and could guide things when words got too difficult.

"Panties too, Books." I shimmied out of my own and tossed them aside, warming at her appreciative glance, her gaze sweeping my body.

I watched her closely and she bit her lip, hooking her thumbs in the sides of her panties, pushing them down until they fell on their own.

"Gorgeous. Now, lay back. I'm going to rock your world."

Chapter Seven
Nicky

My heart beat like a drum. Billie's body was compact, slim, and toned, with just enough curve to grab, and they wanted *me*. My skin felt like it was vibrating from their attention. I still hadn't put my finger on why exactly a craving for them burned through me, but that was a problem for a future Nicky. Current Nicky was a needy bitch who desperately wanted to get laid.

I climbed onto my bed and stretched out over the blankets. Nerves stirred in my belly. My thighs squeezed together, and my clit throbbed with anticipation. Billie looked down at me with blazing blue eyes that made me feel more than a bit lightheaded. I ached to be touched, and, luckily, Billie didn't make me wait too long before climbing to join me, straddling my waist.

They reached out, tracing from my chin, down my throat, through the hollow between my breasts, and down over my stomach to tease the thatch of hair between my thighs. I shivered, goosebumps rising on my skin.

"So beautiful." Billie laid both hands on my belly.

I dug my hands into the pillows at my head. "Please."

"Begging already, Books?"

"I'm not above begging."

Billie chuckled softly and cupped my breasts, teasing the nipples with gentle twists and pinches that had electricity arcing from their touch to my clit.

I squirmed beneath them. "Kiss?"

"Happy to oblige." Billie tilted forward and captured my mouth in a dizzying sweep of heat. I lost track of time, sinking into the taste and sensation of them, breathing in their spicy notes, reveling in their touch. They slid their hands up my arms, wrapping one around each of my wrists, and pinning me firmly to the bed. Their breasts hovered in my face, so I lifted my head to capture the nipple of one and was rewarded by their hiss of pleasure.

"You've got a wicked mouth on you, Books."

I broke away with a needy whine, wiggling my hips between theirs.

"If I say please again, will you touch me more?" I asked.

"That could be arranged." Billie chuckled.

"*Please?*"

Billie released my wrists and meandered their fingers down my body. I tilted my head to the side so they could suck at my throat, moving slowly to drop kisses upon each breast and over my stomach. They nipped over the silvery stretch marks that decorated my skin.

"Why don't you spread these pretty thighs for me?"

I held my breath as I did so, my legs trembling as I opened them to their gaze.

They flashed me a wolfish grin. "Excited? You look like you're a little bit wet for me."

"You should check to be sure," I said in a fit of boldness.

Billie rose up for a moment, their face tipping down to my

ear, hot breath tickling and teeth nipping eagerly. "You ever squirt for anyone, Books?"

I whined and shook my head.

"Good. I'm gonna be your first, then. Let me get you all warmed up."

Before I had a chance to react, Billie's face was between my thighs, their fingers spreading me open and their tongue sliding against my clit. I arched up with a sound that was half cry, half moan.

"Jesus, *fuck*."

"Nuh-uh. We only call my name in this bed. I'm your savior now, Books." They nipped the tender skin of my inner thigh and pressed a searching finger into my pussy. I squeezed around it, hips rocking on instinct.

My skin tingled.

Billie added another finger, curling them inside of me; their thumb rubbing a delicious pattern against my clit that had my whole body trembling. Every breath was accompanied by some pitiful little sound I had no control over.

Billie lifted their head and gave me a cheeky grin. "You sound so good when you're getting fucked, Books."

Any response I might've made was obliterated right out of my head as their tongue returned to its work. I squirmed and bucked, lifting my hips for more.

The orgasm caught me off guard, a cascade of sensation that had my back bowing up and my pussy squeezing Billie's fingers desperately. They coaxed me through it with rhythmic touches until I melted it back onto the bed with a shaky breath.

"Ready for another?"

I'd have been satisfied with one, but the hot, mischievous gleam in Billie's eyes made me curious. I had never had multiple orgasms outside of a solo session, though I certainly wasn't opposed to more.

"I could go for another."

Billie got up on their knees between my thighs. "First, I need you to direct me towards some towels. Don't want you to be stuck with laundry when I'm done with you.

"In the linen closet slash pantry next to the bathroom."

They hopped off the bed and returned a moment later with a stack of two, unfolding both and tucking them under my hips, and letting the rest of the fabric drape over the sheets.

"I'm going to give you a task this time," they said.

"Oh?"

"I want to watch you play with those pretty pink nipples while I turn you into a hot mess. When you get close I want you to pinch them as hard as you can stand and hold it until it's over. Got it?"

Oh god. I swallowed hard. "Yep."

"Just relax, okay? And don't worry about anything. I know what I'm doing, but I need you to not fight it when it happens."

I took a deep breath to calm myself, still feeling my heartbeat pulse through my entire body.

Billie tested out a few different motions inside of me. Some felt nice, and some felt like nothing, then they moved their wrist and the sensation struck me like a hammer so hard I cried out, surprised.

"Holy shit!"

"Yeah, it's a bit intense. That just means I found the right spot. Are you going to be okay with that?"

"I'm definitely willing to try."

I might die in the process, but I wanted to feel it again.

"Just remember to breathe." Billie worked their fingers inside me again, hitting that same spot that made me come apart and lose complete control of my body.

Breathing beyond frantic gasps was impossible, and even my task of playing with my breasts seemed to use up more mental capacity than I had available. I had never felt what Billie was doing, and I was certain that I would be absolutely ruined by the time they were done.

All of my muscles pulled taut, freezing me in place. I barely registered how loud I was. I couldn't stop. It was like I was going to explode from the inside. The intensity kept increasing, blurring everything around me. Billie's hand pressed firmly down just below my belly button.

"Pinch those nipples, Books."

Some part of my brain reacted to the instructions and obeyed with fumbling hands. I squeezed hard, and the burn of it seared, electricity zipping between my fingertips and my clit, ending with the fireworks of Billie's touch.

My vision blacked out, and liquid gushed from between my thighs, my body seizing from head to toe as I screamed. The orgasm seemed to ricochet, rolling through me endlessly, my body pulsing and twitching with each rebound. It faded impossibly slow. The warmth of Billie was pressed to my side, gentle fingers stroking my cheek until I opened my eyes again.

"There's my girl. Have fun?"

My throat felt raw, and my head was full of scrambled eggs instead of functioning brain matter. I giggled, flexing my muscles slowly, making a kissy noise to lure Billie closer so I could kiss them again.

"I think you ruined me," I murmured against their mouth.

Billie laughed quietly. "Sorry, I know it's a bit much. You lay right here, and I'll get you some water."

They were so nonchalant for absolutely blowing my mind.

How was I ever supposed to sleep with someone else after they'd given me the knowledge that I could experience this fresh fire and burning need?

Billie lifted my head and pressed the edge of a cup to my lips. I sipped a bit of it, and that helped the ragged dryness of my throat. I nestled into their arms, needing the contact as little panicky thoughts flickered in the background that whispered this was a one time thing, and I'd never get to experience this kind of desire ever again.

"Rest for a few minutes. You'll be right as rain soon." Billie set the cup aside and curled up next to me, drawing little patterns on my skin. I burrowed close, looping my arm around their waist, breathing in their spicy scent laced with their pack's.

Mine.

The word echoed in my thoughts, even though it wasn't true. Billie belonged to a pack, not to me, no matter how much I liked the idea of keeping them.

I must've fallen asleep because when I woke up Billie was snoring softly. I had no clue what time it was until I heard Spud's plaintive meow from the kitchen. I rolled towards Billie and kissed their cheek.

They opened their eyes slowly. "She lives."

I laughed, the gravelly feeling in my throat finally subsided. "I do. I have to feed Spuddy."

We detached ourselves from one another and I wandered into the kitchen naked to get Spud breakfast. There was a square of paper on the floor on the inside of my door. I picked it up, groaning.

Are you all right? I heard you scream and you didn't answer. Please come let me know as soon as possible.
-Mrs. Poppadakis

Oh God.

All of my neighbors had probably heard me. Another problem for a future Nicky. I scribbled a reply that I was fine, pulled on a robe, and shoved it under her door, retreating hastily back into my apartment.

I gave Spud his extra meal and trotted back to the bedroom where Billie was stretched out luxuriously in my bed.

"I'm sorry I fell asleep before giving you your turn," I said.

"No harm, no foul. I certainly wasn't expecting anything after that. If you're not up to it I know several people at home who will be happy to rail me."

An image of Billie sandwiched between Tony and Jasper filled my head.

"Whatcha thinking about that put that gorgeous blush in your face?"

"Absolutely nothing inappropriate."

"Of course not. You're a perfect lady." Billie patted the bed next to them. "Join me. I'm getting lonely."

I dropped the robe, and climbed up. Billie opened their arms to me and I let myself get lost in them, memorizing their taste and texture as my fingertips wandered down their stomach. Their thighs parted easily at my approach and they licked into my mouth with an eager moan.

I only had experience with myself for this part, but maybe that was enough. They were slippery under my touch, and my fingers dipped inside their body, sliding back over their clit. I had no idea how to replicate what they had done to me, so I stuck with what I knew—plunging fingers, teasing strokes, focused attention on their clit—until their sounds shifted and their hips rocked frantically. I ate up every whimper and sigh, using it to fuel me even when my forearm started to burn, determined to give Billie even a fraction of what they had given me.

The reward of them bucking against my hand while crying out against my skin was everything I wanted. Billie caught my hand when I went to reach for the towel to tidy my hand and dipped my two middle fingers into their mouth, tongue curling around each digit. I gasped, my clit pulsing in response.

Billie pulled my hand free and grinned at me. "Snuggle with me?"

Like I would say no.

I gathered them into my arms and curled against their back. "We can sleep for a few more hours. Spud always settles down after his first breakfast."

Billie cuddled in. "Sounds perfect. How're you feeling, Books? I didn't go too fast for you?"

"You went exactly as fast as I asked you to." I kissed their shoulder. "I...didn't know it could be like this."

"How so?" Billie wiggled around in my arms until they were facing me.

I traced soft circles on their back to anchor myself. "Just having someone so focused on making me feel comfortable, and wanting me to feel good. I'm not used to it."

Billie gave me a deep, drugging kiss, the subtle scent of mint and matcha filling my nose as their hand cradled my cheek. "That just makes me want to sucker punch every one of your past partners."

"They weren't terrible about sex," I assured. "They just weren't...great, I guess? I'm just sort of realizing that now that I have something to compare to. I definitely didn't get flowers, soft cuddles, and multiple orgasms."

"My statement still stands," Billie insisted. "In any case, I'll give you as many flowers, cuddles, and orgasms as you want. I want my partners to live the three S's."

"What are those?" I asked.

"Safe, satisfied, and spoiled." Billie grinned at my laughter.

"Well, I am definitely all three of those. But I wouldn't say no to some more sleep while acquiring more of those promised cuddles."

"Your wish is my command, Books."

When we woke again it was deep into the afternoon. I felt luxuriously rested. I suppose the best orgasm of my life might have something to do with that. My ridiculous little giggle woke Billie.

They stretched slowly and leaned in to kiss me prior to sliding off the bed to collect their phone in the living room and go pee, returning to flop back onto the bed with me. "I think I have messages from the entire pack."

"Did we worry them?"

"They're just making sure that I'm alive. They knew I was with you, but I forgot to let them know that I was getting lucky."

My cheeks flushed with warmth.

"I suppose it's too early for me to invite you to the pack house to meet everyone?" Billie asked.

Anxiety at the suggestion churned my stomach. "Maybe a wee bit early."

"Fair enough. I should probably get home to them even though I'd love to lay here all day with you." They tapped away on their phone. "Tony can pick me up in about ten minutes."

"I can drive you home," I offered.

"My self control can't handle having you that close to home and you not coming in. Best not to tempt me. You rest." Billie kissed my cheek. "So, did this date go as well as I think it did?"

"Yep. Pretty darn good," I said with a laugh.

"Good." Billie took my face in both of their hands. "Does that mean I could interest you in a second date?"

I wasn't entirely sure why the way they held my face made me breathless. Billie's thumbs brushed over my lower lip and my clit tingled. I wanted to answer, but I felt almost completely immobilized by the force of their gaze and the electric heat in those blue eyes.

"How is it possible for you to be this exquisite?" Billie asked. "Use your words, Books."

Their hands slid to cup my neck, fingers tangling in my hair.

"Second date sounds amazing." My voice sounded embarrassingly like I'd been running a marathon.

"Is tomorrow too soon?"

"Will I seem like a hermit with no social life if I say tomorrow's great?"

Billie laughed and tugged my head back, pressing their lips to the pulse of my throat. I was sure they could feel it hammering.

"Your lack of social life is my gain."

I surrendered immediately to the kiss Billie dropped onto my mouth, my body igniting. They nuzzled my cheek with theirs, scent marking me like I belonged to them. I didn't mind that one bit.

I watched them lazily dress, only a little disheartened when my offer to make them coffee was thwarted as their phone pinged, signaling the arrival of their car.

Billie kissed me once more and teasingly bit my earlobe. "You be a good girl for me, Books. I'll see you tonight."

They were gone barely two minutes when a text from Mom popped up.

MOM:
How was your date?

NICKY:
It was perfect :)

I was relieved I didn't have to lie to her this time. Billie really was so much more than I'd anticipated and I was eager to experience more of this beta who had swept into my life and upended all of my expectations.

I climbed into the shower with a smile on my face. Morning couldn't come soon enough.

Chapter Eight
Tony

"Are you even listening to me?"

"Of course, Councillor Harvey." I bit my tongue to keep from saying anything further. The woman was insufferable on multiple levels, not least of which when she insisted on explaining to me the importance of doing the same job I'd been doing for years with zero complaints.

"I need that back by tomorrow afternoon."

She spun on her heel and stalked away without so much as a thank you. Not that I ever expected one out of her. She was probably already counting down the minutes, hoping that I would be late so she could berate me.

Jokes on her because I had yet to be late since starting this job. I popped open the document on my phone to do a cursory check, just to see how bad it was. It was a clear mistake that froze my phone from the sheer size of it.

Of course.

God forbid Councillor Harvey ever be succinct.

I collected a few more assignments from the other Councillors and made my way home with my work for the week. It all could've been done via email, but some of the older Councillors heavily preferred that they see my face when they gave me my work.

Thankfully, the others were more flexible, so that would give me time to get Harvey's work done first. I personally hated rewarding her terrible behavior with expediency, but taking my sweet time would only be trouble for *me*, not her, and, for the most part, I did enjoy this job. Editing documents for the municipality wasn't exactly a thrill a minute, though it did pay well enough and kept me up-to-date on the goings-on of the city.

Every so often I got to do more interesting projects, like the novella I had just finished for a client, but ninety percent of my editorial work revolved around making the Councilors sound competent and clear.

I swung by the address that Billie had sent me and found them standing in the entryway of an apartment building when I arrived. They hopped into the van with a bright, if tired, smile on their face.

"You look like you had a good night," I commented.

"You bet your ass I did." Billie grinned and pulled me in for a quick kiss. "I'm ready for a shower and some croissants."

"Nicky didn't feed you?"

"We got food together after her shift ended, but I bounced before she could feed me again."

"Any particular reason?"

"Hana seemed worried. You know how she likes to reassure herself by seeing us in person. It didn't seem fair to keep her waiting."

"She would've survived," I said, patting Billie's knee. "You'd have had time for pancakes."

Billie shrugged. "I'll have pancakes with Nicky tomorrow."

I raise one eyebrow. "Another date already?"

Billie was a notorious flirt that loved attention, but it had been years since anyone had tempted them beyond a dance or conversation. The fact that they had spent the night with Nicky and were already itching to do so again made me pay attention. I couldn't fault Billie for their taste when it had been them that had found all of us and brought us together.

"What can I say?" Billie stuck out their tongue. "I'm an exquisite lay."

I burst out laughing. "You're not wrong about that. Nicky seemed a little uptight. I'm surprised she found that out so soon."

"I can be very persuasive."

I sighed. "Billie..."

"She didn't need any *actual* persuasion. I promise she was on board with everything well before I got around to asking."

"Good. Because you're kind of a force of nature."

"A force of nature that values consent." They nudged my shoulder playfully.

"Nicky knows about the whole pack, right?"

Billie nodded excitedly. "I told her all about us. She didn't shy away from anyone's scent either."

I tapped the steering wheel. I hadn't anticipated adding anyone new to our mix, but I could trust Billie's instincts for now and get to know Nicky myself. Time would tell if she would end up in our pack like the rest of us had when Billie had blown into our lives like a hurricane.

"How was horrible Harvey today?" Billie asked.

"Just as condescending as every other occasion. I have a rush order from her for a monster project."

"I really need to get you a T-shirt that has that quote, what is it? 'Failure to plan on your end does not constitute an emergency on mine'. Just wear a sweater over it and whip that baby open the next time she pulls this bullshit."

"I could imagine her face." I laughed.

The rest of the trip was reasonably free of traffic considering it was mid-afternoon. The guard at the community gate waved us through, and I pulled up to the home that we all shared: a three-storey brick manor that Billie had inherited from their grandparents. Gabe was in the driveway hand washing his motorcycle in a tank top and ripped jeans.

"Tone it down, babe," Billie said with a laugh. "I can smell that alpha funk from you eyeballing Gabe."

I shrugged. I'd long since gotten over my embarrassment at being wildly attracted to my pack. "If he wasn't out there looking delicious then I wouldn't have to be hungry."

Billie snickered and hopped out as we came to a stop, bounding over to give Gabe a kiss on the cheek. My beta was already gone by the time I got out of the van, and Gabe was standing up, waiting for me. I pulled him into a slow kiss that bathed my tongue in the sweetness of black tea and brown sugar.

"Did our beta get you all worked up?" Gabe asked.

"Nah, that was all you."

Gabe smiled and hooked his fingertips into the waistband of my jeans. "You know how I love compliments."

"And that's exactly why I tell you how perfect you are every single day."

Gabe growled and tugged me in sharply for another delightfully deep kiss. "If I wasn't meeting friends after I finish this little tuneup, I might have to take you upstairs."

"That's okay. You know I'm a patient soul. I'll leave you to your work. I've got to get started on mine, too."

We parted ways, and I found Billie in the living room on Hana's lap. I didn't see Jasper yet, but he was probably still asleep.

"I'll be in my office if anyone needs me," I said as I passed the two of them and headed up the stairs.

Billie had spared no expense when renovating to make sure it suited our pack. They had added in a pool next to the walkout basement and had included a full gym for Hana, a workshop in one of the garages for Gabe, a totally up-to-date kitchen for Jasper, a painting studio for themselves, and a library office for me. As perfect as the house was, we all still made a concerted effort to leave it outside of our working hours so we didn't become a pack of hermits. Of course, in the winter that was exactly what

69

happened, the same for any bad weather really. Home was comfortable, but it was important not to get too stuck in our ways.

I'd grown pretty fond of the new library at the twenty-four-seven community facility, and it was nice to get a change of scenery that was still a quiet space. Now that Nicky was there, I imagined that Billie would be all the more eager to spend time there. At home, the pack tended to leave me be when I closed myself up in my office, and I could blast through the majority of my work, which made the trips to the public library that much more enjoyable since I didn't have to worry about struggling to finish while Billie talked my ear off.

I opened up the Harvey documents, and, after only a page, ice started to settle in my blood. The fucking *audacity* of this bitch. I'd known from the get-go that Councillor Harvey despised the new community facility, but these documents were a new level of fuckery, even for her.

I scanned a few pages ahead.

Any facility that is available twenty-four hours a day encourages illicit behavior. In the time the facility has been open there have been numerous reports of patrons engaging in sexual activity, consumption of alcohol on the premises, and even the formation of a cult.

What the hell was Councillor Harvey smoking? The only way any of those things were true was if her own little cult of followers were the ones doing it to make the facility look bad.

It wasn't my place to get involved in municipal politics, only to copy edit the documents that would become their white papers and bylaws, but damn if this didn't make me want to run for mayor just so I could verbally bitch slap her during meetings.

I started on the copy edits with a sour taste in my mouth, the nausea growing the further I got. It seemed like she was trying to hold hospital funding hostage, with a sole goal of stripping the facility's funding and restricting it to bankers hours. That would be fucking useless. Only a woman who had never needed a community facility like this would make such stupid rules and restrictions.

I worked for a couple of hours until there was a knock at my door, and I pushed down my anxiety to answer it.

"There's food downstairs if you're hungry," Jasper said as I opened the door. "Whoa, what's crawled up your butt?"

I took a deep breath to try to even out my scent. "Just work." I held my arms open for him.

Jasper stepped into my embrace and his purr buzzed against my chest. It was far more effective than anything I could do for myself. Chocolate and cinnamon saturated every breath, and his purr evened out my ill-temper.

"Come for snacks and cuddles," Jasper ordered.

I had zero desire to refuse, so I didn't. Jasper led me back downstairs, his hand in mine, and sat me down at one of the barstools overlooking a tray of fresh sticky buns and a bowl of fluffy icing. He fetched me some coffee and sweetened it exactly to my taste before setting the cup and an iced bun in front of me.

Hana joined me, but with a cup of tea instead of coffee. She tugged her sleek, dark hair back into a ponytail, amber eyes looking me over as she used another elastic to twist her hair into a bun. "Rough day?"

"Just the start of it. I know I'm not really supposed to share, especially since I'm pretty sure Billie's going to bite some faces off if I do, but..."

"Who's going to feel my wrath?" Billie asked, popping up behind me and weaseling themselves onto my lap, straddling me to take up my full attention.

"Councillor Harvey is gunning for Nicky's job."

"What the fuck?" Billie snapped. "Why does she hate Nicky?"

"Not her specifically, but, if she gets her way, all of the evening and night jobs will be gone."

"What a cunt." Billie huffed. "I have time and money, I should run for councilor, or mayor."

I laughed and stroked a hand down their back. "I thought of doing the same. I'm just hoping one of the others has some counter measures prepared."

"Fingers crossed." Billie held up both hands with the first two fingers on each crossed over the other.

"I just got him relaxed," Jasper lamented. "We need happier topics right now."

"I was going to talk to the facility manager about renting some space for classes," said Hana. "That café is going to get so much business if they accept me."

"That means you can sneaky meet Nicky!" Billie prodded Hana's shoulder.

"Such an impatient little beta," Hana tutted.

"That should be a surprise to no one."

"It's not," said Hana, "but I do still think some patience is in order."

Billie's subtle spicy scent filled my nose and I laid my palm over their thigh, squeezing gently. "I might be in agreement with Hana here." I nuzzled Billie's cheek.

"I think our beta could do with some abstention to teach them some patience," said Hana.

Billie whined in my grip. "That's not fair. I have a date in the morning."

I nipped their shoulder. "And no one is saying you can't take care of your date."

Billie squirmed, and my cock rose to attention under the movement.

Hana turned our chair and slid her hand into Billie's hair, pulling them slowly backwards with a fistful until Billie's head rested in Hana's lap. "What do you think, little beta?"

It was impossible for me to miss the flexing of Billie's hips in my lap.

"Do you want to give us control over this?" I asked, setting my fingers between their thighs and pressing firmly until they let out a whimper.

"Answer the question," Hana prompted. "Unless you think you can't handle it."

Jasper watched us with rapt attention, his chocolate and cinnamon scent almost overwhelming as his desire made itself known.

"I can handle it," Billie said quietly.

"Of course you can," Hana murmured, tracing a pattern down Billie's chest until her hand covered mine. "You're a perfect little beta, and *this* belongs to *us*."

Between Billie's shuddering breath, the heat of their cunt beneath my fingers, and the intoxicating scent of Jasper's arousal, it was a wonder I didn't spread Billie out on the counter and order Jasper to fuck them while I fucked him.

Hana's palm on the back of my neck made me jolt.

"We all know I'm not opposed to an orgy in the kitchen, but if we're going to do that we should let Gabe know too."

I still had a colossal amount of work to get done, and that only made me hate Councillor Harvey even more. The woman wasn't even here, yet she was making me cock block myself with my sense of responsibility.

"I'll have to join you for another one later, unfortunately."

"Boo!" Billie protested.

Hana helped them sit up. "Your alpha has work to do. You can join him in his office, or you can stay here with me."

I held my breath as Billie decided. I wasn't quite sure which choice I would've preferred them to make. A meal in Hana's lap, getting teased until they hit their breaking point, or going beneath my desk to tease me until I hit mine.

"That choice is too hard," said Billie.

I looked at Jasper. "What's your vote, omega? Do you want to watch our beta suffer or imagine it?"

Jasper swallowed hard. "I think we all know I'm a visual person."

Hana grinned. "Then it's settled. Billie, you're with me, and Tony can get back to his extremely boring work and think about all the fun we're having down here."

"I have chairs in my office," I said to Hana, "if you feel like torturing us all at once."

Sharp mint and soothing matcha filled my senses. Hana growled softly and hooked her fingertips in my shirt. "If you make that kind of offer, you had better be prepared for me to accept it."

I nudged Billie off of my lap and stood. "I'm always prepared for that. You know where to find me."

I slipped out of the kitchen with my coffee and sticky bun and retreated up the stairs to my office, my body humming with anticipation.

Chapter Nine
Nicky

"Hey there, my lily."

That voice. That *name*.

My jaw snapped tight and a cold sweat broke over my skin. I looked over the edge of my desk to see my ex-fiance Alphonse standing there with the same slicked back dark hair, neat suit, and smarmy smile I remembered.

"I thought you were in Tokyo." The words jumped out before I could process that I should have greeted him first.

His brow furrowed. "I *was*. You were supposed to be, too. In any case, I just moved back."

I hadn't handled our breakup particularly smoothly. He'd been set to move to Tokyo for work to help them establish a new office, and I was supposed to have gone with him. I hadn't wanted to move, but he'd worn me down into agreeing. Every time I tried to bring up that I didn't want to go, it ended in an argument. So, instead of following him, I had used the opportunity of my broken lease to get a new apartment, change my number, delete my social media, and just pretend that none of it had ever happened for as long as possible.

I had never wanted to marry him, either. He'd done a public proposal, and I'd felt so awkward refusing that I'd said yes with the intention of refusing in private, but then he'd gone and announced the engagement online barely five minutes later.

Mom had been so happy...

I'd mailed the ring to his office and gone straight to my parents place to delete his contact off their phones and block his number. My brothers hadn't needed that step and blocked him themselves. Mom was heartbroken over the failed engagement, and I knew that if Alphonse phoned her, she would answer, so I'd used her lack of tech skills against her.

Sure, disappearing into the night wasn't the best way to handle it, but I didn't know what else to do to slam on the brakes when a life I didn't want was careening toward me.

I swallowed back the bile that rose in my throat. "What brings you to the library in the middle of the night?"

"I ran into your mom at the grocery store, and she told me about your new gig here. She was so happy to see me."

I shivered. How the hell do I have a calm conversation with someone after everything that had passed between us?

"Are you doing well?" I asked, struggling for anything else to say.

"Well enough. I'll be even better when you agree to go out with me again. How about breakfast when you're done working?"

"Oh, um, actually I already have a date for breakfast."

I don't think he could've looked any more surprised than if I had pulled out a fish and slapped him in the face with it.

"I...see. That's unfortunate. I missed you while I was away and was really looking forward to spending time with you again. I wasn't expecting you to turn things into an open relationship while I was gone."

I stared at him, at a complete loss for words. True, I hadn't explicitly stated we were done, but how much clearer could returning my engagement ring have been? We hadn't spoken in more than two years.

"Show me the library, he insisted. "You don't mind some company while you work, do you?"

It felt hypocritical to say that I did when I was waiting on Billie and Tony to arrive. I guess I could humour him for a few minutes...

"Sure. There's signs that show you all of the sections. Is there something specific you're looking for?"

"Nope. I'm just here to see your beautiful face."

I pushed down my sense of unease.

"Hey, Books!"

I felt more than a little guilty at the wave of relief that rolled through me when I heard Billie's voice. They bounded up to me and wrapped an arm around my waist. "Who's your friend?"

"I feel like *I* should be asking that," said Alphonse. He thrust out his hand to shake Billie's. "Alphonse Morelli. Nicky's fiance."

Billie squeaked, and Tony's eyes widened.

"Ex!" I burst out. "Ex fiance."

Billie looked to me for some type of guidance with how to respond. I had no idea what to say. I wasn't sure how Alphonse would react if he knew who Billie was to me. And, besides, it wasn't any of his business.

Tony stepped between Alphonse and I, holding out his hand for Alphonse to shake. I relaxed a fraction as he put me out of eyesight and gave me a barrier. Billie put their hand in mine, squeezing gently.

"Good to meet you," Tony said to Alphonse, his voice tight. "I'm Tony and this is Billie. We're friends of Nicky's."

Alphonse stared at Tony's outstretched hand, finally accepting it after a few moments. "You must be *new* friends then. I don't recall her ever mentioning you."

Why would I have? He'd never liked *any* of my friends to begin with, and so many of them had dropped away when I'd dated him. I wasn't going to introduce anyone new to him when we weren't even together.

"Yep," I said, trying to end the conversation quickly. "Pretty new, but I like them a lot."

Alphonse's posture was stiff as he eyeballed both of the new arrivals.

"I should really get back to work."

Please leave.

Alphonse gave me a long look, then nodded. "I'll pick you up for a date tomorrow then."

He was on his way out before my brain could formulate any kind of response. Billie and Tony were looking at me curiously.

Tony opened his arms to me, and I stepped into them without thinking, freezing as he held me there in front of the main desk.

"Are you all right, Nicky?" Tony asked quietly.

"Yeah," Billie said. "You look wigged out."

I curled my fingers into Tony's shirt to anchor myself, breathing in his coffee and caramel scent that had a lingering layer of bitterness to it, slowly fading out the longer we stood here.

"I didn't *agree* to a date with him," I said. "Just so that you know. I told him I was busy, and he didn't take the hint."

Tony set a warm hand between my shoulder blades. "Seems like he's the type of guy who doesn't get hints. Probably not the type who gets direct communication either."

"What's the deal?" Billie asked. "You said he was your ex. Rough breakup?"

"Um. I kind of chickened out on a proper breakup and just never followed him overseas when I was supposed to. Changed my phone number, moved to a new apartment, cut off all contact, and mailed the ring to him." My voice had turned all high and squeaky.

Tony's hand moved higher and settled on the back of my neck. It was weirdly cozy to be in his arms, though I barely knew him. I should be more mindful of the cameras, but I was so comfortable.

"Damn, Books. I'd say that's cold, but that dude had creepy vibes so I don't blame you."

"I haven't *seen* him since. I thought I was home free until he just showed up saying he wanted to get back together and that he talked to my mom. I hate that she just handed out info about where I work."

Tony set me at arm's length, his warm gaze flicking over my face. "Nicky, are you afraid of this guy?" he asked, point blank.

"*No!* No, it's...he's *fine*. He's never hurt me." I shook myself. "Sorry. I really should get to work though. I think your corner is free and I'll come hang out on my break if you want me."

Billie made a *psh* sound. "*If* we want you. What kind of question is that? The answer is obviously yes. You're welcome anytime."

They cupped my cheeks and laid a soft kiss on my lips. I should *really* care more that the cameras could see me, but I just wanted them to kiss me again. Alphonse had shaken me up, and apparently Billie and Tony were what I needed to settle back down.

Billie grinned at me before tugging Tony off to the bean bag corner. I felt better knowing that they were here even though there was really no reason to feel unsafe.

Alphonse had always been all bark. Kind of clingy. A bit judgemental. Desperate to know where I was at all times so his insecurities didn't nag at him, which made him nag at me if I went MIA for more than half an hour. I pinched the bridge of my nose. I didn't want to go back to that. I hated who I'd been with him—neurotic *all* the time, letting friendships slide away to avoid conflict. Him picking a fight with me when I'd rescued Spud had been the final nail in that proverbial coffin. I'd seen my chance to escape, and I'd taken it.

I wouldn't have any friends at all right now if my sister-in-law hadn't pulled me into her little group. Her besties, Meg and Luna, had essentially adopted me when we'd all been in the wedding party together, but I had never reached out again to the friends I'd lost while dating Alphonse.

79

I pushed all those thoughts aside and got back to the set up of one of the day programs, putting up the decorations and making sure that all the resources would be accessible come morning. We were having an ornithologist come in and bringing a few special animal guests. I was definitely jealous of the day staffers, but the birds weren't coming in until noon for a school field trip, and I would be dead on my feet by then. Maybe I'd get lucky and they would do a nocturnal bird exhibit one day when I was working.

Once I'd put together all of the finishing touches, I decided it was time for a break and headed over to where Tony and Billie were tucked together on the bean bags.

Tony saw me first and offered a bright smile that made my stomach flip. "Hey cutie. Having a good shift?"

"Yep. All set up for the birds tomorrow."

Billie scooted over and patted the vacant spot on the beanbag next to them they had just vacated. "Park that booty, Books."

I sank down and tried not to blush too hard when Billie snaked an arm around my shoulders.

"Billie is pretty big on PDA," said Tony. "Best to let them know now if you're not cool with that."

"It's okay," I replied. "I'm just not used to it."

"Do you mind if Tony comes to breakfast?" Billie asked. "I told him about your eggs benny."

"No pressure," Tony added. "I don't want to intrude on your date."

If I was going to keep seeing Billie then it was probably a good idea for me to get to know their pack as soon as I was comfortable. Tony was an easy first addition to spend extra time with.

"Sure," I said. "The more the merrier."

"Have you ever gone out with an alpha?" Billie asked.

"Uh, well, I've spent time with alphas in general. My oldest brother is one. But I've never dated an alpha if that's what you're asking. Just betas."

"Why is that?" asked Tony. He looked at me curiously.

"I dunno, I just never thought I'd be enough for one. I've never dated an omega either for the same reason."

"Oh, *no.*" Tony set his hand over mine and slid it slowly up my arm like he was giving me time to tell him to stop. Then he was cupping the back of my neck, holding me captive with his dark gaze. "No, no. We don't speak about ourselves like that in this pack. You have value no matter your dynamic. You are enough for the right person, and anyone who believes otherwise is simply wrong."

I found myself nodding along to his words.

Billie pressed up against my back and whispered in my ear, "Isn't he sexy when he cares about your emotional well-being?"

I squeaked, my skin bursting into tingles as their combined touch ignited my cellular memory of everything Billie had done to me yesterday. Warmth pulsed between my thighs as if my body was urging me to slip my hand down my pants to soothe the ache there, or simply lay back and let Tony manage it for me.

I couldn't breathe with his gaze on me like that. My skin felt feverish, and every passing second made it harder to remember that I was at my job and that there were cameras in the library.

I had no defenses against feeling like this. No one except these two had ever made me breathless with wanting or made me consider indecent acts at work.

"If you're interested," Tony began, "I could make us breakfast at the pack house. Jasper and Hana will both be at work. Gabe might be home, but probably not. I make a mean pancake, or anything else you might be craving."

I swallowed hard. Going to the pack house seemed like it would be leaving myself open for some possibly regrettable choices. It was hard to think with my heart pounding in my ears and Tony's warm hand on my skin.

Billie tucked a strand of my hair behind my ear. "The pancakes are bomb. Plus we have like a million different kinds of syrup too. And you can meet Roscoe!"

"Who's Roscoe?" I managed to ask.

"He's a little tortie cat that we foster failed with," replied Tony. "He loves people, and if you sit down in the living room for more than two minutes, he'll probably become an anchor on your lap."

"There's no pressure if you come over, Books. I can behave. We'll have some pancakes and a cuddle, and I'll send you back to Spud untarnished if that's what you want."

I couldn't help the snort laugh that escaped me. "I'm not sure how you can say that after this morning. Spud's witnessed some things he can never unsee."

Billie laughed. "That's true. But cats are little voyeurs so he's probably not too traumatized."

Tony's thumb moved softly against my throat, and it stilled the breath in my lungs again.

"We'd love to have you. And if someone comes home unexpectedly, we can sneak you out the back if you're not ready to meet them." He grinned at me.

Even though I was pretty sure he was joking, the reassurance helped anyway. "I could come by for a little while. Spud might hate me for delaying his breakfast, but he's not going to wither away."

"You could bring him," offered Billie. "Roscoe loves other cats."

"I honestly have no idea how Spud would do with another cat. It's just been him and I since he was a baby. He does like car rides though for some strange reason, so I guess I could pick him up and bring him just to see how he likes it."

Tony's hand slid away, and I suppressed a shiver at the loss of his touch, though the goosebumps probably gave it away.

"Sounds perfect," he said. "Can I have your number to send you the address of the pack house?"

"Yeah, okay." He passed over his phone for me to fill in the information, and I handed it back a moment later. Billie looked entirely too excited by this development.

"How long is your break?" Tony asked.

"Fifteen minutes."

"Five minutes left then. Can I grab you a drink from the café?"

"You don't have to do that," I said automatically.

Billie poked me in the side. "Alphas like to take care of people. If you don't have a specific objection, you should let Tony do that."

I didn't say that I was pretty sure that the whole concept was that alphas liked to take care of their *partners* and not simply people in general, but I let it slide and asked for a simple black tea with milk and honey. It also occurred to me that Tony had referred to me earlier as if I were already a member of the pack, and I hadn't even thought to correct him at the time.

I had a feeling that dating Billie was going to be like willingly drowning, and I couldn't quite make myself be afraid of that. Maybe it was about time that I took a deep breath and let myself dive down.

Chapter Ten
Nicky

"Holy shit," I whispered to Spud as we drove into the gated community and rolled to a stop in front of the massive brick home that my GPS *insisted* matched the address Tony had given me. "I guess with five incomes you can afford this level of swanky."

Bushes of blue, pink, and purple hydrangeas nestled beneath the windows on the main floor and the driveway could hold six vehicles easily. I'd expected the lawn to be something akin to a golf course at a place like this, but the majority of it was white clover that abutted a variety of flower beds. A tiny sign at the corner read *'Don't mind the weeds, we're feeding the bees!'*

I booped Spud's nose through the netting of his carrier. He was staring, wide eyed, examining the bits of the world that came into his line of sight.

Billie waved from a set of main floor windows as I pulled up.

"Ready, Spuddy? You have to be on your best behavior, okay?"

He didn't respond beyond looking at me, slow-blinking to show his love. I carried him up to the front door, and it opened before I had a chance to knock.

"You're here!" Billie crashed against me in a hug. Their purple curls were up in a high ponytail that bounced with their movement, and their face was free of makeup, body dressed in indigo shorts and a black tank top. "Roscoe is chilling with Gabe so your little prince can wander to his heart's content during his visit."

The entryway had hanging plants and a gilded mirror as tall as me. I wasn't sure what to do in the face of such a luxury.

I set the carrier down and removed my shoes, letting Spud gain his freedom when Billie closed the door behind us. I'd put him in a harness with an extendable leash just so that I wouldn't lose him in some nook or cranny.

"Your home is gorgeous."

"Thanks! It used to belong to my grandparents. We've spiffed it up since moving in."

"I feel a little out of place being somewhere so fancy."

"Don't worry, that'll go away." Billie grinned. "Would you like the grand tour first, or breakfast?"

"How about a partial tour of the main floor? At least show me where the bathroom is."

Billie laughed and waved me in further. Spud was sniffing away at everything, but a gentle tug on his leash had him trotting along beside me. To the left of the entrance was a large dining room enclosed with double French doors, and sporting what looked like an antique table big enough to fit twenty. Next was the kitchen that equaled my entire one bedroom apartment for size. White cupboards filled the space with light and a shimmering backsplash of white, gold, and black tied things together with the black granite island in the center that was as big as a king-sized bed. A huge raised countertop matched the island, and had white leather bar seating.

Tony was at work at the stove, dressed in red lounge pants and a fitted white T-shirt that showed off his lean muscles. He turned to greet me with a little wave. "You made it! I just started cooking. What can I get you to drink? We have a super fancy machine so I can try my hand at pretty much anything."

"Maybe a matcha latte?" I suggested.

"Hana's favorite," Tony said. "Coming right up."

Billie tugged me along, and Spud followed, rubbing against everything within reach and sniffing excitedly. A kitchen table sat in the soft afternoon light with a round bouquet of white roses in the center. The absolutely massive living room took up most of the remaining space on the main floor with a giant square of dark gray couches, bigger in all directions than a king-sized bed, where the center was all filled in like one huge nest of pillows and blankets.

"No TV?" I asked.

"Projector," said Billie. "The screen drops down from the ceiling."

I choked a little. "You have a living room theater?!"

"Uh, yeah. How else are we supposed to have epic movie nights?"

That was definitely the question of a person who had grown up in wealth.

Billie waved me over and showed me the deck that seemed to wrap around the entire back of the building and overlooked a backyard filled with flowers, lounge chairs, and a hot tub, as well as a covered gazebo.

"Holy shit," I whispered to myself.

Billie giggled. "There's not much else on the main floor except for the pantry and the guest bath. Come on, I'll show you."

Spud and I followed them and they swung open the door on what I assumed would be a powder room, but turned out to be a bathroom with marble floors and walls, a glassed in shower I could probably fit a dozen adults standing without touching, and a clawfoot tub.

"This feels like a five star hotel." I scooped up Spud and kissed his little head just to anchor myself in the moment. He purred away as I scratched his chin.

"Upstairs is all of the bedrooms and the basement is all of our recreation spaces," Billie explained. "Let's get you some breakfast. I bet Spud would like to nap on the couch."

We backtracked, and I set Spud down on the giant couch nest, hooking the handle of his leash under the foot of one of the side tables to keep him somewhat secured. He curled up, completely unbothered, and I let Billie take me back to the kitchen.

Tony set down a steaming cup for me when we both came to lean on the island to watch him.

"What do you think of our abode?" Tony asked.

"It's gorgeous. *Way* bigger than I was expecting."

He chuckled softly and flipped some pancakes from the pan onto a plate, setting it in front of us. Billie fetched us plates and cutlery while I sipped at my matcha latte. Tony's phone buzzed on the countertop, and he flipped it over, glancing up at me.

"Do you mind if Gabe pops down here to grab some pancakes? Otherwise, I can take him a plate."

Nerves jumbled in my stomach. "He can come down. I don't want anyone to feel like they can't be in their own house just because I'm here. That's not very fair."

Billie nuzzled up to me and wrapped both arms around my waist after setting down the plates. "He's not scary I promise."

They stood on their toes and gave me a kiss that sent sizzles up my back. When I pulled away I saw Tony watching us appreciatively in between spooning more batter into the pan. My pussy clenched. I'd never been explicitly watched in the past, but apparently that was something that I was into.

Footsteps coming down the stairs had me turning. An impossibly gorgeous man in a white tank top and ripped jeans with golden skin and tousled dark hair appeared, sauntered across the space towards us. I couldn't help but stare. His easy smile as he approached me had me squeezing my thighs together. I stared at his outstretched hand for a moment, belatedly realizing I was supposed to shake it, and thrust my hand into his grip.

"Nice to meet you, Nicky. I've heard so much about you. I'm Gabriel Hassan. Feel free to shorten it to Gabe."

My tongue felt thick and I swallowed hard. Billie nudged my hip and I jumped, coughing to recover myself. "Nice to meet you, too."

"I'll be out of your hair soon." He picked up a plate and speared three pancakes onto it with his fork, pausing to peruse the syrup collection.

"Stay." The word flew out of my mouth.

Billie looked absolutely beside themselves with excitement, and I caught Tony biting his bottom lip to cover a smile.

"You're sure?" Gabe asked. "I don't want to intrude."

"But *I'm* the intrusion here. I can certainly manage a meal with you here. Besides, I feel like the faster I meet all of you, the happier Billie will be."

"It's true!" Billie skipped across the open space and lifted Spud from the couch, holding him up. "Come meet the little prince."

Gabe turned to Spud and walked towards Billie, giving me a brief reprieve. I inched closer to Tony and leaned against the counter next to where he was working.

"You okay, Nicky?"

"Question..."

"Yeah?"

"Are all of you like ridiculous levels of beautiful? I mean, we're four out of five so far. Is this just a house of secret models?"

Tony cackled, and that had both Gabe and Billie looking over at us. My cheeks flared with heat, and I covered it up by spinning to keep my back towards them, holding out a plate for Tony to deposit the next ready pancakes.

"I think only Gabe has done modeling, but Hana's definitely no slouch in the looks department either."

I was so doomed.

How were they all this pretty?

I bit down a whine, but Tony must've sensed my distress

anyways. He dropped in more batter and then held one arm open to me.

"Come here."

I followed the instructions and tucked myself against him, my skin buzzing as he set his arm around my shoulders. His soothing scent settled my nerves and helped me relax. I drifted in that comfortable altered state in the cocoon of his alpha scent.

Tony was so warm. There were no cameras watching this time, so I let myself rest against him and looped my arms around his waist so I could link my fingers comfortably.

"Better?" he asked, barely loud enough for me to hear.

I closed my eyes and nodded, half drunk on his scent and too relaxed to be awkward about it.

Billie and Gabe seemed entirely occupied lavishing attention on Spud.

By the time there was enough food for all four of us, I was feeling like I'd just gotten out of a massage. Billie patted my butt as they walked by and started fishing out nearly a dozen bottles from the fridge to set on the island. I turned them each in turn, checking the flavors—cherry, apple cinnamon, peach, maple, chocolate, caramel, and every type of berry I could think of. I had only ever used the cheap grocery store syrup that pretended to be maple.

We sat down at the kitchen table, with me between Billie and Tony, and Gabe across from me. I pre-cut all of my pancakes and divided them into sections so that I could taste each of the different syrups.

"Why are you so fucking cute, Books?" Billie asked.

"I'm just being meticulous. I haven't had most of these so how am I supposed to know which one I like best if I don't try all of them?"

Gabe doused his in the apple cinnamon syrup, while Tony was half cherry and half maple. Billie poured some combination of chocolate, strawberry, and blueberry over theirs.

This close to Gabe I could pick out his scent from the mix I remembered coating Billie's skin. Black tea and brown sugar. I pushed down the tingles of desire it elicited. Apparently I had already developed a Pavlovian response.

"How long have you had Spud?" Gabe asked, luring me into conversation.

"Two years," I replied. "He was a little street baby I rescued when he was a couple of weeks old, and we've been together ever since."

"Any story behind his name?"

"Ah, he's a Spud for two reasons."

Gabe listened intently, and even though it was mildly disconcerting to have so many eyes watching me, it was also nice to have the attention. Tony put his hand on the back of my neck, and it became very difficult to care about nerves. I wasn't sure what kind of alpha magic this was. My brother had never been able to chill me out like this, but then I guess there was probably a reactive difference between siblings and potential lovers.

"He was so tiny when I found him, just like a little potato baby." I flushed with warmth at Gabe's smile as I spoke. "And my mom's nickname for me is Patatina, which means little potato. I decided we could both embrace slang terms, so Spud and I are both potato babies."

"Well, you've both grown into majestic beings," said Gabe. "But, in any case, we always appreciate a good potato in this house."

I couldn't help my giggle. "Billie said you're a bouncer? How do you like it?" I asked, sliding into a conversation about work.

"It's pretty good for the most part, but I'm thinking that I'm ready for a change soon. Maybe get into private security instead."

The four of us chatted about our jobs, education, and vacations while I worked my way through all the syrup flavors, eventually settling on a favorite that combined maple and peach with melted butter.

I groaned appreciatively. "I'm pretty sure these are the best pancakes I've ever had in my life."

"Jasper has us all beat for baking," said Billie, "but Tony is the pancake monarch."

"I'm too full to move now."

"Want to have a cuddle and watch a movie in the couch nest?" Billie asked. "After you've digested, I can show you the rest of the house."

The couch sounded like exactly what I needed. "Sounds great."

Tony's thumb tapped against my throat, and I turned to him. "I can carry you over if you're actually too full to move."

My stomach flipped, and I swallowed hard. "What?"

Billie nodded. "He can do it. He's lanky, but he's strong. I get carted around all the time and it's great."

Being carried by the hot alpha I'd been touching most of the morning seemed like the beginning of a very bad idea, one that warmed me from head to toe and overrode my good sense. "Sure."

Tony was on his feet before I could blink. He pulled my chair out and scooped me into his arms, spinning to carry me towards the nest.

The ease with which he lifted me sent a bolt of lust right down my spine to settle between my thighs. His hands squeezed a little tighter, but he didn't say anything about it even though I'm pretty sure he had been able to smell the shift in me.

Spud was sprawled out in the cushions, and blinked one sleepy eye at me when Tony set me down. I buried my face in Spud's fur to hide the flush in my cheeks.

"It's snuggle time!" Billie hopped up into the giant nest and patted the spot next to them for me. I crawled over to join them and Tony sat on their other side, with Gabe on the other side of him. It was becoming increasingly difficult to not focus on the fact that I was in what was basically a bed with three unfairly hot people, one of which I had already slept with, and another that I had definitely thought about while masturbating. Fate was either very cruel or laughing her ass off.

Billie nestled against my side, fingertips inching under my shirt to rest on my bare skin. The nest was probably the most comfortable thing I had ever laid in. Tony pushed some buttons on the remote, and the projector screen descended, lighting up with a rom-com from the early 2000s that would've made me nostalgic under other circumstances, but I was far too distracted by the people around me. Another button push had the curtains closing, plunging us into darkness.

I squeezed my thighs together and shivered as Billie traced patterns on my skin. This was unfair. I wasn't even twenty-four hours out from Billie absolutely annihilating me, and now they were touching me again. Sweat prickled on my skin, and my nipples poked against my bra.

Tony's arm stretched across the back of the nest, his fingertips dangling so that they brushed the top of my shoulder. The touch was so light that any other time I probably wouldn't have noticed, but I was way too primed, and goosebumps sprouted all the way down my arm. The darkness only let my imagination run rampant. It was way, *way* too easy to imagine sliding down and letting the whole lot of them descend upon me.

Billie looked up at me, inching closer until their mouth was at my ear. "Your heart's beating really fast, Books. You okay?"

Saying yes would technically be a lie, but I also didn't want to draw further attention to myself, so instead I nodded. "Yep."

Billie licked along the shell of my ear, and an embarrassing moan snuck out. I tensed and held still, not even daring to breathe, experiencing the turn of Tony and Gabe's heads towards me in slow motion.

Oh, fuck.

"Billie you shouldn't tease your guest," Tony admonished.

Billie huffed and slumped back to their original position. Tony set his fingertips more firmly against my skin, and I tensed again, a gasp sneaking out.

Get it together, girl.

I could feel all of their gazes, which did absolutely nothing to temper my bodily response. Hot people need to stop looking at me right now, or I was going to start getting squirmy.

Billie inched back up. "Want me to take you up to my bedroom?" they whispered.

That would almost be *more* embarrassing. There would be

zero hiding the reason why we'd retreated barely a third into a movie.

The temptation was there.

Even their gentle innocent touches were able to set me on fire. Gabe watched me with interest.

I sucked in a breath and held it, the subtle flavors of their combined alpha scents—coffee, caramel, tea, and brown sugar—lingering on my tongue. If I opened my mouth right now to answer Billie, I wasn't sure what would come out. Part of me wished that I'd had a partner in the past that had elicited this type of response so that I would've had a little bit of background to deal with it now. Instead, everything was brand new and bordering on intoxicating.

I shook my head slowly, as if that might somehow make it imperceptible to the alphas watching me.

Billie pouted. "Okay, let me know if you change your mind."

They nestled in again, this time resting their head into the curve of my neck where I could feel their hot breath straight through my shirt.

Doomed.

That's exactly what I was right now.

Chapter Eleven
Nicky

Every wiggle, every shift to get more comfortable, every
breath made me keenly aware that the person who had basically given me a carnal revelation was plastered against me, and
that the other two in proximity had absolutely been in the same
position with them. Maybe they had even been the ones to teach
Billie.

I squeezed my hand, digging into the blankets beneath me,
and let my fingertips trail along Billie's arm.

Was I sliding down an extremely slippery slope? Yes.

Was I going to hop off this couch, take my cat home, and save
myself some colossal embarrassment? Nope.

Billie squirmed against me, pressing their hips tightly against
my leg. I let my touches linger. I traced up their arm and over their
throat, tucking their hair aside, to run my knuckles on the underside of their jaw. Their fingers kneaded against my skin, inching

down my waist to my thigh. Billie rearranged themselves to tuck their face against my skin. Hot breath puffed against me. Billie let out a whine, and it was as if the air in the room itself froze.

Tony paused the movie and hit another button that turned on a single light, just enough to properly illuminate our expressions.

"I have no issue with the two of you playing, but if you don't want us to join then you should take it up to a bedroom."

I stared at him helplessly, my heart pounding like the entire drum section of a parade.

Tony quirked his head and slipped his hand beneath my hair to hold the back of my neck, as he had done several times already today. "Unless...that's something you were interested in?"

My tongue sat like a lead weight in my mouth. How was I supposed to answer that? Fantasy and reality were crashing against one another. Fantasy Nicky was shouting *'yes fucking please!'* in my head, while Reality Nicky felt like a baby deer about to be eaten by the entire wolf pack.

"Nicky, I'm happy to give you anything you want," said Tony, "but not if you don't use words to tell me what that is."

My heartbeat was one big pulse through my body.

Fantasy Nicky was doing her damndest to throw Reality Nicky under the bus to claim victory. Would it really be so bad if I went for it?

They were all *so* pretty, and they were looking at me like they wanted to devour me. None of my old boyfriends had had that fire in their eyes when they looked at me.

"I'm not very good at the words part," I finally whispered.

Billie grinned up at me and squeezed me tightly around the waist. "The fact that it's not an outright no is making several fantasies come true right now."

"Billie don't pressure her." It was the first time Gabe had spoken in a while, and his voice had my clit pulsing.

Goddamn these alphas and their velvety voices.

"I'm not *trying* to pressure," Billie defended.

"I, um, I've never done anything with more than one person... at the same time, I mean."

95

Gabe and Tony's gazes sizzled. *I* was making them look like that.

"Have you used the sexy stoplights?" Billie asked.

I shook my head.

"It's helpful for people when words are hard, which is a lot of the time for me when these things get going. Green means that you're okay with what's happening and want more, yellow means that we should pause and either talk about what's happening or change what we're doing, and red is a full stop that initiates immediate aftercare."

"Sounds reasonable," I squeaked out.

"Okay," said Billie, "so if I wanted to kiss you right now, what color would that be?"

My whole body tingled. "Green," I whispered.

Billie sat up and moved with a kind of sultry energy that I would probably never be able to embody, sitting directly in my lap. "You can say the colors whenever, and we're all going to respect wait, stop, or anything else that indicates you need a break."

At my nod, Billie braced both hands on the couch behind me and dove in. The sweep of their mouth against mine was like a shot of whiskey that burned all the way down. Knowing that I was being watched ramped up every sensation. I clung to Billie's hips and shivered. Billie pulled away only to push aside my hair and fasten their lips to my throat. I turned to accommodate and found Tony right there.

His thumb traced over my cheek. "Color?"

"Green," I said breathlessly.

Tony was a whole new type of intoxicant as he kissed me for the first time, his fingers curling in my hair, the steady warmth of his mouth dragging me under. I thought I was doomed with Billie, but now I was doubly fucked. Metaphorically...but I had hopes for it being literally, too. The sweet caramel notes of his scent saturated every inhale. My pussy throbbed, the fantasy of the two of them fuelling this delicious reality. I moaned against his mouth.

96

A tentative hand rested on my ankle and I pulled away from Tony.

Gabe was watching me. "Do you want me to leave?"

I shook my head.

"Do you want me to participate?"

Fantasy Nicky was ready to drag him in by his tank top and devour him. "Yes."

I'd been right about Billie ruining me.

Tony chuckled next to me. "Brave girl."

I hooked my fingers into the collar of this shirt and kissed him again before Reality Nicky could gain any foothold. His lips were unfairly soft.

Movement out of the corner of my eye caught my attention. Billie tossed their shirt aside, leaving their top half clad only in indigo lace. I reached out blindly, and Billie linked their fingers with mine, bringing my hand to their chest so I could knead their breast through the lace. Gabe's weight dipped the cushions as he maneuvered himself between Tony and I, resting his forehead briefly against mine.

"Color?" he asked.

I figured that action would serve just as well as a verbal agreement and tipped my face up to claim my first kiss with him. It was just as intense as the others as he slipped his tongue into my mouth, his palm landing on my shoulder and sliding to rest beneath the hollow of my throat, his thumb stroking gently.

Most of my sexual history was as vanilla as an ice cream scoop, but the way his hand trembled, as if he was holding back, made me crave something hell of a lot deeper. The only problem was I didn't know how to ask for that because I wasn't sure how to put it into words. I had read plenty of books that contained all manner of things I'd always been too afraid to try, but they had certainly put ideas in my head. I wrapped my hand around his wrist and inched it up until that palm was against my throat. His fingers twitched against my skin.

"Squeeze or hold?" Gabe asked.

"Hold."

He claimed my mouth again with a burgeoning ferocity that had my thighs slipping together. Billie teased my ear with nips and licks, eager hands sliding under my shirt and into my bra cup. I couldn't move with Gabe pinning me, and somehow that made the sensation of Billie pinching my nipples all the more intense. I'd lost track of Tony until he grabbed each of my ankles and slowly spread my legs open.

I was still fully clothed, but it felt like I had been laid bare.

Billie lifted the hem of my shirt and whispered huskily in my ear, "Colour?"

"Green," I murmured, having pulled away from Gabe just enough to answer. Billie stripped off my blouse and tossed it aside. I should've worn a cuter bra. Beige was definitely not cute enough for my first fourway.

Gabe reclaimed me. The man kissed like it was his entire job. Billie lifted my breast free of my bra and Tony nuzzled it. I put my hand to the back of his head to encourage him so I didn't have to stop kissing Gabe to give anyone a color to keep things moving forward.

That plan lasted for all of two seconds. I broke away, arching against Tony with a moan as he pulled my nipple into his mouth. I panted out curses as he tended to me with an expertise that spoke of long hours of practice. Gabe's hand slid up to hold my chin, turning my face towards Billie so he could lay his teeth against my skin, grazing the scent gland at my throat. I trembled like a foal just learning to walk. We'd barely begun and I was already overwhelmed.

The three of them traded places and switched roles with practiced ease, and I couldn't help but imagine the spectacular flow that must be at work during Jasper's heats.

Sweat clung to my skin as if I'd been fighting a fever.

"Colour, Books?" Billie whispered in my ear.

"Green. So green." Reality Nicky was busy merging with Fantasy Nicky, rationality melting away until all that remained was the bone deep craving to have all of them *right now*.

Tony and Gabe both lost their shirts, and Billie leaned back to let me glide my hands over their exposed skin. They passed me back and forth between them for kisses that made my head swim. Tony's chest had a light scattering of curly hair down the center, while Gabe was pretty much bare.

The two of them picked me up until I was on my knees between them. Gabe's tongue swept into my mouth while Billie and Tony sucked at my throat until I was shaking. Tony set his palm on my stomach and inched his fingertips beneath my waistband. I put my hand over his and pushed it deeper, convinced I was going to implode if someone didn't put their hands on me right now. Someone undid my button and zipper and between the many sets of hands I was freed of my dress pants. I whimpered and flexed my hips.

Gabe pulled away and held my face in his hands. "I want to see what you look like when Tony makes you come."

Oh god.

I was already so wet I could feel my soaked panties sticking to me.

Tony cupped me first.

"Please."

"Please *what*, Nicky?" Tony asked, his voice husky in my ear.

"Please. Someone needs to get inside me before I explode."

Tony chuckled. "Good girl."

The ridiculous needy sound that came out of me at being called a 'good girl' had Gabe grinning at me like the cat that'd caught the canary.

One of Tony's fingers slowly spread me open, and I shuddered at the slick glide. Another finger joined it, sliding from clit to cunt, where he pressed inside with ease.

"Jesus *Christ*." My eyes flared wide, and I used both hands on Gabe's shoulders to steady myself as I pushed my knees apart and rocked against Tony's hand.

"You're so wet, baby girl," he whispered in my ear, biting my earlobe as he finger fucked me, the sound of it audible to everyone. The name made me melt and I whimpered desperately.

Billie appeared in my field of vision and pressed their cheek to

Tony's, slipping their hand down my body to join his. He angled to allow space, so he could plunge into me while Billie worked my clit.

Gabe put his hand back on my throat, his thumb holding my chin in place as he dove in and sank his teeth against my scent gland.

My panting turned to uncontrollable moans to an outright scream as the three of them worked in tandem to obliterate me. My pussy squeezed Tony's fingers, and Billie's inability to let me have only one orgasm carried me up and over another crest before I could catch my breath. Gabe leaned back to watch me as I came, his hazel eyes on fire. It was a vulnerability I wasn't used to, and it made me feel every touch all the more keenly.

When Tony pulled his hand free, Gabe lifted it, the fingers shining in the dim light. He sucked them both into his mouth to lick them clean.

"Holy shit." I squirmed.

Why was that so hot?

"Do you want more, Books?" Billie asked. "I promise the alpha dick is worth it."

I couldn't stop my laughter. It came out sounding a touch hysterical, but I didn't care.

"I'm the only one that's come so far. We should change that."

"I agree," Billie said with a grin.

The four of us slipped off our remaining clothes. They had probably seen one another in the state a thousand times, but it was hard to feel self-conscious when they all looked ready to devour me. Both Tony and Gabe were bigger than anyone I'd had in the past. Not an insurmountable kind of big, but definitely not a glide-right-in size.

"Condoms?" Billie asked me.

Tony smiled warmly. "We're fine with whatever you're comfortable with, Nicky."

"I think I'm okay without them." I'd gotten topped up on my contraceptives last month, and was ready to ride this train to the final station.

Billie wrapped their arms around me. "I'm not allowed to come today unless Tony or Hana give me permission, but I'm loving you getting to play with the alphas."

I looked at Tony curiously. "Why can't they come?"

"All part of the arrangement," Tony said. He crooked his finger, and I crossed the couch nest toward him. His cock pressed against my stomach, and his hands cupped my ass as he kissed me. I lifted my arms around his neck to keep myself aloft.

"How do you feel about being on top?" Tony asked.

"Not my usual spot. I can try."

"I just want you in control. We can trade after if you like, but you're in charge of getting my cock into you."

My pussy clenched, wishing it was there already. "Okay."

Tony kissed me again until I was shaking and desperate to be touched. He stretched out on his back and took Gabe's cock in his hand, his other disappearing between Billie's thighs, the two of them using his hands to take their own pleasure. I lingered a few moments to watch them, transfixed by the way they moved and how easy it all seemed to be for them.

I set a knee on either side of Tony's hips and teased him softly, running my wet slit along the length of his cock. Emboldened by the shudder it drew from him, I took him in hand and circled the tip of him with my thumb.

I braced myself with a palm on his shoulder, wiggling to get a reasonable angle, fitting the tip of him to my entrance. Even being this wet I wasn't entirely sure how I was going to get the rest of him in. I pushed him deeper and breathed through the delicious burn.

"Go slow, baby girl. I know it's a lot."

I whined pathetically at his words. Why hadn't I invested in a bigger dildo? Why hadn't I been able to look into the future and know I'd be in bed with two alphas so I could have prepared?

I moved gingerly, taking him in small increments, rising up entirely and sinking back down to gain a fraction of an inch each time.

"Fuck," Tony hissed. "You feel incredible, baby girl."

101

My pussy sucked him in a little more. The stretch walked the line between exquisite pain and unbearable pleasure. My vision went hazy as I started to fuck him, doing my best to keep going slow when I just wanted to get railed until I couldn't think.

I only managed to take about two thirds of him, but he didn't seem to mind. Billie rolled away from him and slapped the side of the couch. I heard the drag of something against the floor, and they popped up with a bottle of lube, squeezing a dollop into their hand and wrapping it around the base of Tony's cock. His fingers disappeared back inside them and Billie leaned forward, teeth biting against my skin.

Between the two of us we could handle all of him. Billie teased my clit and Gabe climbed up behind me, cupping my breasts, rolling and pinching the nipples as he nipped at my throat. Tony fucked up into me and my next breath came out as a choked up cry.

"Color, baby girl?"

"God, green. Don't stop. No one stop anything."

I couldn't breathe as his cock drove into me, buffered by Billie's fist to keep from going too far. Gabe's breath was hot and ragged in my ear, his cock tucked between my ass cheeks and up my back. That was something else I had never played with, and the curiosity was bordering on insatiable now. Good sense kept my mouth shut, though. If I couldn't take a full alpha dick in my pussy, then the odds of being able to take one in my ass were pretty nil.

Pleasure burned through every cell, and my pussy pulsed around Tony, getting closer to the edge with each passing second.

"Come on, baby girl. Show me what you feel like when you come on his cock."

I shattered. The pulsing beat of my orgasm seized every muscle and stole my breath. He was so much. Tony bowed up beneath me, and my pulsating cunt dragged him in a little more until my vision burst into stars. I only managed to remain upright because of Gabe's grip on my body.

"Tony," I gasped out. "I need..."

"Tell me what you need."

"I'm ready to trade spots."

"Lay down for me, baby girl," Tony said.

I slid off, my pussy aching at the loss. I stretched out, breathless and waiting. Billie stretched out next to me and linked our fingers, bowing up with a cry as Gabe settled between their thighs and fucked into them.

Tony was hovering above me, leaning down to capture my mouth and tuck himself back against my cunt. I braced a palm against his chest.

"Color?"

"Mostly green. Just go slow."

Tony nodded and eased himself into me. I panted and arched off the cushions, spreading my thighs further and digging my fingertips into his arms.

A string of *'fuck's'* left my mouth, and I gasped out as he slid as deep as I could take him.

"Where do you want me to come?"

How was I supposed to make decisions while getting railed? "Options?"

"I could come deep inside this perfect pussy, or here," he said, tracing his fingers down my torso.

"Surprise me?"

I luxuriated in the soft blankets beneath me and the warm weight of the alpha above me. It didn't take long for me to scale the peak of pleasure again, my body craving him and opening to accept each thrust. Billie pulled my hand over and bit the scent gland at my wrist, sending delicious sparks dancing over my skin.

Tony's breathing shifted, and his movements became more erratic. He fucked deeply into me and pushed me over the edge, a burst of heat blooming in my core as he dropped his head, panting in my ear. I dug the nails of my free hand into his ass cheek, whimpering as he bit my throat. I wasn't sure if that was specifically a pack thing, or an alpha thing, but god, I never wanted it to stop.

Chapter Twelve
Gabe

I definitely had not been anticipating my first meeting with Nicky to go that way. The four of us had passed out in the couch nest, and I woke to Spud sniffing my face. Billie was curled up sleeping in my arms, and Nicky was plastered between them and Tony. I didn't usually care about Billie's random crushes, but then most of them didn't end up at the pack house. Something about shyness enclosing a fiery core of untapped desire had piqued my interest a lot more than I'd expected.

The curtains were still closed so I had no idea how much time had passed, but neither Jasper nor Hana were home yet, so it had probably only been a couple of hours.

I kissed the back of Billie's neck, and their stirring sent a ripple through the cuddle pile, waking Nicky and Tony.

Nicky groaned and stretched, and Spud walked over us to slam down his tiny weight down between Nicky and Billie.

"He's as bad as Roscoe," I said, laughing quietly.

"Roscoe is a voyeur," said Billie. "Spud is a polite little prince who waits till we're all done before invading our space."

Nicky giggled and stroked Spud's ears, snaring him into her arms as she wiggled herself more firmly between the others with a happy little sigh. She was a far cry from the buttoned up librarian who had arrived for breakfast.

I watched her body slowly tense as she came further into the waking world, and I reached over Billie to wrap my hand around her wrist.

"How are you feeling, Nicky?" I asked.

"Um...kind of whipping back and forth between bliss and panic, if I'm being honest."

That wasn't difficult to tell given that her scent had soured now that she was fully awake.

"Trade places with Billie."

My beta rolled right over top of Nicky and wedged themself next to Tony, avoiding crushing Spud in the process. The cat protested anyway and slipped away to lay near our feet. Nicky looked at me with wide eyes.

She wasn't *my* beta, but the alpha instinct to soothe and protect was there regardless. I pushed my scent towards her and wrapped an arm lightly over her waist.

"Walk me through your feelings."

She tucked her face against my chest and melted, looping her arm around my back. "It's just a lot. I'm used to living life in slow mode, and I feel like I've been racing since the moment I met Billie and Tony. It's sort of like my body outran my brain."

"And now that we've slowed down again it's catching up to you?"

"I didn't mean to rush you, Books," Billie said, nervously fidgeting.

"You didn't. Not really. Everything we did was something I wanted to do, but it's still a lot to process."

"Could I interest you in a bath?" I asked, tracing over Nicky's cheek.

"A bath sounds nice," she murmured.

"Would you like the others to join us?"

Her moment of hesitation was enough of an answer.

"Billie will survive without you for half an hour," I said. "Come with me."

We didn't keep much for luxurious supplies in the main floor bathroom, so I opted to bring her upstairs to my room where I had everything we'd need.

I climbed out of the nest, not bothering with anything to cover myself, and watched Nicky tuck a blanket carefully around herself like a dress. Her fingers flexed and squeezed the fabric as she stood, looking to me for guidance. I held out my hand and she took it with a shy smile, letting me lead her upstairs. I'd been naked in this house so often I didn't even think about it anymore, but I could feel her gaze on my ass as she followed me.

My room was on the top level along with Hana's, while Billie's, Tony's, and Jasper's were on the second level. Roscoe greeted us the moment I opened my door.

Nicky's eyes lit up. "Oh my goodness! Hello sweet baby." She reached down, letting him sniff her before she gave him some scratches from head to hip. Roscoe would do any work that I couldn't in calming her down.

I got Nicky situated on my bed while I got the bath running. It was more of a hot tub than a bath by size which made it perfect for our needs.

Nicky looked so small wrapped up with her toes sticking out the bottom of her blanket. Roscoe forced his way onto her lap and she stroked his orange and black patterned fur while she waited for me, looking around the room, taking in the space— cream walls with a gray-blue feature wall behind the double king-sized bed, brown leather headboard, earth-toned fabrics, photos of the pack and I reaching nearly up to the ceiling over my desk in polished brown frames, and a handful of landscape paintings Billie had done for me—eyes darting to and fro.

"Do you regret anything that happened?" I asked, sitting down next to her.

She shook her head. "No. I'm just processing. I had fun. It's very different from what usually happens for me."

"What usually happens? Tell me while you pick your bubble bath," I ordered, pulling her towards the bathroom.

Nicky followed me in her blanket dress, cradling Roscoe.

"Well, the past couple years it's just been me. I never quite worked up the courage to start dating again after I called off my engagement. At least until Billie showed up. They made it feel so easy." She picked out some cinnamon bun gel to add to the water. "They're the first one before today to actually be invested in me having a good time without just waiting for their turn."

I listened as she picked her way through her past, telling me about the panicked decisions, the stress and regret, the string of mediocrity she'd dated prior to her ex-fiance that had set a standard for normal in her relationships. All the way to the relief she'd felt when he'd gotten on a plane to Tokyo, and she'd made the choice to vanish.

She traced her fingers through the frothing bubbles.

"I don't know how to be part of something that makes me feel this good," she confessed. "I'd kind of resolved myself to being a spinster."

"Come here," I said softly.

Nicky set Roscoe down and slipped easily into my arms.

I was familiar with this pattern. Hana had dated shit people too, and hadn't known how to grab onto healthier things. When she and I had met, her walls had been a mile high, but I'd taken the time to love her and show her that she was safe. Nicky wasn't as walled off as Hana had been, but the fear and insecurities were there, along with the similarities in their past and their craving for quiet and comfort after big feelings. I knew how to deal with that.

"Spinster life should be a choice, not something you resolve yourself to. Let's get you in the bath to relax."

"I feel so spoiled. My apartment only has a shower." She sighed against my skin. "I'm sorry to be so much trouble."

"You're no trouble. We express our needs in this house and do our best to help one another anyway that we can. Right now, you need some quiet time, and that's okay. Even when Billie's resting their energy isn't quiet, but that's my whole vibe."

"I guess that would be helpful considering you're a bouncer, right?"

"It comes in handy." I nodded. "You should come by the club with Billie and Jasper sometime. It might be a little bit out of your element, but no one will hassle you there."

"I haven't been to a club since college. I could stop by, though."

"Do you want me to leave you be or stay?" I asked, turning her towards the bath.

Nicky fidgeted, swaying gently so the blanket swished around her. "If I'm by myself I'll stew."

"Fair enough. Do you want me in the water or outside of it?"

The question seemed to relax her, which had been my whole intention. Letting people have control of the situation and guide things to their own comfort level was important.

She stared at the bath, then back to me a couple of times. "In the water is fine."

I didn't know her as well as I wanted to yet, and I was eager to uncover the mysteries. She was covering a lot of new ground, and I was more than happy to hold her hand while she traversed. I slipped into the water and got myself comfortable in one of the corners.

Nicky's cheeks flamed pink as she dropped the blanket and stepped into the bath across from me. She found one of the lower seats so she was enveloped to the tops of her shoulders, the tips of her hair trailing in the water. Bubbles covered the surface, obscuring everything except for our heads.

"Better?" I asked.

She hesitated, her cheeks going even darker, and sank into the water a bit more.

"Nicky, I can't help you if you don't talk to me."

She muttered something I couldn't make out, so I prodded her with my toes, prompting her to speak again.

"Could I sit by you?" she finally asked, loud enough for me to hear.

"Of course you can."

She let out a little huff and crossed the bath to sit at my side, still vibrating with nervous energy.

"You can sit closer if you'd like," I offered.

Nicky looked up at me with those beautiful doe eyes, practically begging me with her silence to take the final step for her. I draped my arm over her shoulder and reached beneath the water to turn her so her legs went over my lap and I could cradle her easily.

She squeaked, and this close her scent overpowered the bubble bath. The sour notes were gone, leaving only the rich, spicy sweetness. She really wasn't kidding about her body outrunning her brain. It would be easy to shift her and indulge in that craving, but that wasn't what she needed right now.

I guided her head to rest on my shoulder so she could get the most potent source of my scent, and then I got my purr going. She relaxed bit by bit until she was half asleep and pliant in my arms. I was used to going without sleep for long stretches, and didn't mind staying up for her while she settled.

"Is this Hana's?" she asked, tracing her fingertips over the bondmark on my throat.

I shivered at the tentative contact. "Yeah, that's hers."

"Billie told me a bit about her, and you. You and Hana were together before the pack formed?"

"Yep. Friends for a year, lovers for another. Then Billie found us, and, well, you know how that turned out."

Nicky fussed in my arms, sighing and drawing patterns on my skin. "I feel so out of my depth. Everyone is so nice, but my brain is low-key screaming in the background."

"If it makes you feel better, mine did that too when Billie first rolled up with Tony and Jasper."

"Really?" The tip of Nicky's nose brushed Hana's bondbite.

"Absolutely. It's a massive adjustment all around. Adding three people into my relationship with Hana took a hell of a lot of communication and precarious balancing. Not to mention introducing a pack to friends and family. Not everyone gets it."

"Oh god. I don't know how my family would react." She tensed back up. "I shouldn't be worrying about that. It's been two dates."

I pulled her around so she straddled me, cupping her face. "Breathe for me."

Nicky closed her eyes and followed my instructions.

"If your mind wants to go that direction then I think you should let it. There's no pressure. Allow yourself to experience those feelings. If it only takes you two dates with Billie to get those thoughts going, then who cares who thinks it's too fast? They're just thoughts, and you're allowed to have those. God knows I had them about Hana from the moment I met her."

"But..."

"Listen, I know what it feels like when Billie sets their sights on you. They pour their entire self into situations, and when they want you there is zero question of that, but I also know that can be overwhelming if you're not used to that kind of energy. Billie makes people feel good, and it's normal to want that to continue, and to think about it."

I'd learned to trust Billie's instincts over time. I didn't know what it was about them, but they're damn good at sussing people out, and I can't fault the results of their choices when they gave me my pack.

Nicky snuggled closer. "No one thinks anything when omegas have multiple lovers," she said softly.

"But they do with betas?"

"A lot of people, yeah. They're very forgiving of omegas and their needs. Betas don't have that same drive, the same need to have sex. I wasn't expecting to want it as much as I do."

"For some people that's dependent on their partners."

"It seems that way. I definitely slept with past partners, and I had a good time, but I never really felt...what I felt today."

"Have you ever been with an alpha before today?" I asked, and Nicky shook her head. "You're not an omega, but you'll still respond differently to each of the dynamics. It could be as simple as that."

"Maybe. I've only ever dated betas. But it was just as strong with Billie yesterday, and they're not an alpha."

I stroked a hand down her side and cradled her head with the other, blatantly ignoring the growing response of my body to her nearness.

"I don't pretend to have all the answers, but I do know that Billie is a force of nature. They come into someone's life like a hurricane, shake up absolutely everything, and then you have to decide what to do afterward."

Nicky giggled and laid her palm against my chest, just over my heart. "Sounds accurate. I really like them."

"Me too. Circling back for a moment. No one is going to judge you for wanting sex, or for acting on that desire. We're a pretty sexual bunch, as you might've noticed."

"I might've gotten a *small* clue to that."

"You can hit the brakes whenever you need. Our relationships shift and change so that everyone gets what they need. If that means you want to de-escalate, take out the sexual component, and just work on being friends with whoever you want, you can do that, and no one will think any less of you. Just like no one will think any less of you if you think you'd rather have an orgy every day after work."

Her burst of laughter was gratifying, and she snuggled even closer. "I don't think I would survive that. I'm pretty sure I need a recovery day."

"That's probably not a bad idea," I agreed. "Billie takes us like a champ, but they also have several years of experience with that."

Nicky fidgeted in my grasp. "It all feels so soon. I don't even think it's been a week since I met them, and now I'm naked in a tub with their boyfriend."

"*Technically* I'm closer to husband because we're bonded, but I get your meaning." I laughed and squeezed her tight. "I am very familiar with freight train Billie. We can hit the brakes and you can go at any speed you like."

"How do you slow down in a situation like this? I feel like I've unlocked some inner sex goddess, and she's not a fan of slowing down."

"That's something I have a fair bit of experience with."

"Going slow?" she asked.

"Not quite." I hooked a finger under her chin and lifted her gaze to mine. "Making slow just as fun as fast."

She sucked her lower lip between her teeth. "You shouldn't say things like that."

"Why not?"

"Because it makes me really want to find out if it's true." Her gaze dropped to my mouth.

"Ask."

"Kiss me?"

Her lips were soft and eager against mine. The taste of her was already familiar, a flavor that would be too easy to crave.

Slow might feel like an oxymoron when it was happening while we were naked and after she had just fucked one of my partners, but I was a man of indulgence, and her mouth was the perfect sample of decadence.

I moved deliberately, keeping the pace from running away on us, from letting her newly awakened desires take over. I drank down the little sounds she made. They were an elixir that would haunt my dreams as surely as my need to touch her.

Nicky pulled away, breathless, chest heaving.

"Slow is really hard," she whispered.

"Stand up for me," I said.

She slid off of my lap, rivulets of water sliding down her skin, standing in front of me, completely exposed.

"Good girl. Turn around."

I didn't miss the sharp intake of her breath, or the way her body shook at '*good girl*'.

I set a firm hand on each of her hips and pulled her closer, forcing her legs apart when she backed up against my knees. The scrape of my facial hair made her shiver as I pressed a kiss to her lower back. I worked up her spine slowly until I couldn't reach any further, and then pulled her back to sit on my lap.

Nicky tipped her head back, leaning fully against my chest when I laid my palm over her throat.

"You make it very hard to behave. Billie's a brat that likes to be pushed toward submission. You hand it to us." I nuzzled her cheek softly.

"Submission? I only vaguely know about it from reading spicy books."

"The way you respond. The way you give over control." I traced down the line of her trachea and she sucked in another sharp breath. "Billie likes to be *made* to submit, but I think you like the peace of it. Tell me how you're feeling."

Nicky hummed quietly. "Hmm, relaxed and needy at the same time?"

"Good. I won't take it very far tonight."

"What if I wanted to?"

"You're on recovery time," I insisted. "I want you to be able to walk later, and Tony was already plenty for you. Plus, I need to get Hana adjusted to the idea first."

"I can be patient. You said slow would be just as fun," she whispered.

I bit down on her shoulder hard enough to make her freeze, lifting my head to growl in my ear. "Are you not having a good time, Nicky?"

I gathered her hair into my fist and kissed up the back of her neck.

"*Fuck,*" she gasped.

"I should get you to bed before we both take things too far. Do you want to stay up here with me or go down to the others?"

"Will Billie be upset if I stay up here?" she asked, voice quiet, a touch of nerves coloring the words.

"I think you'll find they're pretty good at sharing. They'll just be happy you're still in the house."

Nicky yawned, as if the mention of a bed reminded her how exhausted she was.

"Have you soaked long enough? Tony will feel bad if he's ruined you."

"Well, if he did, it was my fault, but I think I'm okay for now."

"Perfect." I got the tub draining and slid out of the water, fetching us both towels from the warming rack. Nicky let me dry her off, and she snuggled into my bed, happy as a clam. Roscoe hopped onto the bed and slammed himself down to be Nicky's little spoon. I shoved my arm under the pillows and wrapped the other around Nicky, tucking my palm under her cheek. My cock was still at attention against her ass.

"Do you want some help with that?" she asked.

I nipped her shoulder. "Go to sleep, Nicky. It's not going to kill either of us to wait for another time to get our hands on each other."

Chapter Thirteen
Hana

I stopped dead inside the door, the smell of sex hitting me like a brick wall.

Someone obviously had fun while I was at work. I dropped my keys on their designated hook and kicked off my shoes, wandering into the living room where I found Billie sprawled on top of Tony, the both of them fast asleep. I could smell Gabe, too, and a more unfamiliar scent mixed with the others.

I nudged Tony. He opened one eye and stretched slowly. "Morning, Han."

I leaned down to kiss him. "I can't believe you guys had an orgy without me. Rude."

Tony chuckled, and the combo of sound and movement woke Billie.

Our beta grinned up at me and reached grabby hands to lure me into a kiss, too. "Hey there, beautiful. How was work?"

"Sweaty. Quadruple boot camps and some very competitive clients. Where's Gabe? He usually stays down with you."

"He's keeping our guest company," said Tony, offering me a soft, almost apologetic smile.

"Is this a guest I know?"

"You know *of* her," Billie said. "You haven't met her yet."

I dug my fingers into the back of the couch. I always liked to climb into Gabe's bed after work, but I couldn't do that today if someone I didn't know was in there. She probably wouldn't take kindly to a stranger sliding between the sheets.

"Is it the librarian you've been crushing on?" I asked.

Before they could answer, the front door opened again, and Jasper popped inside. "Oh, hot damn. You guys are ripe." He laughed.

"They're being sexual deviants without us," I called back.

"Well that's inconsiderate when I brought home treats."

"Get in the nest, you two," Billie demanded.

"I should shower first," I said. The workout clothing had done its job and dried quickly, but I was still covered in sweat, and my scalp was starting to itch.

"We already have to do laundry. It's not gonna be any worse if you get in here a little bit sweaty."

I relented and shucked my outfit to join them.

"Jaspy!" Billie called. "Get your cute little butt in here."

Our omega rolled his eyes with a smile on his face as he set the baked goods he'd brought home on the counter prior to stripping down like the rest of us. The four of us bundled together, Billie climbing over Tony to greet each of us with a kiss.

"Where's Gabe?" Jasper asked.

"Upstairs with Nicky," Tony replied, a frown marring his features. "She got a bit wigged out after her first group experience so he took her for a bath and it seems like they're just staying up there for a while."

It had been a long time since Billie had brought anyone to the pack house, and the fact that it was so soon made me infinitely more curious to meet this woman for myself. I curled around

116

Jasper, nuzzling his beard with my cheek. He turned in my arms for a proper kiss before tucking himself under my chin to sleep. The others were out almost instantly, but I was left staring at the ceiling in the dark.

I contemplated slipping upstairs to snoop. Gabe almost never closed his door with only the two of us up there, but now it almost felt like an invasion to even consider walking up those stairs. It was weird for him to not be here with us, and weirder still to be proverbially barred from where I wanted to be. The petulant part of me had me pouting in the quiet. I just wanted to tuck into Gabe's arms for a minute after our hours apart, and I couldn't.

I closed my eyes and willed myself to fall asleep. Success occurred at some point, and when I woke, it was deep in the afternoon, and a cat I didn't recognize was draped on top of Jasper and I.

"Hey there, little stranger." The cat lifted a sleepy gray head and leaned into my offered hand. I nudged Billie with my foot. "Did you get another cat without telling me?"

My beta lifted their head in much the same manner as the cat. "That's Nicky's baby. His name is Spud. Roscoe is upstairs while he visits."

I hadn't been a cat lover until we'd adopted Roscoe. That little tortie had stolen my heart, and there was no going back. Spud looked like he might be a heart thief too.

"We should probably get both of them some food." I untangled myself from Jasper, unhooked Spud's leash from the coffee table, and carried him into the kitchen. "Can one of you grab Roscoe?"

"On it," said Billie as they climbed out of the cuddle pile.

I opened up a can of fancy cat food for Spud and dumped it out onto a plate for him and got his water. "I guess you probably haven't been to the potty either?" I asked, scratching his ears.

I carried him over to one of the concealed litter boxes we had on each level and opened up the door for Spud. He sniffed for a while, eventually climbing inside to do his business, kicking the litter around, and adorably wiping his paws on the floor mat next to the box.

"There's a good boy. Let's get you some breakfast." I carted him back into the kitchen and set down his plate and bowl, where he proceeded to stuff his sweet face. Billie appeared with Roscoe, and the two cats stared at one another warily.

"Roscoe, we got you a little temporary buddy. Want to say hi?" We held Roscoe so he and Spud could touch noses. Neither kicked up any fuss, so Billie put our baby down, and I got him his own plate of food.

They both seemed calm enough that I wasn't worried, which was good because I did *not* want to be dealing with a cat fight for the sake of Billie's crush. Or I guess, given the situation, this woman was also Tony's, Jasper's, and Gabe's crush now, too.

I was the odd one out.

I usually was when it came to romance. I'd been the most resistant to joining the pack in the first place, half convinced that they would charm Gabe away from me, at least until they had made it unmistakably clear in their actions that they wanted me, too. The others had gone on dates occasionally since we'd all gotten together, but they'd almost never brought someone back here.

Footsteps coming down the stairs drew my attention, and it occurred to me that I was butt naked and probably about to meet this person. "Billie."

"Yeah?"

"We can't all be completely naked."

"Why not? We're naked constantly."

"I don't want my first meeting with this woman to be with my tits out," I whisper-hissed.

Billie sighed dramatically and trotted off, returning just in time with one of the robes that must've been left hanging in the main floor bathroom. I whipped it on with seconds to spare as Gabe appeared in a pair of sweatpants, his arm around a brunette bundled in a robe like mine, though the garment dwarfed her.

I assessed what I could at a distance and in dim lighting. Nicky's dark hair hung loose to her shoulders and she leaned into Gabe. No surprise there. His relaxing presence was the main reason I'd been drawn to him in the first place. He'd soothed my anxieties and stress from the beginning, and it sounded like that was what she'd needed after more than half the pack had gotten her into bed.

I couldn't quite put my finger on how I felt about this stranger spending the night with Gabe. I'd never been *particularly* jealous, but Gabe was...different for me. The others had come into the picture as an existing package, and we'd all meshed together really well, but Gabe had always been able to understand me better than the rest.

Billie and the others were already enamored. I hadn't yet fallen sway to whatever charm this woman happened to have over them, and I'd be damned if I didn't stay on my toes to make sure my pack wasn't going to get hurt.

The curtains opened about halfway to let in the light, and I saw Tony set the remote aside. He climbed off the bed and wandered over to greet Nicky, bare as the day he was born. I couldn't hear what he murmured to her, but I could see her smile and the way she relaxed when he hooked a finger under her chin, lifting her mouth to his.

Yep. He was in deep.

Jasper sat up, still half asleep, his hair in every direction. His cheeks turned bright red when he noticed Nicky, and he grabbed one of the smaller blankets around his waist, rolling the top edge until it was secure enough for him to stand up with it. Nicky gave him a shy wave, and then her gaze swiveled to land on me. She tensed immediately.

I didn't want to be at odds with her, but at the same time I was way too comfortable with the status quo. The others were falling hard by the look of things, and I was never one for doing things quickly. I had withstood the force of Hurricane Billie for a whole year before finally agreeing to move in here with them, and even that was fast for me.

I could be pleasant and still remain on guard for the safety of my pack.

I would wait for her to come to me. I stepped over the cats and into the kitchen to get the coffee going alongside the kettle, and took down plates for whatever Jasper had brought home for us.

Nicky watched me from a distance, everyone catching her in a group hug. She was pretty, with that soft and sweet vibe all tucked up in her robe. But I would have to reserve my judgement until I actually got to know her.

"Why don't the lot of you put on some clothes, or at least some robes, so we can have a meal without most of us naked?" I suggested.

I wasn't a prude by any stretch of the imagination, but we weren't exactly a house of nudists—at least most of the time— and I'm sure Nicky would probably appreciate having our clan at least somewhat dressed while she ate.

I turned the oven on to preheat to warm up the baked goods we'd be having.

Billie grumbled their way upstairs with Tony and Jasper on their heels. Gabe maneuvered Nicky over to the kitchen, but she was distracted partway to me by the cats.

"Oh my god! Spuddy, did you make a friend?"

She kneeled down and held out her hand to Roscoe. "Lovely to see you again, petit sir."

Our cat sniffed her fingers, shoving his cheek along the tips to indicate his approval. She scooped up Spud, and Gabe scooped up our baby, the two of them coming further into the kitchen.

"Hana, this is Nicky. Nicky, this is Hana."

I hit the button on the coffee pot before turning fully towards her, my hand extended. "Nice to finally meet you."

She put her hand in mine, and I took note of the warmth and the calluses down her fingers. Her cheeks were hot pink, and she buried her face behind Spud's head, hiding her obvious discomfort by kissing him. "Nice to meet you, too. Billie told me you're a personal trainer. How do you like that?"

"It's a lot of fun most of the time. You should come to one of the boot camp classes."

Nicky laughed. "My arms are strong from carrying books. Absolutely nothing else is remotely fit, and I'm pretty sure a boot camp would destroy me."

Gabe slipped away from Nicky and hugged me with Roscoe sandwiched between us. He kissed me, slow and deep, fully distracting me from the beta in our kitchen.

"Miss me?" Gabe laid an easy smile on me and tucked my hair behind my ear, his fingers lingering as they slid down my jaw.

"Always. Someone was hogging you." I poked his chest playfully.

Nicky's cheeks flushed impossibly brighter. "I'm so sorry. I didn't mean to."

I waved off the concern, staunchly ignoring the little flip in my stomach at her blushing because of me. "Gabe is his own person, and I don't blame you for needing some quiet time after a living room orgy. Can I get you some coffee?"

"Yeah, I'd love some. Thank you."

"Fancy or regular?"

"Whatever you feel like making?" She set Spud back down. "Can I help?"

"Guests don't help," I insisted. I certainly wasn't going to put her to work on her first visit to the packhouse. "Have a seat. Feelings on milk?"

Nicky blinked. "Love it."

"I'll get you a café au lait started, and Gabe can grab you the ten million flavors of creamer out of the fridge."

"It kind of feels like a restaurant here with you guys having so many options for everything."

"All of our tastes run a little bit differently," I told her. "We love all the same bases and mix it up with our sauces and flavors."

"That's nice though," said Nicky. "I grew up in the 'if your parents made it for you, you're going to eat it and love it' kind of household."

121

"I think most of us did too, but that's part of the luxury of being an adult."

I fixed up her coffee and sat it in front of her. She added a splash of hazelnut syrup to the cup and stirred it with the spoon Gabe handed her.

The rest of our pack had returned downstairs, dressed in lounging clothes, and gathered around the bar seats.

"Why don't we eat at the table to give Nicky a little bit more space?" I suggested. "Jasper, can you grab us whatever you brought home?"

Our omega was up on his feet, now dressed in a loose white long sleeved T-shirt and blue checkered pants. He opened up a box of croissants—a mix of plain, cheese, chocolate, and raspberry —arranging them on a tray along with a ramekin of water to steam them while they warmed. He popped them in the oven while Gabe hauled out the eggs and a couple packages of bacon.

"Eggs, bacon, and pastries okay for you Nicky?" Gabe asked.

Nicky nodded. "Absolutely. I love all of those things."

Jasper fetched himself a coffee and sat down with Nicky, adding a hearty glug of cinnamon creamer to his mug. I let Jasper and Tony occupy Nicky while the rest of us worked on the food —me cracking eggs into a mixing bowl, Gabe laying out the strips of bacon on a cookie sheet, and Billie whisking up the eggs as I added them. I kept an eye on our guest while I worked, noting her warm response to their easy touches and the way she laughed at their stories.

The oven timer went off, and Jasper extracted the pastries, arranging them across two dinner plates, offering first dibs to those of us in the kitchen, and setting the rest on the table.

I nibbled at my raspberry confection, standing next to Gabe as he stirred the scrambled eggs in the pan, the bacon cooking away in the oven.

"How are you feeling?" he asked me with a whisper.

I could only shrug. Nicky was pleasant enough, even if she did have my entire pack in her thrall.

"Do you wanna go out on a date after Nicky leaves?"

I leaned into his side, letting his arm wrap around my waist while I looped mine around his shoulders.

"Yes please. Where do you want to go?"

"It's nice today. We could go to the conservatory, or take a walk at one of those pretty trails outside the city."

"Tough choice. I'll have to flip a coin after we eat." I kissed his cheek, letting my touch linger.

"Or, I could take you downstairs and hold the paddles while you kickbox your stress away."

He knew me far too well.

"Have I told you lately that I love you?"

"Before I left for work, but I never get tired of hearing it." He pulled me in and kissed my forehead, though he had to stand on his toes to do so. "I love you, too."

I breathed him in and ignored the lingering scent of Nicky on his skin. I had to trick my brain into not thinking of her as an interloper. I wasn't going to lose anyone simply because they had gotten interested in someone else. They were all mine. And they were all going to stay that way.

Chapter Fourteen
Gabe

I knew Hana too well by this point to let her insecurities lie. She was a creature of habit, and as lovely as Nicky was, she disrupted the flow of things in our home.

After breakfast, I stole Hana away. It would've been a good chance for her to get to know Nicky, but there would be other opportunities. Plenty of them, I'm sure, if Billie had their way. Right now, I needed to make sure Hana felt safe and comfortable with the shift that had happened.

She'd dressed herself in a hot pink athleisure set with a sports bra and three-quarter-length leggings, her hair slicked back into a ponytail that swished behind her as we walked. When we got home she could burn off her frustration, but a walk away from the chaos of the house would be a decent warmup and time to digest.

"Talk to me," I said, taking Hana's hand in mine as we hit the trail.

"Not ready yet."

I nodded. Hana came to things in her own time, and pushing had never resulted in anything except a fight. Instead, we sipped our iced teas while we wandered the boardwalk, pausing every so often to watch the ducks.

"I always forget to bring food for them," Hana said, as she leaned on the railing at a viewing platform over the wetlands.

"I'll add extra frozen peas and corn to the grocery list."

Hana leaned into me, rubbing her cheek against mine, staking her territory with a fresh scent mark. "Thank you for taking me out."

"Gotta take care of my girl." I turned my head to catch her in a kiss, the sweet mint of her scent flourishing.

By the time we finished the boardwalk loop, Hana was only marginally less broody. We talked about nothing important as she drove us back home. Even small talk was good for keeping her from sliding too deep in her own head, so I kept it up until we pulled into the garage.

The tension returned to Hana's body with every step inside. I went in ahead of her and found the main floor empty. Roscoe chirped a greeting to us and wove around my ankles. There was no sign of Nicky or Spud.

"I think she's gone home," I said.

Hana's shoulders dropped before hiking up again a moment later. "Makes me feel like a dick that I got happy about that."

I ushered her further inside. "Nothing wrong with being glad to have your own space. Time for downstairs?"

She nodded, and we swept down to the gym. This was where Hana shone, her insecurities faded and her confidence blazed bright as the sun. All of us were pretty fit, but the only way any of us could ever take Hana in a fight was with a four person dogpile.

After readjusting her ponytail, she picked up the paddles we used for kickboxing and handed them to me. We started off slow, easing into the flow of strikes and movements. Every time we did this I was reminded of how we met—a coed kickboxing class where she had promptly knocked me on my ass.

I'd been gone for her instantly.

A lot of people had tried to flatten me over the years, especially when I started working as a bouncer, but Hana was the only one that succeeded, and there was nothing quite so hot as her pinning me to the mats, sweat making her skin shine, and a satisfied smirk on her lips.

She hit hard. The force of each strike rippled through the paddles and into my hands as I matched each blow. When she lost herself in this it was all I could do to keep up. She shoved all of her power into a kick that had me retreating to keep myself upright.

Now we were getting into the meat of her stress.

Her movements got a bit sloppy as she pummelled the paddles, forcing me back, step after step.

"How was she?" Hana finally asked.

"I think you'd like her," I said, catching a kick that drove me to the edge of the mat. "I bet she would melt for you."

I circled back around and Hana followed in a flurry of strikes.

"Don't play games with me about this." She huffed and puffed, but kept advancing.

"I'm *not*. And I didn't fuck her if that's what you're worried about. You know I don't go that far without talking to you first."

She had never discouraged my exploration with anyone, but she needed a little extra comfort whenever someone new showed up on the scene for any of us. It had been a few years since anyone had made it back to the pack house, so it was an adjustment for everyone. I was more than content with the pack, and, after years with them, I think we had forgotten what it felt like to have those dynamics shift.

"What did you do with her then?" Her next blow slid past the paddle and struck me on the wrist, making me flinch. "Shit, I'm sorry."

Hana stood down immediately and pulled the paddle out of my hand, gentle fingers moving over my arm to test for any damage. She hadn't broken anything, but it was a bit tender to the touch.

"We played a little bit," I said. "It was ninety-percent her with Billie and Tony, but she asked me to stay so I did."

Hana's gaze lifted from my arm to my face. "And after you took her to your room?"

"I mostly just sat with her in the bath. We played a little bit there too. That's why I think you would like her. She reminds me of you in a lot of ways. Old you: when you were less comfortable with who you are. If I thought you wouldn't end up liking her, I would have put down a boundary."

Hana sighed and lifted my wrist to her mouth, pressing a kiss to the skin.

"Maybe we're all just little kids with a new shiny toy," I suggested.

Hana snorted. "I could see that with Billie. Not with *all* of you. *But* you're right. I shouldn't get so worked up because of a single meeting. I just really like how things are."

I dropped the other paddle and pulled her into a hug. "I know. But even if we're not shaking things up with a new person, there's still other changes coming. Our beta and omega are turning thirty soon, and, if all goes as planned, we'll be parents soon. Things won't stay the same forever."

She cupped my face and kissed me with a ferocity that had my cock standing at attention in my sweatpants. When she'd blitzed every thought right out of my head, she pulled back with another sigh.

"I wish I didn't feel this way about Nicky. She hasn't done anything wrong."

"It's okay that you do," I insisted. "We all love you, and if you need to set some boundaries to be comfortable with how things progress, then I'm sure the others will be fine with that."

"I'll decide that later, once I see how deep the others are. In the meantime," she glanced down at the obvious tent in my pants, "I have somewhere you could put that."

I laughed and hooked my fingers into the waistband of her hot pink athleisure pants. "Is that so?"

"Mhmm. Do you wanna wrestle for who's on top?"

"I really, really do."

I already knew she was going to win. It was all part of the foreplay with her. She got me down onto the mats in seconds, and every buck, shove, and grunt had us grinding together and rolling around until I finally accepted defeat. Her hands pinned me down by both wrists, and her weight settled on my chest.

Sometimes when we played this way, I would get pinned down with a pussy to the face, but she needed a little bit more today, and my hips could take a lot more force. She stripped me from the waist down, and I peeled her clothing off of her.

Her skin glistened with sweat, her cheeks were flushed, and her eyes were full of fire.

"I never get tired of seeing you like this."

Hana grinned, and lined me up, fucking hard with one smooth stroke, her pussy consuming me down to the hilt.

My ability to breathe disappeared, and every sensation focused down on the driving force of her cunt. I managed to whip off my shirt before the strength of her thighs could drive me too far forward. We'd both learned the hard way that having sex with her while having a shirt on sometimes ended up with a little bit of accidental strangulation. I relished her power as she rode me into oblivion.

Alpha pussy was vastly underrated. I couldn't be sure if it was *all* alpha pussy, but the grip of Hana's cunt matched the strength of the rest of her body and left me seeing stars. I descended into incoherency between the slick grip around my cock and her hand in my hair that pulled enough to sting.

The sound of her shifted as she rode the fine edge of pleasure and carried us both to the peak. I had the wherewithal to get my fingers on her clit to help her along, but the first touch had her clamping down and sending a perfect searing burn from my cock through the rest of my body. I spilled into her without warning, and she ground down, riding my fingers as much as my cock until she shuddered and came with a ragged cry.

The delirium of pleasure she always visited upon me was fading back slowly. Hana grinned down at me, her hips still rocking to tease me to the point of overstimulation. The only place to move was up into her, and, even though the bucking made it worse, I couldn't quite help myself as I dug bruising fingers into her hips and pushed my way deeper. She finally stilled enough for me to catch my breath.

"Sweet fuck."

Hana lowered her face and nuzzled my cheek. "Come shower with me?"

I nodded. I nearly came all over again when she slid off of me, hips lifting off the mat as far as I could manage to follow her. "God, *Hana*. Go on without me. I'll meet you there."

She stroked my ribs with her toes and gave me the most delicious, satisfied smile. "Don't be too long."

I gathered all of my strength and rolled over, making it to my feet with enough energy to clean up after us. I sprayed the mats down, wiping away our sweat and the smear of cum I had left behind, then joined Hana in the showers.

Her hair was already washed when I arrived, and pinned up with a clip to let the conditioner do its work. She kissed me softly, mouth lingering, tongue delving with a patient pace that warmed my blood all over again.

"Do you want me to wash your hair?" she asked.

"Yes please," I said, both because it felt nice and because it was always part of Hana's aftercare when we played here. Hana took her time shampooing my hair, kneading my scalp and working out the knots in my shoulders before rinsing me down. She soaped me thoroughly from head to toe, hands covering every inch, rinsing me clean again and taking the time to dry me and lotion my skin. I loved her hands on me in any capacity, but nothing quite compared to her dedication to tidying me up after she had ruined me.

I let her comb my damp hair and blow dry it into my usual

style. Afterwards, she sat quietly in turn, slowly relaxing as I blow dried hers for her until it was like black satin falling down her back.

Her tension had melted away by the time we made it back upstairs, and I only hoped she would be able to maintain that for a while. I hadn't said it at the time, but I was pretty sure that Nicky would be making another appearance, and I was probably more excited than Hana would like me to be about that. If Nicky would let us both play, I knew that it would trigger Hana's dominant side. Those giant doe eyes would lure in my beautiful alpha in a heartbeat.

I wouldn't push though. Hana would come around, or she wouldn't, and nothing any of us said would change that.

Chapter Fifteen
Nicky

Work was agony.

How was I supposed to behave *normally*? *How* was I supposed to act like the fabric of my whole existence hadn't been ripped out from under my feet to toss me into a bed with deliciously hot people that made me *feel* things I didn't even know were possible?

I fumbled the book I was trying to return to the shelf, and it fell face down on the floor. "Fuck," I murmured, to no one but myself.

The library was empty tonight except for a few students who had taken over the glassed in study rooms.

Billie and Tony were giving me *space* so that I didn't feel crowded with them popping up every single night. But space gave me room to stew, and I was already far too prone to that to begin with.

I pulled out my phone and texted my sister-in-law on the off-chance that she was awake at two in the morning. The phone rang in my hand barely three seconds later.

"Heyo," Allie chirped. "What's up? Is this a call for your brother to overhear or should I hop out of bed?"

"Preference on him not hearing. I'll talk to him later if I need to." I wedged my phone between ear and shoulder, wheeling further down the aisle to return more books. "I'm kind of up in my head right now, and I just wanted a little perspective, I guess?"

"Ooh, I dunno how good I am at giving that, but I'll do my best. What's going on?"

"Um..."

I hesitated too long, and she let out a giggle. "Is the delay because it's a sexy thing?"

"Shut up."

Allie cackled at the other end of the line. "Details! I need them. But I feel like this needs to be a round table discussion. Should I get Luna and Meg in on this?"

"Sure," I said. "I guess more opinions can't hurt. You think they're awake?"

"No idea. They'll totally answer if I call, though. One sec." Allie got the call connected. Meg greeted us sleepily, but Luna sounded wide awake.

"What's up, babes?" Luna asked.

"Nicky has a sexy problem," Allie replied. "We're round-tabling."

"Ooh. Juicy!" Luna laughed.

"What's going on, Nicky?" Meg asked.

"Okay, so, I started seeing someone." I took a deep breath and shoved a book back where it belonged. "And, they're also seeing people, and I might like those people too, and I'm so out of my depths with it all."

"What's the dealio with the other people they're seeing?" Luna asked. "Casual? Serious?"

"They're a pack. They all live together in this giant beautiful house, and I stayed there last night, and oh my *god*, I don't know how to exist anymore."

"Oh, heck. A pack is pretty damn serious," Allie said. "We're going to need to know everything down to the last juicy detail to properly offer that perspective you ordered."

I filled them in on *some* of the details. They didn't need to know everything that had happened.

"Okay, so what's the problem?" Allie asked.

"You don't think it's all really fast? I feel like I'm going to end up panicking and run away to Europe to find myself a month from now when they get tired of me."

"They're not going to get tired of you because you're delightful," Luna insisted.

"Also," said Allie, "you found yourself when you went to Rome after your first year of university. You also found Stefan while you were there, if I'm remembering that story correctly."

"God, that was ages ago, and also irrelevant," I said with a laugh, maneuvring my cart to another aisle. "I'm pretty sure Hana was not a big fan of me spending the night with Gabe."

"Did she say that, or are you gleaning?" Meg asked.

"Gleaning, but it felt pretty obvious."

"I mean, I guess that's fair if she was a bit weird about it," Allie said. "Like, if Sidney and I had discussed him being able to date other people, and two seconds later he popped up with a woman in our bed, that would be a pretty massive adjustment, right? Maybe she just felt like you were kinda sprung on her."

"That's true. Ugh. I just, I feel like they've got it all figured out, and I'm just like a baby deer tossed in there trying to keep up with the herd before I've even learned to walk."

"The cutest baby deer." Luna laughed.

"It'll take time," said Meg. "If they're a pack they're going to have some experience with each other."

"How long have they been packed up?" Allie asked.

"Six years, I think?"

"*Nicky.*"

"*What?*"

Allie sighed. "They've had six years to figure out their flow, and you're worried about being awkward a few days in? Girl, you gotta take a breath."

"That's why I'm calling *you*." I smoothed down my hair even though it was already perfectly smooth and tucked back. "You're all my breath."

"Well, then you're doomed," Luna said with a laugh.

"Come *on*, that's not fair. I don't have any sisters to ask and none of my beta friends ever dated alphas. Tell me your personal experiences. I need to know what I'm in for."

"I only know things from the alpha side. I never really asked any of the betas I knew in the past," Meg told me.

"I mostly only kicked it with alphas for my heats," replied Allie, "so they all hit me like a ton of bricks with the hormones and all that jazz."

"I've dated the whole sample platter," said Luna. "I don't think I have any particular preference, though Allie's right about the ton of bricks when it comes to a heat."

"What about when you're not in heat? What's it like?"

"Just know that in the answer to that question I'm going to have to talk about your brother," Allie warned.

"Yeah that's fine. Whatever."

"Okay, well, he still hits me like a ton of bricks. Even without the heats we're super tuned to one another, but that could be because we're bonded. I dunno. Alphas have a vibe. A lot of them are very sexy, and they know it, and they've got way better control of their scent than the rest of us, which is very unfair."

"I just wonder if maybe I'm reacting *too* much. Is that possible?"

"Biology is not my forte," Allie replied, "but if you're really freaked out you could always go ask at the clinic. Or you could ask your brother, I mean he's been a nurse forever so he probably knows something."

"But he specialized in omegas. I need someone who knows about betas."

"It's up to you. Dr. J at the clinic is great and she's always doing research and stuff to help patients. If nothing else, she would probably know about a specialist that you could ask.

"Dr. J is great," Luna added.

"I guess that's true. Okay, maybe I'll swing by when work is over just to be safe. I just really don't know what to do with myself. I went from one partner to three at once and—"

"Girl, *what*?" Allie gasped.

"You had a fourway?!" Luna shrieked.

"Shhh! Yes, and I *know*. It's only been four days. If I didn't know any better, I would think I was body snatched."

"Have you considered the fact that they're all just really hot?" Luna asked.

"I was a terrified prude before I got with Sidney," Allie said. "I barely ever played and stuck pretty much exclusively to heats, and now I can basically get railed ten times a day if I wanted to."

My stomach heaved. "That was information I could've done without."

Allie cackled. "I'm just saying. Things can take some drastic turns when you have the right partner, or *partners* in your case. There's different energy and different dynamics."

"I guess that's true."

"Are they attentive lovers?" Meg asked.

"I'm beginning to regret this conversation..."

"Shut up and answer the question." Allie laughed.

"Okay, *fine*. They're all great. I learned too many new things about myself."

Luna giggled. "Yeah, you did!"

"And how invested were previous partners with making sure you were comfy? Were they open to exploration?" Meg asked.

"I mean, not very. We both got the job done for each other most of the time, but it wasn't anything spectacular or beyond vanilla in any way."

"Can I make an observation?" Meg asked.

"Please do," I replied.

"I'm gonna go out on a limb here and say that you're probably a very spicy lady, Nicky, and no one in your past ever

135

unlocked that. You can kind of get a sense of people, and I think you're just finally getting what you need."

"I agree with Meg," said Allie. "It sounds like you had a really good time, and I would tell you not to freak out, but I know it's not your specialty. Have a few more sexy nights, and if you decide it's not for you, that's okay, but it *really* seems like it's for you."

I let out an absolutely pitiful sound and finished shelving the last book on my cart. "Okay, fine."

"*Please* keep us posted," Luna requested. "I want to know if you add the other two to the mix."

I snorted. "You're a terrible little gossip, Luna. I love you all so much."

Allie snickered. "We love you too, babe. I'm being summoned to bed. Have a good rest of your night."

"Sweet dreams."

We all hung up and I rolled everything back to the front desk. A fresh gaggle of university students flooded the library after having gorged themselves on caffeine at the café. At least I wouldn't be stuck with silence.

It was so tempting to text Billie, but they were giving me space and I was trying to honor that even though it made my mind spin in circles.

I finished off my shift, doing my best to lose myself in the work so that I didn't spiral. The day staff arrived ten minutes late, which wasn't entirely terrible since I used the excuse of my shift being over to text Billie good morning.

Kathy and Belinda trotted into the library, their hair wind-blown and their cheeks flushed. "I'm so sorry we're late," Belinda said, gasping as she made it to the front desk. "We carpooled this morning, and there was an accident on the freeway."

"No worries." I ran through the set up I had done for their programs and was more than ready to leave by the time we finished that chat.

I hitched my purse over my shoulder and barrelled out the library doors.

"Nicky!"

I skidded to a stop at the top of the stairs, spinning to see Alphonse standing there with a frown on his face and a hand on his hip. The iced coffee he carried was dripping condensation and only the last quarter of it remained.

"Hey, what are you doing here?"

His frown deepened. "I'm here to pick you up for our date. I've been waiting for over an hour."

I stared at him, incomprehensibly. Even if I had agreed to a date there was no reason for him to wait that long when I didn't even get off work until seven, and the extra time wasn't my fault. Still, the guilt swelled in my stomach and made me vaguely nauseous.

My phone buzzed, and I spared a glance at the screen. A text from Billie asking how my shift had gone.

"I should really get going though. I didn't mean to make you wait."

I wanted to go home and sleep, but Alphonse was staring at me like I'd just kicked a puppy in front of him. He scooped up my hand, and I fought the urge to wrench it out of his grip so I didn't upset him.

"You mean *we* should get going."

That was definitely *not* what I meant. Guilt whispered in my ear. What harm could one date do? I'd disappeared into the night on him, maybe this was like a cosmic re-balancing.

I needed to eat anyway.

I tried to keep my sigh from being obvious and wandered back towards him.

"Okay. Where are we going?"

"I bought all of the ingredients for French toast," he replied, beaming at me like he expected a pat on the head.

Did that mean I was supposed to go over to his place? "I thought you wanted to go out?"

"I thought my place would be more relaxing than a restaurant for you," he said, voice dripping with sympathy. "You always liked quiet evenings in more than out."

I fought down the urge to pinch the bridge of my nose. It was true, but I just wanted to get this over with as quickly as possible. "I would really rather go out."

His eyes narrowed. "I did a whole grocery shop for you, and you want me to just waste all of that and buy you a meal instead?"

Goddamn.

"I guess not." I covered a yawn with my hand.

Alphonse sighed, pulling me closer. "Nicky, I got up this early because you're important to me, and I expected the same level of respect in return. Here's what we're going to do. I'm going to drive you to my place, you're going to enjoy the meal I make for you, we'll have a pleasant conversation, and after that, I'll drop you off back here. It'll be just like old times."

Old times...

The idea made me nauseated.

"Just one meal," he prompted. "I've missed you."

I also really didn't want to go over to his place, but how much harm could there be in French toast?

"I can drive myself."

"Nicky, you don't *like* driving in the city. I used to pick you up for dates all the time."

He tossed his iced coffee in the garbage and walked back over to me, hooking his arm around my waist as he started to lead me down the stairs.

"I would be more fun if we could do this another time," I said. "I had a long night."

"That's no problem," he said. "You're already familiar with my bed. You can have a nap there."

Why did he have a stupid answer for everything? I just wanted to go home and cuddle my cat. People were staring by this point, and it cowed any outward reaction I might have. I let him pull me along, out into the parking lot and into the early morning sunshine. His black sedan was occupying one of the accessible parking spaces.

Gross.

He opened the passenger door for me, and I looked longingly at my little car across the lot.

"Your carriage awaits, my lady."

He watched me intently for so long that I finally gave in and sat down, nerves twitching in my belly. The true crime show I'd watched a couple weeks ago flashed in my head. Never let them take you to a second location. But that was silly. Alphonse wasn't going to murder me.

I worked my thoughts around to calm myself. Alphonse had been a decent cook when we had been together, and he kept his place clean, which was a far cry above a lot of people I had dated.

"Are you enjoying being back in the country?" I asked, for lack of anything else to say.

"I'm settling in nicely, though not quite finished unpacking. You'll be my first proper guest."

I fidgeted with my phone. I couldn't really send his address to anyone when I had no idea what it was or where we were going.

"It's rude to be on your phone while you're with other people, Nicky. I know you know better than that."

"Sorry." I tucked my phone to the side where he couldn't see and sent a tracker pin to the first message my thumb hit, tucking it into my purse while I watched the streets we passed.

"You used to be a much better conversationalist. Surely you have something to say after not seeing me for two years."

My hackles rose. "I told you I was tired."

"That's all right. I can talk for the both of us for a while." He went on to regale me about Japan and his life in Tokyo. We were way farther from the library than I was expecting, across the entire city in fact. My phone had buzzed three more times in my bag, but Alphonse gave me such a look of disapproval that I didn't take it out to see what had been sent.

We pulled up to a neat little townhouse with navy blue siding and white trim.

"It's cute," I said. It wasn't the house's fault that Alphonse lived in it. I'd been mostly silent during the drive, adding appropriate *ooh's* and *aah's* during his story when he looked over at me expectantly.

139

"I think you'll like the inside," he said. "I've gotten a bit more into decorating since we were last together."

I followed him in, clutching my purse to my chest. My phone buzzed again.

He unlocked the front door and waited for me to enter, closing and deadbolting it behind us. Unease trickled up my spine, so I focused on the details. His place was tidy. Colorful art decorated the walls, great quality furniture filled the space, and the kitchen looked recently updated.

"Have a seat at the table," he instructed. "Coffee?"

"Orange juice, if you have it."

He frowned at my response. "You used to take what I offered you."

"I work nights now," I explained. "I don't want to be drinking coffee before I go to sleep."

He nodded, but the tension didn't leave his body. "I'm not sure I like you working nights."

I didn't really give a flying fuck if he liked it or not. "I love it."

"How are you going to work nights when you get married?" he asked, pulling out a carton of orange juice from the fridge and pouring me a glass. "What about when you have children?"

We'd talked about marriage and kids when we were together, but that was mostly because I'd been fast approaching thirty and less because I was jazzed about the idea of either of those things with him.

"Um, well, I'm not engaged and I'm not pregnant so I'm pretty sure that's a topic of discussion for the future and not right now."

He set my drink down in front of me with a little more force than necessary, the sound of the glass clacking against the table loud enough to make me flinch.

"I always got the impression that you were a family woman," he said. "At least until you backed out of our engagement without so much as a word. I didn't appreciate how you handled things Nicky. You could have just talked to me."

I wanted to scream out '*When?!*' because I *had* tried to talk to him and he'd worked around everything to make it seem like my concerns and wants didn't matter.

"I'm sorry that the move made you feel pressured. I'm back now, and we can pick up where we left off. I shouldn't have to move again, and my mom's finally moved back here too, so you'll finally be able to meet her."

"I feel like I missed out on a rather important conversation."

He quirked his head, pulling out a loaf of bread and a container of eggs from the fridge. "What do you mean?"

"Why would you think I'd want to get back together?"

"I thought you coming on this date was you agreeing to restart our relationship. Your mom was very clear when I talked to her that you haven't dated anyone else since I moved away. Why *wouldn't* you want to pick things up again? It's not like you're drowning in opportunities, and you're over thirty now."

"I think I should probably go." No sense giving him any more ideas than he'd already fabricated for himself.

"You're here for breakfast. I've gone through the trouble of picking up all of this food. I'm going to prepare it for you, and then you're going to appreciate it. Okay?"

I should've fought to bring my own car. We were in a pretty new development. How long would it take a cab to get here? My phone buzzed again, and Alphonse slapped the frying pan down onto the stove.

"I'm getting a little tired of your disrespect, Nicky. Turn that off and engage me in a real conversation so this isn't a complete waste of my time. I don't know why I even thought you *deserved* a chance. You're making a terrible case for our re-engagement."

My breath froze in my throat. I turned my phone to silent rather than turning it off and typed a hasty SOS without looking.

Okay. I knew this mood. I could placate him until I got out of here...

"Sorry," I mumbled. "Can I help you make food?"

That finally seemed to relax him. He pulled a pair of plates out of the cupboard and set them on the counter along with two

141

sets of cutlery. "Set the table. I'll give you a tour after breakfast so you know where everything is."

I didn't argue. Instead, I just nodded along and put the place settings on the table. I put us on opposite ends rather than right next to each other to give myself a fraction of distance.

I focused on my breathing to keep myself calm. He was just being a little snippy. That wasn't unusual for him at all. The moment things didn't go his way it came out in his attitude.

It was *fine*.

Everything was fine.

If I thought otherwise, I would cry, and he'd always hated it when I cried. Apparently it 'made the conversation all about me' when I did.

The scent of cinnamon and vanilla from the battered bread hitting the pan made me ache for the pack.

I ate quickly once he set the food in front of me.

"Someone's hungry. I didn't know you liked French toast so much. I'll have to be sure to keep the ingredients on hand."

My meal sat like a lead ball in my gut.

Once he had finished eating, he directed me to the living room where we both sank into the plush leather couch, and he turned on the TV.

"There's a great documentary on modern Paris I want you to see."

Well, that sounded like a *thrill* a minute.

"Cool," I said, not wanting to piss him off.

He got the show rolling and inched over so our legs were touching, swinging his arm across the back of the couch. I held my breath, my skin crawling.

"I'm a little sweaty. Would you mind scooting over?" I asked.

He smirked. "I know a hint when I hear one." His other hand swung around to cup my cheek and dread turned so forcefully in my stomach I almost threw up on him. I shoved him and skittered away.

"I think you've got the wrong idea."

"Oh, *I've* got the wrong idea? You came over to *my* house,

Nicky. What other idea should I have? You don't even want to try to make up for all the bullshit you put me through?"

"You *made me* come over to your house. I wanted to go to a restaurant. Actually, scratch that, I didn't want any date at all, but you guilt tripped me."

His eyes narrowed, jaw tight. "I really don't appreciate you making me the bad guy here. It's not like you put up any kind of fight."

The second he started to get to his feet, I bolted, grabbing my purse off the floor next to my chair in the kitchen. I flipped the deadbolt and wrenched open the door only to have it slammed in my face.

"Nicky, what the fuck are you doing? Why are you acting like you're afraid of me?"

I didn't answer.

My breathing had shifted to little panicked gasps.

I just wanted to get out.

"Please let me leave."

"You're being ridiculous," he snapped. "Go sit down."

"*Please.*"

Chapter Sixteen
Tony

"**G**et in the car!" Billie burst through my door and I bolted awake.

"What?"

"Up! We have to go."

"Billie, what's happening?" I climbed out of bed and hastily threw on the nearest clothes at hand.

"I don't *know*, but Nicky needs us."

That was all the information I needed.

We flew down the stairs and into our van.

"Give me a little info?" I asked, as we pulled out of the garage and zipped out of our gated community.

Billie was practically vibrating in their seat. "She stopped responding to my messages, sent me a location pin and an SOS message."

My beta plugged in their phone and got the directions for me.

We weren't too far away in terms of distance, but it was rush hour, and the main roads were at a stand still. I iron-gripped the steering wheel and wove us through residential streets. Even with the slower speed and longer route, it would be faster than waiting in grid-lock.

"What do you think is going on?" I asked.

Billie tapped out another message. "I have no idea. I just want her to reply. What if she got kidnapped or something?"

As unlikely as a kidnapping might have been, now that Billie had said the words out loud, they were in my head. I took the next turn a little too fast and Billie squeaked, bracing themself on the door. The route kept recalculating as I whipped us through the city on the smaller roads. Each moment that passed without a reply from Nicky had my blood pressure rising.

Billie was glued to their screen, knuckles white as they held their phone. "How am I supposed to give her space when something like this happens? We should have let me cling!"

"We don't know what's happened," I said, trying to assure them. I couldn't say that maybe it was a mistake or maybe Nicky was just busy when the radio silence was accompanied by an SOS and directions.

"Turn right up here," Billie demanded, arm extended, pointing down a narrow alleyway that let us bypass the next set of lights.

Their legs bounced, pouring out nervous energy. I kept all of mine focused on the road. Sweat prickled at my temples. My alpha instincts were being *unreasonable*. They screamed at me to find Nicky and neutralize whatever threat there was. She wasn't *mine*. No matter how loud my instincts were to the contrary.

It took all my self control to not step on the gas. Getting pulled over would only waste precious time. Another road down. More moments of Nicky in some unknown danger with us still too far away to help. I took a deep breath, trying to stay as calm as possible. Billie was ready to go feral in the seat next to me, and I needed to manage the situation when we arrived. My beta was small, but if they got riled they could do some damage. Without knowing the details, I had to assume that a feral Billie would be unhelpful for Nicky's safety.

I reached over and slid my hand into Billie's hair, getting enough of a grip to get their attention. "We don't know what situation we're arriving in. Stay back and let me lead."

"We both know I can't do that." Billie squirmed.

I took my hand back to manage another turn, this one bringing us onto the same street as Nicky's pinned location. I pushed our speed.

"You can, and you will. Don't put yourself in danger," I ordered.

I slowed in front of a navy and white house. Billie was out of the van before I'd even stopped, racing up the walkway and throwing themselves at the door in a series of rapidfire knocks.

"Shit." I threw the van into park and wrenched up the emergency brake, chasing after Billie. The door swung open again as I approached. One look at the tears rimming Nicky's eyes and panic clear on her face activated every alpha instinct I had.

Mine.

I planted my palm on the door and shoved it all the way open, the two betas inside stumbling back.

"Get the fuck out of my house," Alphonse snapped.

"Gladly," hissed Billie. "As long as Nicky comes with us."

I pulled Billie behind me.

Alphonse wrapped a hand around Nicky's wrist, and I locked my hand around his with a growl. "You'd better take your hands off of her before my fist meets your face."

Nicky's eyes widened, and she strained against Alphone's grip to get to me. I squeezed hard, forcing Alphonse to wince and let her go.

He glared at me, his slicked back hair askew, frown marring his face. "This is none of your business. Get off my property."

"Nicky *is* my business."

Alphonse moved to grab her again, and I shoved myself bodily between them. He took a step back. I wasn't overly tall, and the two of us came eye to eye. If it came to a fight, I was reasonably certain I would win with Hana's training, but I wouldn't come out of it unscathed.

"Fine," he snapped again. "Get out. I shouldn't waste my time on an unappreciative cunt anyway."

That spurred my growl once more. "You talk about her like that again, and you'll be missing teeth."

Billie looped an arm around Nicky's waist and pulled her further outside.

She reached out helplessly. "My shoes."

"Back up," I ordered him.

"Like fucking hell. You can take her out, but you're not getting in here. This is *my* home. Fuck off."

Alphonse slammed his front door, and I heard the snick of the deadbolt locking.

I scooped Nicky up so she didn't have to traverse the ground barefoot with construction materials littering the area.

We brought her to the far side of the vehicle, and Billie pulled open the back door so I could set our beta down on the seat.

"Nicky, what happened? Are you hurt?"

She shook her head. I cupped her face in both hands and lifted her gaze to look at me. The second we made eye contact, those tears spilled over, and the dam burst, Nicky descending into sobs.

"Hey, baby girl, it's okay. We're here." I cradled her in my arms, and she clung to my shirt. Billie went around the vehicle and climbed in on that side so they could sandwich Nicky between us. "Nicky, where do you want us to take you? Do you need a hospital? Police?"

She didn't answer right away and continued to cry, but I could hear her trying to get herself under control. "I don't know. I have to go home. Spud hasn't had food yet, and my car is at the library."

Her voice wavered, and she took big gulping breaths.

Billie set their palm on Nicky's chest. "Breathe with me, Books. In," Billie gave an exaggerated inhalation—and Nicky followed suit—"and out."

"I'll get everything handled," I told her. "Is there anyone you want us to call?"

Nicky shook her head.

"Okay. Let's buckle you up and get you home." I did up her seat belt for her and made sure Billie was secure as well before I returned to the front seat.

Our girl was quiet for most of the drive, and I spent the whole trip reining in the burning well of fury that scorched my insides. I wasn't sure if she would tell me what happened, but I didn't need to know the details. She'd been scared and had reached out to us for help.

By the time I pulled up in front of her apartment building, her eyes were dry.

"Do you want us to stay with you?" Billie asked.

Nicky hiccupped softly. "I feel like such a baby for wanting to say yes. It's my own fault all of this happened. I was so *stupid*."

"You're not at fault here," I insisted. "That weasely little fucker is to blame. I don't care what he said to you, he was wrong."

Nicky's big brown eyes looked at me, tears threatening again. She didn't argue, lowering her gaze to her hands. The two of us got her into her apartment where Spud was screaming for his breakfast.

"Billie, can you feed Spud, please?" They went about the task without having to be asked twice. I turned to Nicky. "Baby girl, do you wanna have a shower?"

She nodded slowly. "I'm so tired."

I ushered her towards the bathroom. "Stress takes a lot of energy. Do you need help with anything?" When she didn't answer right away, I offered something different, "Do you want Billie to help you?"

"Yes, please," she murmured.

I switched assignments with Billie, putting them in charge of making sure Nicky got washed up all right. I fed Spud, got the kettle going, and, while I waited, I did a few chores to keep myself settled—putting her dishes away and scooping the cat litter as her sleepytime tea steeped. I couldn't be certain how she might feel about me doing her chores, but if there was less for her to do, then she would be able to rest more.

My betas emerged after about half an hour, Nicky wrapped in a fluffy purple robe, her hair wet around her face. Billie brought a hair dryer and a brush, handing both to me.

The three of us sat on Nicky's couch. She sipped her tea in silence while I dried her hair and Billie held her other hand. By the time I was finished, Nicky was half asleep. She accepted being carried to her bedroom, and we got her tucked under the blankets, one of us lying on each side, Spud joining us to lay at her feet.

I texted the rest of the pack to let them know what happened and where we were. At some point, we fell asleep alongside Nicky, at least until Spud pawed my face to wake me for a second meal. While I was up feeding him, my phone rang.

"Hey Jasper, what's up?"

"How is she?" he asked.

"Sleeping right now. I messaged Hana to see if she'd be okay with Nicky coming over for a while. I'm going to see how Nicky feels about it once she's woken up. I know she's probably perfectly safe here, but I would feel better keeping an eye on her for a while."

"Sounds good. I'll bring her a loaf of focaccia home."

I smiled, though he couldn't see it. "I'm sure she'll love that."

We chatted for a couple more minutes until the exhaustion snuck back up on me. I climbed back into bed after feeding the cat and slept several more hours curled around Nicky.

I woke before her again and found Billie still fast asleep as well. My stomach growled, so I shuffled into the kitchen. We would all need food, but Nicky likely wouldn't want to go out for it. I could order us takeout, though I wasn't certain what all she liked.

She didn't have a lot of food in her fridge, which left few options. My instincts nudged *hard* to provide for her, but since she wasn't providing well for herself with her food supplies, that made it more difficult.

I slipped back into the bedroom and ran a gentle hand over Nicky's cheek. Her eyes snapped open and she stiffened, relaxing again with a soft smile when she recognized it was me.

"Hey baby girl, I'm going to order some food. What's your favorite?"

She closed her eyes for a moment, and, right as I wondered if she had fallen back asleep, she whispered, "I'm really craving some tiramisu."

I smiled and tapped her nose. "I'm happy to order you dessert, but you should have something a little more substantial, too."

She sighed and stretched, a little more awake when she looked at me again. "There's a really good Italian place nearby that has amazing stuffed shells. I don't know what time it is, but, as long as it's after eleven-thirty, they should be making pasta."

I pulled out my phone and got the name of the restaurant from her, placing an order for her stuffed shells and tiramisu, as well as a pair of minestrone soups and a couple of baked lasagnas. We had the option of picking it up in fifteen minutes or waiting an hour for delivery, so I let my betas know and slipped out to fetch our food.

Nicky was considerably more bright-eyed and calm when I returned. I kept my palm on the back of her neck as she inhaled her tiramisu, enjoying the sweet, grateful look in her eye whenever she turned to me for reassurance. She moved closer and ate her pasta with our knees touching.

"Thank you for doing all of this," she said quietly. "I'll pay you back for the food."

"You'll do no such thing," Billie said. "This is for your enjoyment."

Nicky lapsed into silence, picking at the last half of her food.

"Do you want me to pack that up for you, baby girl?"

"I can do it."

"I *want* to do it," I said. She let me gather her container up, and I popped on the lid, putting it into the refrigerator. "How are you feeling now?"

"A lot better, thank you."

"So," said Billie, "I know we're supposed to be doing the whole space thing so you don't feel suffocated by my exuberance, but I would really like it if you would come and stay with us today. Or we can stay here."

"Jasper has more gifts of bread for you at the pack house if you do come over," I said.

Nicky laughed. "Well, how can I refuse in that case?"

"Billie will help you pack up whatever you need for work and for the rest of the day. Spud is more than welcome, and we can drive you to work so you can take your car home in the morning. Sound okay?"

She fidgeted in place. "I don't work tonight. Not until Sunday."

"Stay as long as you like, then," I said. "However long makes you comfortable."

I tidied up while my betas started packing and getting Nicky dressed, beyond grateful that she had called us for help. That woman had wormed her way right under my skin and straight into my heart in a matter of days. I didn't want to think about what would've happened if she hadn't called us, or if we hadn't gotten there in time.

I pushed down the swell of panic and rage.

She was safe now. And I was going to make sure she stayed that way.

Chapter Seventeen

Jasper

I paced the kitchen as I waited for them to arrive. The focaccia I had brought home for Nicky sat on the counter wrapped in plastic. It was such a small thing I could do for her. I hoped it would help.

Tony and Billie had gotten to spend way more time with her than I had. If she was going to stay with us for a couple days, then I could hopefully steal a few hours to get to know her better. I had no immediate opposition to her joining our pack, though it was still too early to say that out loud. She had good vibes, and they made my instincts happy.

The tension in Tony when I had called was easily discernible. My poor alpha. He didn't often let his distress show, but I could tell with only a few syllables that Nicky being in trouble had wrung him out.

Hana waved me over. "Come here, my love."

I abandoned my pacing and climbed onto the couch between her and Gabe. She kissed me softly and stroked my cheeks, their combined scent of sweet tea and mint filled my nose and forced my muscles to relax.

They wrapped me securely between them with their heads resting against mine. I sighed, letting the rest of my tension drain. They made it very difficult to be stressed in this house.

Gabe pulled one of the blankets over us, and I closed drowsy eyes, curling into Hana.

"There's my sweet boy," Hana crooned. "Everything will be all right."

Gabe pressed up against my back, tracing soothing patterns on my arm, his breath warm on my skin.

I heard the van pull in, and I tensed up, extracting myself to walk over to the connecting door to wait.

Hana sighed from the couch and came to join me, Gabe on her heels.

"We shouldn't crowd her," Gabe said.

"Well, if Jasper would sit tight, I wouldn't have to be over here," said Hana.

The door to the garage swung open, and Nicky appeared between Tony and Billie, Spud's carrier in her hands.

"Oh, you're all here." Nicky's gaze dropped to the floor.

Tony waved us out of the way.

I wanted to do something to soothe Nicky, but it felt weird to ask when I knew her so little.

"We're going to take her to Billie's room for a little bit," said Tony. "We'll be down later tonight."

I let them pass, my mouth pulling down with worry. I wanted to be a comfort in this situation, and it tweaked against my omega instincts to not be able to provide that.

The three of them went upstairs, leaving me alone again with Hana and Gabe. It was silly to feel left out, but I felt it all the same.

"What do we do?" I asked.

Gabe shrugged. "Whatever we want until she's ready."

Hana pulled me into her arms. "She just needs time to settle, and then I'm sure she would welcome you being there."

I tried to relax. I sucked in huge lungfuls of her fresh scent to clear my head, but it didn't completely remove the lingering worry.

"Babe, if you're going to be wafting omega distress scents, we're going to have to distract you," said Gabe.

Even as my thoughts focused around Nicky, my body responded to his words. This pack could run a master class on sexy distractions.

"I could get on board with that," I said. It was certainly better than staring at the ceiling and waiting for them to re-emerge.

I couldn't be a very good support for Nicky if I was a ball of anxiety.

"Do you want to stay here?" Gabe asked. "Or do you want to go upstairs?"

"Maybe upstairs," I replied. "We can go to my room."

The three of us ventured up, passing Tony's closed door, and into my own room. I flipped on the lights and dimmed them, leaving everything illuminated in a soft glow. My room was the largest in the house, in order to accommodate the entire pack being in here for my heats. A kitchenette gave us easy access to food so we didn't starve, and the bathroom was spacious enough that we could all wash up at the same time if we wanted to. My bed was the biggest too, leaving enough room for anyone to rest during a heat without being jostled by the fucking.

There was usually someone in my bed, if not the entire pack, and I liked to have any option to keep them all close. The whole space was decorated in warm tones—brown, cream, and terra-cotta—with a plethora of shade-loving plants set out of reach of Roscoe to give pops of color. Thick earth toned curtains were held back with matching ties so that when my heat rolled around we could close them up to make my nest super cozy.

My own little sanctuary.

More tension melted away just from stepping inside. The space was saturated with the scent of my pack.

Hana ushered me in and paused me in front of the bed to strip off my shirt and press my back against her chest, her hand cradling my throat. The doors clicked shut, and Gabe joined us both.

He appeared at my front and claimed my mouth in a fierce kiss that drew a needy whine from me.

It was so easy to give in with them, to let myself fall and know that every one of them would catch me.

"I'll indulge you today if you want," Hana said, kissing the curve of my shoulder. "Would you like that?"

I knew exactly what her indulgence meant. They would fuck me between them, letting me bury myself in her while Gabe buried himself in me. That was the usual way of things with Billie and Tony, but Hana didn't often let herself be on the bottom. I reached around to cup the back of her neck, my mouth still occupied with Gabe.

Her fingers twitched against my throat. Gabe pulled away long enough for me to answer.

"Yes, alpha," I breathed the words with reverence.

The two of them tossed me onto the bed, and I landed with a *whoosh*. My pants and underwear were removed in short order, and Hana stretched out on the satin sheets.

Gabe and I fell to each side of her and slowly stripped her down, mouths worshiping every inch of skin we exposed. The bright, earthy taste of her was like coming home. I took this rare gift for what it was and stole every taste I could, sucking her nipple into my mouth and splaying my hands across her skin.

She looked so beautiful spread out beneath us. It was almost enough to make me lament that I didn't get to see it very often, but then the vision of her rising above me, hips driving me to completion with her skin flushed and her hair swaying, filled my mind.

Gabe peeled away her pants and thrust his fingers between her thighs so that she arched up against my mouth. He stoked her slowly until her hips bucked against his hand, and he gave me a knowing look.

155

"She's ready for you."

Hana spread her thighs for me, revealing her slick center. Her clit sat like a pink pearl, awaiting my attention. I bent towards her and drank down the taste of her, my tongue teasing her until her fingers twined in my hair with a sharp sting as she tightened her grip.

"Jasper," my name came out of her in a breathy whisper.

The perfect sound.

Hana wasn't usually one for softness, or for the leisurely fucks that I experienced with some of the others, and I knew if I didn't get a move on soon, she would pull me up by my hair and clamp those powerful legs around my hips to demand the next step.

When I raised my head, the scent of her was just as strong, her wetness coating my beard so I could carry her with me. She lifted her hips in a wordless order.

I teased her with the tip of my cock until she did just as I predicted and used her heels against my ass to drive me into her. I melted down across my alpha while Gabe fetched a bottle of a lube from my bedside table. I waited, shaking, Hana's pussy squeezing me in a rhythmic fashion while Gabe's slicked cock teased my asshole.

My body welcomed him, opening to the insistent pressure, the stretch stealing my breath. My alphas groaned and flexed, moving me between them as they rode me slowly, inching deeper with each thrust until Gabe was buried to the hilt and I was left panting and squirming between them.

Gabe withdrew almost to the point of sliding free, and I followed him, lifting my hips just to where I might slip out of Hana. I rocked between them until we found the perfect position where I could buck wildly and lose neither of them, driving deep with each so that I lost my breath each time.

Every so often Gabe would catch us both by surprise, fucking hard enough to push a little whimper through Hana's lips. She craved the roughness, while I thrived on both rough and soft.

I squeezed around Gabe's cock with the same voracity that

Hana's cunt squeezed mine, the three of us making a game of passing the sensations back and forth.

Slick friction made it difficult to think. Rising pleasure rolled through my body like waves crashing on the shore.

I pistoned my hips as I lavished my tongue over Hana's skin, sucking anything I could reach. Gabe and I found a rhythm where we could drive into her barely a second apart, where I fucked her and he followed, pushing me that little bit deeper, the force of it giving her what she craved.

As much as I wanted her to come first, I was fighting a losing battle. Omegas weren't designed to last. We were designed to take, to come hard and fast, and drown in whatever our partners gave us.

I let out a soft whine, a warning they both knew well.

"Come in your alpha, sweet boy. Give me everything." Hana's thighs flexed, cradling my hips.

Gabe grabbed a handful of my hair and bit down at the scent gland on my throat. I lost it instantly, spilling hotly into Hana's cunt, my hole spasming around Gabe hard enough to make him grunt against my skin. Pleasure clouded my vision, and my nerves sparked, the orgasm bursting like a popped water balloon.

My energy melted away with it, and when Gabe released his teeth, I collapsed down onto Hana. She cradled me with thighs and arms, her fingers stroking my hair, all the lingering ricochets of pleasure slowly easing me down.

Gabe slid out of me and disappeared briefly into the ensuite. He tidied me up, then stretched out next to me, the two of them rolling me over where I lay dazed on the sheets as Hana climbed up and over, sinking down onto Gabe's waiting cock. I reached over to tease her clit.

She was beautiful in all of her pleasures, and I watched in sleepy awe as she fucked him hard, the bed jostling with every stroke. We'd broken a fair few beds in the past before we started getting them seriously reinforced.

Gabe was lost first, and Hana followed him a moment later, grinding down against my fingers as she came. I lazily stroked my own slack cock as I watched her. Her head was tossed back, her eager cry filling the room.

I sucked in a slow breath.

Hana climbed off and stretched out next to me, my two alphas pressing me between them again. She kissed me until I was dizzy.

"Time to shower," she said. "I have both of you dripping out of me."

I quite liked the image of that and wriggled my way down the bed to push open her thighs and glide my tongue between her folds.

"Fuck," Hana murmured, fisting her fingers in my hair.

The two of them always tasted as good as they smelled, and my own flavor was something I had grown deeply familiar with over the years. I teased her, thrusting my tongue as deep as I could.

"You shouldn't have told him." Gabe laughed.

There was pure fire in his gaze when I looked up from my post between her thighs.

Hana's legs trembled around me. I added my fingers to the mix, using them to fuck her as hard as I could at this angle, using my lips and tongue to suction onto her clit until she swore again and dug her fingers into the back of my skull. Her cunt rippled. I stayed relentless until her body relaxed again and she pushed me away with a shudder.

"I've said it before, and I'll say it again," said Gabe. "We could make an absolute fortune in the adult industry with videos of the two of you."

I chuckled and sat up, hopping off the bed, summoning the two of them into the bathroom with a crooked finger.

"My perfect ass is only for you," I called back.

We rinsed off quickly. None of us had had dinner yet, and my stomach was starting to growl.

My alphas toweled me down and tossed me a fresh outfit of red lounge pants and a cream T-shirt.

"We'll meet you in the kitchen," Hana said, the two of them retreating upstairs to get dressed as well.

I meandered to the main floor slowly, feeling phantoms of their touches as I navigated the stairs. Nicky was still sequestered in Tony's room, but I would get started on dinner anyway.

I was halfway through opening the cans of chickpeas when Gabe and Hana joined me. We worked as a unit to prepare one of my favorites, a Mediterranean chickpea stew with tomato and spices that went perfectly with grilled focaccia.

The rest of our pack and our impromptu guest appeared when I was pulling the bread out from under the broiler. I spared a quick glance at them before brushing melted butter across the crisp surfaces.

"There she is." I offered Nicky a smile and wave as her gaze locked onto me. "Just in time for dinner."

She hesitated for a moment as she walked into the kitchen, but when I held my arm open to her, she sank against me, fingers curled in my shirt.

"Hi," she said quietly.

"Feeling any better, sweetheart?"

She nodded without replying.

"I made you your favorite."

I passed her a fresh slice of the focaccia, and she bit into the corner, a little moan of happiness passing through her lips. "So good."

"Let's get you properly fed so I can hog you during movie night."

Nicky giggled and squeezed me a little tighter. "Sounds perfect."

Chapter Eighteen
Nicky

Staying at the pack house was like something out of a fever dream.

I felt like I was at a five-star hotel with a whole herd of servants waiting to attend to my every need. Not that the pack were servants, but there was always someone at the ready, no matter what I needed.

While we watched a movie, I was wedged in the center with Billie cuddled up to me on one side and Jasper on the other, Tony leaning into him. Tony's arm stretched behind me, and his hand rested comfortably on the back of my neck while Gabe and Hana snuggled next to Billie in the cozy couch nest.

They were the best and easiest distraction I could've ever asked for. We ate together, fell asleep briefly in a cuddle pile, and we even made use of their pool.

It was hard to give Alphonse even a second thought while I

blasted an inflatable ball over the volleyball net strung across the pool in my borrowed purple polka dot bikini.

We paused the game when Gabe had to leave to head to work at the club.

Gabe climbed out of the pool. "You all behave."

Everyone all lined up for goodbye kisses. I couldn't stop my giggle over how sweet they all were, rising up to meet his lips.

"None for Nicky?" Gabe asked.

I hadn't even considered I might be a part of the ritual, but it warmed me that he wanted me to be included, so I swam over to the edge, lifting myself up to accept a kiss on the cheek with his hand hooked under my chin.

It only took him disappearing out of sight for us to resume our game. Hana switched over to lounging on a float in the deep end, only re-entering the fray when the ball went wild and landed close enough for her to punt it back in our direction.

Jasper and I were up by two points.

The luxury of having a pool this size, an indoor one no less, wasn't lost on me. I had gathered that this pack was basically loaded, but seeing it in action was another thing entirely.

Jasper swam underneath me and hoisted me straight into the air with me on his shoulders. I shrieked with laughter and fought to maintain my balance. Tony plunged beneath the water and lifted Billie, too. The two of them walked us up to the net.

"Kiss for good luck," said Jasper.

Billie laughed, and we kissed through one of the open squares of the netting.

"How do we play volleyball like this?" I asked.

"We don't. I feel bad for Hana floating all by her lonesome," said Billie.

"Don't stop playing on my account." Hana waved them off.

"We can switch to Marco Polo so everyone is included," said Tony.

Hana gave a long-suffering sigh, even as she smiled softly.

Jasper tipped backwards, and I crashed into the water with a yelp. I flailed back to the surface and swiped my hair out of my face.

Tony closed his eyes and shouted, "Marco!"

We all yelled "Polo!" and I plunged back under, swimming away as fast as I could. I'd played this game with my brothers when we went to the community pool as kids. It had probably been close to fifteen years since then, and it brought back a vibrancy I hadn't realized was missing.

The game carried on, "Marco!" and "Polo!" echoing off the walls as we splashed around.

"Marco!" Tony yelled again.

Oh shit.

He was way too close.

"Polo!" I cried out, and tried to use the bottom of the pool to propel myself away from his grasp. I wasn't quick enough. He snatched an ankle, dragging me in, an arm around my waist to hold me close in order to nip at my shoulder.

"Caught you, Nicky." His voice was a rough, growly whisper in my ear.

My heart stuttered.

He held me aloft until I could get control of myself so I didn't inhale water from gasping. Heat buzzed between us, but a beach ball to Tony's head broke the moment.

"Hurry up so I don't catch you immediately." I closed my eyes and took up my role as seeker. "Marco!"

The chorus of "Polos" made me grin, and I swished through water, searching them out. They were all a bunch of slippery seals. It felt like I was stuck just trying to find their vague locations forever until my fingertips hit skin and hooked in the string of a bikini. I opened my eyes to see Hana frozen in the deep end with my hand curled through the strap of her top, the fabric pulled aside to reveal one perfect breast.

Oh. Fuck.

Her gorgeous amber eyes examined me. "Good catch."

"Thanks." I swallowed hard and I disentangled myself, doing my best to not grope her in the process. "You're it."

Hana adjusted her top. "We've been in here for three hours. We should probably take a break."

"Cheater!" Billie yelled.

"It's not cheating if we end the game," replied Hana. "I know you won't let me forget it for the next time we play. I need a snack."

Hana hopped out of the pool, and I struggled to not stare at her. Her legs were long and muscled, body toned, and arms absolutely ripped, all exposing the fact that she could probably snap me in half if she wanted to.

I bit down a squeak.

That should not have been a sexy thought, and yet my body thrummed at the idea all the same.

Billie wolf-whistled. Hana ignored the sound and wrapped a beach towel around herself, disappearing into the main house.

Jasper swam over next to me and gently hip-checked me under the water. "What's going on in that head? Your cheeks are red as a beet."

This time I wasn't successful in muffling my squeak.

"You don't have to feel bad for ogling her," Jasper laughed and pushed back his curls. "We do it all the time, we were just behind you so you couldn't see it. She's something to look at, isn't she?"

I nodded silently, still willing my cheeks to return to their normal color. "I don't want to make her uncomfortable."

Billie and Tony joined us. With other people, I probably would've felt crowded. I had already slept with two of them, and that thought prompted me, reminding me that I was pretty interested in making that happen with Jasper, too.

At least in the pool my scent would be muted, so they couldn't immediately tell. Just to be sure, I ducked under the water, popping up between them with a grin. "Are we getting snacks or not? Or," I stretched out my toes and tapped Tony on the butt, "you're it."

Billie and Jasper leapt away from him, and the three of us frantically swam with Tony hot on our tails.

It was a quick game, whoever was 'it' catching their quarry in

163

moments, passing along the burden to the next person. Back and forth, over and over, until Billie jumped at me, their fingers swiping down my back and undoing the ties of my top.

"Foul!" I cried and clapped my hands over my chest with a laugh.

Billie nestled up to me and tucked their hands under mine. "I'll help protect your modesty."

They did the exact opposite when they rolled my nipples between their thumb and finger, tucking their face to the curve of my throat. I pressed a hand over my mouth to muffle the sound I made, but the pool had fallen silent, and, by the sharp intake of breath, it was pretty clear that Jasper and Tony knew exactly what was happening over here.

A reasonable woman would have probably hastily tied her top back into place and left to recover some dignity, but I wasn't feeling particularly dignified when Billie tweaked me again.

The slow swish of water had my nerves on edge. Tony and Jasper appeared in my peripheral vision.

"Billie," Tony said, his voice filled with admonishment. "You were supposed to let her rest for today."

Billie huffed in my ear, but kept their hands where they were.

"I can go," offered Jasper.

I chanced a look at him and was struck breathless by the longing fire in his eyes.

Oh.

That was for *me*.

They all waited for me to decide. It felt almost hypocritical to be awkward when barely two days ago I'd had a four-way on their couch upstairs.

Tony's palm rested on the back of my neck. "Nicky?"

God, why did that stupid hand feel so good? The wild thought of being pinned down with it flickered through my mind, and I sucked in a shallow breath. Jasper watched me with open want in his eyes.

"I *should* rest," I said. "But you're making it very difficult to make rational decisions when you look at me like that."

164

Jasper gave me a charming grin and put his hands in front of his eyes. "Better?"

"No." I giggled. "That just makes me like you more."

My stomach growled obnoxiously.

Tony laughed and gave my neck a little squeeze. "Let's get you some food, and afterwards you can decide if you're going to take mercy on Jasper."

They let me slip out of the water first, and I wrapped a beach towel around myself before the other three of them joined me. I tried in vain to not stare at the obviously tented swim trunks.

I had always been glad I didn't have the potential for a boner, specifically for moments like this. Sure they could smell when I was turned on, but I could do the same to them. It was a relief to not have such a blatant visual indicator for myself, though it did very good things for my ego, considering I was pretty sure both of those erections were for me.

Billie and I shared a shower upstairs to scrub away the chlorine. They were remarkably well behaved, all things considered. We all regrouped downstairs in the kitchen where Hana was grating cheese onto two cookie sheets of nacho chips.

My mouth watered in anticipation.

The others took up their posts as if they all had some secret telepathic communication, each managing a different ingredient to complete our meal—Jasper whipping up a pico de gallo, Billie warming up shredded chicken from the freezer, and Tony mashing up an avocado for guacamole.

Hana passed me a glass of water. "Hydrate. The pool takes a lot out of you."

My fingers curled around the glass and I lifted it to my lips, chugging down a good half of it under her watchful gaze. She gave me a nod of approval and turned back to her task.

"Can I help?"

"No." Hana's amber eyes froze me to the spot. "Drink your water. Tony told me you're supposed to be resting."

I sighed and had a few more sips.

When Hana finished with the cheese and shoved the trays

165

under the broiler, she went and filled three more glasses with water, setting one in front of each of the other members of her pack. She didn't have to tell them to drink, all of them downing their glasses in a few short seconds.

I'd been living away from home for over a decade, and none of my past partners had really had those natural caregiving tendencies. It was nice: to be watched over, to be cared for so diligently, and by so many people.

God. I hoped I didn't fuck this all up.

It was all so new, but screwing up with *any* one of them would bring this all crashing down and I was already dangerously attached.

I sipped my water to distract myself.

Hana got us set up at the table with a tray at each end and a card game in the middle. She briefed me on the rules—lay down your letter cards to make a new word as fast as you can, first one out wins—and set out five pairs of chopsticks so we didn't get our greasy fingers all over the cards.

I had a reputation to preserve. There was no way I was going to lose at a spelling game.

The starting word was FLAN, and the chaos began immediately. I slapped down my cards in quick succession, going from FLAN to FLAT to SLAT to SLAP before anyone else had a chance to play. They each barely got one card in before I slammed down my remaining cards and raised my hands, victorious.

Hana looked at me with an appreciative gleam in her eyes. "Well done."

I flushed under the simple praise and used my chopsticks to stuff a loaded chip into my mouth to cover my reaction.

We played until all the food was consumed and I was giddy from my multiple victories.

Hana cleared away the trays. "We should get you to bed."

I glanced at the clock behind her. Five in the morning was earlier than I usually went to bed, even on my days off, but, now that she said it, I could feel the weight of the day sinking into my limbs.

"I've got to head to work and set up for my first boot camp," Hana announced.

She accepted goodbye kisses from the rest of the pack, offering only a nod to me. Not that I was surprised, but I sucked back in a little pout.

When Hana had gone, it was only the four of us remaining.

"Would it be okay if I took mercy on you a different day?" I asked Jasper.

He laughed and gave me a soft smile, patting my knee beneath the table. "I'll accept your mercy on any day."

"Cuddle pile for sleep?" Billie asked.

I smiled, leaning in to kissed their cheek. "I can never say no to a cuddle pile."

We tidied up, and I let them bundle me upstairs, wedged in between them all in Billie's bed. Spud appeared, from wherever he had been hiding, along with Roscoe, and the two of them took over the foot of the bed.

I had never been to paradise before, but this was coming pretty damn close.

Chapter Nineteen
Nicky

The music pounded like a drum beat, setting the rhythm right down to my bones. We'd gotten into the club that Gabe worked at the moment we walked up to the door.

I tugged down the hem of my borrowed dress. Billie had put me in the purple sequin minidress out of their closet, but I was both bigger and taller than them, which meant the dress was about three inches too short, just barely reaching the curve of my ass and absolutely *clinging* to my curves. Billie was in a sparkly black romper, and Jasper at our backs was in dark skinny jeans and a hunter green tank top with a discrete line of sequins along the neckline.

We hadn't gotten deep enough to find Gabe yet. Every occupant of the club was omega or beta, with the bouncers that kept the peace the only alphas allowed in.

I felt like an imposter while standing among the strobe lights, listening to dance music I didn't recognize. It had been almost a decade since I'd been to a club.

Billie dragged us to the bar where they got us three shots of vodka. I tossed it back, trying not to give away how infrequently I drank, and attempting to avoid coughing at the searing burn as I swallowed.

"One more for luck," said Billie, getting another set of three from the bartender. They tucked a generous tip into his hand and passed our drinks to us. I swallowed back the second shot, already more comfortable with the burn. It warmed me all the way down my throat and sat like a little bundle of coals in my stomach.

Thank god I'd packed a pair of flats. If I was in heels, I already would've tripped over my companions. I'd learned from a very painful experience what liquor and high heels did to me—or more accurately what it did to the people around me. I didn't want to relive the time I had punctured someone's foot after a drinking contest.

I pushed the thought aside as Billie dragged us out onto the dance floor. At least club music all hit similar beats, making it easy to dance to when you were uncoordinated or unfamiliar. I hadn't eaten more than the piece of toast Jasper had shoved on us before we left. Already, the vodka was warming my body and loosening my limbs.

The crowd throbbed around us. Billie and Jasper sandwiched me between them, and I started to heat up for a whole different reason. Billie hooked their arm around my neck, their heels bringing us up to the same height. I leaned in first, taking the kiss that they rained down on me with a moan that I heard even above the music. Jasper's hands were rooted to my hips, our bodies moving to the sway of the music.

I felt only a little bad that Hana and Tony were at home without us, Tony working on his contract projects, and Hana resting until it was time to make her boot camp clients see god in the coming morning.

Jasper kissed my throat, and I sighed happily against Billie's mouth. This pack was like a drug high. When I pulled away, my eyes were drawn to Gabe like a magnet. He watched us from across the dance floor, looking absolutely scrumptious in a rough white tank top.

Billie spun in my grasp and tucked their ass against my hips, taking both of my hands and setting them purposefully on their front, one bracing their stomach, the other brazenly cupping a breast. I squeezed softly, unable to look away from Gabe.

It was hard to draw a full breath when I was surrounded on all sides, the crowd thick and the smell of desire a haze hanging over us.

I'd been here like five minutes and I was already wanting someone to bend me over a table: a very particular alpha, someone who watched me with the gaze so hot I was surprised my clothes didn't burst into flames. A gorgeous omega appeared to steal Billie away for a dance, leaving me with Jasper.

His breath was ragged in my ear. I leaned back, angling myself so I could breathe in the sweet chocolate and cinnamon scent of him. That was dangerous—one whiff hitting me just as hard as the vodka. There was no way that he missed the pitiful sound that fell from my lips or the way my fingers disappeared into his thick curls.

I tried to focus on the dancing. Billie swayed alluringly with their omega partner, and an icy surge of jealousy slithered around in my chest.

Jasper laughed in my ear. "Are you growling at them?"

I shrugged my shoulders. If I was, it wasn't on purpose.

"It's hard to watch at first," he said. "I've gotten used to people finding them fascinating and wanting to be close. Billie's a flirt, but they never pursue anything beyond that without talking to us. Will you let me distract you?"

I nodded without thinking. When a new song began, Jasper spun me around, pulling me into what seemed like a proper dance position. He moved me to the beat, and I did my best to follow the flow of the music and his guiding body. The twirls caught me off guard, leaving me laughing each time we crashed together and maneuvered through the crowd.

I wouldn't have pegged Jasper as a dancer. When he turned me again, laying my back to his chest with his forearms wrapped over my stomach, I noticed the strength of them for the first time. The corded muscle flexed when I laid my hands over them. I guess people got pretty strong kneading bread every day.

Arms like that could ruin a girl.

"You smell so fucking good," Jasper murmured against my ear, nipping the lobe teasingly.

I didn't stop my whine this time. Jasper's cock rose behind me and he pulled me closer still, grinding against me with a fierce little growl in my ear. I wove my fingers into his red curls, his scalp sweaty under my touch.

I lost track of how many songs passed and how long Billie had been gone. Everything centered down to the omega at my back and the ever present throb between my thighs.

When my feet started to ache and my throat burned from the exertion, I tapped Jasper's arms, and he worked us through the crowd toward one of the smaller bars at the back of the club. I didn't make the connection to where we were going until he stopped in front of Gabe and Billie. Gabe watched us with amusement clear in his eyes, and Billie leaned against the wall sipping a brilliantly coloured cocktail.

"He finally tired you out, Books?"

"Just need a bit of a refuel. Where have you been?"

"Watching you grind on my omega in between letting the club patrons grind on me."

Heat flooded my face. "I didn't mean to hog him."

Billie waved away the concern. "I refuse to get in the way of you and Jaspy having sexy bonding time. I've had access to his cake for years. I'm more than happy to share with you."

I swallowed hard, my tongue thick.

"Having fun?" Gabe asked.

"Yep," I said, not quite able to meet his gaze.

"Come on, cuties," said Billie. "Let's get you some refreshments."

Billie ordered me a vodka cranberry with lemon soda so I

could get some more sugar and fluids rather than straight alcohol. At a signal from Gabe, the bartender also gave us each a glass of water.

I was never going to be thirsty again if these alphas had their way. I chugged down my water and sipped more slowly at my drink. The three of us rested together at a small table near where Gabe kept his silent watch of the patrons. The crowd tonight seemed well behaved, and none of the bouncers had needed to step in, that I had seen anyway. It was a shame that Gabe had to work because I was pretty sure he would be able to fling me around the dance floor as easily as Jasper had. Maybe on a night he didn't work we could all go to an all inclusive club so that the alphas could join us.

The sugar, water, and extra boost of alcohol worked their magic, and Billie shoved me back out onto the dance floor with Jasper. He looked at me with that same fire in his eyes. I was far enough separated from yesterday's upset that I didn't stop myself from rising up on my toes to hook my arm around his neck to kiss him. His chocolate scent burst around me and his hands snaked up my back, stroking the bare skin exposed by the dress. His mouth was soft, warm, and eager, sliding against mine with a hot determination, and it was all I could do to keep up. He dropped his hands lower and tugged the hem of my dress back down, cupping both butt cheeks to keep it secure.

"Jasper," I breathed his name, wishing there was somewhere we could go. I was as randy as a teen and ready to drag him into a bathroom.

The house lights went up and back down, a warning for last call.

"Gabe won't be off for a couple hours, but we can get the limo to take us home." He threaded his hands into my hair, loosening my hasty updo.

My clit had been throbbing since he'd first put his hands on me. One word broke through my needy haze. "Limo?"

"We have one on call for tonight. Billie just has to let them know when we're ready."

I hadn't ridden in a limo since prom, and my happy lust-filled brain was very excited to repeat that experience.

"Why didn't we take it here?" I asked.

"Because we wanted it to be a surprise, and post-party limos are always more fun."

I traced a finger down his chest and back up, hooking it in the neckline of his shirt. "Do you want me to take mercy on you while we're in it?"

The soft buzz of alcohol was nothing compared to the desperate pulse I felt like a heartbeat in my cunt. In the light of day, I might've balked at the idea of sex in a fancy car, but I couldn't get the image out of my head now that it was there.

Jasper rocked against me, using his hands to press me even closer. "Won't be the first time I've had sex in a limo. And hopefully won't be the last."

If he shifted just a couple of inches, he'd be touching exactly where I craved. Shame that we were in public and I hadn't had nearly enough liquor to shake loose those particular inhibitions. I could think about it though, even if I wasn't brave enough to do it.

Billie appeared out of nowhere. "Are we staying or going?"

Jasper leaned in and whispered something in Billie's ear that I couldn't hear over the music, though, from the delighted, saucy expression on their face, I could only assume he was informing them of my offer.

Billie sidled up close and kissed my cheek. "Spicy Books is my favorite. Jaspy is going to rock your fucking world."

My skin tingled, my body aching to be touched even though they both already had their hands on me.

I wanted them to ruin me.

This pack was going to turn me into a sex fiend.

It wasn't my fault there were so many things to discover with so many people, especially when they each made me feel safe and desired. What was I supposed to do with that if not indulge in my own needs and curiosities?

"I'll text the limo company," said Billie. "If they're not already here waiting, they shouldn't be more than ten minutes out."

A song I actually knew finally played over the speakers, and I vibrated with excitement, happily forcing both of them onto the dance floor again.

By the time Billie signaled to us that the limo had arrived, I was giggly and giddy, drunk all over again with the experience of the evening more so than the liquor.

"Let's go. I'm ready for my world to be rocked."

Chapter Twenty
Billie

Nicky stumbled adorably to the limo. The driver was waiting and opened the door for us so she could climb into the backseat with a giggle. Her dress rode up as she did so, exposing the cute black panties she had on underneath. I was next in, followed by Jasper, and the door closed behind us. We had the limo for as long as we wanted, and I sent a message to the driver to loop around the city so we had time to play.

Nicky had already pulled Jasper in, the two of them making out on the long side seat. I'd watched them together on the dance floor, torn between joining them and begging Gabe to go on a break to destroy me. Nicky and Jasper were another piece in my fantasy. They were entirely too beautiful and so fucking hot together. I couldn't wait to get in there.

My patience lasted only a couple of minutes. I unhooked the

button at the back of my romper and pulled down the strappy sleeves to let the top portion fall.

"Room for one more?"

They both reached for me without unfastening their mouths from each other. I weaseled my way in, gliding a hand down Jasper's back and nipping along Nicky's throat. The limo smelled like a bakery with all of us wild and ready, the hot, spicy tinge to the air easily as intoxicating as the vodka I'd been sipping all night.

The three of us traded off one another's mouths, the two of them consuming one another before I took a turn with each.

Everyone was entirely too clothed. I freed Jasper of his tank top and ran my hands over his tight little body, his muscles stark and lean under my touch. Nicky hummed appreciatively and wandered her hands over his chest.

"If you let me get those panties off of you," I said, "I can show you one of Jaspy's special skills."

Nicky let out an absolutely delicious sound. Jasper helped her sit up, and she wiggled her hips to the edge of the seat, lifting them so I could tug off the damp fabric hiding her from us.

This was exactly how I liked her—riled up and perfectly needy, desperate to be touched. I pulled one of her thighs open, and Jasper got down on his knees on the floor of the limo.

I hadn't anticipated how much fun having a view of this would be. Sure, I was just as eager as Jasper to get my mouth on that pretty pink cunt, but I was very much enjoying watching Jasper tease her, loving the way her chest heaved as she panted and the way her eyes squeezed shut when he slipped that tongue over her folds.

A lot of my friends had complained about men not knowing where the clit was, but I had trained Jasper extremely thoroughly with that from the very beginning. Someone eager for their partner's pleasure made the very best student.

Jasper lapped at her greedily, and I slid my hand down the front of my romper, giving my own clit a bit of attention. It wasn't quite as good as his tongue, but I would get to play with it later.

I got down on my knees next to him and pushed open Nicky's thighs as far as she could manage. Poor thing was bordering on hyperventilating. She buried one twitchy hand in my hair. I licked her right along with him, our tongues working in tandem like an elaborate French kiss that just so happened to include a cunt in the mix.

Neither of us were doing more than teasing, but that was half the fun. I wanted her incoherent with desire, every bit of her brain shut down except for that primal part that would beg and plead for us to give her more. And by the gorgeous little whines she was giving us, it wouldn't take much more to hit that point. Her legs trembled around us and her hand shook in my hair.

I added my fingers so I could open her up, giving us clear access to that pearlescent little bud that would turn her into a mess. Jasper's tongue slid inside of her and I tugged down the top of her dress, folding the sequins over and popping the clasp of her bra.

"Books, you look so perfect while getting ruined." I stole a kiss, tongue delving as she opened to me. There was nothing quite like the rush of a lover yielding. I laid my hand against her throat like I remembered Gabe doing. Nicky bucked against Jasper's mouth, and I ate up her moan. I slid down to give her some attention elsewhere.

Lips, tongue, and teeth went to work on her. She let loose a string of curses when I carefully pinned her nipple between my teeth and swirled my tongue over it, sucking hard. I only relented when she let out an anguished cry.

"Please," she begged. "Please god, more."

There we go.

We both pulled away, Jasper's beard glistening.

"On your hands and knees, Books."

She looked at me with lust-glazed eyes and scrambled to follow the instructions. I nipped that perfect round ass she exposed, smiling against her skin at her little yelp.

"Are you ready for Jaspy to fuck you?"

Nicky nodded frantically and dropped down to her forearms, resting her cheek on the leather seat.

"Sweet fuck," Jasper breathed. "Nicky, you don't even know what kind of picture you present right now. If the others could see you, they would be so fucking jealous."

Jasper undid his jeans and shoved them down out of the way along with his underwear, his cock popping free and ready for action. I reached over Nicky's ass and cupped her. I already knew she was ready, but I pushed my fingers in anyways, her body opening easily with the invasion of three of them.

"Shit," Jasper whispered. "I wish I could record things with my eyeballs, but lucky for me I'm pretty sure this vision is going to be seared into my memory for the rest of time."

"Our needy little beta is so slippery. I think she needs some omega cock to fill her up." I grinned at them both and extracted my fingers with a slurping sound, getting right in Nicky's eye-line to lick them clean. I watched her face. I could tell the exact moment that Jasper pressed forward by the drop of her mouth and the moan of pleasure.

I sat back to watch them, one hand buried between my own thighs while I split my time admiring their faces and watching his cock disappearing into her willing body.

I was still in orgasm denial, but that didn't mean I couldn't tease myself in the meantime. When I got home I could throw myself at Tony and beg him to let me come, but, for now, I would enjoy Nicky getting all the orgasms I couldn't have.

Sweat gleamed on their skin and I indulged every so often, licking away the salt. I teased Jasper's nipples and used my free hand on Nicky's clit, gratified when her sounds pitched and Jasper grunted from the squeeze of her as she came for the pair of us.

I got her off once more before Jasper's hips started to falter. He pulled out of Nicky and I took him straight into my mouth, pumping his shaft with my fist and drinking down the hot liquid that hit the back of my throat while he cursed and dug his hands into my hair.

I sat back with a satisfied smile.

"On your back, Books. Time to experience Jaspy's other special talent."

She whined and moved on shaking legs, sprawling back on the leather with one foot hooked up on the back of the seat, the other on the floor next to me.

"Do you mind if I get you a little bit bendy?" I asked.

She shook her head and looked at me curiously. I shimmied out of the rest of my romper and dropped my panties, moving to snare both of her ankles, lifting them into the air, and setting a knee on each side of her head.

"Do you wanna give me a little treat, Books?"

"I don't know if I'll be good at it."

"No worries. You can just explore. I'm not allowed to come anyway. I just want to know how amazing that mouth feels." I lowered myself down until I felt her tentative tongue, and then I finished moving her into position, pressing her shins to my chest. Hana had done this to me on many occasions, but it was a whole different level of gleeful intoxication to be the one in charge.

Jasper folded his tank top and tucked it under Nicky's hip. I watched as three of Jasper's fingers disappeared into her. His forearm flexed, and I knew exactly what kind of bliss she was feeling even if her expression of it was muffled by my cunt.

Nicky had no real finesse, but the eager sweeps of her tongue still felt lovely, moreso when she found my clit and went to town.

"You should have a race with her, Jaspy. See if you can get her off before she gets me off."

My omega's brow furrowed in concentration, and Nicky's whole body trembled in my grip from him thoroughly working her over. I pulled in a shuddering breath, Nicky finally finding her stride down there. Her hands cupped my ass and shifted me around so she could get the angle she was seeking. Her tongue faltered as Jasper ramped up.

His hand pressed down on her stomach, and I nipped mischievously at her ankle.

She writhed beneath us, her cries all the more alluring when I

179

could feel them against my wet pussy. I bore down as the scream hit her, and liquid gushed from between her thighs, soaking Jasper's shirt.

I was so fucking close. It killed me to lift my hips, cutting off the orgasm she'd been building for me.

Nicky melted into the leather when I released her ankles and sat down next to her head. She was breathing like she'd run a marathon, and her body still twitched from the lingering ripples of pleasure. Her hair had entirely fallen out of its style, and her face glistened from me.

"You make the prettiest fucking picture right now. An absolute mess that we ruined in the back of a limo."

I fixed her up, putting her bra back on and tidying the dress. I got myself dressed, too, but only in the romper, folding my bra and panties and tucking them down the front of it. I wasn't going to need either of those for long when I got home, anyway. I sent a message to the driver that we were ready to head to the pack house, and barely fifteen minutes later we passed through the gate.

I sent a message to Tony, too, telling him to be ready.

"Jaspy, you can manage getting Nicky up to your room right?"

"Yep. Nicky, do you mind bunking with me tonight?"

Our beta shook her head.

"Good," I said. "Because I've got a very sexy date with an alpha the second I get inside."

Jasper laughed and adjusted his arm around Nicky. As we pulled to a stop, I launched myself out of the limo before the driver had a chance to get out, running barefoot up the drive and through the front door. I didn't even have to call for Tony. He was waiting for me in the entryway with knowing eyes.

I jumped into his arms and lost myself in the taste of him. "Please, god, tell me you'll let me come tonight."

"I'll think about it."

He carried me into the kitchen and set me on the island. The romper shorts were loose, leaving nothing in the way of his seeking fingers.

I reveled in his growl and laid back with a needy giggle. "Take me, Daddy."

His firm grip on my hips pulled me right to the edge. His hands disappeared for only a moment, presumably to free himself from his pajama pants. My theory was proven correct when the tip of him found my entrance and he fucked into me with no resistance. I arched off the counter, my cry echoing over the stark marble.

"Yes, fuck. Just like that, Daddy."

"Did you have a good night, little one? Nicky and Jasper didn't satisfy you?"

I whimpered. "I'm not *allowed* to be satisfied."

"We both know that, but you're not always good at following the rules." He ground his hips between mine and lifted my knees, pressing them to each of my shoulders. "Hold these for me. I suppose if you'd broken the rules you wouldn't be quite this desperate."

"I was *good. Please.*"

Tony withdrew slowly, teasing me with the retreat of every inch, then surging back in, setting a punishing pace. It was exactly what I craved. His thumb teased my clit and brought me right up to that glorious shining edge before pulling away.

"No!" I sobbed. "Please let me come. Please, please, please, please. I can't take it anymore."

Tony laughed and fucked into me so hard I slid along the marble. "I fucking *love* to hear you beg, little one."

He pulled me back to the edge of the counter and resumed his pace, this time letting his thumb finish me off. I screamed into the dark house and bowed up, taking everything he gave me.

When I finally settled, he slid his cock out of me, and he gave himself a few additional strokes, curses dancing on his lips as he came, white ropes of his pleasure splattering my clubwear.

I shuddered. "Thank you, Daddy."

Tony looked down at me fondly as I laid there basking. "I saw Nicky and Jasper sneak upstairs. Where are things at with them?"

"They fucked in the limo on the way home." I grinned. "I'd

say that I wish you could have seen, but I get to be in charge without alphas around and it's fucking *hot*."

Tony laughed and swatted my ass before helping me stand. "I'll have to imagine it until it happens in my presence."

"I doubt that'll take very long. Nicky's taking to everything like a duck to water." I squeezed my thighs together, shivering at the lingering sensations.

"How are you feeling about that?" Tony asked as he peeled my romper off of me, letting it drop to the floor.

"Blissed!" I stood on my toes to kiss him. "I knew I had excellent taste, but I am fucking *loving* everyone else agreeing with me. Plus, I have a *very* good time watching her come undone."

"I have to say I'm quite a fan of that myself." He dipped down and nipped my shoulder. "Get to bed you little slut."

I winked at him and grabbed a handful of his shirt, yanking him down so I could kiss him fiercely, slap his ass, and take off at a run. I cackled happily hearing his footsteps thunder after me.

Tonight was the best fucking night.

Chapter Twenty-One
Nicky

I woke to an aching head and Jasper plastered to my side. Two bottles of water and a container of pain relievers sat on his bedside table. I groaned quietly so as not to wake him, laying a hand over my forehead. I hadn't had *that* much to drink, but apparently even a small-ish amount in my thirties was prepared to kill me.

It took another couple moments to realize what had woken me. My phone buzzed away next to the water bottles and I rolled over gingerly to grab it.

Mom flashed on the screen.

God. No.

I answered anyway.

"Hi Mom."

"Nicola! This is the second time I've phoned you. Why are you taking so long to answer?"

"You know, there's this new invention called sleep," I muttered.

Mom hadn't quite gotten the hang of my night schedule yet.

She scoffed and started chattering away, my head throbbing. Jasper woke in all of the chaos and stretched, looking at me with squinty eyes.

"What's happening?" he asked. "Who are you talking to? Why are we awake?"

Mom gasped. "Nicola! Is that a *man*? Are you sleeping with someone?"

I laid a fist against my forehead as if that would temper the throb from her volume. "Mom, can you freak out a tiny bit quieter?"

"Who is it? Are you and Alphonse back together?"

The inquiry was like a bucket of cold water dumped on my head. Jasper cuddled up to my side and kissed my cheek, removing my sour expression.

I took a deep breath and steeled myself. "No, Mom. We're not back together. And I'd appreciate it if you never talk to him again."

"Nicola," Mom huffed. "That's so rude. Why wouldn't I talk to him? I'm just being polite."

"Listen, I don't wanna get into it right now. Just please don't give him any more of my information, okay? What did you call about?"

"I wanted to know if you would bring dessert tonight. Your father is making chicken parmigiana, so choose something that fits well. Is your bed partner joining us?"

I sighed and flopped onto my pillow, looking to Jasper for answers. He briefly held up a thumbs-up and curled back under the blankets.

"Yeah, I can bring him."

"Excellent!" Mom's voice had brightened considerably. "I can't wait."

"Yeah, me neither. I'm gonna go back to sleep now though. I'll see you tonight."

184

I hung up without giving her a chance to reply and chucked my phone to the foot of the bed.

Jasper flipped the blanket over my head, bathing us in darkness and warmth. "Where are we going tonight?" he asked.

"Family Sunday dinner," I replied with a groan. "Hosted most weeks unless my parents go to Palm Springs or someone is sick."

Jasper laughed quietly. "My parents love Palm Springs. I'm pretty sure they live there more than they do at home." He kissed my cheek again. "Good morning."

I hummed happily and burrowed into his arms in the dark. "Good morning."

Jasper's purr kicked on and he stroked my hair while we dozed. "We should probably drink that water Hana left."

I couldn't stop the giggle.

"What?"

"It's just cute, is all. The silent caretaker." I weaseled out from under the blankets and grabbed both bottles, passing one to Jasper and tapping four pills out of the pain reliever container, two for each of us. I swallowed everything back and leaned comfortably against the headboard.

Jasper kissed his way up my throat until I was squirming.

"I bet if we go downstairs there will be fresh scones," he told me.

"How would there be fresh scones? Did you get up in the middle of the night to make them?"

"No, but usually after we go clubbing one of the alphas will peel themselves out of bed and pick up some tasty carbs for us."

I slid back down to lay flat and pulled the blankets up to my chin, rolling towards him and pressing my forehead against his chest. "I don't know if scones are enough to coax me out of this bed."

"No one is going to *make us* get up. We could stay in here until it's time to leave for your dinner."

I let out a pathetic moan. "No, thank you. I love my family, but I need to be solidly awake with time to mentally prepare if I'm bringing someone over."

"Entirely fair. We could bring Billie for reinforcements."

I kicked my feet like a petulant child. "I don't know if I want to see the look in my mother's eyes when she finds out there's more than one lover."

Jasper laughed so hard my head ached, and I tucked it firmly underneath the blankets. "You know what, that's fair. Not everyone is down with packs. My family was pretty chill about it, but I think that's because I'm an omega. I know the alpha's families can be a little touchy about the subject, and Billie's are a whole other ball of wax."

"Most of my family will be fine with it. My brothers might look at me funny, but that's just because I'm their sister. And I don't think Mom will disapprove necessarily, it's just not a discussion I really wanna have with her."

"Tell me more about your family? I feel like I should know a tiny bit more about you besides the fact that you are the sexiest librarian on the planet."

I giggled and took a big whiff of his chocolate and cinnamon scent to relax myself. "Okay, well I'm the oldest, and I have two younger brothers. Sidney just turned thirty and got married a couple months ago to his bondmate, Allie. He's the only alpha in our family and works as a nurse. My youngest brother is Luca. He's twenty-six, single so far as any of us know, and he's been floundering a bit, bouncing around jobs trying to find something he's passionate about. Um, my parents have been married for thirty-five years, both betas. What else did you want to know?"

"What made you decide to become a librarian?" Jasper rolled me over and laid his head on my chest. I laced my fingers through his hair, absently stroking as I answered his question.

"We lived down the road from my library growing up and I was the biggest teacher's pet in history. Just *really* craved that adult approval. One of the librarians there took a shine to me since I spent basically all of my free time curled up in the children's section reading stacks of books as tall as I was. She warned me it would take a lot of schooling to become a librarian, but I wanted to be the steward of a place like that. One where kids could lose themselves in reading. A little beacon of peace in a world of chaos."

"And here I thought you couldn't get any cuter than you already were." Jasper traced his fingertips over my ribs until I was shivering.

"What about you?" I asked. "Did you always want to be a baker?"

"Not my whole life. It really picked up when I was a teen. My grandmother was a *huge* baker. At holidays she would send every single person home with their own ice cream pail full of cookies. I'm pretty sure she spent almost every day with something in the oven, passing them around to neighbors and friends." His next breath stuttered a little and I stroked his cheek softly. "She passed away when I was sixteen and left me her recipe book. I started baking as a way for all of us to feel closer to her, and it was the look on peoples faces when they ate what I baked that really made me fall in love with it."

"That's so sweet." I wrapped my arms snugly around him. "She'd be so proud of you."

"I like to think so. I wouldn't have my bakery without Billie. They hounded me for years about letting them be an investor until I finally gave in and let them make my dreams come true."

"They have good taste and a good heart."

"Very true." Jasper laughed quietly. "Billie's thirst brings us all together. How are you feeling about the others?"

I fidgeted, sorting through my thoughts. "I really like Tony, too. Gabe kind of makes my brain shut off. And Hana...I can never quite tell if she likes me or not."

"Trust me, if Hana didn't like you, you wouldn't be asking that question. She's just feeling you out right now."

"I guess that's okay. She's so pretty. I don't wanna disappoint her."

"Don't say things like that around her or she'll get ideas."

"What kind of ideas?"

Jasper shook his head. "That's for future Nicky to find out about. I'm not spoiling the surprise."

Chapter Twenty-Two
Jasper

We decided on rosemary shortbread with a sweet lemon glaze for tonight's dessert. Hana meandered by every so often, checking in to make sure I wasn't putting Nicky to work, but I still wanted to share this with her.

Everyone gave us this space, just a little bit of time to bond.

Nicky looked cute as a button in the apron she borrowed from Billie—solid black with sparkly purple text that read *Kiss The Cook*, which I had done the moment she'd put it on.

"What can I do if I'm not allowed to work?" Nicky asked.

"Mostly keep me company."

I had measured out all of the ingredients into bowls in the order I would need them, so at the very least Nicky would be able to pass them to me without Hana eyeballing me too hard. It was nice for Nicky to actually watch me in my element, and I was glad that she enjoyed what I made. I always found that things tended to taste better when you could see the love and work that went into them.

"Did you make shortbread with your grandma?" she asked while I sifted the flour.

"Every December. I'm more of the mind that shortbread is an all-season cookie. Especially when you mix up the flavors. Do you bake with your family?"

"Not very often. My brother is a pretty good baker, and once he got that skill I mostly just mooched off of him. Luca's started making most of the desserts, but Mom likes things to be egalitarian so she passes around the duties between us."

"I don't mind if you mooch off of me. Lucky for you I can be paid in kisses."

Nicky's cheek blushed pink and she planted her lips to my cheek with an adorable giggle.

"Payment accepted."

It was way too easy to see this happening on a regular basis. I already knew that we were sexually compatible, and she'd proven that she was comfortable to be around, plus her interest in me as a person made for a dangerous combination. It was a slippery slope when I'd started to catch feelings with the other pack members.

I stole another kiss for good measure, and Nicky stood on her toes, matching my enthusiasm until I backed her up against the counter where she broke away with a laugh.

Too often, by the time I realized how deep I was, the edge was already out of reach, and I was sliding towards the inevitable. Nicky seemed like she would be a soft place to land.

I got the oven preheating and gave her the task of overseeing the mixer while the icing sugar and butter whipped together. The recipe was simple, and one that I had memorized years ago. But Nicky was mostly a baking newbie, so I explained the process as we went and the point of each of the steps so that we got the fluffiest cookies possible.

I indulged myself, draping my arms around her waist and managing the mixer while she poured the ingredients in turn until we had a dough formed.

"How are your piping skills?" I asked.

"Like plumbing?" she asked.

A traitorous snort laugh escaped before I could stop it. "Not quite, but I'll show you."

I tasked her with holding the piping bag so I could scoop our dough into it.

I squeezed one glossy swirl out onto the cookie sheet. "Your turn. Come here and try."

She accepted the piping bag with nervous fingers and squeezed out an uneven swirl, turning those beautiful brown eyes on me. "Help."

I tidied up the dough back into the bag, made sure the top was twisted closed properly, and adjusted her grip, keeping my hands over hers as we moved in one fluid motion. "There you go, just like that."

She was warm in my embrace, and I couldn't help nuzzling her cheek as I guided her through a few more cookie swirls before letting her finish off the tray.

"I no longer have to wonder how your arms are so strong. This is a lot of work."

I laughed and breathed her in. "Oh yeah. Between piping and kneading, *every* day is arm day. You did a good job Nicky."

She flushed at the praise.

"You can pop those in the oven. Set the timer for fifteen minutes while I tidy our space so we can make our glaze."

I liked her in our kitchen. If she stuck around—and I hoped she did—we'd have to get her her own apron. She turned back to me after completing her task, happy as a little clam.

Too fucking cute.

It took only a minute to load up the dishwasher and get it running. Lemon glaze was always my favorite, perfect for adding that bright pop of sweet freshness. Nicky watched me with a rapt attention as I combined the icing sugar and the lemon juice, dipping a spoon into the mixture for her to test the balance. Her whole face puckered at the first sample and I laughed at her shiver.

"Noted. I'll add a little more sugar."

While we waited for the cookies to finish baking, I got her to tell me about some of her favorite food experiences so I could make sure we added those little touches when she visited. I wouldn't be able to compete with an Italian grandmother, but I could definitely take a stab at making her some cannoli that was just as delicious as the ones she had for her eighteenth birthday. It was no surprise that most of her favorites were Italian, but she had a few fun experiences in college—an Iranian classmate who had invited her over for tahdig, a Greek neighbor who surprised her with treats regularly, and an international fair at school where she had consumed her weight in horchata to stave off the summer heat.

I transferred the baked cookies onto a cooling rack and sent her to go shower.

I set a protective cover over the cookies just in case Spud or Roscoe got curious, and disappeared to shower myself. I added some curling mousse to my hair and I stood in front of the mirror, trimming down a good portion of my beard so it was much neater.

Next, I was facing down my closet. The compulsion to put on a suit when meeting a partner's family never quite went away. Nicky assured me that anything that fancy wasn't necessary, so I stuck to dark wash jeans and a black button down with a silvery pinstripe.

"How come *you* get to go?" asked Billie, popping their head into my room. "I'm the one who found her."

"Because I was the one her mom overheard when she called." Billie pouted, and I leaned over to kiss that expression off their face. "Don't be jealous. I'm sure Nicky will bring you to meet them soon."

They sighed dramatically and flopped back onto my bed, purple curls spreading like a halo around them.

A knock on my door had both of us turning. Nicky slipped inside wearing a ruffly white button down tank top and black dress pants that would be equally suited to dinner and her shift at the library afterward.

Billie sat up, looking hopefully toward Nicky, who beelined over and kissed them softly.

"I want to go to dinner, too," said Billie.

Nicky stroked their cheeks. "Soon. I have to work up a little more courage, but I promise I'll take you to meet them another time." She gave Billie a sweet, slow kiss before turning to me. "The cookies felt cool enough when I checked them. Are we ready to ice them?"

"You bet." I fussed with my hair one more time and finally stepped away from the mirror. We were leaving a bit early to pick up Nicky's car from the library. We'd go together to her parents, and then I would chill out with her at work, along with Tony and Billie before I had to go to the bakery. I picked up the small tote bag I had packed with much more comfortable clothes for work tucked safely inside.

Nicky watched as I added a little dollop of the lemon glaze to the center of each cookie. I gave her the task of adding a round silver sprinkle to top it off. Her tongue stuck out the side as she concentrated.

I hauled out one of my transport boxes and laid the cookies in neat layers to take over to her family.

My phone buzzed, and I perused the readout, seeing an email from the bakery's online order form. I popped it open just to check.

PLEASE SEE THIS IN TIME!!!

Hello! I'm so sorry to be emailing you with so little notice. I was supposed to put in this order last week and I forgot and I'm so worried I'm going to get fired over it. If it's AT ALL possible, I need 200 scones and cinnamon rolls (half of each) for a 5:30am pick up.

I'll pay double for the inconvenience.

-A hopeful client, Alex

Aw, fuck.

"Hey, Nicky."

Her head perked up. "Yeah?"

"Would you hate me forever if I had to bail on tonight?"

She looked a little crestfallen at the question. "Is something wrong?"

"I got a very urgent request for the bakery, and normally I wouldn't entertain something last minute like this, but it sounds like the person might lose their job if I don't do it. We have another massive order for this morning and I'll never manage it all without going in early."

"Oh. Of course. Bakery comes before a brand new friend's family dinner. You do whatever you have to do."

"You are a gem." I cupped her cheeks and kissed her thoroughly. "I'll make it up to you."

"I accept bribes in the form of focaccia." She grinned up at me.

"You got it, sweetheart."

I handed her the cookie box and went to the garage to climb in my car with only a few grumbles. I didn't want to skip out on Nicky, but I also didn't want someone losing their job because of an administrative fuck up. I knew what that fear of god felt like. I replied back to the email as I was sitting in the driver seat, and then pulled out, taking a short trip to the bakery.

Chapter Twenty-Three
Nicky

I fussed with the cookie box, suddenly thrown off balance with the change of plans during today's already ridiculous roller coaster of emotions. Despite the hangover and awkward phone call, waking up with Jasper had been like a dream. A cozy, sexy dream full of cuddles, kisses, and sweet stories that made me like him even more. I'd gotten all mentally prepared for Jasper to meet my family, and now that was yanked out from under me. Mom was going to question why I was showing up alone and I didn't have the energy for that today.

"Damn it smells good up here." I turned to see Gabe coming up the stairs from the basement. He was in workout clothes, and his skin gleamed with a thin sheen of sweat. "Where's Jasper? Aren't you two supposed to be leaving now?"

"He had to make an emergency trip to the bakery, so I'm going to dinner by myself."

"Oh, shit."

"Yeah. I was kind of looking forward to having some back up tonight. Take some of the attention off me, you know."

Gabe wandered into the kitchen and leaned on the counter. "I'm free if you'd still like the company. I'm very good back up."

A ripple of warmth slid through my body at the suggestion. "You're sure?"

"Absolutely. You want me there, I'm there. Plus, free food."

Billie came trotting down the stairs. "What's happening now? Where's Jaspy?"

I updated them on the situation.

"I'll come with you!" Billie offered immediately.

I fidgeted. "I'd love to have you there, but I'm kind of a baby under my mom's scrutiny, and she definitely heard Jasper on the phone. I feel like if I showed up with you, who I could definitely not pretend was the same person...that would lead to a lot of questions that I don't really want to address with my family right now."

Billie pouted.

"I'm sorry." They allowed me to gather them into a hug. "I know that's kind of selfish."

"It's cool." Billie sighed and kissed my cheek. "Gabe's probably better for their first meeting anyway. He's got those calming alpha vibes and I *definitely* do not."

"Just give me five minutes to change," said Gabe. "I'll be right with you."

I watched as he walked away, then as he took the stairs two at a time, disappearing into the upper levels.

"I guess it's too soon to say you should invite your family *here* so we can all spend time with you," said Billie as they fidgeted with the hem of their shirt.

"A bit." I kissed them softly. "Let's make it past the first week at least."

"Okay, fine." Billie thrust out their bottom lip in an extra dramatic pout. "I'll survive."

"If Mom didn't have superhuman hearing, then you'd be the first one over there. She's just a lot when it comes to my love life."

Gabe appeared, dressed much the same as usual, in his distressed jeans and a black tank top tucked under a black button down with gold embellishment at the cuffs. He was freshly cleaned, and envy surged. I wished I could shower that fast.

"Do you want to take the motorcycle, or the sports car?" he asked.

"I've never been on a motorcycle and I would one-hundred-percent choose that if I didn't have cookies to safely transport."

Gabe gave me a smirk. "No worries. I'll get you out on the bike another time."

He waved me towards the garage, and I clutched the cookies to my chest, following after him. Gabe opened the door to a sleek black two-seater and waited for me to get situated before climbing into the driver side.

The ride was smooth as hell as I directed him to my parents house. Every mile we covered tweaked my anxiety a little higher. The last person I'd brought home was Alphonse, and I hadn't planned on bringing over any of the pack this soon.

"Anything I should know about before we go in?" Gabe asked as we parked.

"Would I be the worst person ever if I asked you to keep the pack on the down low just for today?"

"For today, I can, but not if I see them again. I'm proud of my pack, though I also don't want your mother to take to the fainting couch over you gathering yourself multiple lovers this week."

My cheeks burned. I was pretty sure that was going to be a common occurrence for the rest of the night. Gabe held my hand as we walked up to the house, the container of cookies tucked under his other arm.

I knocked on the door, opening it without waiting for anyone to answer. "We're here!" I called.

Mom was there first, followed very closely by my sister-in-law, Allie.

"Nicola, introduce us to your special friend," Mom insisted.

Gabe put out his hand to greet her. "Gabriel Hassan, but you can call me Gabe. It's very nice to meet you, Mrs. Marino."

The rest of the family gathered around, and I smoothed my hand down the front of my shirt to anchor myself.

"Nicola didn't mention you the last time she was here. When did you two meet?" Mom asked.

"We met through friends this week," Gabe replied.

Mom turned to me. "Nicola, what friends are these? Do I know them?"

"I actually met them at the library. At my shift after our last dinner."

Sidney laughed.

"What's so funny?" Mom asked.

"You were so determined that she would never find anyone working nights. And then it took her less than a day after you made that declaration. You're like a reverse fortune teller."

Mom slapped him playfully on the chest. "Mocking your own mother."

"Come in, come in," Dad insisted. "Gabe, what can I get you to drink? We got everything for Italian sodas tonight. Raspberry, peach, or lime?"

"I'll have whatever you're having, sir."

Mom frantically pawed my shoulder and hiss-whispered at me, "Nicola, you found such a polite one."

"Nicky, which flavor would you like?" Dad asked me.

"Peach for me, please," I said.

We left the entryway and got settled at the dinner table. The oven timer dinged, and Dad disappeared into the kitchen. I introduced Gabe to the rest of my family, and pointedly ignored the absolutely delighted expression on Allie's face.

Dad returned carrying a bubbling tray of chicken parmigiana. Luca appeared on Dad's heels with a giant bowl of salad and another of spaghetti noodles.

"Nicola, what did you bring for us?" Mom asked, gesturing to the case in my hands.

"Rosemary lemon shortbread. We made it today."

Mom put her hand to her chest like she couldn't quite handle the romance of it. "Gabe, you bake, too?"

"I don't usually. Nicky was over for lunch, and one of the people I live with owns a bakery."

"Oh, how lovely."

I put the cookies in the kitchen, and we all sat down to dinner once Dad had made all the Italian sodas. I sipped mine happily while Mom focused herself on Gabe. It was mostly basic questions: they asked about his family, and I learned that he was an only child but close with his cousins. I probably should have known how old he was before this—thirty-four—but at least I knew now. I also learned that he had initially gone into trades with a community college to help support his parents through a health crisis.

That fact had won him some major points with my parents.

"What do you do for work now, Gabe? Dad asked.

"I work security downtown," he said.

Dad perked up. "Really? One of my buddies runs a security firm. Which company do you work for?"

"Oh, um, it's a pretty small place."

Dad tapped his fingers on the table impatiently.

"I'm actually a bouncer at a club. Slick City."

"Oh my god!" Allie squealed. "We used to go to Slick City in college! That place is na—I mean, classy. Super, super classy. Very *elegant* atmosphere," Allie finished off, shooting me a grin. "We always had a great time."

My parents looked at her, wildly confused.

"It's a club specifically for betas and omegas. Super safe. The staff makes sure nothing bad happens while everyone is drunk as a skunk."

I chewed my lip, waiting for Mom to have some sort of negative reaction to the revelation, but, on the contrary, she looked at Gabe as if he were some sort of white knight.

"Oh, Nicola, you found yourself a *protector*."

"Exactly," Allie added. "Defender of the drunk and stupid."

Gabe chuckled. "That's definitely one way to put it."

Dad gave a decisive nod and then gestured to the food. "Everyone dish up. The food is getting cold."

Luca was in charge of serving, filling our plates for us.

I nudged him as he sat back with his own plate. "What's new with you?"

"Nothing." His eyes darted to mom briefly and whipped back to me before focusing onto his food. Weird. He was a little twitchier than usual, but I wasn't going to call him out on it in front of Mom. He'd tell me about whatever was making him so nervous when he was ready.

"This food is incredible, Mr. Marino," said Gabe after his first bite of the chicken parmigiana. "And not just because I'm trying to get you to like me."

Dad's cheeks turned pink. "Thank you. That's appreciated."

We were spared some conversation while we all stuffed our faces, but I could see the questions working behind Mom's eyes as we ate.

Allie, bless her, welcomed Gabe into the situation as if they had been best friends for years. Sidney looked at his wife a few times with his own questions tucked behind that dark gaze. Allie knew the details, but I hadn't quite worked myself up to telling him yet. I did still want to talk to him since I hadn't made it to the clinic, though I didn't really want to leave Gabe to the mercy of my family. At least Allie would probably be able to keep them on track.

Tension slowly climbed up my back, burrowing at the base of my skull. My family was being astonishingly good about me springing a surprise man on them, but I just kept waiting for the other shoe to drop.

"Do you like sports, Gabe?" Dad asked as we hit the point in the meal where there were only a couple bites remaining.

Gabe glanced at me briefly, and I tried to give the subtlest nod possible.

"Yeah, for the most part. I don't play much anymore, but I watch the World Cup with my dad every year."

That single fact softened my dad even more. Gabe had an

annual tradition with his father, which told my dad that the family was important to Gabe, beyond basic duty. Family was the biggest thing to my dad, and I couldn't have coached Gabe to answer any better.

"Could I interest you in my signed World Cup jersey I got in Brazil?"

"Absolutely, I'd love to see it."

Gabe was hitting all the bull's-eyes with my family tonight. We polished off our food, and Mom declared a brief reprieve before we started dessert. Gabe went with my dad and Luca into the den, and I snatched Sidney by the wrist, dragging him into the guest bedroom.

"Can I ask you a weird question?"

His face squished up. "I only hope it's nothing about sex now that you're dating an alpha."

I snorted. "Vaguely related, but not really because of him. Okay, a little bit because of him but... So I've already talked to Allie about this, and she said I should talk to you. I didn't wanna be weird."

"Well, spit it out so I don't have to imagine anything unsavory."

"Gabe isn't the only one that I'm seeing."

"Elaborate." Sidney lately crossed his arms over his chest.

"He's part of a pack. I've been seeing a few of the members."

"You little horn dog." Sidney laughed. "I knew you had it in you. So what's the question?"

"I was wondering if you would ask the doctor at your clinic if there's anything weird about, how do I say this... Reacting stronger than anticipated?"

"Nick, you have to give me a little more info to go on."

"It's just, like, I've only ever dated betas, and they were fine, but this pack, even the beta in it, it's like *extra* fine. You know? I feel like my brain fritzes out with the whole lot of them."

Sidney ran a hand through his hair. "What are the dynamics in this pack?"

"Three alphas, one beta, and one omega. And then me, tiptoeing around the edge."

"Okay. I'm not sure off the top of my head, but Dr. J might know more, and if she doesn't, we'll dig into it. I'd still recommend you coming in for an appointment."

"But it's an omega clinic."

"Yeah, and you're my sister. She'll see you if I ask."

I hugged him hard until he let out a little squeak of air. "Thank you."

"No worries. Now let's go back out and make sure Mom hasn't started planning your wedding."

Chapter Twenty-Four
Gabe

Nicky's whole family was a bunch of chatterboxes. In a good way. Her younger brother Luca had followed her father and I into the den, and I'd spent the next twenty minutes listening to the two of them regale me about their trip to Brazil back in 2014 to see the World Cup together. It was almost enough to make me suggest Brazil for a future pack trip except for the fact that Billie wilted in the heat like an unwatered flower and Jasper practically burst into flames in direct sunlight.

Luca was a sweet kid, if I could call a twenty-six-year-old man a kid, and it was obvious to anyone who looked for half a second that Nicky's dad was a loving family man. Mine was too, but we had very little in common. Football had never been particularly interesting to me. My dad loved it, so I had learned, which was proving to be an asset now. I couldn't quite tell if Luca actually enjoyed it or if it was the positive interaction with his father that he craved.

Once their stories had finished and we returned to the main room, I was back under the scrutiny of Nicky's mother. She seemed to like me so far, but I'd seen that sharp, bright gaze on mothers before, the proverbial wedding bells dancing in her eyes. That was to be expected when the middle child got married first. I slid straight over to Nicky and let my arm rest comfortably around her waist.

"When was the last time you brought someone home?" I whispered.

"About five years."

Well that explained it.

I was curious what Nicky's mother would think about her joining a pack, and then cut that thought off. Nicky *hadn't* joined our pack, no matter how easily she slipped into it.

Things had to happen in their own time.

Gradually.

Organically.

The crushing force of expectation couldn't have a place in that decision.

Nicky's oldest brother studied me. He was the only alpha in their family, and I tried to relax under his steady assessment. To be honest, I was surprised he hadn't immediately pulled me aside. Family was like a pack until you struck out on your own, and, while Nicky might not take too kindly to the concept, his instincts were likely nudging him to protect her from a new alpha.

When he did wave me over, I went willingly.

"Take a walk with me?" he asked.

I nodded. Even if I hadn't been inclined, I couldn't have said no without arousing suspicion.

The night wind was a little bit chilly, but I could manage for a short walk.

"So..." he began.

"Are you worried about your sister?" I asked without any preamble as we set off down the street.

Sidney snorted. "Only in some ways. She can take care of herself, but I would be remiss in my brotherly duties if I didn't talk to you anyway."

"I can respect that."

"So, what's the deal with your pack?"

My surprise was only momentary. Mostly I was just glad that Nicky clearly trusted her brother enough to tell him about the situation.

"We're solid. Two alphas besides me, a beta, and an omega. All bonded. Everyone has consistent jobs, except our beta, but they were born into money, so they have a lot of wiggle room to play with passions. We established the pack six years ago, and, so far as I've been able to tell, everyone is pretty fond of Nicky. Hana, one of our alphas, takes a while to warm up, but she's open to the idea."

"So, you're all after her joining you?"

I shrugged. "I'd be happy to have her, but the decision is entirely up to Nicky. I think she's just in the exploratory phase right now."

"She's... I was going to say she's always been patient, but I think it was that she was always a little bit bored. She needed more than she let herself have. Granted, I don't know the rest of your pack, or you, really, but I'll trust her judgement with it. Just don't fuck her up, okay? She's tough, but she's a lot more fragile than she likes to let people see."

"I'll keep that in mind. I have no intention of hurting her."

"I know. I can tell by the way that you look at her. But just know that she's stubborn as a fucking mule, and sometimes that makes her a little stupid. Said with love," Sidney laughed. "She's been caught by that sunk-cost-fallacy in the past. And if she starts missing family dinners, I'm gonna get suspicious."

"I gather there's a story behind that statement?" I asked.

"Just an asshole she used to date. The longer they were together, the less often she came around. And when we did see her, she was always stressed out."

"Is that Alphonse?"

Sidney nodded. "She told you about him?"

"Tony and Billie picked her up from his place. He spooked her, and she's been staying with us."

Sidney stopped dead. "*What?*"

Well, fuck. Apparently Nicky hadn't told him *everything*.

"Why was she at his place? Fuck. I hope she's not thinking about getting back together with him." He ran a hand through his hair and started us walking again.

"She's not. At least, from what I've heard through the pack grapevine. He showed up at her library, and, from the sounds of it, he bullied her into a date. If he makes himself a nuisance, we'll see about having someone from the pack making sure she gets home all right, but we're hoping he got the message to leave her alone."

"I wish she'd told me." Sidney's brow furrowed. He let out a deep sigh as we rounded the corner. "In any case, I'm glad to have someone else in the 'Nicky's well-being' corner. I love her a lot. It was easier when we were kids and I could just punch anyone who was stupid towards her."

"Working security at a club has taught me that some people never outgrow that."

He laughed. "God, I don't doubt that for a second."

We passed the rest of the short walk chatting about inconsequential things. I liked having this opportunity to get a deeper insight into the beta that had swept over us like a storm. Nicky's family loved her, and that quelled a lot of lingering questions about who she was and what the future might mean.

Back at the house, we settled in for dessert with a fresh round of Italian sodas and a particularly vicious game of Monopoly. Once Nicky had snared the final railroad, it was the beginning of the end for the rest of her family. I couldn't hide the amused curl of my mouth as I watched her absolutely trounce them, her in-game fortune ballooning with every round.

She was momentarily distracted by a text that she hastily replied to before rolling the dice. A moment later there was a knock at the door, and her spine snapped ramrod straight.

205

"I'll get it," said Luca. He trotted over to the front door and swung it open, revealing my beautiful omega standing there, looking apologetic, with a box from the bakery.

"I'm so sorry I'm late. I got everything managed as quickly as I could and got the dough in the refrigerator to deal with later."

Nicky's parents stared at Jasper, confusion clear on their faces. Sidney glanced back-and-forth between me and the door, and his wife looked absolutely delighted by the turn of events.

Nicky shot up from her seat and dashed to the door. It was then that Jasper saw me. The color drained from his cheeks. I rose to follow Nicky and set a comforting hand on Jasper's shoulder.

"Nicola, who is this?" her mother asked.

"Um..."

Sidney joined us in the entryway and thrust out his hand to greet Jasper. He swung his other arm over Luca's shoulders. "Nice to meet you. We're Nicky's brothers, Sidney and Luca."

Jasper swallowed hard and accepted the handshake. "Jasper."

"Nicola," her father said. "Explain."

Her cheeks were flame red. "So, about that..."

I briefly dipped towards her ear and whispered, "Do you want me to cover?"

She stiffened a bit more, and whispered back, "No, it's okay."

Nicky took a deep breath and slipped her hand into Jasper's.

"I can go," offered Jasper.

"No." Nicky squared her shoulders and took a deep breath as she turned to her parents. Nerves rolled off her in waves. "Mom, the person you heard on the phone was Jasper. He had to dip out for a work emergency, so Gabe came with me instead."

Her mother scrutinized the three of us. "I don't understand. Which one of these men are you dating?"

"Both?"

I bit down my laugh. Obviously, I had some work to do to remove the question from that statement.

By this time both of her parents were looming in the entryway with us. Her father turned to me. "You're okay with this?"

"More like she's okay with me and him," I explained. "Jasper and I were already together when we met Nicky. He actually met her before me. I was just lucky she's an open-minded sweetheart."

Nicky flushed an even darker red.

"Nice to meet you, Jasper!" Allie said, bursting onto the scene. "What's in the box?"

Her interruption gave Jasper a moment of recovery. "Oh, I brought scones. Apology ones since I missed most of the evening."

"Fuck yeah. Any chocolate ones in there for me?"

My omega extracted his hand from Nicky's grip and lifted the box lid. "Double chocolate, actually. I grabbed a few off the rush order I completed, not that I was taking them from a client. I made extra. Just to be clear."

"You're the baker, then?" Luca asked. "Your cookies were *amazing*! There's no leftovers. I have to get your recipe."

Jasper smiled softly. "Yeah, absolutely. It's my grandmother's recipe."

"Luca," Allie said, nudging him. "Go grab another chair. I'm ready for dessert after my dessert."

Nicky's parents still looked a little unsure, but I figured they were both too polite to prevent Jasper from coming inside. A good thing, too, because I was certainly not going to tolerate them being rude to my omega, and I didn't want things to be ruined with Nicky because of her parents. We would definitely have to ease them into the whole pack idea.

"Come on, babe," I said to Jasper, kissing his cheek. "You can't woo anyone with your wonderful baking while standing in the doorway."

I could see the gears turning in Nicky's father's head. He must've decided on a favorable outcome because his next question was, "Peach, raspberry, or lime for your Italian soda, Jasper?"

Nicky let out a relieved breath, her shoulders dropping a fraction. Tension slid off me at Mr. Marino's quiet acceptance.

"Raspberry sounds amazing," said Jasper. "Thank you."

Chapter Twenty-Five
Nicky

"**C**ome here."

I slipped into Gabe's arms in my parent's driveway, angled out of the line of sight of the bay window.

"You too, Jasper."

Jasper pressed up against my back, sandwiching me between the two of them.

"Deep breath, both of you," Gabe ordered.

I followed the instructions, and a rush of chocolate and tea flooded my system, instantly dispelling my lingering stress.

"Do you think it went okay?" I asked.

"They seemed nice," said Jasper.

"I think it went fine." Gabe tipped my face up to his. "Your brother and sister-in-law are on board; the rest of your family just needs a little time to adjust."

I sighed and stood up on my toes, brushing my mouth against

his. I melted eagerly at the way his fingers curled around the back of my neck and let my eyes slip closed. After a few moments of indulgence, I turned between them to face Jasper.

"Thank you for coming tonight, I mean *both* of you, but *you* took time out of work to be here for me." I cupped his cheek, fingers tracing over his beard. I rose up on my toes again and kissed him slowly until the sweet omega smelled like the bakery he worked at. I settled back with a relaxed hum, savoring the safety of having two of them at my front and back.

Gabe nipped the shell of my ear. "You're going to be late for work if we don't leave soon."

"Okay, okay, I'm going." I gave Jasper one more quick kiss and slipped into the passenger side of Gabe's two-seater.

The trip was smooth and seemed faster than usual, but we arrived at the same time as I normally would have. Part of me felt guilty that we had dropped Spud off at my place on the way to dinner. He'd been so cute with Roscoe lately, and now my baby boy was all alone in an empty apartment. I'd have to see about bringing him over to the pack house again so he could have little play dates.

Gabe parked next to my car that had been temporarily abandoned in the lot. "Start it up for me and park a little closer to the building. I want to make sure it's running fine. But first," he hooked his hand behind my head and pulled me in for a sweeping kiss that instantly turned my legs to jelly and had my clit throbbing.

I leaned into him. My hands curled into his shirt, and it was only after he devoured my needy whine that he sat back.

"Hurry up," he chided teasingly. "You can have one more before you go in, but go park the car in the light for me first."

I huffed and climbed out, starting my car and pulling it around to park under one of the lot lights. It ran just fine, though I hadn't expected it otherwise.

Gabe pulled to a stop next to my car, and I hopped out, leaning through his open window to collect my additional reward. It was *way* too easy to get lost in the feel of him. In the way he made *me* feel. I hummed happily and stepped aside, adjusting my purse on my shoulder.

"Have a good shift, Nicky."

It was on the tip of my tongue to say that he could hang out in the library if he wanted to, but I didn't want to be needy. So I simply walked up to the main doors, turning back to see him wave through the windshield, waiting until I was safely indoors before driving away.

I trudged up the stairs and waved to Miranda, who was sitting at the front desk.

"Hey there, lucky girl." She grinned.

I raised an eyebrow. "I'm going to need a little more context."

Miranda gestured to the bouquet of stargazer lilies on the front desk. "The weekend girls said that these came for you on Friday night."

I stared at the ostentatious bundle of pink and white blooms. Who had sent me flowers at work? I'd been with the pack the whole weekend, and, even if I hadn't, none of them were likely to have chosen flowers that were fatal to cats.

Miranda plucked a card from the center and passed it to me.

My blood turned to ice water as I read it.

Sorry about this morning.

Give me another chance to prove that we're meant to be.

Call me.

– Al

"Are you okay?" Miranda asked. "You look a little pale."

"Super fine," I squeaked out. "You don't happen to want a bouquet of lilies, do you?"

Miranda looked at me curiously. "I can take them if you don't want them. God knows the guy I'm seeing never buys me anything like this."

I crumpled the card and stuffed it into my pocket. "All yours."

"Do I want to know?"

"Let's just leave it a mystery for now. Hopefully it's the last bouquet."

Miranda gathered up the flowers and gave me a quick rundown of her evening. Most of the tables were occupied by university students studying for midterms.

I felt better immediately as I watched the blooms leave with Miranda. I fished the card back out of my pocket. Alphonse's phone number was on the card below his sign off.

I didn't want to contact him. Then he would have my number, and he didn't have a good history with that. We also definitely *weren't* meant to be. Maybe if this was a year ago I might've entertained the idea, when loneliness and depression had been hitting soul-crushing levels, but dating the pack was like a revelation, and I knew with absolute certainty that someone like Alphonse would never make me happy. I was honestly still a little baffled that he thought that *I* could make *him* happy. But then I had never properly understood him. I'd given him three years, and the thought of going back made me queasy.

I pushed it all aside and got down to work.

A little after midnight, Billie and Tony arrived at the library.

I hated that we had cameras watching us because they both looked too beautiful and I could've done with a hug.

Tony leaned on the front desk and gave me an easy smile. "Hey there, baby girl. How was your night with your folks?"

"Partly chaos," I answered. "Mostly good, though, I think. I ended up with both Gabe *and* Jasper after a mixup. I'm pretty sure my parents' brains are going to melt once they find out about the rest of you."

"Well, we wouldn't want that." Tony laughed and Billie squished up next to him.

"I think Roscoe misses your little prince," said Billie. "Poor baby sang us the song of his people all over the house trying to find him."

I pressed a hand to my chest. "Way to double the guilt. I was

211

already feeling bad that Spud's home alone. I didn't mean to separate the soulmates."

"Roscoe is getting babied by Hana," said Tony. "He'll survive."

"There's a lot of people here tonight," commented Billie.

"Yeah, we're coming into exam season."

"I was hoping I could get your help with something tonight, Nicky," Tony said. "I need some of the town's previous bylaws and propositions. Would you know how to access that?"

"Yeah, of course. I can dig up some stuff from the archives. How far back are you looking?"

"About twenty years."

I blinked. "And you need the bylaws specifically from twenty years ago or everything from twenty years ago to now?"

"Then to now, if you can manage it."

I quirked my head. That was *a lot* of paperwork to sort through. "Reading for business or pleasure?"

"Unfortunately neither. Once I have a little more information, I can fill you in on things." He laid that easy smile on me again. "Not being allowed to touch you just makes me want to do it more."

Heat burst in my cheeks.

"I'd be a rule breaker," said Billie, "but I don't wanna get you in trouble. So just know that I'm undressing you with my eyes."

I couldn't help but giggle as the beta's gaze swept my body and settled very pointedly on my chest with a waggle of their eyebrows.

"You two are terrible. Go get your spots and I'll see about getting access to the archives for you, Tony."

I focused on my new task. The library staff had access to all of the documents that have been digitized through the city's history. I just had to find what he was specifically looking for. None of it was particularly well organized, so it might be a multi-night process if I didn't want to get too behind on my other work. The hours passed slowly, and around five Tony and Billie appeared back at the front desk to say goodbye.

"Hana's going to kick our butts at boot camp," Billie said. "Don't miss us too much."

I slipped away from my post and away from the library cameras to kiss each of them goodbye, unable, and unwilling to go the entire night without touching them. They sent me back to work with a pleasant hum of desire in my blood.

I checked briefly on the university students pulling all-nighters first, then got going on the rest of my work: spending the next two hours on programs set up for the morning and re-shelving the stacks of books the university students left behind as they vacated the premises around six-thirty.

I welcomed the arrival of the day staff and gave them a brief rundown of the setup I prepared before I picked up my purse and headed down the stairs to go home. I was *so* looking forward to my bed and having a good cuddle with Spud.

The parking lot was pretty empty, but there were a few staff vehicles for those coming on to start their day. I froze on the side-walk in front of the main doors. A black sedan was parked way too close to my car with only inches to spare, blocking my way into the vehicle. My heart leapt when the driver side door of the sedan opened, and Alphonse stepped out.

I was rooted to the spot, torn between telling him to move so I could leave and retreating into the building.

"Is this where we're at, Nicky? You're back to ignoring me? I send you flowers and I get two days of silence in return."

"I didn't work this weekend," I defended.

He narrowed his eyes. "Then where are the flowers now? They were *expensive*."

I swallowed hard and pressed my lips together, unwilling to tell him that I had given them away.

"Little liar." He sighed. "Since when do you dislike flowers?" Alphonse pinched the bridge of his nose.

I fought the urge to shrink and was only mildly successful, wrapping my arms over my stomach. "I should get home. Can you please move your car?"

"I can give you a ride. You must be tired after your shift."

213

I squeezed my lips shut again and took a steadying breath, my fingers digging into my ribs to ground myself. "Please move your car."

"You're doing that thing again," he said, with another sigh, as he crossed the distance between us.

"What thing?"

"When you get all jittery and act like you're afraid. I don't understand you, Nicky. When have I *ever* hurt you? I send you flowers, I check in on you, I offer to drive you home from work, and none of it is appreciated."

Anxiety clawed its way into my throat and cut off any words I might've thought to say. I had no idea how to respond. Why couldn't I have been selfish and asked Billie and Tony to stay so they would've been here?

Alphonse reached toward me, and it broke through my freeze response, sending me stumbling backwards so his fingertips met only air.

"I can't deal with you being like this right now." Alphonse huffed. "Next time we talk I hope you'll be more respectful."

He climbed back into his car and slammed the door shut, tearing out of the parking lot so fast I was surprised his tires didn't burst.

My hands shook as I fished out my keys and hit the unlock button. I slipped into the driver seat and slammed my fingers down onto the lock button on the door.

Deep breaths.

I was fine. Just...overreacting.

Hot tears slipped over my cheeks, and I pushed down the swell of nausea, gripping the steering wheel like it was a lifeline. I waited in the parking lot for almost an hour, building up the courage to drive home, half worried that he was waiting to find out where I had moved to. The last thing I wanted was him hanging out around my apartment.

I drove slowly, gaze constantly darting to the rearview mirror as if Alphonse was some sort of spy that might be tailing me.

Spud howled at me when I finally got inside. I deadbolted the door and scooped him into a cuddle to settle myself, burying my face against his fur until the sharpest edge of my nerves was worn smooth. I got Spud his dinner, stripped down, and showered, tying my wet hair into a braid before I took Spud to bed, pushing the rest of the world away.

My dreams twisted between the loving embrace of the pack and Alphonse's cold grip.

I woke up sweating, my apartment feeling so lonely after spending the weekend with warm bodies whenever I needed a cuddle. Spud made a difference, but he wasn't capable of talking me down.

I grabbed my phone before I could talk myself out of it, hitting the call button on Tony's contact.

Chapter Twenty-Six
Tony

"Hey, baby girl." I answered Nicky's call on the first ring. "How was work? You're up early."

"Yeah, weird dreams," she croaked.

My brow furrowed. She sounded off. "Nicky, are you all right?"

"Yeah, I just..."

She fell silent, and tension snapped my shoulders tight.

"Nicky, talk to me."

"I shouldn't have called. I'm sorry. You're probably busy. Did I wake you?"

I set aside my work, my focus entirely on the woman at the other end of the line. "If you need to talk, I'm here. I don't care what time it is or what I'm doing. What do you need?"

Her sounds were muffled, but I caught the quiet hitch of breath.

"Do you want me to come over?" I asked.

"I don't want to *bother* you."

"Baby girl, you're not a bother. Give me a few minutes to get organized, and I'll be on my way."

I heard her soft whine as if it was filtered through a pillow. My instincts roared to the surface with an insistent knowing that she was *mine* and that she needed me. "Nicky, I'm going to give you a task, okay? Can you get up and make yourself a cup of tea? Get Spud a treat too. And then sit yourself on the couch until I get there."

"Okay," she said quietly.

I gathered up my things and stayed on the phone with her as I went downstairs, got into our minivan, and made the trip to her.

"I'm here," I said as I arrived. "Remind me of your apartment number so I can get buzzed in."

Nicky gave me the info and buzzed me in. She'd been quiet for the rest of the call, but I had heard her following the instructions as well as her little snuffling breaths. She answered on the first knock at her door and went straight into my arms. I tucked my phone back into my pocket and pulled her close, breathing in her soft, spicy scent. I purred for her and stroked her hair as I ushered her inside the apartment.

I gave her a minute to adjust before I took her face in both hands and lifted it to look at me. "Do you want to tell me what's wrong, or do you just want company?"

"Company please." Her voice was the meekest I had ever heard it, and as much as I wanted to know what had caused whatever this issue was, I wasn't going to push her right now.

"Okay. Let's lock up your apartment. Did you finish your tea?"

Nicky flipped the deadbolt and shook her head. "I'm halfway through it."

I nodded. "Let's sit so you can finish it."

She let me maneuver her back into the living room, where she nestled into my side beneath my arm and sipped her tea. I kept purring and pushed my scent towards her. Little by little she relaxed, the tension melting from her shoulders as she leaned more heavily against me. When she finally finished her tea and set the cup aside, she wrapped her arms around my torso and buried her face against my neck.

"Thank you for coming. I shouldn't have asked you to."

"I offered," I reminded her. "I'm happy to be here for you."

She nodded slowly, and when the tension snuck into her body again, I put my palm on the back of her neck, just the way she liked, and she released a contented sigh that had her melting once more.

We sat like that, falling asleep together sprawled on the couch, until Spud howled us awake for another meal. I laid Nicky out with a blanket and fed her cat, scratching his ears as I returned to her. She was still drowsy so I let her rest with her head in my lap.

I messaged the rest of the pack to let them know where I was. Those that were awake to respond did so with concern, asking after her well-being. I had no answer for them on that account, so I could only tell them that she was safe and that I was with her.

Hopefully, when she woke fully, she would be more ready to talk.

Her fingers curling into my shirt brought me back into focus.

"Alphonse sent me flowers," she said at last.

I held still and silent, waiting for her to continue.

"Lilies," she added. "Even if I'd wanted them, I couldn't bring them home. They're so dangerous for cats. He *knows* I have Spud. Me adopting him was part of the last big fight Alphonse and I had."

I stroked her hair and got my purr rumbling for her.

"He was waiting for me when I finished work."

I tensed instantly. "*What?*"

"In the lot, next to my car." She continued on, telling me about the altercation, her body trembling in my grasp as she spoke. "I don't...I can't go back to that. I—" her voice broke off as she started crying.

"Hey, it's okay. You're safe here." I cradled her, settling her slowly, waiting as she exhausted her tears, until she was hiccuping and sniffling in my arms.

"I didn't realize how miserable I used to be," she said quietly. "Not that long ago I might've gone back, might've let him talk me into it because...maybe I had remembered it all wrong. Maybe it wasn't that bad. But this whole last week is like a spotlight. I used to be so scared, and I didn't realize until I didn't feel that way anymore. I'm probably not making any sense."

"You're making perfect sense, baby girl." I hugged her gently. "I'm so sorry that you went through what you did with him, and I'm glad that we could help you see it, even if that realization sucks."

"Do you know what my life was like before I met you?"

"I can only guess, but I'd like you to tell me."

Nicky heaved a sigh, her fingers curling more tightly in my shirt. "I worked, I came home, and I spent my evenings with Spud. The only thing different in my week was days off, where the whole thing was spent with Spud, or I visited my family. The wedding planning for my brother helped with the monotony, and Allie's friends brought me into their group, but that took some time. I lost pretty much every friend I had in the years I was with Alphonse, and I was so depressed when I finally left that I didn't have it in me to try to make new ones. By the time I felt like I had woken up from everything, it had been so long that I couldn't work up the courage to reach out to the people I had used to love. And the pack just... You all make me feel like I'm alive again instead of just existing, and that honestly scares the shit out of me."

I held her tighter. I bet saying those words out loud to me was terrifying, too.

"Nicky, I don't know what the future holds, and, frankly, I don't care that it's only been a week. You've brought your own brand of light to us and I'm glad that you were brave enough to take a chance."

"Billie makes it pretty difficult to refuse." She laughed softly and turned her face into my chest.

"That they do." I traced patterns over her back to center us both in the moment. "What do you want to do about Alphonse?"

"I don't know. Do I *have* to do something?"

"That part is up to you, but I'm not a huge fan of his behavior thus far. In case you hadn't noticed, I've gotten a little bit protective of you."

Nicky puffed out a breath and somehow managed to snuggle even closer. "I may have noticed. I just feel like such a mess and I hate dumping that on anyone."

"Everyone needs a little extra support sometimes. I'm sure, if you stick around, the opportunity for you to support one of the pack will pop up."

"I hope so. Not that I want anyone to be in distress, but I hope that I can be half as wonderful to the pack as you've all been to me." She toyed with the tip of a loc that hung over my shoulder. "Tell me a story. I need a distraction, and I want to get to know you better."

I sifted through a few of the options in my head. "My whole family has always had the travel bug. I was carted all over the world by my parents and all over the country with my aunt's pack on the back of a motorcycle. It was amazing in a lot of ways, but it also really made me crave roots."

"Really?!" Nicky perked up. "Where was your favorite?"

"That's a bit like asking me to choose a favorite star in the sky." I laughed, trailing my fingertips down her arm. "Cambodia was incredible, so was Mongolia, Chile, Botswana, and Iceland. Honestly, there's something awe-inspiring everywhere that we went." I told her about climbing Kilimanjaro, swimming at the Great Barrier Reef, seeing the countless castles of Europe and the temples throughout Asia. She absorbed every word with rapt attention.

"How did you manage school with all of that travel?"

"My dad was a teacher and Mom was a doctor before they both retired. He handled my education on the road, and we just returned to the states for me to take the standardized tests. While we were globetrotting, Mom would always dip in at clinics wherever she was needed, and we'd stay in spots for a while so it was sort of like having a hundred different homes."

"Did you see much of North America during all of that?" Nicky asked.

"Oh, definitely. My parents went on a lot of trips without me to places that weren't quite as safe when Mom was part of Doctors Without Borders. On those occasions, I hung out with Auntie Angelica's pack. They rode coast to coast, spending winters in the south and summers in the north. One of her pack-mates is also a teacher, so that made things easy for them to keep up with my education, too."

"How did you end up here?"

"Ah, that's Billie's fault, actually."

Nicky giggled. "Somehow I'm not surprised."

"This was a couple of years before Jasper had his own bakery and was working the day shift at another local place. I was in town with Auntie's pack and stopped in to grab some breakfast for everyone. That place had a sit-down area, and Billie was curled up there with a book waiting for Jasper's shift to be over. I flirted with Jasper, and they took notice. It didn't take a lot to convince me to go out with them. I dropped off the food I'd bought with Auntie's pack and told them to go ahead without me, that I'd meet up with them somewhere else. I'd only planned to stick around for a few days. Spoiler alert, those few days turned into six years."

Nicky rose up and kissed me in her slow, sweet way that felt like a drug coursing through my body. "I'm glad you stayed," she whispered against my lips and dove in again.

She sat on my lap, and we indulged ourselves in too many kisses to count until her phone buzzed, and she fetched it off the coffee table to read the message. "Would I be the worst if I dipped out in the next half hour?"

"Nope." I sat up, searching her face for clues. "Is it good or bad news?"

"Just an appointment I've been waiting on. There's a cancella-tion, and they can take me in an hour."

"Speaking of appointments, and you don't have to answer, but did you ever attend therapy to process everything with Alphonse?"

"I should have, but no."

"If you're open to it, I might consider looking into it. You'd probably feel a lot better once you've worked through things."

Nicky nodded, not saying anything further. We passed the next stretch of time with more stories of my childhood travels while she got ready for her appointment. I felt lighter when we finally parted ways: Nicky to her appointment and me back to the pack house.

She'd relaxed considerably over the course of my visit, and that calmed my instincts to soothe her. I had succeeded there, even if I couldn't solve the root issue, but, if Alphonse was going to make himself a problem, then that fucker was just begging for me to introduce my fist to his teeth.

Chapter Twenty-Seven
Nicky

"Thank you for seeing me."

"Of course." Dr. James smiled at me. "I'm glad we could fit you in. Why don't you walk me through what brought you here today?"

I did so, explaining my huge jump in libido and what already felt like a burgeoning codependency. Dr. James listened quietly, taking notes on her laptop.

"It just feels like I'm out of control. Isn't it weird to have such a strong instant connection with that many people?"

The doctor smiled indulgently. "Not at all, especially in a pack situation. I've done plenty of research on the subject so I can give my patients comprehensive answers. When you think about it, all of the people involved in this pack are compatible with each other, so it stands to reason that if one of them discovers they're compatible with you, then that would probably follow through with the rest of the people involved, or at least most of them."

Each of her words untangled knots of worry in my gut. It didn't alleviate all of my concerns, but she did have a point, and that helped.

"Do you mind if we do a quick hormone test?"

I offered up my finger to be pricked for the clinic's rapid test, jolting as the needle punctured my skin. I sat with bated breath as the doctor stuck the test strip into the droplet of blood that beaded on my fingertip. The end of the strip turned a bright greenish-yellow and Dr. James showed me where that fell on the guide.

"I have no baseline for you," she said, "but this result is very high for a beta. It's not quite in the omega range, though it is close. I'd be curious what your levels were prior to getting involved with the pack, since that can have an influence."

"What does it mean to have high levels for a beta?" I asked. None of the health or biology classes I'd ever taken really discussed the minute details of these things.

"Ah, that's something else that I wanted to discuss with you since your brother spoke with me."

The doctor didn't look concerned, so I smushed down the rising panic. "Oh?"

"I've been working on a new study with other medical professionals between the omega clinics and the general beta healthcare system. Through that, we've come up with a model we're calling the Dynamic Spectrum Theory. Essentially, we believe the dynamics are on a spectrum, with alphas at one end, omegas at the other, and betas filling in the majority in the middle. We're proposing that portions of the beta population are what we've dubbed *unexpressed* alphas and omegas."

Was she telling me this because I was one? "What does that mean?"

"They're basically people who fall at the far end of the spectrum, but for whatever reason never presented as alpha or omega. Their hormones still technically fall within the beta range, but they lean heavily to one side. Now, given the results we have here, I would put you in the range of an unexpressed omega.

"That's not to say that someday you'll spontaneously present," Dr. James continued. "It hasn't happened in any of our research, anyway, but you would be more likely to have stronger reactions than other betas towards alphas and omegas. Obviously, this isn't definitive, but it is a possibility given how you've described past relationships with betas and the immediate change when you got involved with a pack. And I want to be clear that none of this belittles any type of relationship that you form with people. Sexual compatibility has a lot of factors, and hormones are simply one of those factors. From your anecdotal evidence, I would venture a guess that the pack making you feel safe and desired would have just as much, if not *more* impact than your hormonal predispositions."

The surge of information left me momentarily stunned, and I simply sat with it, giving my brain some time to process.

"How would I know for sure if I'm one of the unexpressed?" I eventually asked.

"Given that the research is still in its infancy, short of volunteering to participate in the study, I would have no way to confirm for you. At least not right now. The important thing, Nicky, is that there's *nothing* wrong with you. You would not *believe* the amount of omegas that come through my clinic and betas, through the clinics of my beta colleagues, who feel like their world is completely upturned when they finally get involved with a partner who understands them."

I fidgeted in my seat. "I guess that's a relief. What about safety?"

"Do you have concerns about your safety with the pack?" Dr. James' brow furrowed.

"No. I just haven't had very good judgement in the past, and it's making it a little hard to trust myself right now."

"In that case, I would suggest that you open up the lines of communication, both with the pack and someone outside of that group that you trust. That could be a friend, a family member, a medical professional, whatever makes you most comfortable. If you feel like you need additional monitoring, that's something I can arrange for you with one of the beta clinics, and, if you'd like to participate in the study, then you would have regular communication with me as well."

I hummed softly. "I see why my brother likes working with you."

Dr. James laughed. "He's a good boy. The clinic always runs a little smoother when he's on staff. So, what steps do you think you'd like to pursue?"

"The study does sound interesting. What's all involved?"

"I'll have the front desk print you out an information packet that goes over all the details, but essentially we would collect your history—including your romantic and sexual history—and you would go through a round of diagnostics so that we have a baseline of information to work with, then you would come in regularly for additional testing and short interviews so that we can monitor any shifts and fluctuations in your body overtime. There's no rush on any of it. I know you have a lot going on, so just take your time and decide what's right for you."

"I think I'd like to. I should probably mention it to the pack that I'd be participating, since they'd come up in the interviews."

"Yes." Dr. James nodded. "I'm sure they would appreciate the head's up. You're even free to invite others to come interview with me to see if they'd be compatible with the study's parameters. Your other brother is a beta isn't he? And you said there's another beta in the pack?"

"Yeah, Luca's a beta. Billie, too. I can mention the study to them. Could I ask about one other thing while I'm here?"

"Absolutely. What can I help with?"

"I'm, um, I was wanting to look into a therapist. I have some stuff I need to work through and I was kind of putting it off, but now seems like as good a time as any. I don't want to be dragging my mountains of baggage into the future, wherever that leads me."

Dr. James patted my hand. "I know plenty of wonderful

options. I'll have the front desk print off a list of local therapists and their specialties as well as some that are a little further afield, but do phone and video sessions, if you think one of those might suit you better. I'm proud of you, Nicky. It's not easy to admit when we need help, and I hope you achieve all of your goals with therapy when you find the right match."

I warmed at the gentle praise. Getting set up to make the leap was so easy I almost regretted not asking my brother for help sooner, but I couldn't be mad at my past self. Waking up in the light made looking back at the shadows that much more difficult. I hadn't known how dark it once was until someone flipped that switch.

After I left the appointment, I took myself out for a milkshake, sent a message to Luca and Billie to let them know about the study, and passed along Dr. James' contact information if they were interested. I messaged Tony, too, thanking him again for being so wonderful today. I was already craving climbing back into his arms, but at least now I wasn't *quite* as worried there was something wrong with me for feeling that way so soon.

I tried my best to focus on other things for the rest of the day. I had to reestablish some kind of schedule for myself, spend some time with Spud, and re-calibrate myself to spending time alone so I could at least pretend at independence.

I streamed a sitcom for most of the evening while I deep cleaned my apartment.

A knock at the door had my shoulders leaping up to my ears, tension radiating through my body. I checked the peep hole first and relaxed instantly when I saw it was only my neighbor.

"Hey Mrs. Poppadakis," I said as I opened the door. "What's up?"

"I made a bunch of spanakopita for my son and I thought you might like some."

"That sounds amazing! Thank you."

"Excellent. Let me grab you a plate." She disappeared back into her apartment next-door for only a moment, reappearing with a paper plate wrapped in plastic that she thrust into my hands.

Spud came trotting up to the door and yowled at her in greeting.

Mrs. Poppadakis laughed. "Hello there, little man." She scratched his head, and Spud arched up to accept a long stroke down his back.

"Do you want to come in for some tea?" I offered.

"Oh, thank you, dear. But my son will be here to pick me up in about five minutes. He just moved back to town from overseas. This is the first time we're both living on the same coast since before I got remarried, and it's been nice to see him again."

"No worries. I hope you have a good time."

The older beta gave me a one-armed hug and a beaming smile. We parted ways, and I sat down at my little kitchen table, scarfing down half the plate. She probably would've been tickled to see me blitz through her food so quickly. I should figure out a recipe so I could share something with her, too. Maybe Jasper and I could make shortbread again.

I quietly chided myself. I wasn't supposed to be focusing on the pack tonight. I had to be able to go at least a few hours in my own company without my thoughts wandering back to them.

A bit after ten, my phone alarm went off to remind me to start getting ready for work. I slipped into some dark purple dress pants and a black cap-sleeved blouse and pinned my hair into a loose chignon. I gave Spud a generous portion of food and kissed his perfect little head before setting off to the library.

I drove a loop around the building when I got there to make sure Alphonse wasn't parked, though I wasn't sure I would be able to tell his car from any other. The parking lot was pretty full which boded well for witnesses, just in case. I parked where I could see the windows of the library and made a quick exit from my vehicle to the front doors in my comfortable ballet flats.

Miranda waved to me as I approached the front desk. The smile faded from my face when I noticed another bouquet of lilies waiting for me. Miranda's gaze shifted from me, to the bouquet, and back to me again.

"Okay, now you *have to* tell me what's going on. Why are flowers making you look like you've seen a ghost?"

I took a breath to steady myself. "Problematic ex. He recently found out where I work."

"Yikes. Do you want to mention it to Patricia?"

"Yeah, I guess I probably should. I don't want her to think that I'm encouraging gifts being sent to work for me." I had hoped that the flowers were a one and done situation, but apparently that wasn't going to be the case, which meant I'd have to update our facility manager.

Miranda nodded. "Definitely. I'll let the day staff know to take anything they want home if more comes from him. Then you don't even have to see it."

"Perfect. Thank you."

We chatted for a few more minutes. There were about thirty patrons spread around the library. A good portion were more university students still studying, and the rest were an amateur astronomy group that would be taking to the roof once the meteor shower started. I was only a *little* jealous that I couldn't leave my post to go watch it as well.

I started off my night with re-shelving and going through a fresh box of donations. There was no sign of Billie or Tony, and I tried not to think about how strange the library felt without them.

My phone buzzed.

TONY:

Are you safe, baby girl?

Yep

I've got a library full

Are you coming in tonight?

TONY:

After Jasper goes to work

Do you mind if Gabe and Hana come too?

NICKY:

You're all welcome anytime <3

I focused back on my job, some of which included hunting down those bylaws Tony had asked for so I could have some ready when he arrived. The university students were particularly needy today, but I didn't mind. It certainly helped pass the time.

In between helping patrons, I dug out a bunch of our old poster boards on how to properly research for a third grade class we had due in the morning. That was one thing that I missed from working days. The kids were always so cute.

My heart gave an excitable skitter when my alphas and beta swept into the library. I was going to let go of the fact that I had called them *mine* and just push onward. Hana and Gabe looked around, surveying my little kingdom.

Hana's long, dark hair was tied up in a high ponytail, and she had a cozy white zip-up sweater on with charcoal athletic pants below. Gabe was in his same signature look, and it made me briefly wonder just how many pairs of distressed jeans and tank tops he owned. Tony was in the same jeans and cashmere as I had seen him in this morning, and Billie was in a lacy black dress with fishnet tights, the perfect little goth.

"The astronomy club is hogging your corner," I told them. "But they should be going up to the roof any minute."

I fell silent under the heat of Hana's gaze. Her dark eyes flickered over my face, and I tried to keep my breathing steady.

"That's okay," said Tony. "We'll have a wander around in the meantime."

The three of them went off. Hana stayed behind.

"Hi," I said softly.

"You look at home here," Hana commented.

"Thanks, I love it. I'm glad you came tonight. I was hoping we could maybe spend some time together? You totally don't have to. I get that I'm kind of hogging your pack, and you probably don't like that, but I—"

"Nicky."

I snapped my mouth closed.

Hana gave me a small smile. "Funny you should ask, because I have a favor to ask you."

"Oh?"

"I'd like you to go on a hike with me."

Oh god.

My cardio was pathetic. But I didn't want to disappoint her. "Sure, I'd love to."

Maybe *love* was a bit of a stretch. While I was certainly eager to get the alpha to like me, I wasn't sure that revealing how bad of shape I was in would do that.

"I only have a sunrise boot camp on Thursday. Can I pick you up from work for our hike afterward?"

I supposed it was probably too much to hope for her picking a later date so I could at least *begin* training myself. "Sure, that sounds good."

Her eyes narrowed, scrutinizing me. "You don't have to agree, Nicky. I'm not going to be mad if you say no."

I squeaked. "Why would you think I don't want to go?"

"You responded twice with 'sure' and you touched your hair six times while answering."

I didn't know I had such obvious tells.

"It's not that I don't want to go. I do. I just haven't gone on a hike in a *long* time. I don't know how much I can manage."

"I'll pick an easy route for us. I'll be coming off of a class so I'm not going to make you climb Everest by any means."

She rewarded me with another soft smile when my shoulders dropped down. "Okay, I think I can probably manage that."

"Good. I'm looking forward to getting to know you."

What if she got to know me and didn't like what she found?

Hana sighed, and for the first time, looked a little nervous. "Look, I get it. I know I'm not the most open person, but I don't want you to be uncomfortable around me. The pack likes you, and I want to give whatever this is the chance it deserves for them. So I'm going to try, okay? And if I go overboard, just let me know. I'm working on getting better about receiving critique."

Damn, she was adorable, gorgeous...tall. I wanted to climb her like a fucking tree.

"Can do. I guess we both have things to work on. I'm trying to get better with communicating my needs."

The heat in her eyes took me by surprise. I stopped breathing for the brief moment at the inferno that was leveled on me.

"I should leave you to your work," she said. I watched her retreating back and shivered.

I spent my breaks with the four of them after they reclaimed their corner. Hana left for work at five-thirty, and the closer to the end of my shift it got, the more often I wandered to the windows.

This time I had parked on the other side of the pole so that my driver's door couldn't be blocked, but, just like yesterday, a black sedan sat next to my car. It was only twenty minutes until my shift ended, and while I couldn't tell who was in the vehicle, I could see that *someone* was.

Billie came up behind me. "What are you looking at?"

I jumped as they spoke.

"Wow, someone's twitchy today."

232

I startled again when Gabe and Tony appeared from around one of the stacks. Tony put a hand on my shoulder and looked out the window with me.

"Is that him again?"

"I think so."

Gabe's low growl had heat pooling in my belly.

"What's with this guy?" he asked.

From his reaction I could only assume that Tony had given them some of the details. I wasn't crazy about my vulnerability being shared, but, considering Tony had rushed to my emotional rescue this morning and he and Billie had physically rescued me from Alphonse before, I didn't blame him for keeping the others in the loop.

"I don't have any answer for that," I said. "This is exactly why I moved and changed my number after he and I broke up. I'd even transferred to another library location."

I let out a frustrated sigh. I couldn't do that this time. This facility was the only one in the city to have a twenty-four-hour program and I was loving working nights. I hated that I even had to contemplate changing my job because of him.

"He sent lilies again. I had Miranda take them home and I'm going to talk to the facility manager. Maybe we can start refusing the deliveries."

"That might piss him off more," Gabe said quietly. "I would see about just having them be redirected. Let him waste his money while we see what kind of escalation he's willing to pull."

"I'd be willing to pull his ears off his fucking head," Billie hissed. "No one's allowed to treat my girl the way he does."

I warmed head to toe at being called their girl, even though it was amid threats of bodily harm to my ex.

"We'll get you home safe, Nicky," Gabe said.

The dread over seeing Alphonse waiting for me was edged out by the gratitude I felt to the three wonderful people surrounding me.

"Thank you." It was on the tip of my tongue to ask if one of them would stay with me, but I refused to be a burden. Alphonse didn't know where I lived, and, even if he did, he couldn't get inside with the building security. I just needed a cup of tea and a solid sleep. Not an absolutely gorgeous babysitter to coddle me.

Before work ended I emailed Patricia and explained the situation with the flowers to keep her apprised, and ran over the program set up with the day staff as they arrived.

Tony, Billie, and Gabe moved around me like they were my own personal Secret Service as we exited the building. When Alphonse tried to get out of his vehicle, Gabe slammed his door shut to keep him in place while I climbed into my own car.

"Nicky, what the fuck is this?" I could hear Alphonse yell through the two layers of glass between us.

I pulled out of the lot with instructions to message the pack when I had arrived home safely. They blocked Alfonse's way so I had extra time, but I still took a roundabout route back to my apartment, parking around back to be out of sight of the road, and I deadbolted the door behind me when I got in. Spud greeted me with a meow-scream, and I tapped out my message to the pack while I fed him.

Why couldn't Alphonse just leave me alone?

Chapter Twenty-Eight
Nicky

"Nicola, you'll never guess who I ran into at the grocery store today."

I took a sip of my coffee, letting Mom chatter away on the phone. She was always telling me about people she encountered that I barely remembered. Sometimes it was an old teacher or classmate or neighbor that had moved away, and I had to pretend to be excited so I didn't appear rude to her.

"Who this time?"

"Alphonse! He was buying the ingredients to make puttanesca and asked me if you still like it."

My blood ran cold.

Mom continued, completely oblivious. "He seemed distressed. Something about an incident at the library. Oh, and goodness, the poor dear told me that his great aunt had passed away and that he was going to be flying to Tuscany for the funeral."

My thoughts ricocheted like ping pong balls in my head. Mom had talked to him again after I told her not to. Alphonse was out of the country. Maybe he would be gone for weeks.

I could dream, anyway.

"Mom, I asked you not to talk to him anymore."

"Nicola, maybe you have the emotional fortitude to not talk to someone who starts crying at you in a grocery store, but I do not. Besides, it was only for a few minutes."

"Did he say how long he was going to be in Italy?"

Please be a really fucking *long* time.

"Not that I recall, but I would assume at least a week. That flight takes half a day, and he wants to be there for his family. So sweet. Why did the two of you not work out again?"

"Mom I—" I sighed. "Alphonse is not as nice as you think he is. He's just a good liar. I'm not telling you to not talk to him for no reason."

"If I don't have context then how am I supposed to know how to react properly? You're my little girl, Patatina, and I hate how we've drifted apart these past few years. Talk to me."

"It's not really easy for me to talk about. He and I didn't work out because I was miserable. He's the type of person that grinds you down slowly until you don't even realize how much of yourself is missing."

"Nicola, did he hurt you?" Her voice had turned to ice on the other end of the line.

Usually her mama bear mode came out at inappropriate times, but in this case it only made me love her more.

"Not physically. I just want to avoid him and he's making it *really* difficult." Another ping-pong ball thought smacked me in the forehead. "Were you shopping at your regular grocery store?"

"Of course," she said. "You know I'm a creature of habit."

"Mom, Alphonse doesn't live anywhere near you. Why would he be at *your* grocery store?"

Unease turned my stomach.

"How should I know that?" she asked.

Frustrated, I sighed again. "Mom, I don't know how safe he is and I don't want him to involve you in whatever the heck he's got going on. Please don't give him any more information about me, okay? He's already been showing up at the library since you told him I work there. And I guess there's always a chance that he's harmless, but he's kind of freaking me out."

"I'm sorry, Patatina." Her voice softened. "I wish you had told me about him. I won't tell him anything else. How are your boyfriends doing?"

I couldn't help but smile at the change of topic. We talked about much more pleasant things for the rest of the call, and hopefully that would be the last she saw of Alphonse.

By the time I hung up I was emotionally depleted.

The one bright spot was that I wouldn't have to look over my shoulder for the next week. It was a relief to be able to message the pack and let them know that they didn't have to put themselves out to stay with me during shifts or escort me to my vehicle in the morning.

Another phone call followed a moment later, Billie's name flashing across the screen.

"Hey!" I chirped.

"Hey, Books! Do you think I could interest you in dinner at the pack house? We're ordering Indian tonight."

"That sounds *delicious*."

"You could bring your little potato prince if you want. He and Roscoe can have a sleepover!"

I couldn't stop the laugh that sprang from my lips. "I can do that. What time should I come by?"

"We're putting in the order at six. You're welcome to come over whenever your heart desires."

Spud hopped up next to me and sniffed the phone, rubbing his cheeks vigorously against the edge.

"Okay. I'm probably going to have a quick nap, and I'll get through a couple chores before heading over."

"Can't wait!"

My heart was lighter when we hung up. I stretched out in bed, and Spud hurled himself down against my back. Setting my alarm for two hours, I curled up to get a bit more rest.

When I woke, I packed up a bag with some work clothing and did a few chores—dishes, vacuuming, and cat litter—and packed up Spud in his carrier to make the trip over to the pack house.

Relief and excitement clashed together as I stepped through their doors, immediately welcomed with a kiss on each cheek from Billie and Jasper. I let Spud free, and Roscoe galloped off of Hana's lap to greet him. We all watched our fur children sniff all over one another before taking off like bats out of hell.

Tony nudged Billie and Jasper out of the way to claim me for himself with a slow, easy kiss, holding my chin between his thumb and forefinger.

Gabe was standing watch over a simmering pot of masala chai on the stove. I slipped under his open arm and breathed deep of the combination of his alpha scent and the bubbling concoction. Being here was like a weight had slipped off my shoulders. It was too easy to fall into the rhythm.

Hana appeared in my field of vision and handed me a glass of water.

I couldn't help but giggle. "Thank you." I wasn't particularly thirsty, but I sipped it anyway because it seemed to make her happy.

We ate dinner like one big family in the dining room, our order spread across the giant Lazy Susan in the middle when it arrived, masala chai poured into every cup. The chatter was ceaseless, someone always picking up the conversation the moment it lulled, and, even though I didn't participate in all of it, it was nice to simply let the words wash over me. Hana talked to me a lot more than I'd been expecting, pulling me into a chat about gardens—the pack was contemplating some extensive landscaping come summer—and luckily I'd read enough books to keep up.

At eight-thirty, Gabe had to leave for his shift. He worked his way down the line, claiming a kiss from each of us on his way to the garage.

"Assembly line kisses are way cuter than they have any right to be," I commented after the door had closed.

"That's just because *we're* all cuter than we have any right to be," said Billie.

The remaining five of us tucked in to watch a couple of episodes of a show I had seen when it first aired years ago, and, when I had digested, Billie stole me away upstairs to change for work for just long enough to leave me ruffled and needy, the knowing eyes of the others making me blush when I stumbled back downstairs in my work clothes.

I found Spud and Roscoe curled up in a ball together in one of the cat beds in the corner of the living room. "You be a good boy for everyone, okay? Mommy will pick you up in the morning."

I kneeled to kiss his head, giving Roscoe a little love as well, before I got my own assembly line of kisses on my way out to the car. Hana still hung back, but she did give me a brief hug, which I counted as progress.

There were no lilies waiting for me at the front desk this time, and my shift went by in a peaceful blur, filled with program set up and bending the rules for the university students so they could inhale their espresso at the library tables while they studied. There was no Billie and Tony tonight, which worked out decently when I had to comfort one of the students who burst into tears from the exam stress. The beanbag corner made the perfect spot for her to rest and recover.

Morning blazed bright through the windows, and I double checked to make sure there was no black sedan waiting for me. I left the library with a pep in my step. When I arrived back at the pack house, Tony managed to coax me inside for some pancakes. Of course, pancakes made me extra drowsy, which made it even easier to convince me to stay there to sleep.

I passed out, sandwiched between Billie and Tony, and woke only briefly when Jasper arrived home from the bakery and climbed in next to us.

I slept like a rock.

The pack was far too inviting. We lounged in Billie's bed, indulging in fevered kisses and wandering hands. Being surrounded by the three of them was intoxicating. When the wandering hands ended up with the four of us naked, I just let myself experience it.

Tony slid into me from behind, Billie's mouth consuming my desperate sounds as eagerly as I consumed theirs when Jasper fucked into them. I lost track of who had hands where. Fingers dug into my hip and hooked under my knee, others kneading my breast as I drowned in the sensation and the fog of their combined scents saturating every breath.

I shuddered as Tony's movements slowed, and someone thrust their fingers between my thighs to tend to my clit. Tony groaned behind me as my cunt rippled around him, my body rapidly scaling the peak of pleasure.

"Fuck, baby girl." Tony hissed in my ear and enclosed my throat in his hand. "This pussy is going to ruin me."

"Good," I said between panting breaths, squeezing tighter on purpose, "because that cock has already ruined me."

The orgasm crashed over me, and I pawed uselessly at Billie and Jasper, trying to gain some kind of foothold as I slid down that sharp peak. Jasper lost it a second after I did, and I devoured the sound Billie made as his hips snapped into them. Tony locked an arm like iron around my waist, his hips speeding back up. Billie's wicked fingers were back to work immediately, even as Jasper flipped them over, his face disappearing between their thighs.

I willed my body to open, to fit everything that Tony was prepared to give me, but I wasn't *quite* there yet.

I let out an *oof* as Tony drove into me. Jasper's eyes locked onto mine a moment before his hand reached out and wrapped around the base of Tony's cock to create a buffer between us, pushing Tony over the edge as he fucked through the combined grip of Jasper's fist and my pussy as it spasmed again.

I slipped into a haze, Tony's hips moving gently to ride out the wave. Billie's shriek of pleasure as Jasper finished them off pulled me back to the surface, and I was flushed with needy heat all over again when I caught sight of their hands in Jasper's hair and their hips bucking wildly against his mouth.

By the time we finally settled, we were a sweaty, sticky mess, and I gave a happy hum, dragging Billie and Jasper closer so I could kiss them both and craning my head back to kiss Tony.

I must have fallen asleep again because the next time I opened my eyes there was only Jasper in bed with me, pressed against my chest with my head tucked under his chin.

I stretched experimentally, gasping at all the lingering phantom touches from our morning romp. Jasper made a displeased sound and hugged me tighter. I had no idea what time it was, but I did feel fully awake, and my bladder was protesting.

My stomach growled. I slid my hand slowly up and down Jasper's back. "You have to let me up. I'm hungry and I have to pee."

Jasper sighed dramatically and rolled over. Billie's black sheets were draped artfully over him, exposing the lean muscles of his chest, but obscuring the rest of him. I slid out of bed and tiptoed into the ensuite to relieve myself and wash up with the borrowed supplies Billie had set out for me. I should just keep an overnight bag in my car so I didn't have to borrow so often.

I found my clothes scattered across the floor, my panties clinging to the edge of the bed on the blankets. Jasper sat up, watching me with an appraising expression.

"Hardly fair that you look good enough to eat when you just wake up."

I climbed back onto the bed, crawling across the mattress towards him.

He caught me in a searing kiss. "Don't get me started again or you're going to be very late for breakfast."

I nipped his bottom lip. "What a tragedy that would be."

I cackled as he flipped me over and settled his hips so his freshly awoken cock could tease its way inside of me. I grabbed a handful of his ass cheeks, digging my nails into the globes of flesh as I thrust up with my own hips and dragged him deep with my hands.

A sound halfway between a groan and a whimper sounded in my ear when Jasper dipped his head to suck on my earlobe, sliding to do the same to my throat.

The gorgeous omega fucked me into the mattress. He came before I did and hoisted my hips close, angling just enough so he could fit his fingers between us to coax me, with diligent attention to my clit, to join him. Arching under the command of his experienced hands, my pussy squeezed him so tight he hissed. I melted flat onto the bed, breathing hard.

Jasper kissed me, sliding free of my body and convincing me to shower with him.

The rest of the day passed with a communal meal on the couches, all of us tucked into a bowl of stew while we watched the first of the Lord of the Rings Trilogy, Extended Edition.

Bliss settled right down to the marrow of my bones.

I agreed to Spud having another sleepover, and left him with the pack to change out my clothes at home and gather up an outfit for tomorrow.

My first one-on-one outing with Hana.

How bad could it be?

Chapter Twenty-Nine
Hana

Nicky braced her weight against a tree, wheezing quietly. I turned so she didn't feel like she had to hide her discomfort. We were barely one-third of the way through the first section of the climb.

Apparently, I needed to readjust my own views of what was easy.

The sweet beta that had entranced my pack was *struggling*. She had already consumed all of her water, so I ushered her over and offered her the straw to the three-liter pouch I carried in the pack on my back. It brought her into close enough proximity that I could smell her sweat mixed with a hint of vanillin and nutmeg. She slurped the water gratefully, and I set an arm around her waist to steady her.

"We can turn back," I offered.

"No, no. I can do it." She dropped down, putting her hands on her knees, sucking in sharp lungfuls of air.

"We're not even halfway up the hill, and then there's the whole way down."

Nicky moaned pitifully and wiped the sweat off her brow. "Stupid hill. My life has been too stationary for this."

My life was the opposite of stationary. My entire job revolved around movement, and my preferred quality time with the pack usually involved carting them out to some form of nature.

"If you can make it in a few more minutes, there'll be a rest stop at the halfway point."

Nicky huffed and pushed herself back to standing. "One more drink first."

She sidled up close to me, probably unconsciously leaning quite heavily against me, and she sucked down a few mouthfuls. I had been intending to talk to her for most of the trip, but she wasn't quite at the level of a shape that was required to carry on a conversation while hiking. That was okay. I could wait until we reached the top, or the bottom, if she changed her mind.

Her face was flushed pink. It was a mild day, but sweat gleamed at her temples. If she wanted to be stubborn, I could indulge that for now. Even so, I kept an assessing eye on her, unwilling to let her actually hurt herself for her pride.

Nicky dragged herself up the hill next to me. I maintained a deliberately slow pace, relieved when the rest stop finally came into view. She sank onto the bench there, and I gave her a few moments to catch her breath then offered her more water after drinking my own fill.

She'd been so nervous when we started out, but the nerves were completely drowned out as she had tried her best to keep up with me before succumbing to her burning lungs and what was obviously a stitch in her side, given the way she dug her fingers into her ribs.

I set a palm on her shoulder. "I promise I won't think any less of you if we go back."

She looked at me, those round brown eyes filled with fiery determination.

This beta was stubborn. It was a quality that I could appreciate given that I definitely shared it. Gabe noticed those similarities in us and had encouraged me to give Nicky a chance, so I had. I'd been intending to anyway, but his gentle nudges had sped up my asking her.

"If you're interested," I said, "I could do some private sessions with you at the pack house. We could work you up to hill climbing."

Her gaze flickered down my body for a half second before rooting on my face. "I can't ask you to do that. That's what you do for work."

I laughed and hooked her chin. "If you think I don't enjoy watching people sweat, then you clearly don't know me very well yet."

Nutmeg and vanillin overwhelmed her sweat for a brief moment, and she snared her bottom lip between her teeth.

In the right circumstances, guiding people through a workout or a fight was foreplay for me. Watching them sweating, struggling, and pushing themselves to do exactly what I told them to do might make me a bit of a sadist, but I didn't let that diminish my enjoyment.

"I could teach you to fight, too, if you like."

Nicky made the most delightful, helpless sound when I pulled her lip from between her teeth with my thumb.

"You've got good fire. We should put it to good use. Are you ready to keep going?"

Nicky nodded. I gave her another drink, and she stared up at me, her lips wrapped around the flexible straw connected to the waterpack. I could see the allure. Gabe had said that I would like her, and her desperate to please attitude, which some people might find off-putting, was a definite perk in my books.

"How are your feet?" I asked.

"A little achy, but I don't think there's any blisters."

"Good. Let me know if you think that's going to change."

We set off onto the trail again, and it wasn't long at all until she started to wilt once more. To her credit, she didn't complain, and I made no comment on her heaving, gasping breaths as she worked to keep up with my leisurely pace. Starting off on flatter terrain probably would've been a better idea, but then I wouldn't have been able to see her stubbornness at work.

After one slope that was a little grueling, even by my standards, the trail started to level off as we neared the peak. I'd let her hold my hand for the steepest portions, dragging this poor sweaty beta for as long as she insisted we go. Nicky sat in a patch of grass not long after the hill.

"Sorry." She flopped backwards gracelessly and I sat next to her.

"Walk me through your body," I instructed. "What are you feeling?"

She whined a little and put a hand on her forehead. "Pretty sure a blister is making an appearance. My shins feel like needles. Every bit of my legs are achy. My lungs are on fire."

"Why did you come with me today, Nicky?"

"Because you asked me to."

I shook my head. "Why did you come?"

Nicky fidgeted with the grass, plucking blades and rolling them between her fingertips. "Because I want you to like me."

There we go.

"I never said I didn't."

"Yeah, but you never said you *did* either. I'm erring on the side of caution."

It is difficult to fault her for that logic. "To be fair, I hadn't decided either way yet. I'm leaning toward liking you, now. Not just because you're out here with me though."

She rolled on her side and looked up at me. "What did I do?"

"The most important part is that the rest of the pack likes you and I'm pretty into trusting their judgement. I like your grit." I pulled off her socks and shoes, and, while she looked startled, she didn't stop me. I checked her over for blisters and found a couple of angry red marks. There was always a little first aid kit in my pack when I went anywhere, so I cleaned the area and applied a couple of bandages so that the blisters wouldn't get worse. She didn't say a word when I set her foot in my lap and dug my fingers into her shin, though she did make a lovely groan.

"Magic fingers."

She slumped back onto the grass, and I worked her through the worst of the pain.

"We're about fifteen minutes from the top. You can either walk yourself or you can contribute to a hard-core workout for me."

She lifted one eyebrow in question.

"I can piggyback you the rest of the way."

"Oh god. My brain says no, but my body says 'yes please'."

I laughed and patted her leg, scooping the other one into my lap to tend to her protesting muscles there.

"Well, listen to your body for now. I brought some snacks for us to eat at the top before we go back down."

Once I was a little more satisfied with the tension in her legs, she put her socks and shoes back on. I passed her the water pack to sling over her shoulders and dropped into a squat.

"You're really really sure about this?" she asked.

"Would I be down here like this if I wasn't?"

Nicky huffed and climbed on. I stood sharply, and she clung to me, arms over my shoulders and her legs locked around my waist. I adjusted a little, keeping my hand over her crossed wrists so she didn't slide back and choke me, and then we set off.

Now I was *actually* sweating. Between Nicky's added weight and the incline, I had to put in some effort. She was squirmy, and still breathing hard in my ear as we walked. Her scent had picked back up, adding to the fragrance of the forest around us.

As we crested the top, the trees parted, revealing a huge viewing platform. We were the only ones there, and I sat Nicky down in the shade on one of the benches.

She was looking at me with a particular sparkle in her eyes.

"What?"

"Nothing. It's just..."

I bent down, leaning into her personal space. "Hmm?"

"I don't get carried that often. It's always a little hotter than anticipated."

The statement caught me off guard, and I released a full belly laugh that had Nicky blushing from her hairline and down her chest where it disappeared beneath her tank top.

"Sorry," she mumbled.

"Don't be. It's cute."

That made her blush even worse.

Damn Gabe for being so correct.

Still, just because she enjoyed being carried didn't mean she was interested in any more than that. She was already sleeping with the rest of the pack, but that didn't mean anything for her and I. A shame, really, because I knew a thousand ways I could ruin her, and every one of them would bring out that blush.

She squirmed under my attention. "You said you brought snacks?"

I fished out a pair of the granola bars Jasper and I had made a couple months ago and stashed in the freezer. She scarfed it down eagerly, and I took my time nibbling mine as I surveyed the sweeping valley below the viewing platform.

I gave her some time to recover before I turned more fully toward her. "What's your goal with the pack, Nicky?"

"Goal?" she squeaked. "Am I supposed to have one?"

"Some people would." I shrugged. "We're an obviously wealthy pack. It wouldn't be the first time someone has tried to get in good with one of us."

"To be fair," she said, "I was minding my own business at work. Billie was the one who snared me into all of this. I didn't know anyone had any money until I showed up at the house. Everyone's been so nice, god, and so pretty. I don't even know what to do with myself most days."

I laughed again, and Nicky's ears turned pink.

"You're an honest sort of person aren't you?"

"I try to be." She shrugged. "I don't want anything from anyone. I'm just enjoying the time I have, however long it ends up being. I feel wooed a hundred times a day, and it's not helping things that I sleep so well at the pack house. And now Spud and Roscoe are buddies. Sometimes it feels like I'm just dreaming and none of this is actually real." She rubbed her legs. "Though the shin splints are really supporting reality right now."

"What do you want with *me*, Nicky?"

Her breath turned shallow, and her eyes widened. "What do *you* want with me? I think that's a better question."

"I don't know about better," I mused. "Maybe more dangerous."

Nicky swallowed hard. "Dangerous?"

"I'm a little more...intense with my lovers than some of the rest of the pack is."

"Oh?" Nicky's voice cracked.

I hid my smile by taking a drink. I tucked one of the hairs that had escaped her ponytail behind her ear and set my palm on the back of her neck like I had seen Tony do to her.

"I think we should approach things slowly. There's a lot that Gabe and Tony can teach you, and neither of them typically take things as far as I do."

"Slow is okay. But you can't say something like that and not explain. How do you take things far?"

I shrugged. "I enjoy a rougher experience and playing with items that might make a newbie uncomfortable."

"Like what?" She shifted in place, her thighs flexing as she squeezed them together.

Interesting.

"Restraints are a favorite. Ropes, harnesses, spreader bars, collars."

Nicky squeaked again, her face lighting up with pink that hadn't faded from her last blush.

"Not everyone wants to be tied up and used."

She made a small sound that I couldn't quite discern the meaning behind.

"You'll be better off playing with Gabe and Tony if you want a firm hand. Neither of them have anything on me, and I don't want to scare you."

"But—" She snapped her pretty mouth shut.

"You seem like you're brand new to most of this, but I've been watching you with the others, and I think you'd like it one day."

Her scent overwhelmed the forest around us until that was all I was breathing. Her dark eyes gleamed, and she was back to chewing her bottom lip.

"Curiosity is not a good way to tempt me away from something."

I stroked my thumb down her throat, indulging myself in the way her mouth parted. Maybe I wasn't trying to tempt her away from anything. I was more curious than I'd been willing to admit. The craving to undo her, to watch her struggle to follow orders, was like a fire in my blood. I slid my hand up and cupped the back of her head.

Her gaze leapt between my lips and my eyes, and her fingers curled around the bench beneath her. I gave in a little, tipping close enough to inhale along her throat, reveling in the way that she shivered.

It was very possible that a few choice words and touches would have her melt enough that she would let me bend her over the viewing platform and let her serenade potential interrupters with the sound of her pleasure. I swallowed hard against my imaginings. Just because she might doesn't mean I should test that theory, delicious as it was.

I pulled back and smoothed her hair. "Are you ready to start back?"

"Yeah, sounds great." Her voice cracked again.

Chapter Thirty
Nicky

I was doomed.

So utterly, ridiculously doomed.

Every inch of my body was singing, and it took all of my willpower to not turn my head and kiss her. She smelled so good. Bright mint and earthy green tea that woke up all of my senses. I'd thought I was going to combust when she carried me piggyback, but apparently the true risk of combustion was her hand in my hair and her face at my throat.

I was *not* equipped to deal with this.

I stumbled after her down the hill. Heading down I had momentum on my side so it wasn't such a slog. My muscles still protested, but they were easier to keep quiet this time. I was going to need a *long* soak to recover.

Hana let me cling to her as we worked our way down the steepest portions. My brain had fritzed when she picked me up, and part of me really wanted it to happen again. What was it about being hefted around like a princess that did it for me? None of my beta partners had ever bothered to try it.

I was determined to make her proud on the trip down. I had new blisters forming by the time I skidded to a stop at the bottom of yet another hill. If I mentioned them, would she sit me down and tend to me as if I was some priceless treasure again?

Her words circled in my head for the entire walk. Images flickered through my brain. I had never used restraints, but I had seen them on occasion, and it was all too easy to apply those concepts to myself. The thrill that zipped through me when one of the alphas held me by the hair or with a palm draped over my throat seemed small in comparison to the torrent of desire that roared through me at the idea of being trussed up at their mercy.

I shivered. My thighs squeezed together, the light pressure against my clit doing absolutely nothing to calm the tempest that pounded in my chest.

I had already had a few carnal revelations in regards to this pack. Maybe I was due for another.

We reached the bottom of the final hill where the trail leveled out, snaking its way through the trees until its eventual end of the parking lot. Hana sat me down on the bench there in the shade. She dropped down to a squat to bring herself level to me.

"How are you feeling? Anything else I need to tend to before we head home?"

My heart tripped at the use of home. Silly, really, considering it *was* her home. How long would it take before my brain associated the pack house with that word, forgetting the little apartment that had housed me the last three years?

"Nothing major," I replied.

Hana gripped a firm handful of my calf, and I hissed as she dug into the muscle. "We'll get you into the hot tub. It'll help."

"Are you going to join me?"

Her amber brown eyes flashed. "If you'd like."

I nodded.

I would *very* much like.

She was difficult to read. While things between us seemed to flow a little better now, it still wasn't as easy with her as it was with some of the others. I wanted to change that.

"I'll message the pack so they can get it set up by the time we're back."

I stood up again with her assistance and held my breath when our chests bumped together. She was definitely the tallest in the pack, having a good six inches on me, which fed the urge to tuck myself under her chin.

I didn't.

My brief respite on the bench only made my body more aware of how much work I had put in on this walk. It felt like I was stepping on glass, and I hobbled a few steps before Hana sighed and passed me her pack again.

She dropped down in front of me. "Hop on."

I obeyed, even as I whimpered. "It's not fair. I was going to make you proud of me on the last half of this."

Hana laughed quietly as I climbed onto her back and clung to her like a koala.

"You *did* make me proud. You don't have to be effortless at something for me to be impressed with your determination to finish. You did good today, Nicky." She adjusted her grip on me. "If you're brave enough to go again with me, I'll pick an easier route."

I warmed at the simple praise and smiled all the way back to the car.

My feet throbbed as I sat in the passenger seat. I would've thought they would be used to having my weight on them all day considering how much of my library job involved standing and wandering around, but apparently none of that compared to the strenuousness of a hike.

We stopped for smoothies on the way back. I tried to pay, but one intense look from her cowed me, and I accepted the creamy peach concoction she purchased for me. Hana had gotten the same for herself. Her favorite, she'd said, watching my reaction when I took the first delicious sip. I drank it greedily on the remainder of the drive.

She carried me into the pack house which got instant attention from Gabe who was fixing himself a snack in the kitchen.

"What happened?"

"Overdid it a little," I said. "I don't really need to be carried, but my feet are grateful."

Hana held still so he could untie my shoes to set them by the door. I slid down to the floor, hissing as I made contact, and was instantly princess scooped up by Gabe while Hana removed her own shoes.

"Let's get you rinsed off so you can enjoy the hot tub," Gabe said.

I let him carry me away, looking at Hana from over his shoulder. Gabe's shower had a wide, luxurious bench in it. I made zero complaints as he stripped me out of my sweaty clothes and got me situated under the water stream. I didn't bother with a full shower since I was going to be soaking in chlorine, but I wanted to get all of the sweat off first.

When I was relatively clean and dressed in a borrowed swimsuit, I was carried back down the stairs and out into the backyard where Hana was already waiting in the hot tub.

Billie and Tony were asleep, and Jasper wasn't quite home from work yet, so it was just the three of us.

"Do you want me to join you?" Gabe asked.

I glanced at Hana, and she gestured back that the choice was mine. I wasn't sure if she would be more likely to open up if he was there.

"If you want a dip, you're more than welcome," I said.

He and Hana exchanged a long look. "Just for a bit. I'm about ready for bed."

Hana and I were alone while Gabe went to fetch his swim trunks. We weren't sitting very close, but we were near enough to put impure thoughts in my head. Not that that was difficult after our conversation on the hike.

"Pass me your feet," she ordered. "If it gets to be too much, you can tell me to stop."

I lifted them both and set them on her lap where she dug merciless knuckles into my foot that was somehow both ticklish and agonizing.

"Hold still," she crooned. "It'll feel better in a minute."

I huffed and puffed, doing my absolute best to keep my squirming to a minimum as she coaxed a ridiculous opera of mewls from me.

"You're doing so well," she soothed. "Deep breaths."

The tension in my foot released with a *pop*, and I melted against the hot tub, head resting on the edge.

"Better?" she asked.

I nodded weakly and resumed my valiant struggle when she scooped up my other foot to give it the same treatment. I jumped when Gabe kissed my cheek.

"Am I interrupting?"

Hana hit the magic spot in that foot too, and the tension drained with a pitifully loud groan out of me.

"Nope," Hana said cheerfully. "Climb on in. I bet Nicky's shoulders could use some attention."

He slid into the water next to me, briefly leaning across the hot tub to kiss Hana before gathering me into his lap. "I'm impressed. The first time Hana dug the knots out of my feet I almost cried. I did feel like I was walking on clouds afterward, though."

A near hysterical giggle slipped free when Hana moved those viciously strong hands to my calves.

Gabe chuckled in my ear, soothing his hands over my shoulders and arms, sliding up to find the ever persistent knot at the base of my skull.

"Someone's a little tense," he murmured.

I melted helplessly between them, surrendering to their expertise, my knots and muscles no match for them. The sun crept its way into the backyard as we sat there in the bubbling hot water, and it was only when it got to the point that it started to spear my eyeballs that we decided to end our soak. Every inch of me felt like jelly barely holding itself together.

Hana's hand snaked through the water until it sat just above my knee. "You should get some sleep."

"Where?" I mumbled.

I didn't want to bother anyone that was already asleep, and, if there was a guest room in the pack house, I wasn't privy to its location.

"That depends on if you want to sleep alone or with someone, and with who," she replied.

It was unfairly hard to think between my mental exhaustion from my shift and my physical exhaustion from the hike followed by the warm—and painful—bliss of the hot tub.

"Just put me anywhere and I'll pass out."

"Why don't we all get showered and we can bunk down in my room," offered Gabe.

Some worried little part of the back of my brain flared to life at the thought of sharing a bed with Hana. I was equal parts nervous and interested in the quiet intimacy of sleep near her.

I nodded sleepily.

"Do you want me to carry you again?" Gabe asked.

"Let me see how strong my legs are first."

I made it up exactly one flight of stairs, my body deciding that was enough for today. This house was far too tall for post-workout soreness. I thought Gabe might scoop me up, but Hana lifted me first. There was a whole lot of skin-to-skin contact with us in bikinis, and, while it did set a quiet fire beneath my skin, I had no energy to do anything about it.

I was vaguely conscious through a quick shower, managing a shamefully messy French braid before I tumbled into the bed wearing a tank top and boxer briefs borrowed from Gabe's wardrobe.

Hours later I awoke in a fog, sandwiched between the two alphas. Hana's legs tangled with mine, her shorty pajamas leaving almost as much skin exposed as her bikini. One of my arms had fallen asleep, and, now that I was awake, the tingly sensation was impossible to ignore. I wriggled like a caterpillar between them until their sleeping forms shifted enough for me to roll over.

I was getting way too comfortable sleeping surrounded by people. My own bed was going to start feeling like a deserted island, where I was left to drift without the warmth and weight of other bodies to anchor me.

Oh well.

That was a problem for a future Nicky.

Chapter Thirty-One
Billie

I had to admit, I hadn't been expecting my spontaneous crush on the pretty librarian to spawn a massive pack-wide crush.

Nicky let us hog her until her Thursday shift. Friday was spent in her own apartment, taking back her little prince for the night so she wouldn't be too lonely. We got her back for the weekend, though.

I got the guest room in the basement all ready for her so that she had her own space in the pack house, even though she slept in my room on Saturday morning and in Jasper's the next.

When Sunday afternoon rolled around, she had sheepishly asked Jasper and Gabe if they wanted to go to another Marino family dinner. I wasn't particularly familiar with jealousy, but damn if it didn't get my knickers in a twist that they got to go instead of me. Hana and Tony had distracted me while the others were out, but the fact that we three were total unknowns to Nicky's family poked at me.

"Give it time," Tony had said.

Anyone who knew me was fully aware that patience was *not* one of my virtues. But I tried.

Tony and I were back at the library with her that night, the tables filled with students, but we had staked our claim in our corner early. Tony was eyeballs deep in work and had been pouring over financial statements and bylaws in a good portion of his spare hours, leaving very little time for me to get the attention I had come to expect. I curled up most of the night to read in my bean bag, taking breaks to indulge in Nicky's presence whenever she came over to visit.

There was no sign of her assface ex when her shift came to a close. She went home without us. Logically, I knew she couldn't spend *all* of her time with us, but it didn't stop me from wishing for it. It would've been silly for her to have her own place and never use it because she was with us. But I wouldn't be dissuaded from luring her whenever I could.

BILLIE:

Could I interest you in a painting or pottery date?

NICKY:

You gonna pretend to be the dude from Ghost if I say yes to pottery?

BILLIE:

It MIGHT have crossed my mind ;)

XD sign me up

I had everything for pottery in my studio—except for a kiln—which I'd neglected to really show her in full since we'd spent so much time in the common areas or bedrooms, but it was my special space in the home, and I wanted to share it with her.

Monday night melted into Tuesday morning, and thankfully, I had sleep to keep me occupied until the afternoon when Nicky would arrive. I prepped a snack plate with chopsticks so even if we were wrist deep in clay we could have a bite if we wanted to.

The doorbell rang, and I bounded down the stairs, flinging open the front door to launch myself at Nicky in a hug. She let out an *oof* from the impact, wrapping her arms around me a moment later.

"Good morning to you, too." She laughed and let me usher her inside. "Where's everyone else?"

"On a hike. It's just you and me for a little while." I grinned and tugged her upstairs to the studio.

My space was tucked into a corner, with two of the walls all windows to let in the natural light. The other two walls were stacked with shelving, partially finished paintings, and rows of canvases waiting for attention. A potter's wheel sat in the furthest corner with tarps laid around to protect the flooring and contain the mess that accompanied the process.

"This is gorgeous!"

Nicky scampered around the room, looking at the paintings hung up and the plethora of supplies I had tucked everywhere. It was a bit chaotic, but it suited me just fine. I had enough space to work and knew where everything was, which was the most important part.

I got her outfitted with a smock, and she twirled adorably in the mass of fabric. The initial part of pottery wasn't exceptionally thrilling, but Nicky was an avid student as I sliced off a chunk of clay and patiently taught her how to wedge it to smooth it out.

"Throwing is fab for getting out your frustrations. Just whack it down in the middle of the wheel."

Nicky slapped the clay down a little off-center, and I had her do it a few more times until we got it exactly where we needed it to be.

"There we go! Now, let's get it properly sealed and smoothed out."

My arms weren't *quite* long enough to get her into position from behind, but that just meant I got to squish myself completely against her. I kissed her throat as I adjusted her grip on the clay. Nicky shivered and angled her head to give me better access. I gave her a nip before focusing back onto the task at hand, helping her smooth the clay further to eliminate the bit of wobble we had happening.

I taught her how to cone the clay next, and we played with it until her movements were surer and the clay responded how we wanted.

"How're you feeling, Books?"

Nicky laughed. "Well, I no longer have to wonder how your arms were strong enough to obliterate me on our first date."

I cackled and snuggled tighter against her back. "If you end up liking pottery, we can do more dates like this, and you'll have surprisingly strong arms too."

"I always did like it, but I haven't done it since I was a kid. Most summers Mom would toss us into some sort of art class. I usually chose the multi-variety ones that covered a whole ton of options, but we didn't get to play with a potter's wheel in those. Just hand forming."

"Now you've got me imagining baby Books all covered in clay. What did you make?"

She wiggled against me, turning to kiss my cheek.

"It was supposed to be a dog, but you couldn't really tell.

None of the legs were quite the same length, and its head was nearly the size of its body."

"I bet it was hella cute."

I moved her into the next phase of opening the clay so we could make a little bowl. We smoothed out the bottom, and then I rearranged her hands for pulling up the walls.

"Holy shit," she whispered as the clay lifted. "It's so perfect."

I nudged the clay and ruined the design.

Nicky let out a squawk. "Nooo. Why did you do that?"

"We're going to do it again," I said. "You know the most basic steps, and I want you to get the feel for it without my hands all over you. Half the fun of this is playing around."

She puffed out a breath, and I climbed off the stool behind her to come around to her front. "I got so excited it was so beautiful."

I drew her into a kiss. "You'll make another that's equally beautiful. The amount of times I've fucked up a project right at the end is too damn high, but you just have to roll with it. Clay can be a little bitch. It's all part of molding it to your will."

I fed her some popcorn while she fussed around with the clay and assisted her as needed to get it under control. Her tongue stuck adorably out the side of her mouth when she concentrated. It made me want to eat her up.

"You're doing great, Books." I grinned.

"I like the feel of it. So smooth." She laughed and opened up her clay ball into a bowl shape. "Question."

"Hmm?"

"You said this place used to be your grandparents' home, right?"

"Yep. They built it when their company really started booming, and I inherited it."

"Would you tell me more about them?" Nicky asked as I helped her with the final phases of shaping her bowl and tested the base thickness with my potter's needle.

"There were three of them; Hazel, Maria, and Albert, they started off as business partners and became a tiny pack. They were all betas, and while they were totally ruthless when it came to business, they were huge sweethearts with me. My mom was their only child, and I'm the only grandbaby. They all passed when I was twenty-two, a little before Jasper and I met the rest of the pack."

Nicky lifted her head and took her hands off the clay. "Did you lose them all at once?"

"Ah, yeah," I said slowly, grief climbing up my throat. I tended to get by well enough if I didn't think about it too hard, but every so often it hit me like a truck. "It was a plane crash."

Nicky wiped her hands on her smock, rising off her stool to hug me. "I'm so sorry, Billie."

I snuggled into her arms.

"They made sure I was taken care of, and I try to use the money in ways that would make them proud of me. The house was the biggest thing they locked down for me. I'm not allowed to sell it or have any other name on the deed until I turn fifty. They didn't want Mom to get her hands on it, and they luckily set aside a good chunk of change to cover all the expenses of running a house this big."

"Why would your mom try to get the house?"

I sighed and curled my fingers into her smock. "Because my mom tends to be a selfish bitch at the best of times. I spent most of my childhood living with my grandparents because she wasn't very interested in parenting. Everything had to be for her no matter how negatively it impacted someone else. I'm still not sure how she turned out that way, but they knew how she was and took a lot of steps to keep her out of my finances."

"What about your dad?" Nicky asked, cuddling me softly.

"He's not any better. He won the lottery very shortly before meeting mom. The two of them just roll around in their money. And, like, I get that I was also born into privilege, but at least I acknowledge it and try to do better. Those two are like the gold-toilet kind of rich."

Nicky pulled me back over to the stool and had me sit on her lap. "I'd say you've definitely made your grandparents proud. You put your money to good use to make a beautiful home for your pack, and you made Jasper's dreams come true. I have no doubt you'll do even more wonderful things in the future."

"Thank you," I said softly, swallowing back a fresh rise of emotion.

"Where are your dad's parents in all of this?" Nicky asked.

"Oh, um, they actually kind of joined a cult a few years back. Last I heard they were part of a commune down in Belize."

"*What*?!"

"Yeah. Cults like pulling in people with money. My dad gave them a bit from the lotto win, and the recruiters came snooping. I've only actually met them twice, and I haven't had any updates since I got disowned."

"My family seems so boring by comparison," Nicky mused.

"Be glad for that. Interesting isn't always good." I gave her a long kiss to shake myself properly out of the sharp edges of grief and pulled her back to the potter's wheel to finish up her project.

I helped her tidy the bowl she'd made and used my wire to slice it off the wheel so I could set it aside to dry.

"Now what?" Nicky asked.

"Now it air dries. Takes a couple days, and then you can decide if you'd like to paint it before glazing it, and then I'll take it to a little studio downtown that has a kiln. You made a very cute bowl. Excellent first try."

I set the bowl on one of my shelves and pulled Nicky back into a kiss. The taste of her chased away the memories, anchoring me firmly back into a much more pleasant reality.

She stayed for dinner before heading home to prepare for work and feed Spud. I worked on some of my paintings so I didn't crowd her at work, but by the next day I was itching to see her again and asked Tony to take us both to the library.

I trotted after Nicky in the stacks, stealing her time for myself while she re-shelved a cart full of books. Her dark brown hair was pulled back in a ponytail today instead of her usual chignon.

"Do you want to come over in the morning?" she asked. "I could make us breakfast."

Warmth flooded my chest. "Fuck yes. Sign me up immediately."

Nicky laughed. "I know it's not as fancy as the pack house..."

"If it's yours then I love it," I proclaimed. "Besides I can ruin you in your bed just as easily as in mine."

I was rewarded by her cheeks bursting into flames. She made a little choked sound and hastily shoved a couple more books back onto the shelf.

"Do you think there's enough room for Tony?" she asked.

"If we cuddle, there's room for anything," I replied.

"That's true." She fidgeted with the cuffs of her blouse. "A sandwich of people doesn't take up much room."

When her task was over and she had to return to the front desk, I returned to Tony with a bounce in my step.

"What's got you so happy?" he asked.

"You and I are going to have a sleepover at Nicky's."

"Oh, are we?" His easy smile had me grinning back at him.

"Yep. She offered to make breakfast, so if there's anything in particular you want we should hit an early morning grocery run."

"Instead of her making her cook for us, we could pick up some food from that Filipino place we both love. I bet Nicky would enjoy some tapsilog."

"Oooh, you are so right. That gave me an instant craving."

At quarter to seven, we placed the order. There was no black sedan waiting for her, a constant relief to all of us. Tony and I picked up the food and met Nicky at her place.

Spud ignored all of us in favor of his breakfast, but once he had inhaled his food, we were all gifted with some side rubs against our ankles. We ate at her little kitchen table, with barely enough room for our plates with the food occupying the rest of the space. I had never lived in a place like this except when I was in the college dorms, but most of the pack had come from similarly humble beginnings.

Once we were well fed and Spud was given enough attention that he slunk away to lay in his bed, we retired to Nicky's bedroom. I'd had full intentions of coaxing her beautiful scream out with my face between her thighs, but she had yawned about fifty times over breakfast, so, instead, the three of us curled up and slept our way into the afternoon.

It felt weird to say that waking up next to her never got old when it had only been about two weeks, but I thought about it every time. I buried my face in her hair and breathed in her soft scent of spices and old books.

The smell of the coffee pot finally drew me out of bed, with Nicky on my heels. Tony stood in the kitchen, shirtless, with his locs still wrapped in the blue silk scarf he'd brought with him, looking absolutely scrumptious. He'd lined up three cups next to Nicky's coffee machine that was percolating loudly.

"Oh," said Nicky. "Let me even see if the milk is still good. I haven't been home enough to get through my stuff before it expires."

She pulled out the carton triumphantly, the date marked on it giving us another two days of grace until it was destined for a drain. It was all a far cry from our espresso machine and fridge full of flavored creamers, but it was equally satisfying while we snuggled up on her couch and watched some terrible daytime TV.

"I don't suppose we can lure you to stay with us after your shift tonight?" I asked.

"Tomorrow," she promised. "I'm going to get far too spoiled staying with you. Besides, I've been neglecting a lot of chores. I want to get this place in order so I can stay with you for a few more days."

Damn her sound logic.

I was a creature of indulgence, and even though I constantly tried to have more patience, it was an ongoing struggle. Still, I would let her have her space. Clinging to her like a barnacle and demanding she stay all the time wasn't going to be good for the long-term well-being of our relationship. I wanted her to continue liking me.

"Would you like some help with your chores, Books? I have a pottery class this evening, but you can borrow me until then."

"You don't have to stay and help me with chores," she said. "I

266

kind of like to nerd out when I clean. Headphones, loud music, terrible dancing. It's all part of the zone I get into. It's nice to vibe by myself sometimes, at least now that I have an alternative."

Tony laughed softly. "That sounds adorable. While I'm sorry to miss it, I'm glad you're able to find a comfortable balance. It's not always easy in situations like ours. Takes a lot of work sometimes."

We didn't get to stay for the evening, but we did convince her to come get tacos with us at a place we saw down the street within walking distance on our way here. Once we were all sufficiently fuelled, we parted ways: Tony and I back to the pack house and Nicky back to her apartment.

"You're doing better about this than I expected," said Tony.

"Rude," I said with a laugh.

"I'm serious. We don't call you Hurricane Billie for no reason. I can see that you're trying and I'm proud of you."

My cheeks warmed and I murmured a 'thank you.' I ruined the moment by asking, "When's the asshole due back in the country?"

Tony shrugged. "Any day now, probably. Not like he handed over his itinerary."

"I hope he asphyxiated on a hunk of mozzarella while he was over there."

Tony snorted. "You're not the only one wishing for his early demise."

I grinned and nudged him playfully. "I enjoy when we're both vicious over the same thing."

"If you make one of mine cry then my moral compass takes a bit of a nap."

"Hot."

Tony rolled his eyes, smiling anyway. "Come on, I've got more work to do."

Chapter Thirty-Two
Tony

"Hey, stranger." Nicky scratched her fingertips over my shoulder and plunked down next to me on my beanbag. "No Billie tonight?"

"Jasper took them on a date night, so it's just you and me."

"I have a proposition for you," she said.

"What *kind* of proposition?" I asked with a wink.

Her cheeks turned pink. "Okay, I hear it now. It's not a sexy one. I was wondering if you might be interested in being one of our featured careers. We're doing some outreach with a few local high schools and one of the community colleges. Most of the people we have on board are trades and some of the standard 'I wanted to be that when I was six years old' kind of jobs. But I would really love to get some more creative careers involved. Editing work would be perfect, and a lot of students might not know much about it. I also think it would be really cool if you

268

could talk to them about balancing travel and education, for the ones who are eager to spread their wings and see the world."

"Yeah, absolutely! I'd love to. What's all involved?"

Nicky gave a squeak of delight, practically blinding me with her smile at my agreement. She walked me through the program that was part informational, part mentorship, and would take about four days of my time outside of preparation. "I'll be coming in to help as well. I think you and I will have some crossover with the students that are interested in book-related careers."

I hadn't really considered mentorship before, but now that Nicky had broached the subject, the idea was definitely something I wanted to pursue. For all the strides the world had made, a lot of parents were still very unsupportive of careers outside of standard fields.

The grin she put on my face was untamable. "Thank you for thinking of me."

"I'm just glad you're excited about it. Not everyone is thrilled about donating time to kids, but I had a good feeling about you."

"I would've killed for a program like this when I was younger. People shitting on English degrees with no imagination for the careers it could lead to gets very old."

Nicky laughed. "I don't doubt that. Mom was *baffled* when I told her how much school was needed to become a librarian. People know nothing about my job, either. I'm kind of hopping into the project part way through. Miranda's been working on the set up for a couple months and finally brought me on board."

I set aside my work task for the moment, and Nicky and I sketched out a brief plan for our involvement in the project. It was exactly the fire I needed to bring back some of the joy in my career that copy editing bylaw propositions didn't quite provide.

Her little smile and quiet laughter was ever-present, the light in her eyes dancing as her pencil flew over her notepad.

She was entirely too cute when she got into full librarian mode.

"Do you want me to reach out to some of my contacts in the publishing industry?" I asked. "I'm not sure how many of them would be available to participate, but I can brush up on some things so I can at least answer if someone asks."

"Oh my god! That would be great! I knew you were the perfect person to ask about this." Her head perked up from her notes. "The program is being distributed throughout the year, with different industries grouped together. Do you think Jasper might be interested when we get to food services?"

"I'm pretty sure he'd be ecstatic. Jasper loves kids, especially ones that will listen to him talk."

Nicky giggled and made herself a note at the top of the page. She stayed far longer than I would've expected with her break times, but maybe the library counted this towards work. By the time she retreated to set up for the day programs, we had a dozen pages of notes between us.

I probably would've said yes no matter what. The ability to say no to that woman was disappearing rapidly.

I drafted up a few emails to some of my preferred industry contacts explaining the program and asking if they had anything they might want to share. Even if none of them responded, I was going to do my best to make the experience a success.

My brain protested when I went back to my copy editing. Councillor Harvey was a rambler and had dumped another stack of work on me with a very short deadline. Thankfully the other councilors were a little more forgiving.

Towards the end of her shift, I caught Nicky at the windows staring out at the parking lot.

"Anything?" I asked.

"Not unless he got a new car." She sighed and slumped against the glass. "This was so much easier last time when I changed jobs while he was out of the country. I don't want to leave this place. I just want him to leave me alone."

"Maybe he got the message," I suggested. "It's possible that Italy made him reassess his priorities. Maybe he'll never show up again."

"I want to be that optimistic." She laughed softly and stood on her tiptoes to kiss my cheek. "What's your plan for the morning?"

"Just a bit more work before bed," I replied.

"A little Belgian waffle shop just opened up down the street and it looks amazing. I don't suppose I could entice you to get some with me?"

"I could be persuaded." I offered her a grin and tidied an escaped strand of her hair behind her ear, ridiculously pleased when she nuzzled against my hand.

I checked the time on my phone. "I'll start packing up my things. Hopefully your morning staff aren't late."

"Sounds good. I'll wrap up my stuff. Be at the front desk when you're ready?"

"You got it, baby girl."

The day staff was on time, and with Alphonse still MIA, Nicky and I decided to walk to the waffle place. It was barely five minutes away, but the wind was crisp this early in the morning, so she tucked against my side for warmth. We shared two waffles— one with poached eggs, bacon, and Hollandaise sauce and another with strawberries and hazelnut spread—at a small table in the back corner.

Nicky shoveled a piece of waffle into her mouth, and I caught her chin between my fingers, licking some of the hazelnut spread from the corner of her lips. Her sweet vanillin scent burst. I smiled against her skin, softly kissing her lips, then sat back so I could watch her. She looked like she was about to spontaneously combust as her gaze darted around the restaurant with her cheeks flaming.

"You look far too inviting when you turn that color."

My statement only turned her a brighter shade of fuchsia.

We finished off our food, and I won the battle for who got to pay. The trip back wasn't any warmer, and I took advantage of Nicky's proximity, draping my arm around her shoulder as we walked.

I kissed her up against her car before I got her inside the vehicle. She rolled down the window after I closed the door. "I don't suppose I could also persuade you to come over for a little bit? Or a sleepover if the pack won't miss you?"

The suggestion warmed me down to my toes. "I'd love to. Do you want me to drive with you or take my own car?"

"Whichever you prefer. I don't mind driving you back here to get your car later if you want."

"Let's do that then." I slipped into the passenger side and pulled her in for a kiss, one of those slow, deeply indulgent ones that made you feel like you're up in the clouds.

I let my palm rest on the back of her neck as she drove, and inside her apartment we were greeted by the familiar sound of Spud demanding his breakfast. Nicky scooped him up and delivered a dozen kisses to the top of his head. I kicked off my shoes and went to grab him some food since I already knew where she kept everything. Spud inhaled his meal, and Nicky drew me into the bedroom.

"You planning on using your feminine wiles on me, baby girl?"

"That may have been part of my intentions in inviting you over." She gave me a shy smile, and, when I gestured her over, hopped straight into my arms. I caught the underside of her thighs and tipped my head up to meet her mouth.

She was all sweetness as she melted under my attention. When I walked her over to the bed, tipping forward so that she landed with a *whoosh* with me on top of her, she gasped. Our combined scents filled the small space, and she mewled happily beneath me.

"I thought *I* was supposed to be using my wiles," she said, voice breathy.

"I'm plenty seduced, but if you'd like to work a little more of your magic, I'm not opposed."

"I don't think I've ever properly seduced anyone before. What do you like?" Her expression was so bright and earnest as she asked that question.

I gave a low chuckle. "Oh, baby girl, I don't know if you're ready for that conversation."

She wiggled beneath me. "You and Hana never want to tell

me things. Quit making me curious about things I don't know. *Tell me.*"

I raised up just a little and put my thumb over her lips, trailing slowly over her chin and down her throat, so she tipped her head back with a soft whine that pitched higher when I laid my palm down to pin her in place.

"There's a lot that I like. I love everything we've done, but I don't think any of us have played with you the way we might play with one another."

Nicky's breath had turned to panting, and she rocked her hips against the bulge of my jeans. "I want to. Show me?"

There went my ability to say no. I wanted to please her, and there were so many ways I could do that. I would start with giving her exactly what she asked for.

"I can do that," I said. "Same rules apply. Tell me words for slow and stop."

"Yellow to slow." Her hands dug into the sheets below her. "Red to stop."

"Good girl. I can show you a few things. If you like them, we'll keep them, and if you don't that's fine too. Do you mind if I root around your place and see what I can find to use?"

"I don't know what you're looking for, but go ahead," she said.

I nodded, already sifting through the possibilities. "Strip down for me and wait. I won't be long."

I left her in the bedroom and did a quick scan of her apartment, slowly gathering supplies: the paraffin candle and lighter on her coffee table, a feathered cat toy, the ice cube tray from her freezer, and a couple of skinny scarves from her closet.

Her eyes were round and curious as I set my stock pile down on her bedside table.

She kneeled on her bed completely naked, knees pressed together, almost in a proper starting position except that she was hunched forward like she was trying to hide the full scale of her beauty from me.

That simply wasn't allowed.

273

"If you have any toys, now would be the time to bring them out for me to see. You can tell me where they are and I'll get them. Be sure to sit up, too. One part of playtime is showing yourself off. Shoulders back."

Nicky shifted into the proper position and directed me to her bedside table. There wasn't a lot to work with, but something was always better than nothing. I extracted the hot pink toy and the little bottle of lube she kept with it, setting both next to the rest of the things I had acquired.

I cupped her chin, and her gaze flickered up to mine, those dark eyes lit up with a war of desire and uncertainty.

"Ready?"

"Yes," she said quietly.

"Since this is your first time, we're going to make it extra clear. Say it like you mean it."

"Yes, I'm ready" she repeated, her voice a touch more forceful this time.

"Good girl. How do you feel about me tying you up a little?" I held up the scarves I'd gathered. "Blindfold and light restraint, okay?"

She nodded, but at the raising of my eyebrow, she added, "Yes. I trust you."

"My brave girl." I cupped her cheek and kissed her softly. "Know that I don't take that trust for granted and I won't let it be misplaced. I'll keep you safe."

She smiled up at me and lifted her face for another kiss, pulling away with luminous eyes. "I know."

I used one scarf to gently bind her wrists and the other to cover her eyes. The shift in her was instant, her breathing picking up as she got squirmy.

"Color?" I asked.

"Green."

I moved on to the next task, using the barbeque lighter to get the candle melting. The cat toy would take on a new function while we waited for our temperature play items to be ready.

She jolted at the first touch, the fluffy end brushing her cheek.

I traced it over the curves and planes of her body, letting her adjust to being without her sense of sight so she could focus on touch. It didn't take very long for her to relax into it.

"I'm going to lay you back, okay?"

"Okay," she murmured, letting me maneuver her up the bed and stretch her legs out.

The feathers traced over her toes and ankles, taking a serpentine route up her legs before teasing each perked nipple in turn. Her squirming resumed, the feathers rounding her breasts, slipping in alternating patterns along her throat and the curve of her waist, crossing just above the thatch of hair between her thighs.

I spared a glance at the candle. It was melted enough to start.

"Nicky," I said softly. "I'm going to try something new, okay? Have you ever played with hot wax?"

"Does dipping my fingertips in it as a kid count?"

"We'll go with yes. This will be like that except on the rest of your body. Is that fine?"

"Yes."

I fetched a towel from her linen closet and worked under her body. By the time I had finished she was shivering in anticipation, her thighs squeezing together, her nipples pebbled and asking to be touched. Who was I to deny them?

I leaned down and sucked one between my lips with a swirl of my tongue. Nicky let out a shocked moan and arched, thrusting it deeper into my mouth. I kept at it, teasing it while she writhed beneath me. When I pulled away, she let out an impatient sound.

The ice cube tray had melted a tiny bit, just enough to make them easy to release and give them a good slide. I cracked one free and touched it to her lips. Her little shocked noise was perfection.

I let the ice slide down the midline of her body, her arch at the sensation sending it careening straight to the crux of her thighs. They opened up at the first touch of cold and I rescued the cube as it dropped to the towel below.

"How was that?"

"Cold," she said with a laugh. "But fun?"

"Good. You relax and we'll see what else is fun. Hands over

your head." I climbed onto the bed and settled between her knees. There were a few sights in this world that undid me, and a lover spread open like this, trusting and needy, rocked me to my core every time.

I brought the ice cube to one of her pert nipples, and Nicky's arms snapped down as if to protect it, returning them to their proper position a moment later.

"If you move those hands again or you try to close your thighs then you're not getting an orgasm from me today," I warned.

She whined, and her fingers curled into her pillows as if that might keep them there no matter what.

I traced the ice along her upper thighs, and they quivered. A simple touch here and there—cheek, shoulder, stomach—kept her unsuspecting. With a few more innocent ones, I snatched a second ice cube as quietly as I could and tapped it against her pink folds.

She squeaked and bucked, but kept her thighs open like the very best girl that she was.

I set the cubes aside for a moment to give my fingers a break and picked up the candle. I sprinkled a few drops onto the inside of my bicep to test the temperature, and, deeming it safe, I tipped it, sending a cascade of hot melted wax down her chest and stomach.

Nicky's gasp made me impossibly hard. The long, beautiful arch of her body was decorated in splashes of white. She slumped down, breathing hard.

"Color?" I asked.

It took her a couple more breaths to answer. "Green. I've never felt that before."

"If you like it, we have much more extensive supplies at the pack house to play with."

She rolled her hips, silently begging for a little more tradi-tional attention. I ran my thumb through her slickness and rounded her clit until her whole body quivered. I fetched the ice with my free hand and touched it straight to her clit, holding only for a couple seconds before dragging it over the rest of her core, teasing her entrance and letting it slide down the cleft of her ass to land on the towel below.

"Are you okay to keep playing?"

Her head nodded excitedly. "Yes, please."

My purr rumbled in my chest. I couldn't wait to get her back to the pack house and introduce her to so much more.

I toyed with her while we waited for more wax to melt, the feather teasing her, the ice surprising her, all while she did her best to maintain her position to keep herself perfectly spread open for me.

"Please," she said, shaking head to toe, fingers clutched desperately into her pillow.

"What do you want, baby girl?"

"I still want to play, but...I really want to come too."

"Lucky for you I'm an accommodating person."

I picked up her pink dildo and teased her entrance, slowly thrusting until the whole length of it was wet from her and buried as deep as it could go. Her hips flexed, and she serenaded me with a perfect symphony of desperate moans and little gasps.

"That's it, baby girl. Sing me a song." I gave her some time with just the dildo fucking into her while my thumb attended to her clit until her sweet mouth dropped open with a cry and she shuddered head to toe.

I sat myself more comfortably and pulled her hips onto my lap, spreading her thighs open further and leaving the dildo right where it was.

"Baby girl, what color would playing with your ass be?"

She squeaked, and though I had just worked her to an orgasm, her cheeks flamed even brighter as if the question was somehow more embarrassing for her than coming apart in my hands.

"Green." She said it quietly and tipped her head so that, despite her eyes being covered, she wouldn't have been looking in my direction.

"What do you say I flip you over and we can play a little with that?"

"Okay."

I turned her onto her stomach easily. "Ass in the air for me."

She wiggled around and got herself into position, the dildo sliding free, the glistening pink toy shining obscenely on the towel below.

"Do you mind if I fuck while we're playing?"

"That depends on which hole you're planning on using." Her nervous laugh made me smile.

"Baby girl, you can't even take all of me in your pussy yet. I'm not gonna push my luck with your ass today."

"Then you can do whatever you want." She buried her face against the pillow she had clutched to her chest.

Ordinarily, those would be dangerous words, but I was committed to easing her into things. My cock sank into her like she was home, and I groaned at the squeeze of her cunt.

That feeling never got old.

I grabbed two ice cubes and let them each slide down her back while she tensed, pussy snaring me tight as the rest of her body reacted to the chill. Fetching the bottle of lube, I squeezed a dollop onto her asshole, using my thumb to gently work it inside as her breathing sharpened and she rocked her hips against me.

"You're doing so good, baby girl. I'm gonna start going in okay? You tell me if you need to stop or slow."

She offered a nod, adding a hasty, "Yes."

I pressed the tip of my thumb in, pushing and retreating in equal measure until it had disappeared to the first knuckle. Her asshole squeezed my finger, and she rocked her hips encouragingly.

"More," she begged.

I added more lube and pushed back in, following it with a slow thrust of my hips. My movements were idle and easy to let her adjust and find her own rhythm. As I gently fucked her, I added more ice cubes, drawing patterns on her skin until she was ready for me to set them aside to fuck her in earnest. I kept my strokes shallow to avoid her discomfort and simply enjoyed the slick drag against my cock.

"Perfect little cunt. You feel so good, baby girl."

Every thrust forced a gorgeous sound through her lips, and it was a constant battle with myself to hold back as her body welcomed me. It was easy to tell by the clench of her and the increasing pitch of her vocalizations that she was close. I fetched the candle and let the cascade of melted wax pour over her skin in a gorgeous splatter that painted her as mine.

I reveled in her cry and pulled her up, reaching around to toy with her clit until she came apart. She pressed her bound hands against her mouth to muffle the sound, but there was no reaction she could hide from me. I fucked into her hard and helped her lower back down so I could slide out, running my cock through my fist to add my own art to the wax that turned her into my personal canvas.

"Dear god," Nicky mumbled a few moments later.

"Did you have fun?" I asked, sitting down next to her.

"Yep."

I laughed quietly. "You lay there and I'll clean you up."

I wiped her down and collected the half melted ice cubes, dropping them in the sink before I fetched a butter knife to tease the hardened wax from her skin with the flat edge. By the time I had finished, she was looking at me with burning eyes, so I indulged her with my face between her thighs until she came for me again.

I tucked the two of us into bed. "Thank you for playing with me, baby girl."

She turned in my arms and kissed me deeply, pulling away with a cheeky grin. "Thank you. I can't wait to play at the pack house."

Sweet girl didn't even know what she was asking for. But she would find out soon.

Chapter Thirty-Three
Gabe

I smeared cream cheese over my bagel and settled in for our monthly pack meeting.

"Okay, first up," said Tony, "Jasper, any updates for your heat?"

Our omega shrugged and stacked some salmon lox onto his bagel. "I haven't noticed any shifting yet. I have an appointment at the clinic in a couple weeks to see where things are at."

"Good. We'll circle back to your heat in a minute, but first I want to ask how everyone is feeling with the whole Nicky situation?"

I swiveled my gaze to Hana. I was fine with the trajectory of things, even if I was mostly on the outer edge of it, but Hana had had the least time to get to know Nicky so far, and I wanted to make sure she was comfortable.

Billie thrust their hand into the air, and Tony chuckled as he called on them.

"I like her," said Billie. "Granted, I'm pretty big on crushes, but this one feels like it's ballooning since she got involved with more of us."

"I like her, too," said Tony.

"Me three," said Jasper. "I'd like her to stick around."

I set my hand on Hana's knee beneath the table. Knowing her, she would bow to the majority, but that wasn't particularly fair no matter how much I was interested in getting to know Nicky more.

"Hana what do you think?" I asked.

She fidgeted with her glass, spinning it in between her hands. "Nicky seems genuine from what I can tell, and I enjoyed the time we spent together, but beyond that I haven't finished forming my opinion. My priority is always going to be the pack. I'm worried about what will happen if her ex-boyfriend becomes a real problem."

Most of my job involved de-escalation and protecting the vulnerable. Despite the fact that I have been a bouncer since Hana and I got together, she had never actually stopped worrying about my safety. The early makings of a stalker in Alphonse was putting her on edge, not that I blamed her. People were unpredictable, and while it didn't sound like Alphonse had gotten physical in the past, that could always change.

"I understand your concern," I said, taking her hand in mine, "but even if Nicky wasn't on a trajectory to joining the pack, I still wouldn't want her to face that alone. Regardless of who she ends up with—whether that's some of us, all of us, or none of us in the end—I still want her to be safe."

Hana watched me carefully, her amber eyes focused on mine. "I wouldn't suggest that we abandon her to an unhinged beta. I just don't want it putting any of you in danger."

"Hana, if you don't like her you can just say so," Billie grumbled. "You can be honest with us."

"I *am* being honest with you," said Hana. "Besides, if I genuinely didn't like her, would that even stop you?"

Billie let out an indignant squawk.

Tony held up both hands to quiet us. "I think we're getting a little off topic."

"I don't think we are," I said. "Nicky is a big change for the pack no matter how far deep we are in things. Better to clarify things early than to wait until something is irreversible."

The five of us were already bonded no matter where Billie's crushes led them, and that fact wouldn't change. We had all built a life together and we were happy. Shifting things around warranted a real, proper conversation that wasn't just momentary check-in's as we went—sooner rather than later, given how quickly Nicky was slipping into the empty spaces we hadn't realized were there.

Billie took a long drink of their orange juice, eyes laser-focused on Hana. "If you really didn't like her and weren't comfortable having her around, then I would stop seeing her. It would *suck*, but I would try because I love you and I love the life we have together. I just can't shake the feeling that she belongs with us, too."

Hana sighed. "I love you too, and I appreciate that you would try. I'm not going to ask you to do that, though. I'm just being a mother hen. I do need more time to get to know her, though."

"That's fair." Billie slipped out of their chair and climbed right onto Hana's lap. "I'm sorry if you felt rushed. I want you to be comfy with things."

Our beta had always been touchy. Any uncertainty or conflict drove them straight into the nearest arms. Hana cradled them softly and kissed their cheek in reassurance.

The rest of the meeting went fairly smoothly, each of us giving updates on work and anything else that might influence our schedules, Tony adding in our shifts and classes to our family calendar.

"Okay, circling back, since we addressed the elephant in the room and since it might happen before our next meeting: Jasper,"

Tony said, focusing on our omega, "do you want Nicky to be present for your heat?"

"If things keep going how they are, then I'd love to have her. You don't think that will be too overwhelming for her?"

Tony's smile turned mischievous. "I think she'll surprise you."

"That sounds like someone has *gossip*," said Billie.

"Not gossip exactly, but we should make sure we're topped up on our supply of paraffin candles."

The four of us stared at him, and my brain was instantly filled with images of Nicky spread out, her skin decorated in droplets of wax. Given the fact that our entire pack suddenly smelled like a gourmet coffee shop, I could only assume that the others were thinking something similar.

I'd had a vague inkling that Nicky would be into more than she was aware of, considering her response to being maneuvered by her hair or held still with a hand at her throat. I was eager to find out more. She and I may have slept naked together, but we hadn't crossed any additional boundaries. I would probably wait for Hana's cue to take things further with Nicky, though that didn't mean I couldn't indulge my imagination in the meantime.

Our meeting came to a close, and I took Hana out for a walk in our gated community.

"Thoughts and feelings?" I asked her.

"Tony knew *exactly* what he was doing when he brought up the candles."

I laughed. "One-hundred-percent. Are you planning on doing anything with that information?"

"That really depends on if she wants me too." Hana shrugged. "I mentioned it on my walk with her, but that's as far as it's gone."

I raised an eyebrow. "Did you, now? How did she react to that?"

"Positively, from what I could tell. But I'm pretty sure I need at least one date with her before I tie her up and ruin her."

I slipped my arm around her waist. "Do you want that ruining to be private or would you like a little assistance for it?"

Hana purred. "You know I always love when I have your assistance."

I kept her talking as we walked, teasing out her interests and expectations. Orchestrating things might go a bit far, but at least, if I knew what she wanted, then I could guide things away from any wayward paths.

"Are you sure you don't want to go with them tonight?" I asked.

"I don't want Nicky to feel like we're crowding her," Hana replied.

"I don't think she minds having us visit her at the library. You only have one boot camp in the morning, don't you?"

Hana nodded.

"I'm not saying this to rush you, but that might be a good time to see if you can take her out for a breakfast date. One where you don't have her climbing mountains so you can carry on a proper conversation."

Hana snorted. "I'll consider it."

I pulled her to a stop so I could steal a kiss. "That's all I ask."

We did a second loop around the community, and I simply indulged myself in alone time with Hana. She was always more relaxed outside and in a quiet environment. I had never once doubted her love for our pack, or for me, but I did acknowledge that she was an introvert who needed her time and space to be happy.

The next few hours passed peacefully until I had to head into the club for work.

It wasn't even an hour past the club's opening when a young omega approached me, eyes panicked in the flaring lights.

"Can you please come help us?" She laid a hand on my arm and her fingers shook. "These guys won't leave us alone."

She looked a little like a much younger Nicky, with the same dark hair and wide, brown eyes. It sent a kick of adrenaline into my blood, and I followed her back the direction she'd come, sending word out over my earpiece. Another of the bouncers flanked us as she led us through the crowd to where a handful of intoxicated beta men were all over a group of college girls that were trying to extract themselves

I clapped a hand onto the nearest man's shoulder. "Leave them alone."

He spun, taking an immediate swing at me, but I was used to this song and dance, and he wasn't faster than me. I caught his wrist and pulled him off-balance, sending him straight to the bouncer behind me. One down, three to go.

The others were just as feisty. I got near the second, and he hissed at me. "Fuck off, man. We're just having a little fun."

One of the omega women whimpered, and I muscled my way between her and the beta plastered to her. I spared a glance to my coworkers who had already pushed the first beta out of the facility. Focusing back onto the man in front of me, I caught his punch and spun him, wrenching his arm behind him. "If you don't want an assault charge on your record, you and your friends will leave immediately."

He struggled in my grip. "Fuck off."

One of the others tackled me from behind. The girls screamed and scattered, the crowd properly taking notice of the altercation amid the music and dancing. They pushed to the edges and gave us room for me to flip the man over my head to roll and pin him face down on the ground. I had had enough training with Hana that I never worried too much about my well being at this job, even if I didn't always make it out of these situations totally unscathed. Another of my coworkers dealt with the final beta, and we hauled the group of them outside to await the police.

Barely ten minutes passed between the beginning of the intervention and the arrival of the cops to take away the troublemakers. I waded back inside. The air pulsed with energy, a sexual haze blanketing the guests as they tossed back their shots and gyrated to the music. They had already forgotten any disturbance.

Much like being the only sober person at a party, being a bouncer at a club never failed to feel like an almost surreal experience. I shook off the lingering adrenaline rush from the altercation and moved back to my post. The original omega who had approached me came back to thank me and assure me that her friends were okay now.

The night wore on. Luckily, the rest of it was par for the course: arranging taxis for anyone who couldn't walk straight and fending off the dozens of people that tried to hit on me.

When my shift finally came to a close around four in the morning, I detoured away from my path home and went instead to the library. I kept my smile to myself when I saw Hana's little red car in the lot. Apparently, she wasn't the only one unable to stay away.

I debated leaving them to it, but then I saw our minivan too. Tony and Billie were probably already up there. I parked and joined them, greeted by a bright and welcoming smile from Nicky as I crossed the library threshold.

"Hey! I wasn't expecting you tonight."

I stuffed down the urge to lean across the desk and kiss her. Fucking cameras ruining the mood. "I won't be staying long. I just wanted to see you."

That brought out her blush.

"Is Hana here tonight?" I asked.

Nicky nodded. "She's taking me on a walk in the morning. A much flatter one than last time," she said with a laugh.

"Good. I hope you'll have some space in your schedule for me soon."

Her blush crept down her throat and disappeared beneath her shirt. "I could make some time."

"Tomorrow morning? Ladies choice on what we do."

"Sounds great!" she said, her voice cracking.

"Perfect. You think about what you'd like to do with me." I winked.

The burst of her scent and the little squeak she made were far too satisfying. I left her to her work and wandered over to see the rest of the pack.

"Fancy meeting all of you here."

Hana blushed just as beautifully as Nicky, and she ducked her gaze as if I had caught her with her hand in the cookie jar. "A bunch of my clients had to cancel this morning, so we rescheduled the camp."

"What are you all up to?" I asked.

"Making my eyeballs bleed while I help Tony look over financial statements," said Billie.

"Oh? What are we looking for?"

"So," said Tony, "you remember how I mentioned that Councillor Harvey was trying to strip the funding from this facility?"

I nodded.

"She has no actual plan for the money after that. That seemed a little weird to me, so I've been doing some digging, and it seems like every time she starts gunning for funding to be cut from something, that money just disappears. I've been poring through the city's financial statements and..."

"You think she's embezzling?" I asked.

"It certainly looks that way," said Tony. "But I have to be able to *prove* it before I can say anything. I'm really not sure if this is a case where others are involved and they're all splitting the money or if their accountant is simply negligent and hasn't noticed. I don't want Nicky to lose her job over this, but I also don't want to lose *my* job by reporting Harvey for something I can't prove."

I nodded along. "That makes sense."

"But if you *did* lose your job," said Billie, "you wouldn't be in any danger. You're bonded to your sugar beta."

Tony snorted. "I guess that's true. I'll get as much information as I can and take the case to the council."

"Do you need any help?" I asked.

"Yes, please" Tony replied. "I'm up to eyeballs in both work and hunting this information down. I've been going through the bylaws, too, trying to match up the finances with measures proposed by Harvey."

"Give me whatever you want me to look for and I'm on it," I offered.

The four of us pored over documents until Nicky was

finished work. I gave Hana a good luck kiss and sent her off with a playful smack on the ass. I wasn't sure if she was going to need any luck, but it certainly couldn't hurt.

Chapter Thirty-Four
Nicky

"Y ou're sure you don't mind stopping at my apartment first?" I asked.

"Comfortable shoes are important," Hana replied. "And far be it from me to deny a cat their breakfast."

"Spud thanks you for your patience."

Hana grilled me, gently, about my dating history on the short drive back to my place, and I told her about the whole stupid mess with Alphonse. I parked in my usual spot when we arrived. Bravery pushed me on, and I hooked my arm through Hana's as we walked towards the door.

"So not only are you *cheating* on me, but you don't even have the decency to be discreet about it *or* to be there for me when a family member dies?"

I froze on the spot, my head whipping around to see

Alphonse in the front seat of his car, the window rolled down. Three stripes of angry red decorated his cheek. What on earth?

"I never took you for a slut," Alphonse snapped, his voice dripping with disdain.

Hana pushed me immediately behind her. "She's not cheating on you because she's not dating you, you delusional fuckwit," Hana spat back.

Panic and nausea clashed together so fiercely I almost threw up right there on the pavement. Alphonse knew where I lived. Oh God. How did he find out?

"Nicky, get inside," Hana ordered as she marched over to Alphonse. "If you don't leave her alone then I am *very* ready to introduce you to my uncles upstate that own a hog farm."

I wanted to retreat, but my feet wouldn't move. I was pretty sure that Alphonse was more bark than bite, as sure as I was that Hana was deadly serious in her statement.

He drove off, tires squealing. Hana turned back to me with narrowed eyes. "I told you to get inside."

I opened my mouth to reply, but all that came out was a sob. It cracked open the dam, unleashing a torrent of tears and panicked gasps that I couldn't stem. Hana wrapped her arms around me, and her purr filled my ear.

"It's okay. I'm here. I'm not going to let him touch you." She pried my keys out of my clenched fingers and maneuvered me inside the building with a firm hand around my waist.

When we arrived at my apartment, the door was ajar. I shoved out of her grip and pushed my way inside.

"Spud!" I screamed. "Spuddy, where are you?!"

I dashed through the space, ignoring the chaotic mess that Alphonse had left behind, every thought focused on finding my baby. He was nowhere visible, and I checked under each piece of furniture, growing increasingly desperate.

If Alphonse did something to him, I would never forgive myself. He hated my poor kitty. I choked on another sob and dropped to my knees, dry heaving in the middle of my living room.

"Nicky," Hana clapped her hand on the back of my neck. "I need you to breathe."

"I can't—I—Spud's, he's..."

"We'll keep looking for him. Maybe he's still in the building. I've called the police. They said they already had an officer en route, so someone else probably called earlier."

Hana kneeled down next to me and wrapped her arms around me in a comforting embrace. Her warmth was an anchor, but I couldn't be calm, not when my baby was in danger.

A knock at the door drew my attention; the uniformed officer, a brunette omega, greeted me from the doorway. "Are you the occupant? Nicola Marino?"

I nodded my head and hiccuped, stumbling to my feet with Hana's assistance.

"And you are?" the officer asked my companion.

"Hana Tanaka. I'm a friend of Nicky's."

The officer nodded. "I'm Officer Lansbury. We got a call about a break and enter from a Mrs. Alexandra Poppadakis."

"She's my neighbor," I said. "You passed her apartment on the way in."

"Does it look like anything has been stolen?" Officer Lansbury asked.

"I haven't checked. My cat is missing. That's the only thing I care about."

Officer Lansbury nodded again. "Do you have any idea who might've done this?"

I swallowed hard. "Alphonse Morelli. We saw him in the parking lot before we came up. This isn't the first time he's stepped over the line, either."

"Have you reported him in the past?"

I shook my head.

Officer Lansbury frowned. "That makes things more difficult for us. Anytime something happens you need to report it so that there's a record. Since you've given us a specific name and alleged that the burglar was seen on the premises, I'll call in for the forensics unit to do a sweep. Please don't touch anything further."

Hana held me protectively.

"What if he hurt Spud?" I asked.

"Her cat," Hana explained. "He's shown animosity about the animal in the past."

Officer Lansbury added that to her notes. "We'll keep an eye out. You can wait here. I'm going to talk to your neighbor for a moment."

Officer Lansbury went next door, and I could hear her talking with Mrs. Poppadakis. Then I heard the sweetest sound in all of existence. The screaming meow of Spud asking for his breakfast. I lunged out of my apartment and rounded the short gap between our doors to see my wonderful neighbor with my baby in her arms.

Mrs. Poppadakis took one look at me and ushered me inside. "Oh, honey." She enfolded me in her arms with Spud between us. That got my crying going again.

"I'll make a note that the animal is safe," said Officer Lansbury.

"I heard the commotion and found your little man all puffed up in the hallway. Scooped him right up, deadbolted my door behind us, and called the police."

"Thank you, thank you," I blubbered all over her.

"Of course, dear. I'm sorry I didn't get a look at who it was."

"I know exactly who it was." I hiccupped again. Suddenly the marks on his face I had seen made sense. Cat scratches. "Officer Lansbury, if you can catch Alphonse—"

"I'm sorry, did you say Alphonse?" Mrs. Poppadakis asked.

"Um, yes? Why?"

Mrs. Poppadakis stared at me like she'd never truly seen me before. "Alphonse Morelli?"

My breath came short. I nodded.

"Oh...that boy! Dear, that's my *son*."

"Your *what*?!"

Hana and Officer Lansbury looked back and forth between us.

"I think maybe this requires some explanation," said Officer

292

Lansbury. "Do you have time to speak with us, Mrs. Poppadakis? Ms. Marino has alleged that your son broke into her apartment."

"Yes, yes, of course. Oh, heavens. Please, come in."

I walked in like a zombie. I'd never actually been inside of her apartment. Cradling Spud, we sat down at her kitchen table, and I couldn't help but feel my skin crawl knowing that Alphonse had been in here.

Mrs. Poppadakis sighed. "Why would my son want to break into your apartment, dear?"

"He, uh, we were engaged a couple of years ag—"

"*Engaged*?! Why didn't he tell me about you?"

"I...don't know." I swallowed past the lump in my throat. "He told me that his mom wasn't really around, but that I would probably meet her at the wedding."

"Please continue, Ms. Marino," Officer Lansbury said, prompting me.

"Sorry. It, uh, it was a weird breakup." I explained my disappearance to end the engagement. "He found me recently, wanted to start things up again, and I didn't want to, which wasn't an answer he liked. He's been showing up at my work, went out of his way to find my mom, and we saw him in the parking lot on our way in."

"Did you see your son today?" Officer Lansbury asked.

"No, not today. He has a key to get into the building, though, in case I need him."

"Does your son have any history of aggressive behavior?"

"He—" Mrs. Poppadakis paused, sniffling, then breaking fully into tears.

I patted her shoulder awkwardly. Hana grabbed a box of tissues from the side table by her couch, and set it in front of her while I got her a glass of water. When she recovered herself enough to speak, she looked at me with so much pain in her eyes that it froze me to the spot.

"I so hoped that he wouldn't turn out like his father." She sucked in a sharp breath and sipped at her water. "I left my first husband when Alphonse was young. We moved states, got a restraining order and everything. I saw flickers of his father in him as a teen. He would…sweet talk, I suppose you could call it, until he met resistance, and then he would become cruel. Cruel and clever, just like his father, to get his way. He didn't often raise a hand, that I know of, at least. He was good at getting his way before things got to that point." She sighed, wiping at her wet cheeks. "When Alphonse was in college, I moved across the country with my second husband who passed away last year, so I'm afraid I haven't had a lot of close contact with my son prior to moving back here. He told me recently he was dating someone and that I would get to meet her soon, but he hadn't told me more than that."

Officer Lansbury took notes diligently.

"Did he hurt your little man?" Mrs. Poppadakis asked, reaching out to stroke Spud's fur. "I heard the poor little thing scream like the dickens."

I cuddled Spud and ran my hands over every inch of him to assure myself that he was okay. He made a little squawk when I touched his hip, and I tested it again to be sure, prompting another squawk and him wiggling to change position.

"I think Alphonse kicked him. He doesn't like me touching his hip."

"Spud gave as good as he got," Hana said. "Alphonse had cat scratches on his face when we saw him. He probably got them when he tried to hurt Spud."

"I'll amend potential animal abuse charges in addition to a break and enter," Officer Lansbury said. "You can stay if you'd like and wait for the forensics unit. We'll be in contact with the building manager in any case. We can seal up the suite and have them give us access another day with your permission."

A warm hand pressed onto my shoulder, and I turned to see Hana. "I would suggest you have a quick look and see if there's anything that he stole, and after that, we'll take Spud to the vet to get checked over. The building manager can handle this just fine if you're comfortable with that."

"Yeah that sounds good," I nodded.

"All right," said Officer Lansbury. "Do you have somewhere you can stay?"

"She'll stay with me," Hana declared, drawing Spud and I into her arms.

I gratefully leaned against her. My parents would let me stay, and so would my brother and sister-in-law, but all I really wanted now was to curl up with the pack and Spud and forget that all of this shit had happened.

We got everything sorted, and I signed off on the form the building manager sent me via email, waiting until Officer Lansbury had sealed off my door with plastic and police tape.

"I'm so sorry, dear." Mrs. Poppadakis pulled me into a hug. "Please let me know if you need anything, but...I understand if you never want to speak to me again."

I stared at her, realizing for the first time that I probably wouldn't be able to have a friendship with her anymore. "I...think I need some time."

"Of course." Mrs. Poppadakis sniffled. "I'm so sorry, dear. Please be safe."

"Thank you for your time and cooperation," Hana said sharply, bundling me away.

She drove while I sat in the front seat cuddling Spud. His regular vet was just opening when we arrived and was able to sneak him in. Poor thing was spooked all to hell, but the X-rays revealed nothing broken, just some bruising that he would heal from.

"Thank you for being with me," I mumbled, toying with Spud instead of looking directly at Hana.

"You're welcome. I texted the pack to let them know the situation. You're welcome to stay with us for as long as you want."

"How am I going to go back to my apartment after this? What if they don't charge him?"

"Nicky, don't worry about that right now. The important thing is that both you and Spud are safe. We'll figure out the rest later."

As the adrenaline faded away, I could only nod, the energy to do any more than that entirely depleted.

I wasn't up to eating, but Hana did insist that we stop for smoothies on the way back, and I sipped mine in the car until I could work myself up to going inside the pack house. I had nothing with me, no supplies for Spud, and no way to get back into my apartment. With a sigh, I let Hana escort me inside, where the whole pack, save Jasper, was waiting for us. I fell into their collective embrace and lost it all over again.

Soothing voices were surround-sound, and arms cradled me from every direction.

"I'm so sorry."

"Nicky, you have nothing to be sorry for," Hana insisted. "Why don't you give Spud to Billie so he can have some breakfast, and we'll get you changed into something more comfortable?"

As much as I didn't want to let go of my little boy, it wasn't fair to keep him hungry for my own comfort. Billie cradled him like the treasure he was and scooped him some extra fancy wet food. Hana carried me bridal style. I was too drained to resist, so I simply curled into her arms and let her do what she wanted.

Upstairs she got me out of my work clothes and into a borrowed pair of her pajamas.

She cupped my face in both hands and lifted my chin until I looked at her, drowning in those perfect amber eyes.

"You did very well today, Nicky. We're going to fix this, and until we do, we're here for you. Whatever you need."

I nodded slowly and tipped forward into her arms, looping mine around her waist and tucking my face against her throat. "Right now I just need this."

"Then you have it."

Chapter Thirty-Five

Jasper

"Pack meeting in my room."

I woke to Hana's whisper in my ear and carefully inched myself away from Nicky. She had slept on the main floor in the couch nest with Spud curled on her pillow like a little gray fuzzball. I didn't blame her one bit for wanting to be easily accessible to him. We'd set up everything he might need close by so he didn't have to walk too much with his tender hip.

I draped an extra blanket over Nicky and tiptoed up the stairs on my alpha's heels. The others were already in Hana's room when we arrived, scattered around her space with Gabe perched at her desk, Billie on the foot of her bed, and Tony leaning against the wall.

"I changed my mind about everything," Hana said as I closed the door behind me.

"In a good direction or a bad direction?" Billie asked.

"I want her in," Hana said. " I was ready to tear that fucker's spine out through his nostrils when he made her cry. *Fuck*. Every alpha instinct I've ever possessed wanted me to commit homicide."

Hana didn't get into feral moods like this very often, but there was something about her ferocity that made her absolutely breathtaking. Alphonse was lucky he'd been able to drive away. If she'd have caught him *inside* Nicky's apartment, he probably wouldn't have been able to walk out of it.

While we had taken turns last night getting Nicky settled, Hana had updated us on all of the bullshit Alphonse had pulled. I was only a *little* bit jealous that the entire rest of the pack had gotten to play protector while I had been at the bakery every time this asshole had shown up.

"Do you think she would stay with us?" I asked. "I'd feel better with her here. A gated community offers one extra step of protection. I'm sure her family would take her in a heartbeat; it would probably only be a matter of time before Alphonse found out where she was staying."

Hana crossed her arms, her brow furrowed. "I just hope the cops catch him. He doesn't really have plausible deniability with how good Spud got a slap in."

Gabe rose up from the desk and hooked his arm around Hana's waist, pulling her into a soothing hug. "I'm going to install a motion sensor doorbell with a camera. I'm happy to have Nicky stay with us, and I think a little extra security step will make everyone feel better."

"Ugh! This is so dumb." Billie flopped back onto the bed. "Why can't this asshole just accept a simple 'no' and leave our girl the fuck *alone*?"

"Pretty sure he thinks Nicky is his property," I said. I had been lucky to find Billie and Tony as early as I had, but as a teen, I had run into similar issues with possessive assholes. None of them had gone as far as Alphonse did, but I had heard plenty of stories and knew that there were a lot more steps he could take if you really wanted to. If I had anything to say about it, he wasn't going to get the chance. Nicky had suffered enough.

"So what do we do?" asked Tony.

"I think we should focus mostly on getting her settled," I replied.

Before she'd gone to sleep that morning, I had helped her craft messages to her family and her job so that they were kept in the loop. Her boss had given her the night off, with the evening librarian and one of the day librarians each taking half of her shift.

"We should take her to pick up some clothes in case the forensics team is slow," I said. "We already know that she feels safe here so we just need to make it feel like home. Wherever she ends up staying, I want her to be stocked up on whatever she needs."

The others nodded.

"Okay," said Hana. "If she's up for a shopping trip, I'll take her out, and if not, I'll grab her measurements and pick up some things myself."

I smiled knowingly at her. Alphonse might be good for nothing, but he had tripped the protective side of Hana, and that had tossed her over one of her final hurdles. By the time the danger had passed, she would like Nicky on her own terms.

Alphonse was a braver man than I was. A pissed off Hana is not something I would ever have the courage to face down if she wanted my blood. Luckily, I have never been on the receiving end of her ire.

"I bet she would like it if we picked up some stuff for Spud." I said. "His own cat bed, his favorite treats. We can make it feel like home for her baby, too."

"Jasper, you're a genius," Billie said with a laugh. "You can never go wrong spoiling a girl's cat."

Tony snorted. "Pretty sure that's true for both kinds."

Billie collapsed into giggles.

I checked the time on my phone. "We'll have to get her up soon to make it to the stores before they close."

"I can look up some that are open until nine if we want to let her sleep," offered Gabe.

"Let me go test the waters," I said. "I'll see if she's feeling up to it or if we need to wait a bit."

I left the pack and skipped lightly down the stairs until I hit the main floor where Nicky was curled up and Roscoe had overtaken the spot I had vacated. I dropped down to my knees in front of her and traced my fingertips over her cheek.

"Nicky," I whispered.

She stirred, but she didn't open her eyes.

"Nicky, it's time for breakfast," I whispered again, getting a little bit touchier, and threading my fingers into her hair.

She jolted with a squeak, instantly relaxing when she recognized it was me. "Hey," she murmured.

"How are you feeling?"

"Gross. Exhausted." She sighed and stroked Spud's fur.

"Don't forget Roscoe. He'll feel left out if he doesn't get attention too." I gestured behind her, and she rolled over to pet him and kiss the top of his head.

"Where is everyone?" Nicky asked.

"Just upstairs. We wanted to know if you were feeling up to a quick shopping trip to get you some outfits for the next few days while forensics works through your apartment."

She made a pitiful groan. "No, but I guess I need clothes."

"Hana offered to pick some things out for you if you don't want to go. You're totally welcome to stay here with the rest of us."

Nicky sat up and scratched her head, trying in vain to smooth down her sleep tangles. "I can't let her do that. I'll get up."

She moved slowly but did indeed get herself up. We had put some toiletries into the main floor bathroom for her, and I hung around nearby in case she needed anything. She looked far too cute in her borrowed pajamas.

"You sit with the cats, and I'll let the rest of the pack know that we're ready while you change." I opened up the blackout blinds to let some light in and scampered back up the stairs, returning with the rest of the pack at my heels.

Nicky wasn't feeling up to much eating, but I did coax a slice of toast with peanut butter and strawberry jam into her alongside a glass of milk.

I hadn't anticipated the entire pack going on this shopping trip, but I think we all felt better keeping Nicky in eyesight.

We did our best to make the shopping as smooth as possible, picking out items in the sizes she had given us so all she had to do was try things on and pass us the rejects. I found her the coziest sweaters and pajama sets. She let me tug the cashmere over her head, taking little breaks to snuggle into my arms that had my heart pounding and my purr kicking into gear to soothe her. I couldn't quite describe what it did to me—knowing that she found comfort in me, that I could help her the way I helped the rest of the pack. The others let me take the lead in that regard, ushering Nicky about and letting her cuddle against me with my arm over her shoulder as we walked between stores.

Hana picked out her shoes, and the other alphas got her snacks and drinks, held the bags, and kept anyone from crowding our group. Billie was a ninja with paying, leaping up to the cash register with anything Nicky had agreed to buy and having it bagged up and ready to go by the time Nicky emerged from a changing room. She had exhibited mild distress after finding out Billie had bought everything for her, but our beta could be persuasive, and Billie had worked Nicky around to accepting all of the clothing purchases in exchange for a cup of frozen yogurt.

With all her clothes picked out, we made a couple stops to pick up all of her toiletries she'd need before swinging by the pet store where we got some extra toys, two new cat beds, a new carrier, and a half dozen packages of Spud's favorite treats. If Nicky had been in a better state of mind, she probably would've put up a lot more fuss over everything we convinced her to buy, but the stress made her malleable, and we were able to successfully get her everything she needed without too much trouble.

"Nicky," I said as we stood in line to get some crêpes. "Would you like to invite your family over for dinner? It doesn't have to be today. That would be cutting it a little bit close, but maybe tomorrow? I bet they would feel better seeing you."

301

She looked up at me, her big brown eyes slightly red rimmed. "I'd love that, thank you."

"Good. We'll handle everything. You're just in charge of passing along the information."

We spent the rest of the evening making sure that Nicky was as comfortable as possible. Prior to her abrupt arrival, we had been discussing potentially converting the playroom upstairs into another bedroom rather than have her options be sleeping with one of us or staying all the way in the basement by herself. That was still in the works, but it would take some time to transition all of the equipment downstairs and get it set up as a real bedroom. And also, no one wanted her to feel pressured over the fact that we were putting in a bedroom with her in mind.

I had always been the sort of person where I liked someone or I didn't. First impressions went a long way with me, and no one had ever recovered from a terrible first one in the same way that no one had ever really managed to pull the wool over my eyes since I had grown into an adult. Maybe it was naïve of me to assume that my feelings for Nicky would never change for the worse, but planning to have her included in my future made me feel better.

When Tony had asked if I wanted her to be part of my heat, that had only cemented it for me. I could've easily gone through a heat without her, with the support of my existing pack, but my instincts had chimed up at the question.

I wanted her to be there.

I wanted her to be part of us.

Hana flipping her switch the way she had was a relief. I couldn't argue with omega instincts in much the same way you couldn't argue with a heart. Both wanted Nicky, and with Hana slipping down that slope with the rest of us, I could let both imagine what the future might hold.

I couldn't wait for Nicky to feel safe enough that she would be able to imagine it, too.

Chapter Thirty–Six
Nicky

The one plus about stress was that it tended to override my self-consciousness.

My parents were going to meet the pack.

Last week that might've sent me into a tizzy, but today I couldn't be bothered with what they might think.

Sidney and Allie were the first to arrive. My sister-in-law tackled me into a hug, my brother following closely. He wrapped us both in his arms. I wasn't quite as weepy as yesterday, and when I pushed down the swell of tears, they actually cooperated and stayed down.

My brother moved along the line of the pack, shaking hands with everyone and getting introduced to the three he hadn't yet met. Allie followed suit, and by the time she had made it down the line herself, my parents and youngest brother had arrived.

Mom squeezed me so tightly my back popped and I wheezed

at the squish of air from my lungs. Dad hugged me too, equally as tight, and kissed my cheek.

Luca weaseled his way in for his own hug. "I'm glad you're safe," he whispered in my ear. "This place is crazy fancy. What if I break something?"

That drew a laugh out of me. "You'll be fine."

I turned to my parents. "Mom, Dad, this is the pack that I'm dating. You already know Jasper and Gabe." I gestured to them and then to the rest of the line. "This is Tony, Hana, and Billie."

Mom's gaze flickered over them and back to me with wide eyes. "*All* of them? Nicola, that's so many."

"What she means," said Dad, lightly elbowing Mom, "is that she's very pleased so many people have taken an interest in making our daughter happy."

Oh, thank god.

At least one of them was going to be cool about this.

Dad attached himself immediately to Gabe, who seemed to hastily look up information on whatever soccer game my Dad had just mentioned to him.

"You look familiar." Mom eyed up Hana for a moment, and realization lit up her eyes. "You taught that wonderful fitness class I attended a couple of months ago with some friends from our neighborhood!"

Hana took that as her cue and engaged my mother in conversation while the pack led everyone into the dining room to sit at their massive table. Mom seemed happy enough, which was a huge relief that she had something to focus on besides me, and having someone she already knew would hopefully help her adjust to the whole idea.

I sat between my dad and Allie, the pack across from us, with Luca next to Jasper, where my brother was busy asking about the recipe for buns Jasper had used for tonight.

The pack had produced quite the spread. I'd made tiramisu under Jasper's guidance while the others had put together a charcuterie board, a tray of eggplant Parm, orzo pasta salad, jazzed up lettuce salad with orange segments and toasted almonds, and a roasted pork loin.

"Do all of you cook?" asked Mom as her initial conversation with Hana lulled, and she took in all the food laid out.

"With varying skill levels," said Gabe. "We usually take turns, but tonight was a team effort."

"Who cleans?" Mom looked around, probably noticing the lack of dust bunnies and gleam of the surfaces.

"We have a service that comes by twice a month for regular cleans and every quarter for deep cleans," said Billie. "Otherwise, we're all in charge of keeping our own spaces tidy."

Mom grilled them on their jobs and hobbies and the history of the pack. I could tell by the tiny smiles she kept hiding that Mom was impressed, not only by their fabulous home but also by the warmth that they offered. When she asked after Billie's parents and that particular story came out, I thought Mom was going to climb over the table to hug Billie. Mom had always metaphorically adopted our friends growing up if they didn't have a great home life, and it was nice to see that compulsion hadn't faded.

As we filled our plates with the main events, Dad set his hand on my wrist. "Nicola, have you heard anything from the police yet?"

"No, not yet. I don't know if that's a good or bad sign."

"Forensics is scheduled to come in tomorrow," said Hana. "We should hopefully get an update after that."

"You're sure you don't want to come home, Patatina?" Mom asked. "We're more than happy to have you."

"I like it here," I said. "Plus, Alphonse knows where you live already."

"You're welcome to stay with us if you ever need to," Sidney offered.

Allie nodded her head. "Anytime. We'd love to have you."

I didn't really *want* to leave the pack house, but I couldn't depend on them just always wanting me around. At some point it would probably be a good idea to find a new apartment. The lease on my current place would be up next month, so I didn't have to renew.

"If this stuff with Alphonse drags on I could stay with you."

Guilt swelled instantly in my belly at the crestfallen expressions that swept over the pack. At least that made it clear that they wanted me to stay. For now, anyway. They had all said as much, but saying and feeling weren't the same things.

It was at least relieving to know that I had places to go. I certainly wasn't keen on going back to my apartment, even when forensics had finished up with it. Alphonse had gotten in once, and he could get in again. It would be better all around if I simply took everyone up on their offers to stay, let my lease end, and find a new apartment.

The rest of dinner went pretty well. The pack was good at charming people, and even with her initial reservations, Mom was all smiles by the time the meal ended.

My family was given a tour of most of the house, minus the private spaces. Allie walked with her arm hooked through mine during the tour, whispering a commentary of how cute the pack house was and how lucky I was to get to stay there. Roscoe became the biggest hit of the tour when the floof deigned to bless us with his presence after we had invaded his nap space in the basement. That spurred the whole conversation about animal rescue, since Roscoe had been a foster fail and Sidney worked with a dog rescue on occasion to foster orphan litters.

Luca hung back with Jasper for most of the tour, walking behind the group. I overheard Luca peppering Jasper with questions about his bakery. I'd missed out on a lot of things with Luca since moving out. We were seven years apart, which was a lot when one party was going off to college while the other had barely hit puberty. If he wanted to make a friend out of Jasper, then I was certainly not going to dissuade it.

Mom sidled up to me while we were showing everyone in the backyard. "Patatina, they seem like lovely people."

I didn't *need* her approval, but it certainly made me feel better to have it. "They are. I'm glad you like them."

Mom nodded. "All of your struggles with Alphonse are my fault. I'm so sorry my dear. I'll never speak to him again unless it's to give him a piece of my mind."

"You didn't know," I said. "If I had been a little less tightlipped about everything, then we could've avoided all of this."

"Well, in any case, I'm very sorry. I'm glad you have a safe place to stay with people who are kind to you. I don't pretend to understand how betas fit into packs. It's certainly not something I would've ever pursued for myself, but their other beta seems happy, and you seem happy too. That's the most important thing to me."

"I appreciate that, Mom."

Mom nodded again. "You can bring whoever you like to family dinner. I can't promise I'll do everything right, but I can promise to try."

I kissed her cheek with a wistful sigh. "That's all I can ask."

It was full dark by the time my family departed for the evening, and I felt a lot lighter.

Hana approached me, her fingers fidgeting. "Nicky, I'd like to teach you how to fight."

Chapter Thirty-Seven
Nicky

This was a terrible idea. My limbs weighed a million pounds, and my sweaty hair clung to my face.

"You're doing very well, Nicky," Hana crooned.

"Doesn't feel like I am," I said, gasping even as I ate up the praise. I hadn't landed a single hit, but I'm not sure that I expected to during all of this.

"Do you think it would help if you had more of a visual aid?"

"I don't know, maybe?"

Hana nodded decisively and tapped away on her phone. A few minutes later, Gabe came down the stairs into the basement where we were practicing, dressed in some sweat shorts and a tank top. My brain tripped happily. It was honestly unfair how gorgeous he was.

"Your model has arrived, ladies." He grinned and took his position in the middle of the mats.

"Nicky," Hana said, "don't worry about Gabe. He's had plenty of experience with being thrown to mats by me."

Gabe winked at me, and even though I was already sweating, I was still far too aware of the heating of my cheeks.

"Okay," Hana said, "Gabe come at me."

A flare of adrenaline licked up my spine as Gabe charged her. He was met with her dropping down and hefting him by the legs straight over her head. Gabe recovered quickly, and she blocked some of his blows, sidestepping the others. I held my breath as she advanced on him, and then he was the one who had to try to block and avoid.

She caught him in some whip-fast maneuver, and he ended up flat on his back again with her knees on each side of his chest and her hands bracing down his wrists. His body heaved beneath her, and they rolled. Even when he managed to get on top and pin her, it lasted only a couple of seconds before she used some kind of witchcraft to get herself back on top and flip him over, firmly pinning him with a knee to his spine and his arm wrenched behind him.

"Holy shit," I whispered.

That was *way* hotter than it had any right to be.

Hana let him up, and Gabe gave me a cheeky grin from his place sitting on the mats.

"You'll be able to do the same with some significant training," said Hana. "But to start with, we're going to work through the basics that will do the most damage and give you the most time to escape. The main thing you want in a fight that's not planned is to get away from your attacker. You don't want to give anyone a chance to get their hands on you, okay? If it comes down to it, you want to deliver some fast hits to key areas, and then I want you to run. Come on over here."

I committed her words to memory and crossed the mats to stand in front of the two of them, Gabe climbing to his feet.

"There are several important points to aim for," Hana explained. "Alphonse and Gabe have the same basic structures, so you're going to want to hit here, here, and here," Hana said,

309

pointing to Gabe's nose, stomach, and crotch. "Other good spots are the eyes and throat. Ultimately, anything tender or a little more delicate is going to be where you want to hit. I'm hoping if we can get some good practice, then your brain will link back to that instead of panicking if an actual situation occurs."

Hana showed me how to move, alternating between use of small weapons like car keys and application of certain techniques: how to hit with the most force, how to strike with the heel of my hand, and how to kick without knocking myself off balance.

"You really think he's going to attack me?" I asked.

"Hard to say." She shrugged. "But I would rather this be training that you have and not need than training that you need and don't have if it ever comes down to that."

"Okay, that's fair."

I didn't think my anxiety levels could handle him actually turning violent towards me.

"Now, come over here," Hana ordered and tapped her toes on a spot in front of Gabe. She stood directly behind me, moving her hands down my arms to adjust mine into the proper position, moving me slowly through a strike, repeating to each of the vulnerable points on Gabe's body. We did that three times for each while I struggled to force down the rebellious thoughts that popped up from being entirely surrounded by two rather alluring alphas.

"Good," said Hana. "Now do each of them yourself in slow motion so I can do corrections."

I followed the instructions, doing my best to move exactly like she had shown me. She tweaked my positioning and made me go through the motions until she was satisfied and I was about ready to keel over.

When she finally called for a pause and passed me a bottle of water, I almost wept with joy.

"You've got a good grasp of things," said Gabe. "There's a lot to learn with all of this, and it does take time, but at least with some foundations you have a better chance if anything comes up.

Take a couple more breaths, and then I want you to come at me with proper speed."

I suppressed a whine and set my water aside, shaking out my limbs. Gabe's hazel eyes watched me intently, and he reacted the second that I moved, blocking every blow with ease and grabbing my wrist on the final one to pull me off-balance. He caught me before I face planted.

"That's a good point," said Hana. I wasn't sure what point she meant, so I waited for her to continue. "Tomorrow we'll work on grappling. If someone gets you down on the floor, I want you to be able to fight your way out."

"Assuming I can move tomorrow," I said with a laugh.

"We'll make it work as best we can," she replied. "I'm not expecting you to win fighting competitions, I just want to get you to the point that you can land a punch."

"I'll do my best," I promised. "How much longer are we doing this?"

"You can be done right now, or you can do one more set and try to hit me."

I huffed, pretty sure that going after Hana would end even worse than going after Gabe, but I didn't want her to think I was copping out. I fell into position and did three quick strikes, each of which she blocked. On the fourth she caught my wrist like Gabe had, but instead of unbalancing me, she used it to spin me and trap me against her chest.

Heat burned through my body for a whole different reason than exertion.

"Good job, Nicky," Hana said in my ear.

"But I didn't land a single hit."

I ate up the praise anyway.

"Effort still gets rewarded." Hana purred and gave me a squeeze. "Let's get you showered, and then we can sit in the hot tub. I'll give you a massage before bed if you'd like."

I pushed that particular thought aside, and as soon as she let me go, I disappeared into the showers next to the gym. It was an open situation, and I kept my gaze firmly planted in the wall in front of me while Hana and Gabe stripped down and joined me. I washed up quickly and wrapped myself in one of the giant fluffy towels that were available. It was only then I remembered I hadn't brought a bathing suit down.

"Give me a minute and I'll run and grab my swimsuit from the new things we bought."

"You don't have to if you don't want," said Hana. "None of the neighbors have any view of the hot tub, and it wouldn't be the first time it's had people in it without suits."

My cheeks burned. "Are you two going to wear suits?"

I scanned them, both alphas wrapped in the same fluffy towels that I was.

"If you want us to, we will," replied Gabe.

It seemed almost a little silly to ask for Gabe to put on the suit when I had definitely seen everything he had to offer already. I hadn't with Hana, but she didn't strike me as the demure and modest type.

I'd had four new people get up in my business in the last month, so maybe *I* wasn't the demure and modest type either. "No suits is fine."

The three of us went out the doors of the walkout basement, got the hot tub cover off, and set the jets to bubbling. Gabe moved one of the chairs over for us to drape our towels on for easy access to get out, and I held my breath as I dropped mine down to slip into the water.

One part of my brain demanded I stare at the sky as they slid in, and all the other parts demanded that I ogle. In reality, they both moved so fast that I barely got a glimpse.

Hana settled in with a happy sigh. "Nothing like a good soak after a workout."

I swished my fingers through the eddying water. "Thank you for trying to teach me how to fight. I'm sorry I'm not better at it."

Hana waved me off. "We all start somewhere."

"Did you know," Gabe said, "that Hana used to participate in underground fights?"

"I did *not*! That sounds dangerous." And sexy.

The image of a hot, sweaty Hana obliterating her competition was really doing something for me.

"Oh it was," said Hana. "But it did pay for school and all my groceries for a while."

"I wish I could've seen it."

"I'm pretty sure we have some terrible quality video of it somewhere. I could dig it out for you."

The thought of watching Hana fight made me squirmy. "If it's not too much trouble."

"Come here," said Hana.

I scooted closer, swallowing hard as I settled myself next to her. She shuffled me around and dug her fingers into the muscles of my shoulders.

"Oh god," I groaned.

Hana found every knot and then ruthlessly demanded its eviction while I wriggled and whimpered, breathing hard as she brought my rebellious body to heel. When she paused, I slumped and basked in the relief.

"How are your legs?" she asked.

"A little stiff, but not too bad," I answered.

"I'll stretch you out a bit once we get back inside." She set a palm on my knee. "Do you mind if I check for knots here?"

"I've never noticed any in my thighs before. Go ahead."

Permission was a mistake.

She found knots almost immediately, and I hit her in the face with one of my boobs when I jolted forward, hands plunging into the water to protect the tender spot.

Hana laughed. "Sorry, was that too hard?"

"Wee bit," I said, panting, cheeks flushed with heat.

Gabe slid over to me. "Would you like a distraction while she tenderizes you?"

"Distraction sounds good."

He slid right beneath me and settled me on his lap. "Just breathe. I'll keep you from flailing."

One of his arms locked around my waist, and his other palm laid over my throat, tilting me back to rest my head on his shoulder. I tensed when Hana put her hands back on me, but melted just as quickly as Gabe's thumb rubbed softly on my throat while he murmured soft praise in my ear.

Hana worked her way down my legs, and my squirming had Gabe's cock rising to attention, tapping at me as my lap kept it trapped. My skin felt like it was buzzing, and I kept my bottom lip snared between my teeth to stop any wayward moans.

It was the strangest mix of a satisfying, productive pain with a firm embrace, whispered praise, and a hint of promise. My hips rocked against him, and his hissing breath in my ear only made me hotter. Hana worked back up my legs, and my thighs parted of their own volition, letting Gabe's cock spring up between them.

Hana laid her hand over my stomach. "Nicky, do you want to tell me what's going on in that head right now?"

I sucked in a breath. "Nope, not really. There's nothing good going on in there."

Gabe chuckled in my ear.

"Would you like me to tell you what's going on in mine?" Hana asked.

I perked my head up, Gabe's grip on my throat relinquishing. "Maybe..."

"I was thinking how proud I am of you." She traced delicious patterns on my skin and then her fingers wrapped around my ankle. "I was also thinking that I wonder if you make all of those delightful sounds in bed, too, or only when I'm hurting you."

I squeaked.

"What would you say the answer is?"

I squirmed in Gabe's lap.

"I can answer that question," said Gabe.

God. I was so fucking doomed between the two of them.

"I'd rather Nicky tell me, but I can certainly venture a guess," Hana said.

I swallowed hard. "They might be something you could recreate with some more pleasant attention."

"I thought so." Hana gave me a mischievous smile. "What are the odds of that happening?"

Was she...asking about the possibility of sex? I'd had more conversations about this in the last month than I'd had my entire life, and I still wasn't used to it.

"Um, they're pretty high, I'd say."

"And how would you feel if I kissed you right now?"

A pathetic keening whine was the most coherent answer I could offer.

Gabe's fingers traced my throat. "Use your words, Nicky."

These people and their goddamn words. My brain wasn't equipped to process vocalizations during times like this.

I nodded, hoping that would be accepted.

Hana's low growl set off fireworks in my belly. "What did Gabe just tell you?"

"You can kiss me," I squeaked out.

"Good girl," Gabe whispered in my ear. Goosebumps burst over my skin.

I froze as Hana glided through the water toward me. She cupped my cheek and brought those perfect plump lips to mine, a soft sweep to start before turning ferocious at the first sign of my acceptance.

I had thought that I knew what it meant to experience a devouring kiss, but apparently my previous experiences had fallen short. Hana seemed intent on consuming my soul through this kiss, and it lit up every nerve in my body, set my clit to throbbing, and put my heart to a rhythm that felt more buzz than beat.

When she pulled away, it took my brain a few moments to catch up. I was breathless and incoherent, held up only by Gabe.

"How far do you want me to go, Nicky?" Hana asked.

The wild part of me that had been through multiple carnal revelations wanted to see this through to the end right now, but I didn't want to pressure her.

"How far do *you* want to go?" I asked her.

Hana let out a low laugh. "Little beta, I could devour you right now, make you come so many times you forget your own name. But, like I told you in the past, I don't want to scare you, so

315

if you need to hit the brakes or give me an end point, now is the time."

How the fuck was I supposed to say no to a statement like that?

Maybe I *wanted* to forget my own name.

Maybe I was just curious enough to let her do anything she desired.

Chapter Thirty-Eight
Nicky

"No brakes. At least not yet. I know my colors."

The absolute glee in Hana's eyes almost made me rescind my statement, but I was far too curious to stop now.

Hana's fingers walked up my leg extra slow, presumably to give me time to decide if I was okay with it. I wiggled on Gabe's lap, and when her hand reached my thigh, she diverted under the water to take his cock in her grip. The movement of her sliding over it brushed between my thighs, and both he and I groaned.

She tipped her head and laid her teeth over my scent gland, biting down.

A breathy *'fuck'* left my mouth. Gabe licked over the other side of my throat and I nearly came in his grip when he bit down there too, pleasure skittering over my skin and focusing down to my throbbing cunt.

I bucked hard in his lap. His cock brushed against me, and I almost lost it all over again when Hana's fingers dipped into the water and tapped quick beats over my clit. I shuddered and writhed between them.

"Have you taken a full alpha cock yet, little beta?" Hana asked.

"N-No, not yet."

Hana purred and rubbed her cheek against mine. "I'll have to train you in that too."

"How?" My brain was rapidly losing its ability to formulate complex thoughts.

Gabe's teeth danced over my skin again, and I gasped.

"We have our ways," said Hana. "You have to be a very good girl for them though."

Gabe chuckled. "It's fun to say isn't it?"

"Oh yes." Hana laughed. "I very much enjoy having a good girl to apply the phrase to."

Her fingers ceased their tapping and moved to a slow glide that had me restless and moaning. She circled my entrance but never dipped inside, and when I gave a desperate whine and tried to rock my hips against her hand, that only made her laugh again.

"She's going to make you beg," Gabe said in my ear. "And when you give in, she'll give you more than you think you can handle."

I shivered head to toe at the prospect. If anyone could take me apart in body and mind, it would be these two.

Hana devoured my mouth again until I was dizzy and playfully nipped my bottom lip. "You don't have to beg just yet, princess. I'm a patient soul."

Gabe's chuckle had goosebumps rising over my skin. "She is in some ways, but I've seen how she's been watching you."

"Nicky," Hana said, kissing my cheek, "how much do you want our beautiful alpha to fuck you tonight?"

A whole heck of a lot.

"My whole body feels like a bowl of Jell-O. I want it, but there's no way I can give as good as I'm getting."

A dark look passed over Hana's eyes. She traced my cheeks,

her purr rumbling. "I certainly have some ways around that if you're interested."

I nodded like a bobble head. "I'm open to suggestions."

She kissed me again and dug her fingers into the back of my neck. "I'm going to go upstairs and get some supplies. If you change your mind while I'm gone, just tell Gabe. And if you want to continue, then I want you to kneel on those mats without a stitch of clothing and face the mirrors. Okay?"

My face was on fire at her statement. I nodded anyway.

Hana hopped out of the hot tub naked as a spring day and disappeared into the house. That left me alone with Gabe.

"How are you feeling, Nicky?"

"So needy I might die." I laughed. "And more than a bit intimidated."

"Hana can be a lot, but she's a good listener, and she pays attention," he assured me. "Let's get you rinsed off and into position."

He briefly showered me off, and I let him dry me off, too. At the sound of Hana on the stairs, I sank to my knees in front of the mirrors just like she had told me. I wasn't in the habit of examining my body too closely, but I couldn't help myself as I waited for her, noting the little rolls of my tummy and droop of my breasts outside the confines of a bra. The only time I ever really struggled with it was when I was in a changing room trying to find something to accommodate my waist-to-hip ratio. My body did the jobs I needed it to, for the most part, and I loved it. I only hoped it was up to whatever tasks Hana was planning for me.

I could clearly see Gabe behind me, just as naked as me, with his cock standing proudly. I hadn't yet had the privilege of getting it inside me, but it seemed like tonight that was going to change.

I looked curiously at what Hana carried in her arms, but I couldn't quite discern what anything was from this distance.

"There's my good girl," she crooned. "Exactly where she's supposed to be. How do you feel about being tied up a little?"

The idea sent a thrill through me.

319

"Tony did a little bit with scarves at my apartment. I'm open to trying it again."

"Good," Hana purred. She set everything down next to me and held up a pair of leather cuffs. "Arms behind your back."

I switched position, holding my breath as she wrapped the leather around each wrist and hooked them together.

"What color is a collar?" She held up a slim piece of black leather with studs and 'O' rings.

"Green?"

She nodded and fastened the leather around my throat. The insides of both the cuffs and collar were soft and fuzzy, comfortable in a way I hadn't expected. I shivered as she hooked a chain through a ring at the back of the collar and let it hang down my back as she maneuvered my wrists so that my elbows were at right angles with one wrist on top of the other. She hooked the chain onto the cuffs, and I quickly found that, if I let my arms drop, they pulled down the collar. Not uncomfortably so, at least not immediately, and I made a mental note to stay as still as possible.

Hana held up two little devices with bells hanging from the ends that I didn't recognize.

"What are those?"

"Nipple clamps!" she said cheerfully.

My face burst into flames at her explanation.

"These ones are adjustable so you can have them as snug as you like. I'm going to put them on you now."

I swallowed hard. "Okay."

My breathing shifted from relatively calm to outright panting as she cupped one breast and fed the nipple into her mouth, teasing it to pertness with her tongue while I let out an embarrassing litany of moans. Hana's eyes glittered as she raised her head and put one of the clamps to my nipple.

"You let me know at what point it shifts to pain," she ordered.

Staying still was a lot more difficult than I had anticipated. Every inch of me shook with the effort, and fire arced from my nipple down to my clit as Hana let the clamp close around me.

"Pause," I gasped out.

320

Hana kissed me briefly. "Good girl." She adjusted some spinning piece that held it exactly where I had said stop. The little bell jingled joyfully.

She focused on my other breast, and although that nipple was already perfectly at attention, she still swirled over it with her tongue until I was squeezing my thighs together. The clamp went on in the same manner as the first, and I squeaked out a stop when it became fractionally too much. Hana adjusted accordingly and then sat back to survey me.

The bells jingled with every breath. I focused back on Gabe's reflection and found him lazily stroking his cock as he watched the two of us.

Next Hana laid out a thick plank of plastic.

"What's that for?" I asked, just barely keeping it together.

"This." She picked up a reasonably large dildo from the pile with a suction cup base and slammed it down onto the plastic so it stood upright. It was only marginally smaller than the alpha at my back.

"Oh god."

"That's what you'll be saying once I get you on it." Hana grinned and fetched the lube bottle she had brought with her, squeezing some down onto the shaft. She spread it around and reached towards the crux of my thighs. "Open."

I inched my knees further apart and groaned as she thrust her fingers into my slick center, leaning close so that she could bite my throat again above the collar. My body trembled. Soft curses tumbled from my lips, and I cried out a little when she withdrew her hand.

My groan pitched into a whine when she slipped those fingers into her mouth and licked each of them clean.

"I'd say you're wet enough. Let's get you on this temporary cock." She patted my ass cheek. "Up."

I did my best to obey, and she slotted the tip of it against my entrance.

"Down when you're ready."

I rocked my hips to ease it into me. I took my time even

321

though my legs shook to do so. Every inch had me mewling, and by the time I had gotten as far as I could go, I was out of breath.

"What color are we at?" Hana asked.

"G-Green," I gasped.

"Good girl. I'm going to overwhelm you a little." Hana flicked each of the dangling bells. "Maybe a lot, but I think you can take it."

I wasn't entirely sure what exactly she meant, but I wasn't about to complain.

Hana held up a bulb with a flared base. "We're going to see about getting us into your ass. Lean forward for me."

I tipped forward, but my exhausted muscles were not enjoying keeping me upright. "Help?"

"Since you're being so good, I suppose we could let Gabe assist."

Hana crooked a finger, and Gabe followed. He kneeled down in front of me and took the brunt of my weight. Cold lube dripped between my cheeks, and Hana rolled the toy in it before pressing the tip to my asshole.

"Remember your colors," she said quietly, pushing it in. I wiggled around pitifully, and Gabe stroked a soothing hand down my back. The bulb wasn't particularly large though still bigger than the thumb Tony had put in me. When it slipped through the rings of muscle with a *pop*, I relaxed instantly. Hana pushed against it once, sharply, and the whole thing started to buzz. I yelped and settled into a moan.

"Now all I can think about," said Hana, "is watching you get dicked down in both holes."

I let out a breathy laugh. "Not the first time I've thought about that happening."

"Then that's something we'll work on in your training. Now, I want you to fuck yourself on this dildo until it has an easy glide, and then I'm going to watch Gabe's cock disappear inside of you."

I shivered. Gabe helped me raise myself up and sink down again. I focused on relaxing until the movements were fluid and the only noise around us was my sharp breaths and the sound of my cunt being used. Being able to see myself, on top of being watched and bound, made everything exponentially hotter. It felt oddly voyeuristic to see the toy slide into me, to see the sway of my breasts and the furrow in my brow as I concentrated on staying upright. When I rose back up again, Hana sat her palm on my stomach and stopped me. She slid the plank away.

"Gabe, it's your turn," Hana said with a grin.

He stretched out on the mat next to me, and it took all of my strength, with Hana's help to balance, to get a knee on each side of his hips.

"I don't think I'm strong enough to be on top right now," I murmured, limbs shaking.

"Don't you worry about a thing, princess," Hana crooned. "We'll take care of everything."

Gabe set a gentle hand on each of my hips, and Hana lined up his cock for me just as she had done with the dildo, nipping at my earlobe as I lowered myself down.

"Sweet fuck. You're so tight," Gabe hissed.

I didn't point out that pretty much any cunt, except an omega in heat, would probably feel tight to an alpha cock. I'd made it about three-quarters of the way down when I had to tap out.

"Good job, princess." Hana bit my shoulder. "Now the real fun begins."

I was almost worried as to what that could mean, considering I was already trussed up and sitting on alpha dick. Hana brought over a white wand that buzzed ominously. Then she got on her knees behind me and grabbed my chin, setting her chin over my shoulder. The bright mint of her scent enlivened me, pulling me from the haze where my mind happily retreated with all of the physical sensations warring for attention.

"Look how fucking perfect you are," Hana said. "Watch."

She pressed her hips flush together with mine and brought the wand to my clit.

I didn't quite recognize the sound I made. Entirely helpless with nowhere to wiggle away, I was caught in a torrent as my cunt

323

squeezed Gabe, my ass squeezed the bulb, and too-intense plea-sure rippled out from my clit to the rest of my body with all the force of a hurricane. I was lost in seconds and faced with my slack-jawed expression as the orgasm dragged me under.

"We're going to show you what it's like to play with alphas," Hana whispered in my ear.

She gave me a second of reprieve, in which Gabe fucked up in to me and I choked out a cry. Then the wand was back against my clit. Hana braced her hips beneath my ass and used her own leverage to raise me up and press me back down on Gabe's cock. The movement of it stole the breath from my lungs. Between the vibrating bulb in my ass that she nudged with a thrust, Gabe's cock stretching me to the limit, and the wand dragging me up the sharp, steep slope of pleasure, I was entirely done for. The orgasms hit me back-to-back.

Hana and I rode him as one. She maneuvered the bulk of my weight and used her powerful hips to lift me with every thrust, keeping her arm wrapped firmly around my waist while the other held the wand, unrelenting. The bells on my nipples added to the music of our bodies. Gabe's hands wandered over my skin, a finger hooking through the other 'O' ring on my collar. My gaze flickered wildly between my own reflection, where Hana watched me with a gorgeous smirk, and Gabe's hazel eyes, which were ready to burn right into my soul.

Pleasure seared through me, my cunt pulsing around Gabe until I could scarcely breathe. We didn't stop. Hana kept me moving through it all until I'd come almost a dozen more times like that, convulsing in her arms as I screamed.

When I finally begged for rest, she held me in place, and Gabe took over fucking up in to me from below with bruising hands on my hips. Hana held me at just the right height so I could experi-ence as much of him as possible, but high enough that he didn't have to control the depth of his thrusts.

"Please, please," I begged. "I can't take another."

"One more for luck," Hana breathed into my ear. "We can't leave you with thirteen."

Every cell in my body was a live wire.

The wand tipped me over the edge again, and I barely had the energy to cry out as my pussy clamped down on Gabe once more. This time, Hana finally did let the wand fall to the wayside. She tipped me forward to let my weight melt against his chest and nudged me up so that my face was tucked against his throat. Rich tea and sweet brown sugar saturated every inhale. I huffed him like a drug and sucked at his scent gland.

I could see in the mirror that she sank down on him herself, taking the wand to her own clit as she fucked him with a strength that I was almost afraid to eventually have turned on me directly. Gabe's body tensed the same time she cried out, the two of them coming together while I laid in a limp heap on top of him.

While I floated in a haze of endorphins, Hana pulled the bulb from up my ass, undid the cuffs and collar, and rolled me onto the mats on my back.

"Color?"

My brain moved like molasses in winter. "Sleepy green."

Hana chuckled. "Let's get you to bed then."

I was barely coherent as they gathered me up and wiped me down, brushed my hair, and bundled me into bed. I fell asleep sandwiched between the two of them, and as I tried to gather my thoughts, I realized that Hana was pretty close to her claim of making me forget my own name.

Chapter Thirty-Nine
Hana

Nicky slept for a solid eleven hours after her first playtime with Gabe and I. She was still snoozing when he had to get up and leave for work, waking only briefly to accept a quick kiss then falling back asleep again immediately. I had taken the opportunity to grab a few snacks and some water, slipping back into bed with Nicky before Gabe left. I sat there for nearly three hours until she stirred, which was not all that thrilling, but I certainly wasn't going to let her wake up alone after all of that.

She wiggled next to me and stretched with the groan, burying her face against the pillow.

"Rough night?" I teased, setting a palm on her head.

She bolted upright with wide eyes. "Okay, I guess my very intense dream was actually real." Nicky dropped her face into the pillow, and I could hear her muffled laughter.

"Very real," I replied.

Nicky lifted her head and glanced around. "Where's Gabe?"

"He already had to leave for work. He woke you up for a goodbye, but I don't think you fully made it to the waking world."

"I guess not." She pouted adorably.

She inched a little closer, so I patted my lap. Nicky squirmed across the remaining distance and laid her head on my thighs, draping her arm around my waist.

"How are you feeling?" I asked.

Her proximity made me worry less that she had regrets. I would give her whatever attention she needed to make sure that she was comfortable.

"I feel a little bit like I've been hit by a truck. But also still a little bit blissed."

I smiled down at her. "That happens. I'll give you another bath, and I'll do a much nicer massage for you once you've eaten."

Nicky sighed and nestled her face against the blankets draped over me. "I don't think I can move."

"Lucky for you, I planned ahead. Come sit yourself on my lap."

Nicky moaned and groaned at the movement, but she did as I asked, sprawling her legs over me, tucking her forehead against the curve of my throat, and accepting the bottle of water I held out.

"Drink up. I grabbed a couple of tangerines to tide you over."

We settled into the quiet intimacy. I peeled the tangerines for her and passed her segments that she ate in between sips of water. I had gotten used to caring for the pack after intensive playtime, though each of them tended to require different things. Nicky was obviously a cuddler, and that was something easy I could provide for her. Since it was our first play time, I would keep an eye on her for most of the day, doting on her and trying to keep her stress as low as possible.

We stayed in our little bubble of peace until her hunger overrode what the tangerines could assuage.

"I'm not sure who's home right now or if there's any meals in progress," I said, "but I'll see what I can rustle up for you."

"Am I allowed to help yet?" Nicky asked.

"Getting there," I promised. "But not today. Your orders are to rest. I'm sure you could convince the cats to give you a nice cuddle while I get us some breakfast."

I carried Nicky upstairs like the limp noodle princess that she was, wrapped only in a blanket. Billie and Tony were snuggling in the couch nest, so I deposited Nicky between them.

Tony pulled me in for a kiss on my way to the kitchen. "You look well-rested," he commented.

"I had a stimulating evening," I replied.

"I'm glad." His fingers cupped my cheek, sliding through my hair. "It looks like Nicky had a good time, too."

Our beta snuggled into him sleepily.

Billie grinned up at me like the cat that caught the canary. "Welcome to Team Nicky."

I snorted, but couldn't quite keep the smile off my face. "Are you two hungry?"

"Nope, we ate already," said Billie.

I left the three of them together and went to the kitchen. As I flipped bacon in the pan, I let myself sink into my feelings. A lot had happened that would normally have pushed me to the edge of my tolerance, but my own struggles with change were shoved aside to accommodate crisis mode. The initial height of the crisis had passed, leaving a lot of space for Nicky to settle into the gaps and giving me a distraction while feeding my deepest desires. She'd been so perfect coming apart for me. So trusting.

I set the bacon onto a plate with a paper towel and poured the scrambled eggs in next, stirring absently. Nicky brought a different dynamic to our lives. In a good way. She was soft and sweet, ready to melt, eager to please, and exquisite in a way I couldn't quite describe. I didn't know how things would go in the future. All I knew was that I didn't want to give her back when this was all over.

Adding some toast and sliced apples to the plates along with the eggs and bacon, I returned to the couch nest to provide my new lover with sustenance.

Tony wiggled over to make space for me, and I settled next to Nicky so I could feed her bites while she half-watched the interior design show they had on the TV.

I had almost forgotten the simple pleasure of a partner who slipped into the adorable *'take care of me'* mode after I had completely ruined them. The others of the pack were more resilient at this point, though I made sure they still got special attention. Nicky reveled in it. She was like a little baby bird as I fed her, and she didn't protest one bit over all three of us snuggling up to her.

It was a break that we all needed with the stress of her asshole ex. Here she was safe. Here we could take care of her. And I was just grateful that she didn't seem bothered by us wanting to do so.

After she finished eating, I fetched the massage table to fulfill my promise to her. She stretched out with a sigh.

"This isn't going to hurt, is it?"

"Only a little. I won't be digging deep on anything."

I squirted some oil onto her skin and spread it around, taking my time to coat every inch of her that I could reach. She made the most delighted sounds as I gently stretched her and very lightly worked her muscles until she was limp and pliable.

"Me next?" Billie asked, watching us over the edge of the nest.

"How could I ever say no to you?"

Billie laughed. "You say no to me all the time. But I will definitely take advantage of Nicky putting you in a good mood."

I rolled my eyes and waved Tony over to gather up our limp princess. She went without protest and snuggled back up in the nest in his arms while Billie stretched out on the massage table in her stead.

"Did you three have fun?" Billie asked, gaze gleaming with excitement.

"Yep."

"Do I get to know what kind of shenanigans went on?"

"Nope."

"No fair," Billie whined. "I want in on hot pack gossip."

"When Nicky is a little more coherent, you can ask her." I dug into the muscle of Billie's butt cheek and they hissed, tensing around my hands until the tightness gave way, and Billie sank back down with a happy sigh.

I was curious how long Nicky's current state would last. She had done very well for her first time, so that only made me more interested in how much she would be able to handle the more she let me play with her. I wasn't particularly into pain, but pleasure and overstimulation could be their own kind of torture. Even though that was my usual preference, I wouldn't mind a slower pace with her, just to let her explore and to let me learn all the secrets her body held.

Patience held its own rewards, and I could be very patient when I needed to be.

Chapter Forty
Nicky

"Hey there, beautiful."

I opened my eyes to Gabe pressing a kiss to my forehead. I was pretty sure I'd been floating on an endorphin high since the hot tub.

I had no idea how much time had even passed since then. I'd been stuck in a delightfully hazy mindset during the times when I was awake; otherwise, I was socked out completely.

"Hey," I whispered and nestled into his chest. "How was work?"

"Long. I may have been mildly bitter over the fact that it made me get out of bed with you still in it."

I giggled and tucked my face against his neck, pressing a soft kiss to his skin. "But now I have you back."

"You do." He sighed and held me snuggly.

At the rate I was going, I'd feel practically touch starved when it was time for me to go back to work. The entire time I had been here, someone was touching me, and I had grown used to the simple contact, began to crave it and the intimacy it afforded us.

I breathed in his tea and brown sugar scent. He was slightly damp, but not sweaty, and I wondered if he'd showered when he'd arrived home.

The lingering fragrances of the entire pack clung to my skin. At some point while I had drowsed in the couch nest, Jasper had joined us too. I looked around and found him curled up on Tony and Billie's laps. Hana sat on the other side of Gabe, watching me with a soft expression that made my stomach flip a moment before it started to growl, and several eyes turned towards me.

"Hungry?" Gabe asked.

"Maybe a tiny bit."

"What can I find for you?"

Even though I *did* want snacks, I didn't want him to move. I burrowed closer. "I kind of want cupcakes, but I don't think we have any."

Jasper perked up. "I could provide that. They don't take very long to make."

"Oh god, don't tempt me." Now that I had suggested it, it was the only thing my brain wanted me to put in my mouth. Food-wise, at least.

Jasper was already getting up. "Nope, too late. Cupcakes are happening. Chocolate cake and vanilla buttercream okay?"

"*So* okay," I replied, mouth already watering.

"Do you want me to make you some tea while we watch Jasper work his magic?" Gabe asked, tipping my face up so he could nuzzle my cheek.

"Yes please." When I sat up, it was then that I realized I still didn't have a stitch of clothing on. "I should probably get dressed."

"Entirely up to you," said Gabe. "At this point the entire pack has seen you naked, so there's no pressure either way. Do you want me to grab you one of the robes?"

"A robe sounds like a good compromise on clothes."

332

I exchanged my fuzzy blanket for a fuzzy robe and trotted after Gabe toward the kitchen. Hana eyeballed me pretty hard, so I didn't open my mouth to offer to help. Instead, she parked me at one of the barstools and put herself on the one next to me so close, the stools were touching. Billie sat on my other side, and Tony sidled up against my back, wrapping his arms around my waist.

"Cozy, baby girl?"

I hummed softly and leaned against him. "Very. I'm pretty sure this is the most relaxed I've ever been."

Gabe ended up making a whole pot of tea, and he distributed the steaming cups to the pack.

I mused on the turn my life had taken as I stirred a bit of honey into my tea. The change of jobs from day to night hours had had my mother fretting that I would never meet anyone, and instead, the universe blessed me with not one, but *five* incredible people.

It felt so easy.

I wasn't sure if it actually *was* or if I would discover something in the future that would rob me of these simple joys. Some dark little voice in the back of my mind whispered that it could happen so easily. No one before had led to happiness, so what were the odds of this leading there too?

I shoved down that thought. Worrying about the future would only ruin today, and I'd had enough todays ruined lately.

Billie leaned over and kissed my cheek. "You look delightfully well fucked. Got that whole peaceful vibe."

My cheeks warmed, and I took a sip of my tea, hissing as it scalded my tongue. I really had to stop doing that around Billie.

Without a word, Gabe set down a carton of milk in front of me. Hana added a splash to my tea for me, which brought it down to a drinkable temperature. I was getting way, *way* too spoiled staying here.

The younger me might have worried about losing my independence, but at thirty-three I cared a whole lot less about that. I had been independent for years already, and I was ready to be taken care of. I was pretty good at taking care of people too, and I had no intention of taking advantage of anyone's good intentions, but neither was I going to deny them if they wanted to care for me.

We talked about the latest book-to-movie adaptation—which looked horrendous from the book lover's side and gorgeous from a cinematic perspective—that had been announced while Jasper whipped up his batter, filled up two muffin trays, and popped them in the oven. It didn't take long until the entire kitchen smelled like baking chocolate.

There was something so indulgent about this. More than the shopping spree or the club and limo or the *ridiculous* amount of orgasms I had accrued from this pack, *this* was what I liked best. All of us together.

Hana relented a little bit on her orders and let me spoon icing sugar into the mixer for Jasper, which also let me cuddle up to him. I got to lick the beater, too, getting instantly transported back to my childhood. Nothing quite compared to chocolate cupcakes and buttercream frosting. Of course, I would have to wait until they were combined, but my tongue was plenty satisfied for the moment as it navigated the twisting bars of the beater.

All eyes were on me as I set it down.

"Damn, Books, what that tongue do?" Billie snickered.

I couldn't help laughing, which set off all of the rest of them.

We only let the cupcakes cool to the point that they didn't burn our fingers. Everyone got their own and split them apart so that the steam wafted from between the perfect chocolaty halves. Jasper dropped a dollop of icing onto each of our cupcakes, and we scarfed them down before it even had a chance to melt.

I wiggled happily in Jasper's arms.

"We should do this more often," said Jasper. "It's been a while since we've made illicit middle of the night cupcakes."

"Ten out of ten, agree!" I chirped, licking the icing off of my fingers.

Jasper leaned across the counter and kissed my sweetened lips. "Do you want another one?"

"Like that's even a question." I kissed him again and reached grabby hands towards the tray of still cooling cupcakes.

Jasper grinned and acquired another confection for me. I made absolutely ridiculous noises while eating it, but that was just part of the cupcake experience. If you're not making ridiculous sounds, then your cupcake is simply not delicious enough.

The rest of the night passed with more cupcakes and Pride and Prejudice while we all snuggled up again in the couch nest. Being with the pack was like a never-ending sleepover and I dreaded having to go back to real life.

I pushed that rebellious thought away and snuggled deeper into Hana's arms, pulling Gabe closer so I was totally smushed between them.

Heaven had a location, and it was this couch.

Chapter Forty–One
Nicky

Work went by surprisingly fast. There was no sign of Alphonse when I got there, and he made no appearances during my shift or after. Tony and Billie had joined me at the library, and I spent my breaks snuggled up in the beanbags with them.

I stopped by the clinic to do my interview and the blood tests with Dr. James. All together, it only took about half an hour, and I left feeling good about myself, like I was contributing to a better future for betas. Like today, every Monday morning I would pop in, though all the subsequent appointments would be much faster, with similar information from the interview being things that I recorded myself and submitted monthly.

My phone rang, and I fished it out of my purse.

I didn't recognize the number.

"Hello?"

"Hello, is this Nicola Marino?"

"This is she," I replied.

"Hi there, Nicola, this is Detective Cameron with the forensics unit."

"Oh, hi. How can I help you?"

"I just wanted to let you know that we weren't able to find any DNA evidence of Alphonse Morelli having been in your apartment. The only DNA we were able to match were those that you had told us had been there previously. We coordinated with your landlord to get your door replaced, and we've taken quite a few items into custody to do further testing, but the labs are backed up, so that may take a while. Officers were also sent to Mr. Morelli's home, but we have yet to actually locate him."

"I see," I said, voice tight. "So what does that mean for me?"

"While the DNA evidence doesn't prove that he was in your apartment, we do have video footage of him in the parking lot on the date of the break in as well as in the lobby, where it looks like he let himself in with a key. Technically, this evidence is circumstantial, but Officer Lansbury will be in further contact with you for how to proceed."

"Am I allowed to return to my apartment now?"

"At this time, yes," Detective Cameron said.

"Okay. Thank you."

I hung up, feeling numb. They knew Alphonse had been in the building and that someone had forced their way into my home.

Fucking *circumstantial* evidence?

Why didn't we have cameras in the hallways?

There was no way I could stay in that apartment again. I had already started emotionally detaching myself from it the moment he'd touched that space.

I tapped out on an email to my landlord to let them know that I wouldn't be renewing my lease. Whether that resulted in me staying with the pack, staying with family, or getting a new apartment remained to be seen. Prior to all of this nonsense, I had been trying to keep *some* semblance of space. Any place that I could stay would only provide me with a guest room at best. And as comfortable as those guest rooms would be, they weren't *my* space.

Sometimes a girl just wanted to veg without people around.

Stupid Alphonse ruining everything.

Moving was such a hassle, but I would have to get on that. A storage unit would be the easiest for most of my things. I guess I would have to talk to the pack about staying a little while longer. And I could probably talk to Sidney about sneaking into their place while he and Allie were at work so I could have some alone time. Not that I didn't love spending time with the pack—I adored it—but I still needed that quiet space to breathe where it was just me and Spud.

I was ready for bed, but I wanted to get as much done as possible so I could collapse face-first into my pillows without guilt.

I dialed my brother first, hoping to catch him before he started his shift at the clinic.

"Hey Nick," Sidney answered. "What's up?"

"Just checking in on your offer to let me stay with you," I replied.

"You're not staying with the pack?"

"I will if they'll have me, but I was hoping I could maybe use your place for some chill time. I love hanging out with them, but they are not a quiet bunch."

Sidney laughed. "Totally fair. You're welcome whenever you want. I'll get the guest bed and bath all set up for you, and I'll leave you spare keys at the front desk of the clinic for you to pick up whenever you're free."

"Have I mentioned recently that you're the best brother?"

"Don't let Luca hear you say that." I could practically hear the grin in his voice.

"Luca can be the best *baby* brother. Besides, it's not like I can stay with him when he still lives with mom."

"Oh, he's looking at moving out. I talked to him about it yesterday."

"Sweet. It's about time that kid got some independence. What the heck is Mom going to do with her empty nest?"

"Your guess is as good as mine," Sidney replied. "He gave her plenty of extra time to get used to the idea."

"I'm sure Mom would love me to stay with her," I said. "If Alphonse didn't already know where they lived, then I might consider it, though I don't think Mom would be very good at giving me any peace either."

"Nope. You are very correct about that. Do you wanna come over for dinner tonight? It can just be me, you, and Allie."

"Sure, that sounds great."

"Cool. I'll text her and let her know, and I'll scrap leaving the keys at the clinic. You can just grab them tonight, then. I get off at five, so you can come over anytime after that."

"Will do. Love you."

"Love you, too, Nick."

Well, that was one step dealt with.

I detoured on the way to the pack house, stopping in at *Go with the Dough*.

Jasper was working in the back when I arrived. A blond man with a smudge of flour on his cheek greeted me.

"Welcome to *Go with the Dough*. What can I get for you?"

"An adorable red-headed omega?"

Jasper turned and caught sight of me, dropping his task and rushing up to the counter. "Nicky! What brings you to the bakery?"

He looked so cute in his hairnet. I wouldn't have thought it was possible, but Jasper pulled it off. I grinned and leaned up against the display case to accept his kiss. "Just running some errands, and decided I wanted to see you."

The blond man laughed. "The famous Nicky? Jasper hasn't shut up about you for weeks."

My beautiful omega flushed pink. "Shut up, Yan."

A woman joined us, and Jasper rolled his eyes. "Oh good, Rita's here, too."

I couldn't help laughing. "I personally think it's cute that you talk about me with your bakery staff."

Rita's eyes gleamed. "We've been wondering when we'd finally get to see you."

"Everything I've said is good, I swear," said Jasper.

"I believe you." I gave him a reassuring smile.

"Go have a break with your girl," Rita said. "We can hold down the fort for a few minutes."

Jasper seemed conflicted for a moment before nodding decisively and untying his apron. He slipped out to the front of the bakery, tugging me outside and pulling me into a proper kiss. He tasted as good as his bakery smelled.

"Can I sleep in your bed today?" I asked.

Jasper reacted as if I'd handed him a bouquet of flowers. "Of course you can. I like having you in there."

"I like when you slip in next to me." I kissed him again, basking in the soft sweetness of him. A more selfish person would've convinced him to come straight home, but he still had over an hour of work left.

"Have you eaten yet?" Jasper asked.

I shook my head.

"Come in and pick anything you want. Should I bring you some focaccia home?"

I brushed my lips over his and traced his jawline. "Yes, please."

I tucked myself in for a hug, just savoring his proximity for a few minutes until I'd soaked up enough calm that I could let go again. Jasper took me back inside and fed me a raspberry croissant.

"I'm at my brother and sister-in-law's for dinner tonight," I told him.

Jasper nodded. "I'll bring two, then you can take one over and still have some leftovers for yourself."

"Brilliant." Stealing one more kiss, I headed to the pack house with a satisfied stomach. Tony, Billie, and Gabe were all in the kitchen when I arrived home. I greeted them each with a kiss and covered an insistent yawn with my hand.

"I'm going to crash. I'll be in Jasper's room if anyone needs me or wants to join."

"Dibs!"

I laughed as Billie hopped off their chair and followed me upstairs.

The two of us stripped down and snuggled up in the middle of Jasper's bed.

Billie was my cuddly jetpack. They were asleep almost instantly, their breath turning slow and even in my ear. I passed out a few moments later and woke briefly to Jasper climbing into bed. I snuggled in, breathing deeply. Somehow his chocolate and cinnamon scent seemed even sweeter than usual. I didn't last in the waking world for long, and when I woke again, it was almost time for me to head out for dinner.

I groaned and stretched, wiggling my toes and weaseling my way deeper into Jasper's arms. The omega held me tighter but didn't actually open his eyes. I traced patterns on his chest and let myself float for a few glorious minutes in the cloud of his scent. Billie wiggled at my back and pressed a kiss to my shoulder.

"Are we awake?" they asked.

"Barely. I should get up."

"*Or* you could stay here forever." Billie snuggled closer.

"As tempting as that is, I do have to get dressed for dinner at my brother's."

"Family dinner?" Billie asked.

"Tiny one. Just the three of us. It's been ages since we've gotten to hang out."

"I suppose I can suffer through your absence for that." Billie laughed and gave me a tight squeeze then rolled over so I had space to sit up.

Jasper made a sound of protest and pulled me back down. He kissed me breathless before I was allowed to actually make it out of the bed. Of course, at that point it took a lot more willpower to manage.

Poor planning meant that all of my outfits were in the downstairs bedroom and I was very naked two floors above that. I snatched one of the smaller blankets that made up Jasper's nest and wrapped it around myself like a dress, collecting my discarded clothes from the floor. I swept down the stairs, waving to the alphas gathered in the kitchen as I disappeared down to the bottom level to get ready for my day.

It felt weird to be leaving the pack house all alone, but I was genuinely excited to hang out with Sidney and Allie. The drive to their place was only about twenty minutes, and Allie opened the front door before I even had a chance to knock. She crashed against me in a fierce hug, Sidney appearing at her back to bundle me into his arms, too.

"Quit hogging my sister," Sidney said with a laugh.

"It's not my fault that you're too slow to be first."

"And how am I supposed to keep up with you bounding at the door like a rabbit the second you hear car wheels?"

"You're not. Just accept my victory." Allie grinned, and the two of them ushered me inside.

"We ordered Thai food," said Sidney. "It should be here soon."

Allie and I took up our spots at the dining room table while Sidney finished preparing some Thai iced tea for us.

"How's everything?" she asked.

"Pack stuff is good. No real updates on Alphonse, so I think I have to move out of my apartment."

Allie hissed. "That fucker better hope I never see him because I will open a whole can of whoop ass on him."

"You'll have to get in line for that," said Sidney as he set the three glasses down on the table for us.

"Sidney said you're going to stay with us for a bit?" Allie asked.

"Sometimes. Before all the Alphonse fuckery, I was still staying at my apartment a few days a week. It just feels a bit early to contemplate moving in with the pack."

"For *you*, maybe," Allie said with a laugh. "I saw those faces when everyone offered to let you stay with them instead. They like you a whole heck of a lot."

"You don't think it's too fast?" I asked, sipping my iced tea.

"We're really not the best people to ask about timelines," said Allie. "We had an accidental bonding, so we're out of the norm, and to be fair, I was already immediately ready to climb all over him."

"The point is," said Sidney, "that things can go as fast or slow as you want. There's no timeline that anyone has to follow. If it feels right, then go for it."

"I want to, but I'm a worrier." I chewed my bottom lip.

"Worry if you need to," said Sidney. "But don't let it stop you from living the way you want. I may not have spent as much time with you in recent years as I should have, but I would have to be lacking in every sense to not know that you're happier now than I've seen you your entire adult life."

The doorbell interrupted my response, and Sidney went to get our dinner. We spread it out, family style, and snared bites with our chopsticks.

"What are you really worried about Nicky?" he asked.

"I don't even know if I know," I confessed.

"Do you like everyone in the pack?" Allie asked.

I nodded.

"And everyone in the pack likes you?"

"Yeah. I wondered for a little while, but that's *definitely* all cleared up now."

"My personal vote," said Allie, "is to just go with the flow. If you ever decide you don't like it, you can leave. Our guest room is always open for you. If they make you happy, then be with them."

I fidgeted with my chopsticks. "You make it sound so simple."

Allie shrugged. "Sometimes love is a lot simpler than people think it is."

I mused on the statement while we ate. They got me familiarized with the guest room and gave me my own set of keys. The space was clean and quiet, and given their propensity to having foster pups run around, neither of them had any issue with Spud joining me here.

"Give me a list of anything you might need," said Sidney.

343

"We'll pick up some things for you and Spud on our next grocery trip. Then you don't have to worry about carting stuff back and forth.

"You two are seriously the best."

Allie laughed. "I love when people recognize our greatness."

Sidney hooked his arm around his wife's neck and kissed the top of her head. "It's truly a wonder how you manage to be so modest."

Allie giggled in his grasp, and that set off my own laughter.

Tension flowed out of my body the longer I stayed with them. I liked having another place to go to with people that I loved. It relieved a lot of lingering pressure and made the idea of letting my apartment go that much easier.

"I'll probably try to sell off my furniture. Do you mind if I keep some boxes in the guest room?"

"Consider that room yours," said Sidney. "You can keep whatever you want in there."

I sucked back the sudden swell of emotion. I must've been a saint in a past life to be blessed with so many wonderful people in this one.

I stayed with them for a few hours, but as much as I loved them, I was already itching to get back to the pack. I would only have about an hour with them before I had to leave for work, but I would take any moments I could grab.

Tony was the only one downstairs on the main level when I got home. It looked like he'd already started work, sitting at the kitchen table with his laptop and stacks of paper around him.

"What are you working on?" I asked. I hooked a finger under his chin and lifted it to steal a kiss.

"Something you should probably know about, actually." He sighed.

"Oh?"

He showed me several highlighted portions, and I read them over, letting my brain parse the information.

"None of these financials match up."

"Exactly," said Tony. "I've been tracking the finances of the city alongside the bylaws and proposals that you dug out of the archives for me. A little over twenty-six million dollars has disappeared over the last twenty years."

My eyes widened. "What the hell?"

"It all coincides with funding that Councillor Harvey has managed to strip from projects she doesn't agree with. And her current target is the facility where your library is."

"*What*?!"

"She's been busy trying to push through a budget cut. Something ridiculous about twenty-four hour facilities breeding immorality."

"But it's a *library*." I gaped at him.

"Councillor Harvey is not a rational woman. Not a very nice one either. I was going to take this information to the Council."

"That's so much money. Do you think she would get arrested?"

"I don't know," said Tony. "I would hope there would at least be an investigation and resignation. Unless, of course, the other councilors are in on it, and that twenty-six million has been padding their pockets."

"Do the messed up financials match up with any of their proposals?"

"Maybe? I've only been digging into Harvey because she started gunning for the library."

I nodded slowly. "Why didn't you tell me earlier?"

"Mostly confidentiality issues. No one is supposed to know about that, but now that I have actual proof that something is going on, I feel a little bit safer telling you. I wanted to say something sooner."

I nodded again. "Okay, that's fair. Will this put you at risk? Harvey is one of your clients, isn't she?"

"Yeah, she is. Both of our jobs are on the line if she succeeds. If she doesn't get arrested, she'll be pissed right off that I tried to expose her. I also don't think she'll stop pushing, which means the pilot project would get nuked. Success with one would probably have her targeting other twenty-four-hour facilities too."

"Is there anything I can do to help?"

"To be honest, I don't know. It might be good to hint to the facility manager to start gathering some reports that show the value of keeping the building open twenty-four hours."

"I can do that. We always make note of the number of guests overnight, and all of our tracking programs for the books and computers have timestamps. I know it's a little sparse during my shift, but the facility isn't dead by any means." I growled. "I can't believe she's going for a fucking library. They're sacred spaces."

Tony laughed softly and pulled me onto his lap. "I agree with you. That's why I've been digging through these records until my eyeballs bleed. I might've worked a little bit harder considering what you stand to lose, but there's no way in hell I was going to let her do this without a fight."

I let myself lean into his embrace. "Thank you for fighting for us. The library means a lot to me."

"Pretty sure that library means a lot to all of us now. We'd have never met you without it. And it doesn't matter who or what comes after you," he said, voice strong. "I'm always going to fight for you."

Chapter Forty-Two
Tony

"Thank you for bringing this to our attention," Mayor Carlisle said to me. "You've been so thorough."

"I didn't want to come with you with unfounded accusations. I just don't want Harvey taking advantage of her position, and I definitely don't want her to rob the city of such a valuable space."

Mayor Carlisle nodded and pinched the bridge of her nose. "Between you and me, I've been suspicious of her for a while. She gets on her high horse about the stupidest things. But there's only so much I can do given that we're both elected officials. I'll have to go through the proper channels: get a quiet background investigation going so she doesn't catch wind of it and cover her tracks. Something like that usually takes months, so you're unlikely to hear any updates for a while."

I nodded. "Is there anything else I can do?"

"No, you've done plenty already, Mx. Agani."

I *mostly* trusted the mayor, but I had still made copies of everything that I was handing over. I had no proof that she wasn't also involved no matter what she said. I wanted to believe that none of the other councilors were involved, but Harvey had been getting away with this for twenty years which meant no one was safe. Billie had harped on me, wanting me to submit my findings to one of their lawyers just to be safe, and I'd relented, dropping off all of my research with the lawyer before arriving for my meeting with the mayor.

I sighed.

Why couldn't people act with integrity?

I didn't want to wait months for results. Who knows how much damage Harvey could do in the meantime? Maybe even telling the mayor would lose me my job. I'll bet even if she doesn't like Harvey, she wouldn't be happy with me rooting around, despite most of the information being publicly available. It would be illegal, sure, but plenty of illegal things happened all the time, twisted around so they couldn't be prosecuted.

The pack had supported me doing this, even knowing that we could earn enemies. Harvey had a lot of connections at both the city and state level, and pissing her off without being able to bring her to heel with the legal system was a dangerous move.

Returning to the pack house with a new stack of assignments, I sat down to work in my office. That didn't last very long. Billie appeared to chastise me for working extra hours.

"I will literally pay you to take a break," they said.

"You'd pay me for a lot of things, but I still like having an actual job," I reminded them.

Billie fussed and climbed onto my lap. "I'm not going to let you work a fourteen hour day. It's just not going to happen. Now, why don't you put this down and take me on walkies?"

I laughed. "Okay, fine. But you have to let me work when we're at the library tonight."

"Excuse you, I'm always perfectly well behaved at the library."

I chuckled. "You and I have different definitions of perfectly well behaved."

Billie hopped off my lap and tugged at my arm until I relinquished my workspace.

I admitted quietly to myself, once I was out in the sunshine, that it was exactly what I needed. There was a beautiful marshland near our property, and we walked the short distance to it.

"When do you think we'll be able to convince Nicky to move in full-time?" Billie asked.

"Pretty sure trying to convince her is only going to slow that process down."

Billie huffed. "But I like her living with us. I'm not going to apologize for wanting her to be there all the time."

I snuck my hand under their hair and held the back of their neck as we walked. "No one is asking for you to apologize for that. Nicky will come to things in her own time. You learned that with Hana, and you'll learn it with Nicky, too."

"*Fine.* What about Jaspy's heat? When are we talking to her about that?"

"That'll be up to Jasper," I said. "If he wants her there, he has to ask."

"Well, he better get a move on, then. Isn't he due to start in a couple weeks?

I nodded. "Yep, he is."

"You're his alpha," Billie said. "Can't you encourage him a little harder?"

"I know that you don't like to wait for things, but this is not something for either of us to handle. The circumstances of Jasper's heat are up to him. You have to give him the space to have that conversation on his own."

Billie huffed.

"Okay, but then you have to distract me. Tell me about your meeting with the evil councilor."

"It was with the mayor, but I can do that." I updated them as we walked.

"Ugh. You have *proof*. They should hurry the fuck up and yeet her into the sun. Nothing moves fast enough for me." Billie shoved their hands into their pockets. "I should just finance a private facility so the government can't say a damn thing about how long it's open."

"You know, if you actually did want to, that's something you could do. A lot of the pack could certainly make use of the space."

Billie looked like I had flipped on a lightbulb in their brain. "You're *so* right. How did I not think of this?"

"Just don't run too fast with it. There's a lot of permits you have to get for a project like that."

"But how cool would that *be*?! I have enough money for it."

I pulled them off the path of a pothole. "If you still want to pursue it after Jasper's heat, then I'll help you with your business plan, okay?"

Billie squeed and threw their arms around me. "Fuck yeah! You're the best."

"I know." I laughed.

Billie kept me out in the sunlight for a solid hour before they finally allowed me to take them back home. The rest of the pack was up and about when we returned, and since I knew Billie was unlikely to hold their tongue for very long, I pulled Jasper aside to talk to him.

"Billie's been asking me when you're going to talk to Nicky. I have to admit I'm a little curious about that answer as well."

"I haven't figured things out that far yet," Jasper said. "She's already arranged to not stay with us full-time, and I just worry how she might react if I ask her to be part of a heat that would require her to be here *all* the time. I don't want to be too needy and freak her out."

My poor omega.

I pulled Jasper into an embrace. He needed a lot of care, but so did every omega. I couldn't imagine Nicky shying away from doing everything she could to make sure that Jasper felt safe and loved.

"You'll never know if you don't talk to her," I pointed out. "Nicky likes you. That's blatantly obvious."

Jasper melted in my arms. "I know. It's just been so long since I've had to invite anyone to be a part of my heat."

"If you're worried, you can always tell her that she doesn't have to stay in the nest the entire time, right? Every part of the house will be unoccupied, so if she needs a break, she can walk out the door."

Jasper sniffled. "I'm worried that, if she walks out during the heat, I'll freak out. Like she's rejecting me even though I know right now that's not what it is. I don't know how well my brain will handle it during."

I held him tighter. "You're a tender heart. I'm sure the last thing Nicky wants is to hurt you, but in any case, you still have to talk to her, because if she's not going to be part of your heat, then we have to tell her that none of us are going to be available, and she'll have to make other arrangements."

Jasper stiffened in my grasp. "I don't *want* her to make other arrangements. I want her to stay with us. The closer I get to my heat, the harder it is to ignore."

I could only sigh. Our pack had thrived because of our ability to talk to one another, and while I thought we had been pretty clear on wanting her with us, I couldn't be sure that any of us had specifically said so. That would have to change. I didn't personally anticipate any issues. If they *did* arise, I knew that they would be painful given how attached we had all gotten, but I still maintained that it was better to know early than when it was too late. I couldn't push anyone to move faster or slower than they were willing to go, no matter how much easier life would be.

I held Jasper, soothing him as best as I was able, though Nicky's acceptance was the only thing that would truly assuage his worries.

I would give him a week. If he didn't talk to her by then, I would have to intervene for all of our sakes.

Chapter Forty-Three
Nicky

S pud wandered around Sidney and Allie's place, checking out his new temporary digs. The place was so quiet. Honestly, maybe a little *too* quiet. It was like my ears kept listening for sounds of a pack, and when it came up with nothing, the silence screamed at me.

I turned on their TV for background noise and climbed into bed.

Spud hopped up next to me.

"Hey baby, do you miss Roscoe?" Spud chirped, and even though I knew he couldn't understand the question, it still sounded like an affirmation that made me feel guilty. "You'll get to see him soon. We're just here for a couple of days."

Tomorrow I would have to forsake some sleep. I had movers booked to take my furniture out of my apartment and into my parents garage so that I could sell it, or keep it if I changed my mind on not getting my own apartment. That was pretty unlikely though. Even these few hours all alone in a home was a stark reminder of how little I had going on before I'd gotten involved with the pack. I didn't want to force activities for the sake of taking up time to fill those spaces, either. I wanted to find things I enjoyed in my own time when I was settled again.

I loved my alone time, but the oppressive silence of today was grating.

I lay back and huffed out a breath. Apparently, I couldn't be pleased.

At least no one minded me taking my space, which was good, but my fingers itched to pick up the phone and message the pack.

I restrained myself.

It was silly to get into a tizzy on my first night away from them. I couldn't spend every night with them for the rest of forever, no matter how tempting that seemed. I had gotten too used to people, and I would just have to adjust again.

I woke to the front door opening and froze, panic shooting through my body until I heard Allie call out.

"Nicky, I'm home!"

I relaxed instantly and shuffled out of bed still in my pajamas to greet her.

"Hey girly. How was work?"

"Mostly good," she replied. "A little weird. One of our very cute coworkers asked Luna out, and she turned him down. I joked that she had to have a secret partner to not be interested, and she got very cagey about it. Now I feel like she actually does have someone she's hiding. Besties are supposed to tell each other everything."

"Why won't she tell you about it?"

"Your guess is as good as mine." Allie shrugged out of her blazer and tossed it over a chair. "I'm sure she'll tell me something eventually. I'm just not particularly patient when it comes to gossip."

"I'm sorry I don't have anything to tide you over in the meantime."

"Oh! You sort of do. I was going to ask you about the omega in your pack. What's happening with his heat?"

"I have no idea, why?"

"Well, unless he's on long-term suppressants and suddenly decided to stop liking you, I assumed you were going to be a part of it at some point. Granted, I don't know a ton about pack dynamics, but I also kind of assumed that they were all involved in stuff like that."

I fidgeted, suddenly awkward. "I've never asked. Isn't that something he would want to share with his established pack?"

Allie shrugged. "I shared a bunch of mine with Heat Helpers. Every omega is different in what they want. Might be good to think about, though. You don't want to be a deer in the headlights when it comes up."

"But I'm a beta. What would I even *do* for his heat?"

Allie sighed deeply and patted my shoulder. "Be there for him? Help the others? Rail him senseless with a strap on?"

I choked at that last response.

"You don't think your presence would be a comfort?" Allie asked. "Plus, think of all the play time. The work is being shared, and an omega only has so many holes, so there's going to be free pack members at any given time."

My face burst into flames. "Allie!"

"*What*? I'm just being honest. I'm gonna look it up." She pulled out her phone and tapped away. I was almost dreading what she might find, even as my curiosity reared its head.

Allie giggled at her screen, and though embarrassment burned deep in my belly, I wandered over anyway to see what she was reading.

"What is it?" I asked.

"It's just some stuff from a magazine, so it's probably not *super* accurate, and it depends on a specific pack, but it sounds like you would be in for a very good time if you were part of it."

"Okay, but I need more info."

"It says that the omega's hormones during a heat will have a heavy influence on *everyone* who has continuous proximity with them, even betas. Obviously, it'll have the highest effect on alphas, but you'll get to experience what they call a *heat high*."

"That sounds intimidating." And more than a little anxiety inducing. I'd avoided most intoxicants just because I liked to be in control. I couldn't avoid that if I was involved in a heat.

"It sounds *awesome!*" declared Allie. "I'm a little bit jealous that I'm the source of it and not the experiencer."

Sidney came home before she could tell me anything else. "Hey, ladies! What are you two up to?"

"Learning about pack heats!" Allie bounded over to him and hopped straight into his arms.

Sidney looked skyward. "That's not a situation I want to think about my sister in."

"But you're such a good source of information," said Allie, nuzzling his cheek.

He made an uncomfortable groan. "I will answer specific questions, but note that I am doing so under duress."

Allie cackled.

"If it makes you feel better, you're not really who I want to be asking," I said with a laugh. "Your wife is springing all these things on me."

"Yeah, she does that." Sidney grinned. "It's good for you to know, though. If you're involved with an omega, you should know how to take care of them even if you won't be the primary caregiver."

Allie nodded excitedly. "See, exactly." She hopped out of his arms and shoved her phone at me. I read over the article while she stared at me gleefully. I also memorized the title of another article that was linked at the bottom about how to pleasure an alpha of any gender so I could look it up later.

It only made me more curious about what the actual pack dynamics would be. There were so many options, and while it definitely all centered on the omega, they had quotes from a bunch of people in packs that said the love was shared around. As Allie had so succinctly put it, an omega only had so many holes.

My brain filled with a million filthy images of what could happen during a heat.

"When do you think his will be?" I asked. "I need time to mentally prep."

"Hard to say," said Sidney. "Probably in the next few months. Allie's are every eight-ish months."

"How long do they usually last?"

Sidney shrugged. "Depends on the omega and how many heats they've had previously. Between the ramp up and the wind down, we usually like to give them two weeks to fully ride it out. The intensive part of the heat itself shouldn't be more than a week."

I stewed on the info. That was a long time to put out my coworkers. No one really liked covering for the night shift anywhere, and I already felt guilty enough even thinking about general vacation, let alone adding a heat leave on top of that.

"I'll do some more research and ask you about any specifics I can't find information on," I said. "Fair?"

Sidney nodded, and I sat down with my phone to learn. My whole body flushed with warmth. Anxiety clashed heavily with interest, and I wasn't sure which would win out in the end.

Chapter Forty-Four
Billie

O ne of the main perks of being independently wealthy with no real job is that I got to be on call for anything that Nicky needed. While the others had to do things like take care of responsibilities and *sleep*, I got to swoop in and be the hero. I might be a tiny little beta that got overlooked by the rest of the world at first glance, but no one argued with my bank account.

It was nice to get some one-on-one time with Nicky, too. We packed up all of her personal things into a set of suitcases I had purchased for her while the movers loaded up her furniture on their truck.

What she didn't know was that while she was busy staying with her brother, I had employed an interior decorating team to redo the upstairs bedroom for her. I wanted Nicky to have her own space so she didn't feel like she had to run somewhere else to get it.

My wallet had gotten quite the workout, but it was all part of the rush. I also took the opportunity to get a classy as hell greenhouse put into our backyard that included a lounge area so we could snuggle down with the plants no matter the weather. I'd been meaning to put one in for years, but now seems like the perfect time.

Ordinarily, I didn't flex my dollars too hard, but building Nicky a sanctuary in our home created a special kind of high. I only hoped she would love it as much as I did. As much as I was growing to love her...

I had also used those dollars to hire a private security firm that posted guards at every entrance to her building while we handled the move. It was an expense I would've paid a million times over because I wanted her to feel safe. Even if Alphonse happened to show up, guns blazing, the guys I had hired him would take him out in a heartbeat.

"Do you want to get some froyo after?" I asked Nicky.

"A thousand times yes. I need the energy boost."

She looked so darn cute with her hair in braided pigtails to keep it out of the way and dressed in an old T-shirt and sweats. Nicky yawned again, and I took the chance to see if I could swoop in with another assist.

"How would you feel if I hired a cleaning company to come in after us? Move-out cleans are a lot of work, and you look like you could use a break."

Nicky wavered for only a moment. "That would be amazing, actually. I was kind of dreading it. Hana's workouts are no joke."

I cackled. "Boy do I know it. You'll be able to bench press me without blinking soon."

I had snuck down onto the stairs to spy on them a few times. Hana was always ruthless when she was on a mission, but damn if she didn't get results. It had only been a bit over a week since Nicky and Hana had started to work together on her self-defense skills. It was more than a little hot to watch Hana flipping and pinning Nicky, though I did feel a *wee* bit bad because I was all too familiar with that burn of well worked muscles.

Even with Nicky staying at her brother's for part of the week, she had been meeting up with Hana every day whenever they could grab time, much to my jealousy. I had no reason to hog her when she was away from the pack. Until today, anyway.

"Do you want to take a break now and go?"

Nicky surveyed her apartment. "I guess we could go for a little bit. All the important stuff is packed up."

"Cool. We can have the boys pack up the rest."

Nicky's exhaustion made her pliable, and since there was absolutely nothing wrong with letting the movers do their full job, I was okay pressing my advantage to get her to take a break. My whole pack was a bunch of workaholics, and sometimes they needed me to fuss at them to surface for air.

I took her to a cute place nearby and grinned at her the entire time as she loaded up her frozen yogurt with berries and chocolate shavings.

"Oh my god, so good." She moaned after swallowing her first bite.

I laughed. "Sexy sounds are how you know it's the best food."

Her cheeks turned pink, and she snuggled against my side. "Thank you for helping me today. I liked spending extra time with you, even if we're surrounded by movers."

"You're totally welcome, Books. I've got surprises for you when we get back to the pack house."

"Oh?"

"Nope! They're secret surprises. You're gonna have to find them for yourself."

There was a lot that I wanted to say to her, but they weren't my topics to bring up, so instead I struck up a conversation about books. Discussing the finer points of monster romance as an allegory for the outsider got us through the rest of our frozen treats.

When we got back to her apartment, the movers had already finished. The relief in her was palpable when she realized there was no more work to be done.

The movers loaded up her suitcases and boxes of her personal items into our minivan. As we exited, I had one of the security guards drive Nicky's car and one drive our minivan while Nicky and I rode in one of their sleek black SUVs with tinted windows. I refused to take any chances with her fucker of an ex out there.

Truthfully, if it wouldn't have crossed several boundaries, I would have hired the security team to follow Nicky around full-time, but I was pretty sure she'd have some negative feelings about that.

Our drive back to the pack house was entirely uneventful. Almost a pity. I half-hoped that Alphonse would show up just so I could have the satisfaction of watching security faceplant him into the concrete.

Nicky was barely awake by the time we arrived. She stumbled into the house, and I sent her up to Jasper's room, where our omega was probably already asleep. Then I directed the movers to take Nicky's things up to her new, secret room.

Under orders to be as quiet as possible, the team of them trekked up the stairs all the way to the top level. I should really look at getting an elevator put in...

Quite a few things that were being carried up Nicky would have no need of, like her bed linens, but those could be set aside and maybe used at her brother's if she still wanted to stay there. I'd gotten her a pack-sized bed, just like the rest of us, and a fresh bedding set that was twirling around in the dryer right now.

Hana popped her head into Nicky's new room. "Need any help?"

"Always. I bet she'd be a lot less weird about you and I putting her clothes away than the movers."

Hana and I went about the task, filling the walk-in closet with Nicky's scant selection of clothing. As we worked, doubt crept in.

"Do you think she'll like it?" I asked.

"If she doesn't, I'm sure it would just be a knee-jerk reaction. You've made her a gorgeous space, and that's been what she's looking for, right?"

"I know." I sighed. "But I still worry. I really want to keep her."

"Well, I hardly think that giving her her own room is going to chase her away."

I chewed my lip and gave in to the swell of emotion, tucking myself into Hana's arms.

"I like her a scary amount."

Hana laughed softly. "You and me both. I wasn't expecting it. I don't think *any* of the pack was, but here we are. You know if any of us thought this was a bad idea we would've said so."

"Oh, I am painfully aware." I chuckled and stood on my toes so I could huff her mint and matcha scent. "None of you are slow on correcting me when I overstep."

"That's just because we love you," Hana assured. "Now, how many hours have you been awake?"

I shrugged. "I dunno. Eighteen, nineteen, maybe?"

"Right. You need to get to bed."

"But I'm helping."

"You can help after sleep. I'll get the others in here, and we'll get it totally finished so you don't have to worry about anything."

I pouted and Hana nipped my bottom lip.

"Get."

"I don't suppose I could persuade you to come to bed with me?" I stood on my tippy-toes and teasingly licked at her collar bone.

"Even when you're exhausted, your thirst knows no bounds." Hana laughed even as she pinched the bridge of her nose. "Okay. But just one orgasm. I'm not letting you weasel your way into staying awake for extra time."

I grinned and jumped into her arms. "I accept your offering of a singular orgasm."

Even though she rolled her eyes, Hana carted me off to her bedroom and dropped me back onto the mattress.

"If you brat to make this longer, I'm gonna send you to bed without anything. Got it? I have no qualms with putting you back on denial."

"Frankly, I'm offended at this accusation that I wouldn't behave." I stuck my tongue out at her for good measure.

361

Hana huffed and tugged my leggings off, tossing them over her shoulder. She raised an eyebrow at me. "No underwear? Really?"

"Just trying to be prepared."

I sat up and raised my arms expectantly. Hana stripped off my T-shirt and tossed it to join my pants, but left my lacy bralette in place.

"Lay back, hands behind your head, knees open. If you move from this position, then we stop."

"Yes ma'am." I stretched out, tucked my hands beneath my neck, and popped my ankles as far apart as they could get.

Hana's growl sent a delicious shiver over me. She disappeared briefly and returned with a small handful of toys. Anticipation skittered over my skin. She tucked two buzzing bullet vibes into each bralette cup, and I hissed at the zing of sensation.

She pushed my thighs open to the point where my muscles started to burn and I arched off the bed, waiting for her to take things further. Getting herself into position, she propped my hips on her lap.

My clit was gifted with a few tender strokes before a quick slap made me jolt.

"*Fuck*," I gasped out.

My whole body shook as I restrained the urge to move.

"Good little beta."

I held myself taut as a bow string as her fingers explored me. There was no pattern to follow or warning when the teasing, probing touches were replaced with the delicious, sharp sting of her striking my clit.

I wanted to squirm and writhe, but not as much as I wanted to keep going. Sometimes playing with Hana was a full body workout just to stay still.

She picked up a thick, blue dildo, lubed it up, and turned on the vibrating function, teasing my clit with it. Hana shifted me around so she had unobstructed access and pushed it inside of me slowly while I whined and desperately held my position.

Each thrust knocked the breath right out of me. Hana's hips

might be stronger than her arms, but that meant nothing when I was being stretched open and the flared base smacked my clit with each movement.

Hana's free hand pinched my nipple to the vibe in my bralette cup and grinned innocently at me as I swore like a fucking sailor.

"Am I losing my touch, little beta?" Hana asked. "Usually you're biting back your begging at this point."

"Just—" I keened. "Just trying to make it last." I cried out as she buried the dildo to its hilt and ground the base against my clit.

"Dangerous." Hana hummed, biting her lip as she traced my thighs. "You know how I love breaking you."

"Better—" I panted, "try harder then."

Before I could blink I found myself face down in the blankets and felt the sharp sting of her hand on my ass cheek.

"Ass up, beta."

I wriggled into position. It wasn't the easiest task with my hands still laced behind my neck. Hana rustled around, and I knew it was coming. The blue dildo slid out of my cunt and appeared in front of my lips.

"Better keep you quiet so the movers don't know what we're up to."

I moaned and opened my mouth, tongue bathed in the flavor of my own body. One of the alpha-sized dildos tucked into the strap-on prodded me next and I had only a single slow thrust to adjust. Hana's hips met mine, and I bit down on the dildo in my mouth. She retreated and snapped forward with the force that shifted my whole body. Her fingers locked around my hips, and then it was all I could do to keep breathing as she ruined me.

Hana on a mission was an exquisite thing to behold. I might not be able to see her in this position, but I could feel the raw power she exuded.

My cunt squeezed her strap-on, and the slam of the base against my clit finally pulled me over the edge. I screamed around the toy in my mouth, every muscle seizing as she rode me to exhaustion.

I whimpered softly, and only then did she slow, my pussy aching with emptiness as she slid free.

"You didn't last as long as I was expecting you to."

I grumbled and shivered, whining around the dildo. She freed my body of all of the toys and set them aside, rolling me onto my back. I lay there panting, muscles still twitching in the aftershocks of pleasure.

"Maybe I'm out of practice. You should fuck me more often so I can up my stamina."

Hana laughed and rolled her thumb over my clit. I jumped at the contact. She stroked firmly, each one making me twitch.

"Are you feeling neglected?" she asked.

"Not really, I just love when you obliterate me."

She slapped my clit again and chuckled at my yelp. "Little pleasure slut. Maybe I'll put you and Nicky in the spreader bars and see which one of you can last longer."

I moaned at the thought and flexed my hips. "No fair! You're going to give me a case of blue clit talking like that."

"Good." Hana grinned down at me. "You're cute when you're frustrated. Now go to bed."

I didn't point out that I wouldn't be able to fall asleep with every nerve singing. Instead, I nodded and waddled my way to her bathroom to wash up before climbing into her bed and sinking into the silks in the cloud of her scent that clung to the fabric.

Chapter Forty-Five
Nicky

Jasper rolled on top of me and smushed me into the mattress.

"Hey there." He grinned and ran a line of kisses up my throat.

I sank into the sweet affection. "Hey there, yourself. Someone's affectionate today."

"That's because it's surprise day," Jasper said.

"What kind of things happen on surprise day?" I asked, tracing my fingers over his jawline.

"Hopefully, a very happy Nicky." He looked so cute with his brown eyes all bright and eager.

I locked my limbs around him. "Well, this is a very good start."

The door cracked open, and Gabe slipped inside, coming over the curl against my back. "I was going to steal a few extra minutes of sleep if you two weren't awake yet."

I wiggled, pulling the two of them tighter around me, sighing happily as their arms cocooned me. "Don't let us being awake keep you from a nap."

"Nah." Gabe kissed my shoulder before kissing Jasper over me. "Now that you're up it's time for surprises. Are you hungry now, or do you want to wait until after?"

"If they're quick surprises, then I can do those first, but the two of you are depleting my motivation for getting out of bed."

Gabe laid his palm on my stomach and pressed me closer. "If the others weren't waiting on us, then Jasper and I could do a few unspeakable things to you."

I tipped my head back as he walked his fingertips up my body to lay his hand at my throat. Jasper picked up my wrist and kissed the scent gland there, teeth scraping over it until I was shivering between them.

Gabe's phone beeped, and he sighed, his hand retreating to check the message. "Billie is getting impatient."

Jasper snorted. "That's their baseline state."

"Come on," I said. "You two can do unspeakable things to me later."

I climbed out of bed dressed in my barely there shorty pajamas the pack had purchased for me. Jasper pulled on a pair of black boxers so we were both at least partially clothed, and we followed Gabe upstairs. He did a series of knocks.

Jasper hugged me, spinning me so I was facing away from the door.

"Ready?" Gabe asked me.

"Yep."

Jasper put his hands over my eyes, and the two of them walked me inside the room. I hadn't actually been inside it, but I had gathered that it was some sort of playroom.

They pulled me to a stop, and I could hear Billie's excited squeal, their body slamming into mine. Jasper removed his hands, and I stared at the space for several moments. It wasn't a playroom. It was...

A bedroom.

Stacks of bookshelves lined one wall, filled with a rainbow of spines and trinkets that I slowly recognized from my apartment, including the bowl I'd made with Billie, though it was shiny and glazed now. The bed was as big as all of the others in the house with more than enough space for the pack to share it. Rich plum curtains hung from the windows, and a storm gray cat tower sat in their gap. I didn't notice Spud at first until his little head popped up.

"*What*? Is this..."

"Yours?! Yes!" Billie shouted. "Do you like it?"

My tears formed faster than my words. I caught their concerned expressions before the world wavered, and I gave over to the sobs.

They made me a room.

They wanted me to *stay*.

Why the hell couldn't I stop crying?

The pack crowded around me in one giant hug.

"Do you hate it?" Billie asked, nuzzling my ear.

"I love it," I choked out.

They waited until I had cried myself out, and then a bottle of water appeared in front of me. I gulped it down gratefully. Hana held up a box of tissues, and I used them to dry my eyes and blow my nose, tossing them into the tiny waste basket that Tony had fetched. Damn, they were efficient.

I took a few deep breaths. "I don't know what to say except to babble 'thank you' until the end of time."

"Can we give you a tour?" Billie asked.

I nodded, distrusting my voice again.

Billie hooked their arm through one of mine, and Tony held my other hand.

"We let Billie's hurricane powers go wild," said Tony. "What do you think, baby girl?"

"It's beautiful." The space was easily the size of my old apartment, open and airy and all mine. "I can't believe you all did this for me."

My own small collection of books was scattered among the

shelves, and the rest looked to be the entire back catalog of every author from my own collection and a ton of new releases I hadn't gotten to yet. There were at least a dozen nooks and crannies set up for Spud, though it would appear that the cat tower was his favorite, so he could look out the window. The curtains were a soft velvet that were already decorated with cat fur.

The walk-in closet was mostly empty except for my very small new wardrobe.

"I'll help you fill it up, if you want," said Billie.

"You don't have to do that. You've already done so much."

Billie made a sound of protest. "*Please*. I have the money and I want to do this. I will yeet money at anything that makes you happy."

That got me sniffly all over again. Tony pulled me into his arms, hand on the back of my neck, his purr rumbling in that perfect way that got me all melty. "You deserve all of this and more, baby girl."

They shuffled me over to the en suite bathroom. It was pretty much identical in design to every other bathroom in the house—marble floors, a massive tub, and a glassed-in shower big enough for the whole pack. Tropical plants hung here and there, adding pops of color to the white stone. A gorgeously fluffy set of purple towels was neatly stacked on some of the shelving, and all of my new toiletries were lined up like little sentinels along the sink.

"The bedroom door has a lock too," said Hana, appearing in the mirror behind me. "In case you get sick of us."

A weird half laugh, half cry sprang out of my mouth. "Literally no chance of that happening."

Even so, it was nice to have the assurance.

I kissed each of them in turn. "Thank you so much. I love it. I love everything. I love y—"

Nope.

I wasn't going to haul out that declaration quite this early.

It hung in the air anyway.

Billie nipped my earlobe, whispering, "Don't think I didn't notice."

My heart pounded, but I was spared having to explain anything when Roscoe appeared from behind the curtains and screamed for some attention. I scooped up the little tortie.

"My goodness. Someone has some opinions."

"I'm pretty sure that Roscoe is going to be over the moon to have Spud nearby more often," said Tony. "And just in case the thought is flicking around in your head, you don't *have to* stay with us, but we would really love it if you did. If you'd be more comfortable at your brother's, that's okay. This space will be here for you whenever you want it."

God.

There were the waterworks again.

I wanted to stay.

Jasper and Gabe nestled around me, the three of us giving Roscoe some love while I collected myself.

"Is there anything you want to change?" Gabe asked.

"We tried to pick everything based on what we knew already," Jasper added, "but anything can be redone if you'd like something else better."

"It's perfect," I insisted.

"We have another new spot," said Billie. "This one is much less likely to make you cry, but it's still pretty cool."

I laughed pitifully and wiped my eyes. "Lead the way."

The group of us trekked down to the walkout basement, and it was then that I noticed the fabulous glass greenhouse that now occupied the backyard. We stepped inside. The air was thick and warm, with plants tucked into every nook. They were still small, but it was easy to see how they would take over the space in a short while. The center of the greenhouse held a large, round couch covered in pillows that would be absolutely divine in the winter. It was the perfect place to curl up and forget the chilly wind outside.

"This is gorgeous. And smells like heaven," I said.

"Since we're down here," said Hana, "do you want to see what used to be in your room?"

The playroom.

369

"Yes, please."

Back inside, they swung open the door to the prior guest room. I stopped short. My eyes darted to every space, unsure where to settle.

"Questions?" Gabe asked. "Comments? Concerns?"

"I don't even know where to start," I choked out.

Neatly organized shelves took up one wall and were filled with what I could only describe as the stock of a sex shop: toys of every caliber and color, rows of candles, leather items I had never played with, and a wall of hooks that held a variety of cuffs, collars, and harnesses.

I squeezed my thighs together as my brain helpfully supplied the memories of when Hana had put the cuffs and collar on me and when Tony had poured wax on my skin.

There were a few pieces of furniture with sharp angles or sweeping curves. I could only assume that they were for sex, considering the room they were in and the fact that they didn't look like any couches I had ever seen.

Hana sidled up to my back and pressed a kiss to my hair. "When your brain restarts, let me know what your thoughts are."

I let out a squeak.

I couldn't stop my wandering gaze. Curiosity warred with what I thought was a healthy dose of anxiety over the many, *many* possibilities this room offered.

Tony's warm palm settled on the back of my neck, and the tension slowly leaked from my body.

Magic alpha hands.

"I don't even know what everything is," I finally managed to say.

Hana purred. "I'm more than happy to acquaint you."

Tony chuckled and traced his thumb along my throat. "Don't overwhelm her."

"But that's what I do best." Hana gave me a sassy smirk. I was already well acquainted with *that* concept.

"I think I need to look around without five sets of eyes staring at me," I said. It was way too much pressure with everyone watching me. "I also definitely need to be fed before any 'overwhelming' happens."

"I guess that's fair," Hana said and patted my butt. "Upstairs with you then. Tony can make us pancakes."

My mouth instantly watered. "Am I allowed to help?"

Hana cupped my cheeks and kissed me deep and slow. "You can help."

The rush of emotion almost set me off again. "Really?"

She combed her fingers through my hair. "Yeah. If you accept your room, then you're not really a guest anymore. You're one of us."

One of them.

One of the pack.

I threw myself at her, and she caught me without stumbling. It seemed silly now to have worried that at one point she never liked me.

"Group hug again!" Billie yelled. The pack gathered around us, and I breathed them in. They really were like a gourmet coffee shop and bakery.

They smelled like home.

"After we eat, I think we should christen my room," I said. "Break in the bed."

Billie chuckled. "I have thought of very little else since I put in the order for it."

"Okay," Hana said. "Nicky needs to eat. Disperse the hug."

We ventured back upstairs, and I joined Tony in the kitchen, where he prepared the batter while I stood like a soldier with my spatula to flip pancakes on the griddle.

We worked in an assembly line—setting out the syrups and the plates, stacking fresh pancakes, and filling the griddle with more batter—until we had enough food to feed a small army. The dining room table was covered, and we all packed close together to eat.

Pancakes had never tasted sweeter.

Nothing was going to ruin this.

Chapter Forty-Six
Jasper

I found Nicky in the greenhouse with a book. She'd only been staying with us full time for a week, but seeing her curled up among the plants made it seem like she'd been here forever.

"Hey, Jasper, what's up?" She tucked a bookmark between the pages and set her book aside, leveling all of her attention onto me. Tingly warmth flowed to my body. The clinic had already confirmed for me that my levels were starting to go up, but even if they hadn't, my reaction to her would've been a hard and fast clue.

I'd been avoiding asking her if she'd be part of my heat. It didn't matter that we were all reasonably sure she would agree; the possibility of a rejection had frozen the words at every single attempt. I was running out of time, so I'd have to bite the bullet and let the pack baby me if the worst happened.

"Can I talk to you?" I asked.

"Yeah, of course." She scooted over on the couch and patted the space next to her.

I took a deep breath and sat down, pulling her into a cuddle so I didn't have to look at her directly. Nicky shifted and snuggled in tighter.

"Is everything okay?"

"Probably."

I couldn't stop my brain from spiraling into the worst possible outcome.

Her fingers combed through my hair. "Talk to me."

"I have a really big ask. And it's okay if you say no. In fact, I totally get why you might, but I've been quietly freaking out about it for a little while."

"I can't answer if you don't ask me." She kissed my throat and nuzzled her nose against my scent gland.

"My heat is coming up really soon. I want you to be there, but I don't want you to feel pressured or that you have to."

She froze in my arms, and my heart dropped down to my toes.

Nicky pushed away to look at me, and I could see the anxiety in her gaze, feel the tension radiating through her body.

"Jasper... I want to be there for you, but..." Nicky swallowed hard. "I don't think I'm ready for that. A heat is so important, and it sounds really intense. I know it's an all-or-nothing, that it wouldn't be fair to you if I had to leave during it, and I don't want to risk it. I just..."

I nodded since I couldn't bring myself to form actual words. Every instinct screamed inside of me, begging *me* to beg *her*. She was supposed to be there.

Nicky stroked my hair, and I barely felt the touch.

"Are you mad at me?"

My tongue weighed a thousand pounds. I shook my head. I wasn't mad. Devastated, yes, but not mad. My eyes burned, and my chest constricted, like steel bands had locked my ribs in place.

"I'm so sorry, Jasper. I talked with my sister-in-law about heats, and I've been doing research, and it all sounds like it would be too much for me right now. I don't want to fuck things up for you. I really want you to have a good heat experience, and right now I don't think that I would add to that."

I still couldn't bring myself to speak.

"Should I get one of the others?"

I tightened my grip on her. I didn't want her to go *anywhere*. Holding her now wouldn't stop her from leaving me, and it wouldn't undo the fact that she didn't want to be part of my heat, but I couldn't let go.

Bone-deep sorrow crept to the surface.

It was probably more than a little bit stupid to be seeking comfort in the source of my pain, but here I was.

At the very least, she made no move to extract herself and stayed there with me without a word until the sun had dipped below the horizon.

Hana found us out there. One look at us, at the stricken expression I'm sure I must've had on my face, and her hackles were up.

"What happened?" she asked.

Nicky finally pushed away from me, and I was able to see the red rims around her own eyes.

"Nicky's not staying for the heat," I said.

My voice sounded foreign to my ears. The words cracked, and I snapped my mouth shut to swallow down the distress whine that tried to sneak free.

"Should I go?" Nicky asked. "I feel like I should go. I read that being close too near to the heat can set expectations for the instincts. I don't want to make things harder."

It was definitely too late for that, but I didn't want to force her to stay. I sat on my hands so that I didn't reach for her.

"Go back inside," said Hana. "I'll sit with him."

Everything in me protested as Nicky retreated into the house. Hana was with me the second Nicky passed her, and she pulled me straight into her arms, unleashing the torrent I had held at bay. I ugly cried. Sobbed on her until I couldn't breathe, and then I kept sobbing until my head throbbed and my throat burned.

"It's okay, baby. We're all still here."

374

That only made me feel worse. I had so much love and support, and I felt like an asshole that I wasn't satisfied with that.

Hana scooped me up as if I were a child. I was carted back into the house and up to the main floor. Nicky was in the kitchen with her small rolling suitcase at her heels next to Spud's carrier. Gabe had already left for work, but Billie and Tony were with her. Neither looked particularly happy at this turn of events.

Trying to force her to stay would only make things worse. I didn't want her to be part of my heat because she felt like she had to be. I wanted her to be with me, with us, because it was what she wanted most.

Hana set me on my feet and kept a steady arm around my waist. "Do you want to say goodbye or go upstairs?"

The others were watching us. Nicky looked almost as devastated as I felt, but it wasn't stopping her from leaving.

"Upstairs please."

I might regret it in the morning, but I couldn't make myself go through a goodbye right now.

I should've asked her weeks ago, before I'd gotten so close, before the hormones turned me into an emotional mess.

Too late now.

A few minutes later I was tucked in my bed with Hana, Tony, and Billie around me. My sheets still smelled like Nicky, and that wasn't helping my emotions to settle.

"Do you think she'll be safe?" I asked. I didn't like the idea of her being out of sight of the pack for so long with Alphonse still out there.

"She'll have her family," Hana said.

"She promised to do check-ins until the heat starts, too," said Billie. "I don't understand why she doesn't want to stay."

"That's because you have a decade of experience with heats," Tony reminded them. "Nicky's never been part of one. And it's better for her to leave now than for her to freak out during a heat when none of us are in the right mind to help her."

Billie sighed. "Okay, if you want to be all logical about it."

"I agree with Tony," Hana said. "If the heat was happening six months from now, or later, then her answer might've been different. But heats are intense. We all know that. It's a lot even when there's only one other person involved, let alone when there are five of us. Plus she's only been with max three of us at a time, and this would be a several days long orgy. I'm not happy that she's not going to be there, but I understand."

I knew everything they were saying made sense; however, my instincts didn't give a flying fuck about rationality.

They all cuddled around me, giving what comfort they could. I only hoped that when the heat actually hit me I could manage with having my pack incomplete.

Chapter Forty-Seven
Nicky

"I feel like such a dick." I slumped down onto Sidney's couch. Allie pushed a cup of tea at me.

"You're not hurting him on purpose," said Allie. "If you're not ready, you're not ready, and you'd be doing no one any favors by trying to force yourself."

I grumbled and sipped my drink. "I hate all of this. Why can't I just be okay with it?"

"Nick, there's no sense beating yourself up about this." Sidney nudged my shoulder. "What's done is done, and when his heat is over, you can all talk."

"But what if they don't want me back?" The concept of it made my throat burn. I set aside my tea and buried my face in my hands. "What if I fucked everything up and they all hate me?"

"Then they're not the people you thought they were," Sidney

said firmly. "I don't care how casual some people are about their heats. Even in my line of work, it's a big deal to share with someone. Omegas are vulnerable during that time, and if you can't be a good caretaker to them, then you shouldn't be there. And the rest of that pack knows that too, or they should."

Allie nodded along. "It'll be okay. If they kick up a huge fuss over this, then I'm not above throwing hands."

The thought of Allie trying to take on Hana was enough to make me laugh. "Please don't."

I sank back into melancholy. Spud was as displeased as I was. Poor little thing was not a fan of being parted from Roscoe. I sighed. It was only for a couple of weeks. Tony had said that he would let me know when the heat was over. Part of me dreaded walking back in knowing that I had let Jasper down.

"Finish your tea," Allie ordered. "You're not allowed to be sad *and* dehydrated."

I wished I had left on a day when I worked and not the start of my break. There was nothing to distract me, no way to fill my time, and that left me far too much space to think about Jasper.

When Sidney and Allie went to bed, I was left alone and awake in a silent house. Time crept by with every second making itself known.

I sat on the couch and absently pet Spud until he got tired of me and went to go lay in his bed. I tipped over on the couch and indulged in a good cry. The sobs shook my whole body, and I did my best to muffle the sound on one of the couch pillows. Self loathing burrowed deep, hooking its claws into my chest.

Soft footsteps came down the hall, and my brother appeared in a housecoat.

I sat up sharply and wiped my face.

Sidney sighed and sank down next to me. "Do you want to talk?" he asked.

I sniffled. "I don't know what there is to talk about. I'm abandoning my omega when he needs me because I'm a chickenshit."

Sidney snorted and put his hand on my shoulder. "You're not

a chickenshit. But I think it does speak some pretty loud volumes that you called Jasper *your* omega."

Heat rushed into my cheeks.

"What scares you about it?" Sidney asked.

I shrugged. "I don't know. Everything. I don't like feeling out of control."

Sidney nodded slowly. "You *are* a bit of a tight-ass. So you're worried that the heat will make you lose too much control?"

"Basically. What's it like? Being on the outside of one?"

"Well, I know you've never done ecstasy, or you wouldn't be this uptight, but I knew a fair few people in college who did, and they always compared it to that. I've never taken it myself, but I've looked up the effects."

"That's not making me feel any better about it."

"I know, but I'm not trying to make you feel better. I'm trying to make you understand. Obviously, things would be different for you than for me, but with so many people involved, it could be comparable." Sidney sighed and scratched his head. "The basics of it are that you're going to be very awake and energized, very warm, and extremely horny."

He laughed at the face I pulled.

"I know you don't wanna think about that part with me, but it's still true. There's a reason they have underground clubs for people to indulge in omegas in heat. It's a drug hit with no negative side effects."

I fussed with my cuticles and grumbled to myself. "I wish I could relax about this more."

"If you bit the bullet and participated, Jasper's hormones would do that for you. But Nick, I've said it before, and I'll say it again. You don't have to do this. Jasper has plenty of caretakers."

I swallowed back the response that *I* should be one of them. "I think it's all harder because I feel like I'm letting all of them down and I've gotten too attached."

Sidney looked at me curiously. "You're going to have to explain that last part."

"How so?"

"You're dating a pack. Were you planning on doing that casually?"

My shoulders leapt up to my ears. "I hadn't really thought about it. They came out of nowhere, and I rolled with it."

Sidney flicked me in the forehead, and I clapped my hand over the tender spot.

"Ow!"

"You're too smart to be this much of a dumbass," Sidney said with a laugh. "You need to think about this a little bit harder. Because, if you're intending to stay with them, there's no such thing as too attached. What do you want, Nick?"

"Quit trying to make me examine my inner desires."

"Nope. Do you see a future of just you and Spud, or do you want to be with that pack long-term? Do you wanna live there? Bond with them? Marry however many of them you please? The time for rolling with it has kind of passed."

I groaned and stole one of the couch pillows, hugging it to my chest. "It's all happening so fast."

"Yeah, I'm not surprised about that."

I quirked my head, surveying his expression. "Why?"

"You hooked up with a polyamorous pack. They know how functional relationships work, and they know how to integrate new people into an existing framework. Presumably, they're good at communicating, at least with each other, for things to be working as well as they are. You stepped into something with people who know how to make space and take care of each other. Be honest with yourself about how much you want to be a part of that."

"I don't know how I feel about you taking over the title of smartest one in the family."

Sidney chuckled. "We all have our strengths. This just isn't one of yours. You don't have to tell me what you decide, but I'd love it if you would give it some thought so I don't have to wake up to the sound of you sobbing."

I frowned. "I didn't mean to wake you."

He moved to flick me again, but I was able to dodge this time.

"I don't care that you woke me up. I care that you're hurting. You can inconvenience me as much as you want, and your well-being will always be the part that I care about."

I tipped towards him and snuggled under the arm he lifted to hug me. "I love you."

"I love you too, Nick. Do you want me to stay up with you?"

"No, I'll be okay. And I'll think about what you said."

"Good." He kissed my forehead and gave me a squeeze. "Sweet dreams when you get there."

I sighed and flopped down over the couch as he retreated to his bedroom, feeling sorry for myself. Was Jasper okay? Were they all secretly mad at me for leaving?

I picked up my phone, my fingers itchy to text them, but I set it right back down again. The effects of the heat still freaked me out a bit, and there was no sense in reaching out and making this break harder.

Spud's interest in me renewed, and I fell asleep to him curled up and purring on my chest after staying up long enough to not completely fuck over my sleep schedule.

When I woke, I was tucked in bed, disorientation washing over me, alleviation arriving a moment later only to be replaced by an empty ache in my chest. I felt hollowed out. My craving for the pack burned deep.

Allie and Spud were on the couch when I emerged from my room.

"Good afternoon, sunshine," Allie chirped.

I waved half-heartedly and dropped myself down next to her.

"You look a little rough," she said.

"I feel it." I gave Spud a scratch, starting his little engine.

"Do you wanna go get some ice cream?" Allie asked.

"Sure. Anything to make the time go by faster."

I washed, dressed, and ate a piece of toast so it wasn't straight sugar going into my stomach. Allie turned it into a shopping trip, but I was grateful that she seemed dedicated to distracting me. We got our ice cream and bought some new swimsuits that were on discount for the season, and I got a new pair of cozy boots. Laden with our purchases, we stopped for a meal at a pasta place, where I stuffed myself on spaghetti and meatballs until I could hardly move.

"Feeling a little better?"

"Much, thank you. I needed this."

"We should have a girls night! I can call Meg and Luna. Do you want to invite anyone?"

My brain flipped instantly to the pack, but I stamped that down. "I could invite one of the girls from work."

"Yes! Message your people, I'll message mine, and we can go to this cute cocktail bar I've been dying to try."

I had Miranda's number, but I hadn't actually used it yet. It was mostly there to let her know if I happened to be running late. I messaged her anyway.

Three hours later the five of us were clinking glasses in a sparsely lit fancy bar. I'd borrowed a little black dress from Allie that I barely managed to squeeze into, and she'd opted for a terra-cotta jumpsuit that set off the warmth of her skin and contrasted with her dark curls that spilled down her back. Luna was in a pink minidress, with a sparkly headband tucked into her riotous blonde curls and blue eyes gleaming with mischief. Meg and Miranda had unknowingly both chosen a gorgeous hunter green that looked beautiful on them.

Luna kissed me hard on the cheek. "Feels like a million years since I've seen you."

"Only three months."

"That's a long-ass time, Nicky." Luna thrust her glass in the air. "To the sexiest bunch of ladies in history."

I laughed and clinked my glass against hers, taking a sip of my appletini. I tried not to think about how nice it would be to have Billie and Jasper here, too, for another evening of dancing. I loved my friends, and it wasn't fair to them if I was wishing someone else was there, but the absence of the pack was an ache I couldn't soothe. Being away felt wrong. The appletini helped a bit, and both Allie and Luna had a similar overwhelming chaos energy to Billie that swept me away.

They both made me dance with them before passing me to Meg.

"Talk to me, Nicky," Meg said, dipping low to my ear. "How can I help?"

I put my arms around her and snuggled in. "I don't think anyone can. I'm just being a baby."

"Healthy boundaries don't make you a baby. You know, I still haven't been part of a heat."

"Really?" I lifted my head, examining her face in the strobelights. "Why not?"

Meg shrugged. "Never felt right, yet. And if it doesn't feel right for you to take that step right now, then I'm certainly not going to judge you for it."

"Thank you," I said, hugging her tightly.

Miranda appeared, giggling at our side, and a moment later Allie and Luna joined us as well, the five of us dancing until I was breathless. It wasn't the sexually charged dances I'd shared with the pack; this was distractive chaos.

Miranda fit in great, and all my worries that we weren't close enough or that maybe she would be too much of the shy librarian stereotype to enjoy herself were for naught. She laughed along with the rest of us.

It didn't hurt that Luna was the master of bringing in new people so they felt comfortable.

We ate and drank and swapped dating stories, the energy of the evening filling me up with a lightness I desperately needed.

"All right down to business," Luna declared. "Who's on the prowl tonight? Meg? Miranda?"

She wiggled her eyebrows at me.

"I'll wingwoman," Allie said.

"Aren't you on the prowl, Luna?" I asked.

She waved me off. "I feel more like assisting tonight. Now, who are we getting laid?"

Miranda burst out laughing and playfully nudged me. "I like your friends. They're fun."

"Does that mean we're helping you?" Luna asked.

"I haven't done a bar hook-up since my early twenties. I'm pretty sure I'm a little too rusty for it."

"Nonsense!" Luna said, slapping her hands on the table. "We will un-rust you with some quality hot people. What's your preference?"

Though it felt a bit like prying, I looked at Miranda curiously. She was a beta, too, and this topic had definitely never come up at work.

"I'm an equal opportunist," she said. "My last boyfriend was an omega, but I'm open to anything."

An idea struck me like lightning.

"Can I bother you with some questions about that?"

Luna bounced in her seat. "Nicky's got an omega boy on tap."

"Sure," said Miranda. "What do you wanna know?"

"Did you share heat with him?"

"Yep, though just one before we split. He hired a Heat Helper because I was not even close to being in shape enough to keep up with that."

"What was it like?"

Miranda chugged the rest of her cocktail and set the glass down hard on the table. "Hottest experience of my whole fucking life."

My face burst into flames.

Luna high-fived Allie.

Meg laughed and waved down a waiter to get us another round.

"Seriously though," said Miranda, "while it was fucking hot, I definitely overdid it. Pretty sure I pulled something in my hip. I should've done some bootcamps or something to prepare. You're thinking about being part of a heat?"

I nodded.

"Start training now, then. Get as well-fed and hydrated as you can in the days beforehand."

"It's in the next week or two."

"Oh..." Miranda trailed off. "Yikes. Well, never say never. You could make it work, you'll just need some recovery time. I fit a smaller dress size when I came out of the heat. Can't say I recommend that, I was shriveled up and parched as the Sahara."

I stewed on the information while Luna pulled focus back to happier topics, and scanned the bar patrons until she found someone she deemed cute enough.

"There. Tall, dark, and gorgeous." Luna pointed out a woman that would've towered over all of us, except Meg, dressed in red sequins and high heels, with smooth brown skin and a halo of curls.

"Oh my god! Yes, please." Miranda chuckled. "She's way too pretty."

Luna sprinted across the dance floor in the center of the bar, skidding to a stop next to the woman. She let out a laugh and allowed herself to be pulled back towards our table. Even in the dim light, I could see Miranda's cheeks lit up like pink neon.

"Selene, this is our sexy beta, Miranda. Miranda, this gorgeous specimen of an alpha is Selene. You should both go dance."

We watched the two of them head out onto the dance floor before we collapsed into giggles.

"Luna, I swear, you have some kind of magic power," I said, chuckling.

Luna grinned and wiggled her fingers. "Leave no friend unlaid is my philosophy. Miranda made me like her enough that that policy now applies to her."

"So when do Luna and I get to meet your pack?" Meg asked. "Allie's been feeling way too special being the only one who's met them."

"Oh, maybe next month, if they all still like me by then," I replied, my mood slipping.

"Are you anticipating them not liking you soon?" Meg asked.

"No, no, no," Allie said, tapping at the table. "We're not talking about the pack tonight; we are distracting Nicky from being sad."

"You all should come to yoga," Luna declared. "I've got a super sexy aerial yoga class I've been teaching."

"Since when do you do yoga?" I asked.

"Since I realized how hot I look in the pants. I finished all the training a few months ago, and now I get to be the yoga teacher that everyone lays their lusty eyeballs on."

"I could check it out. And you," I said, with a wink. "I've started getting a little bit more serious about my physical health, and if I don't do something while my trainer is occupied, I'm gonna lose all my progress."

Luna squealed. "Then it's settled! You can come to all my evening classes, and I'll make sure you're all buff and flexible."

"Come dance with me," said Meg. "We'll work on your cardio."

I let Meg tug me out onto the dance floor and spin me around to the high tempo pop song that was playing from the speakers. Meg was beautiful, as tall as Hana, but dancing with her made me miss my pack. I swallowed that down and tried to focus on the music. Meg spun me so fast I needed to hold her to stay upright. I giggled in her arms, and when I tripped over my own feet, she caught me.

"Whoa there, girl." Meg laughed and wrapped her arms around me. "Do you want to go for another spin or get another drink?"

"Are water and snacks an option?"

"Always." Meg escorted me back to the table, and we passed Miranda tearing up the dance floor with Selene.

"Keep our married lady company," Luna ordered. "Meg is going to show me a good time out there."

The two of them bounded back onto the dance floor, and I settled in next to Allie. "You don't want to dance?"

"I will, but I'm going to let one of them get tired and settle down first. Someone has to guard our food and drinks."

We got another tray of finger food and glasses of water for all of us. I didn't make it back onto the dance floor, but I was able to successfully distract myself from the storm of emotions that I was keeping at bay. Loud music and happy friends were a good remedy for now.

When the evening finally came to a close, with Miranda and Selene going home together, we parted ways: Meg taking Luna home and Sidney picking up Allie and I.

I stayed up for the sake of my sleep schedule, plowing through a book and thankfully not waking my brother with crying this time.

Hopefully, tomorrow would go as well.

Chapter Forty-Eight
Gabe

"How's he doing?" I asked.

"Not amazingly," said Billie. "I wish I could fix it."

"You and me both." I tucked my beta into a hug and kissed their forehead.

"I really thought my info dumping at her about my first heat with Jasper while she was packing to leave would be enough to calm her down about it."

"You tried," I said. "That's all we can do. Do you think Jasper's up to some company?"

"I doubt he would say no to you."

I slipped inside Jasper's room, where my omega was fussing around with his nest. He'd been wandering in and out of our rooms all day gathering up laundry, blankets, and pillows as he saw fit to fill his space with our scents.

I kissed his cheek, catching him off guard and making him jump.

"Would it be better or worse for you to get some things from Nicky's room?"

Jasper's bottom lip wobbled. "I don't know."

"Do you want me to go up with you and see?"

He flexed his fingers against the blankets. "What if she doesn't want us in there?"

I pulled out my phone and sent her an inquiry text. There was no sense in Jasper making himself work with hypotheticals when I could find the answer. A reply buzzed a moment later.

"Nicky says you can take anything you need."

My poor omega sucked in a shaky breath.

I sat next to him and cupped his cheek. "I know that you're hurting, and I want nothing more than to be able to fix it, but this is the best that we can do for you right now. Can I bring you up to her room?"

Jasper nodded and swiped at his eyes.

I could still remember the first time he asked me to be part of his heat. There had been a sense of honor to be asked, but it hadn't outweighed the nervous anxiety that I wouldn't be able to give him what he needed. I didn't begrudge Nicky the fact that she didn't feel ready to be included in something so important, but I hated seeing Jasper like this.

"Come on. Let's get your nest fixed up."

I pulled him off the bed and into my arms, kissing him until the sour notes of his sadness faded in favor of his usual sweetness.

"You know I love you, right?"

"I do." He sighed. "I love you too."

We took the journey upstairs slowly, pausing outside of her room for another series of distracting kisses until he felt strong enough to push through that barrier.

I stood by his side as Nicky's subtle, spicy scent billowed out in the whoosh of air from the doors opening. Jasper whined softly and pawed at his chest.

"She should *be* here."

"I know."

I walked with him as he let his instincts guide him, his fingers curling around a sweater from her hamper and the soft sheets we had bought for her. It took both of us to remove them from the bed, and Jasper wrapped himself in them like a many-layered cape.

"Are you home from work for a while, or are you going back until your heat starts?"

"Home for now. I'm sure I would burn things if I tried to go to work now."

I kissed his forehead. "I'm glad you're getting some rest."

I didn't have the same luxury. I would be stuck at work until I got the call that Jasper had gone into heat. It was hard to take proper advantage of heat leave when we never knew exactly how long his heat would last or the day that it would start. Sometimes he hovered at higher levels for a week before tipping over, and others there was barely a couple days of warning. Luckily, the pack schedules made it possible for there to always be at least one person available to him.

I turned to a knock at the door and found Hana watching us. She glided towards us and wrapped Jasper in her arms.

"Hey there, baby." Hana kissed the top of his head.

She was always the one to stick closest to him in the early phases of his heat, though I was never one-hundred-percent certain if that was because of her protective instincts or if it was to make sure that her body was ready for him. Tony and I had the advantage of having cocks at the ready, but Hana needed the continuous heavy dose of Jasper's upcoming heat hormones for her body to start its own shift to accommodate his needs.

"Did you find everything you need?" she asked.

Jasper shrugged under his sheet pile.

Hana sighed. "I want to be mad at her for this, but I know that's not right."

"She'll be here for the next one," I said.

At least, I hoped so.

If participating in heats was going to be a dealbreaker for her, then it would be a long recovery for all of us when we had to end

390

things. We couldn't date her and have her leave like this for future heats. Jasper would be a mess, and as much as I despised the idea of breaking things off with Nicky, we would have to do that for him. I only hoped that she would come around.

Hana and I got Jasper back to his room and sat nearby while he arranged his new acquisitions into the nest.

If I could argue with his omega instincts and rationally explain why Nicky wasn't there, then this would be so much easier. Jasper liked Nicky too much and felt too safe for his primal omega brain to stay objective.

I'd been feeling that pressure myself. Coming home to her being here felt right, and though alpha instincts weren't quite the same, mine still nudged at me all the same. Nicky was pack, and pack belonged together.

I didn't know how strong the pull was for betas. Billie had been the one to bring us all together, but their personalities are drastically different, so I'm not sure that any information Billie could give us in that regard would be relevant to the situation.

The primal depths of my instincts wanted me to go and find Nicky, toss her over my shoulder, and drop her into Jasper's nest for him. Lucky for all of us that my rational brain was able to override that. I itched to see her, to put my hands on her and assure myself that she still wanted us.

My omega was going into heat, and he was in distress. Both of those things were like a banshee in my ear, demanding that I fix it.

I gave in.

"I need to go for a walk," I said. "Will you two be okay?"

Jasper nodded and burrowed deeper into Hana's arms.

"Go," she said. "We'll be here when you get back."

GABE:

Can I come see you?

391

She followed her reply with her brother's address.

Instead of a walk, I ended up on my motorbike, zipping through the city and winding residential roads until I pulled to a stop in front of Sidney's house.

The door opened as I got off the bike, and Nicky wandered out in a pair of jeans and a fuzzy sweater, her hair down with the tips curling softly. Her eyes had a hint of redness like she'd been crying not long ago. That wouldn't do.

I hadn't planned anything on the way here, hadn't decided if I wanted to kiss her senseless or beg her to come back with me.

I settled on kissing her, swinging my leg over the bike and meeting her approach. She stood up on her toes and locked her arms around my neck, letting me melt into her, devouring her until I was drunk off her taste. She still wanted us...wanted me. That soothed the deepest instincts, even if it was only a temporary fix. I couldn't ask her to come back, and my brain, slowly being steeped in Jasper's pre-heat hormones, wasn't quite capable of thinking of anything else to say.

She let out an *oof*, and I realized I had backed her up against the garage. Without missing a beat, she lifted one leg, and I hooked my hand under her thigh, giving her a boost as she jumped the rest of the way. I braced us and sank into her touch.

A honk behind us had my heart leaping right into my throat.

"If you two are going to get freaky, make sure you do it indoors so you don't get a public indecency charge," Sidney said as he swept out of his car. His wife hopped out of the passenger side.

"Cool bike!" She grinned. "Are you going to take Nicky for a ride?"

I set Nicky back on her feet, enjoying her squirm of discomfort at being caught.

"If she wants to go," I replied.

"Definitely better than staying here and getting gawked at," she said teasingly.

I passed her the spare helmet, and the light flickered back into her eyes as she accepted it. She looked perfectly adorable with the massive black orb engulfing her head. "I'll have her back before curfew."

Sidney laughed as I climbed back onto the bike, and Nicky settled herself behind me.

We took off together. The snug hold of her arms and the whipping wind did a lot to recalibrate me. For the moment, things were the way they were supposed to be.

I drove until my fingers started to cramp and pulled to a stop at a viewpoint for the mountains.

Nicky hopped off, her eyes bright, energy high. "That was so fun!"

She looked so perfectly delicious and so wonderfully receptive as I parked the bike and stalked towards her. I reveled in the heave of her chest.

"Do you want to play, princess?"

Nicky nodded breathlessly. "Play how?"

I caught her chin. "Run. And, when I catch you, I'll show you exactly how much I'm going to miss you while you're away."

She trembled in my grip and spun on her heel, taking off down the trail that led to the river. I gave her a few seconds headstart before setting off.

My alpha instincts were running on high, and though I couldn't drag her back to the pack house, I could satisfy them this way.

There was no one else at the viewpoint, and I pushed myself into a run, my strides eating up the distance between us. Towering oak trees and thick firs lined the trails, weaving all the way down to the river. Nicky disappeared around a bend, obscured by the branches. Her cardio still wasn't up to snuff to outrun me, and I knew she wouldn't last long. She was already slowing as she came into view.

A quick glance behind her, seeing me close, had her picking up speed, and the endorphins of chasing down a willing lover buzzed in my blood. I was close enough to hear her labored breathing as she charged ahead, her feet slapping against the gravelly trail.

"Run, little beta."

Nicky's scent exploded, wafting back to me as she scrambled up another path.

A few more moments and I surged forward, wrapping an arm around her waist and using our momentum to spin her so we didn't come crashing down. She was flushed in my grasp, whining desperately as I pressed her up against one of the oaks.

I held her jaw snugly and forced it up until she had to stand on her toes, sliding my palm down to pin her to the tree by her throat. She shook, doe eyes wild, lips sweetly parted as she struggled to catch her breath.

"You're a temptation," I said, tugging aside the neck of her sweater and laying my mouth on her skin, "and I'm ready to give in."

Nicky squirmed perfectly. Her gasp as my teeth raked over her was exactly what I craved.

"Pants off, princess."

I leaned back to watch her trembling hands undo the button and zipper of her jeans and shove the stiff fabric over the curve of her ass while she whimpered beautifully. She stepped out of her shoes and onto the soft moss, and, while I kept her pinned with one hand, I wrestled off her clothing with the other until she was bare from the waist down against a backdrop of the forest and twisting river.

I buried my fingers between her thighs and drank down her sighs, thrusting into her wet heat as she gripped my jacket.

"Did you like being chased?" I bit her lip and licked over the tender spot. "Your pussy says that you did."

Nicky moaned, thighs shaking around me. "Yes. I liked being caught, too."

I pushed my own pants down and freed my waiting cock from

my underwear, hoisting her up to press her against that tree with my hips. I bit down on her throat, teeth grazing her scent gland as if I could will a bond into existence and bind her to my body and soul.

Grinding against her, I angled my cock to slide into her, fighting against every instinct and forcing myself to go slow. She writhed in my arms, her ankles locked around my waist, pushing me deeper.

Nicky did a bit of her own devouring, branding herself on my lips. Each gasp she puffed against my mouth as I fucked into her fed my basest instincts. I let my cravings guide me until she was mewling and her cunt pulsed around me.

"Yellow," she whispered. "The bark is hurting me."

I dragged myself out of the haze of lust long enough to let her down and spin her so she faced the tree, stripping off my leather jacket and laying it against the bark for her. She buried her face against it and cried out as I slid back in and reached to tease her clit.

"Better?"

She nodded frantically, her pussy spasming around me and letting me know she was close. I held her by the throat and nipped her earlobe.

"Anyone could see you right now. Getting fucked in the woods by your alpha, desperate to come." I breathed in the sweet spice of her. "Tell me you want it."

"I do," she keened. "I want it so b— *fuck*."

Nicky lost it. Her cunt convulsed, and I sucked in a sharp breath, working her clit and scraping my teeth over her throat as she bucked in my arms.

I fisted a hand into her hair and craned her neck so I could suck a mark onto her skin, my own little brand. My fingers kept up their work, and I rode her until my own pleasure pushed me over the edge, burying myself as deeply as her body would allow and stroking her until I had made her come one more time.

"Gabe!" Nicky keened, pressing her hips to bring me a little bit deeper.

We stayed there against the tree until she had caught her breath. It was only then that I slid free and kneeled down to help her into her panties, kissing one rounded ass cheek on the way up. We both righted our pants, and I wrapped her in my leather jacket, pressing her against the bark to consume as many of her kisses as I pleased and leaving her lips plump and her eyes bright with desire.

Nicky hooked her arms around the back of my neck and grinned up at me. "I guess I have a couple new kinks to add to my list." She burst into giggles and buried her face against my chest.

I cupped her through her jeans. "And how do you feel about carrying me around with you?"

"Three new kinks, then." She pulled me in for another kiss.

With the lust and adrenaline starting to fade, reality threatened to roar back in. My fingers snuck around her throat and squeezed gently until her doe eyes widened and her whole body shivered. I wanted to stay right here.

Her breath came in quick little gasps. "Gabe?"

I loosened my grip. "I'm not looking forward to being separated from you. You belong with us."

Begging her to stay was on the tip of my tongue, but I bit it back.

She wavered, gaze dropping, her fingers curling into my shirt.

"I'm not saying that to pressure you, but I thought it needed to be said. We're going to miss you."

She opened her mouth and closed it again without speaking, wrapping her arms around my chest and nuzzling my cheek. "I don't like being away *at all*. I just don't want to make it harder for Jasper." Nicky turned, whispering in my ear, "I'm going to miss all of you, too."

I hugged her for the longest time before finally stepping away. "I should take you back and get home to Jasper. I shouldn't have left, anyway."

"Why did you?"

"A few weeks without you freaked me out. You and I haven't had as much time together as I'd have liked, and I think part of me worried that we'd become distant while you're away. I needed to top up on you to last me through that." My answer made her smile even beyond the sadness that echoed in her eyes.

"If you'll all have me back again after this, I promise I'll be ready next time." She kissed me softly. "A few weeks apart won't change how I feel. I— The pack is so important to me."

I pulled her in for another kiss, drinking in the soft sweetness of her before reality prodded at me again. "Come on, let's get back."

We picked our way along the trails to return to the viewpoint and climbed onto my bike, starting the twisting journey home. She clung to me the whole way, and when I dropped her off, I spent far too long breathing her in and sucking another mark onto her skin while she squirmed in my arms.

Unease settled into my bones as I drove away.

All of the pack was home and waiting for me when I arrived. I sidestepped them all and went upstairs to shower. They all likely knew where I had been, but that didn't mean I was going to bring Nicky's scent to Jasper's bed, not when I didn't know if that would make things better or worse.

Tonight she was just for me.

Chapter Forty-Nine
Nicky

"Hey, what's up?" I answered Tony's call on the first ring when he called the next night. "Is everything okay?"

"Not really," he said. "I don't want to bother you, but I'm at the hospital with Billie, and I thought you would want to know."

Panic roared through me like a freight train. "Oh my god! What happened?"

Tony sighed. "They tripped on the stairs. We're pretty sure they have a concussion."

"Oh, shit. What can I do? Can I come to the hospital?"

"We'd love to see you," Tony said softly.

"Send me a pin. I'll be right there."

I still had a couple of hours until I needed to start work, and I'd be damned if I was going to let work get in the way of making sure that Billie was all right.

I messaged Miranda to let her know I might be late, and followed up immediately with a call to my boss.

"Hi Patricia, I'm sorry to bother you this late."

"Not a worry. What's going on Nicky?"

"One of my partners is in the hospital. I'm heading over there now."

"Oh my goodness, I'm so sorry. Take the night. I'll stay at the library until morning."

"Really?" Relief hit me like a truck. "You're amazing. Thank you so much. I'll keep you updated."

"Please do. Take care."

I threw on a sweater and shoes and hopped in my car, letting my phone direct me to Tony and Billie.

They were still in the emergency room when I arrived, and I raced to their sides.

Tony seemed pleased to see me, and it loosened one of the many knots in my stomach I'd been harboring since I'd left the pack house. I gave him a quick hug first before looping my hand through Billie's. They had a giant goose egg on their forehead and looked totally out of it.

"Hey, honey." I kissed their cheek. "How are you feeling?"

Billie whimpered, their grip like iron in my hand. "Everything is wiggly. I don't like being dizzy."

"Nicky."

I turned to Tony, taking in the worry lines between his brows and the way he chewed his bottom lip.

"I really hate to ask, but I think I need to. I have to stay here with Billie, and Gabe is short-staffed at work, so he can't leave quite yet. Jasper is going to be in heat any minute now, and only Hana is there with him. Our food service order got fucked up. We were heading out to get some temporary supplies when this happened. Could you..."

"Oh god, of course. I'll get whatever you need." Nerves at seeing Jasper right now were overridden by the fact that my pack needed me.

Tony's shoulders dropped. "Thank you. I'd ask you to stay here with Billie while I did all that, but..."

The moment he tried to pull away Billie's unfocused gaze shot to him, tears glimmering. "Don't leave me. Don't..."

"He's not going anywhere." I kissed Billie's hand. "They're going to take really good care of you. I have to go get some things for Jasper, but Tony will be here with you."

Billie's glassy eyes flickered between me and Tony before they groaned and closed them. Tony caught me in a kiss that warmed me all the way down to my toes.

"Thank you," he said again. "Jasper will be in the nest with Hana. You can leave everything in the kitchen, and I'll bring it up to them when I get home. They don't have to know that you're there at all."

I hugged Tony, burrowing into his arms and breathing in his coffee and caramel scent while tucking my nose against Jasper's bond bite. Craving for the pack sank into my bones. I didn't want to leave Tony's arms, but Jasper needed me, and if I was too chicken to join his heat, then I could at least do this task for them.

I left a few minutes later with a list of what they needed. The hospital was nearby where my parents lived, so I went to their usual grocery store. The only cashier on staff this late waved to me as I entered the store. I waved hastily back and beelined for the section for premade high calorie meals perfect for omega heats. I grabbed a stack of them as well as a bunch of fruit and a few containers of pastries that couldn't compete with Jasper's but would be easy calories. I wanted to rush through the purchase, but the cashier was slow as molasses, and nothing seemed to want to scan, so he typed every single item in by hand until I was ready to scream.

As soon as I paid I dragged everything out to my car at top speed, dropping it all into my trunk and racing away to the pack house. The guard at the gate let me through, and I zipped down the street, coming to a stop in their driveway.

The house was dark.

I unlocked the front door with the key they had given me the same day they'd given me my bedroom. Struggling my way inside under the weight of the groceries, I dropped it all in the entryway and stood, huffing and puffing to catch my breath.

The varied scents of the pack hung in the air. Jasper's scent was heaviest among them, all sweetness thickened with desire like a syrup pouring down my throat. I shook my head and steeled myself, taking the bag of apples I'd bought into the kitchen to wash.

Fixing the hurt I had caused would be as easy as walking upstairs... I hated being away from the pack, and even though I was nervous as hell, the thought of leaving this house again without making things right felt wrong. I wasn't sure how far gone Jasper would be, if it was possible to talk to him or if I would fall face first into the heat high, but it was a risk I was willing to take, to make sure that he knew how much I loved him.

I froze. I hadn't fully admitted it to myself, but the truth was there. I'd been falling fast and hard for this pack, and they meant so much to me that I couldn't even begin to comprehend a future without them. If I needed some extra care on the other side of things, I knew the pack would step up to help me.

Staring at the ceiling, I tried to pluck up the courage to carry everything upstairs. Tony had said I could leave it all in the kitchen and go without anyone else knowing I was here, but who knew how long it had been since Jasper and Hana had eaten? What if they were hungry? It was a flimsy excuse at best, though it was enough for me to override some of my trepidation and gather everything up to take it to them.

I bundled the clean fruit into a bowl and set it into one of the grocery bags, hooking everything over my arms to trudge up the stairs. My lungs burned by the time I reached the top. Apparently, lugging around fifty pounds of groceries overwhelmed what little bit of cardio I had gained with Hana's workouts.

I crept towards Jasper's room in the strangely oppressive silence. I managed to open Jasper's door with my elbow, taking a deep breath, bolstering myself to take the final step.

My arms burned as I shoved my way inside, trekking over to

401

the kitchenette to unload everything. I was *not* fit enough for this. The scent of his heat hit me like I'd walked into a brick wall. Sweat prickled instantly on my skin, every inch of me tingling. My first instinct was to breathe as deeply as possible, sucking in more air until my body throbbed.

The curtains around Jasper's nest were closed, but now that I was in here and not moving, I could hear his whimpers and panting breaths and the slick sound of what was probably Hana fucking him.

I bit down on a whine.

Need pulsed like a heartbeat in my cunt, and my skin burned. I shoved the meals into the freezer, leaving the fruit and pastries on the counter. I braced myself, shivering head to toe. My initial apprehension was being quickly drowned out by the burgeoning desire that wracked me.

Jasper cried out and I spun around, staring at those closed curtains. My feet carried me over of their own volition. Standing on the edge of everything was too much. Ready to dive in, I reached out to part the fabric.

I moaned, hands shaking at the sight before me. Hana's body had completed its temporary shift to accommodate our omega's heat needs, her clit swelling up to rival an alpha cock. It disappeared in measured thrusts inside of Jasper.

Mine.

Why had I ever tried to deny that?

Jasper whimpered and reached for me, and I couldn't hold myself away from him any longer. Our fingers laced together and I climbed onto the bed, claiming his mouth. I groaned. His skin was as warm as sunlight, and every breath was saturated with cinnamon and chocolate and desire. It rippled through me like a tsunami hitting the shore.

"You came," Jasper said when I pulled away.

"I'm so sorry, Jasper. I'm still scared, but I hate being away from you."

Hana snared a handful of my hair, not hard enough to pull, just to keep me in place and get my attention. She growled low in her chest, adrenaline soaring through me. "Stay or go, but decide now. You can't leave him again if you don't go now."

No part of me wanted to leave. Being away from the pack didn't feel right, and leaving Jasper when he needed me wasn't an option.

I kissed him again and wrapped my fingers around his cock. "I'm here."

Jasper choked on his breath as my hand moved, and Hana renewed fucking into him, releasing her grip on me. I licked over Jasper's scent gland. He tasted so good and smelled even better. Every second I spent in his presence eroded my lingering resistance, unraveling knots of fear and insecurity.

I could surrender.

They would catch me.

He came with a sharp cry and spilled over my fingers.

I was so hot. I tugged at my clothes, peeling them off and throwing them to the side, drowning myself with sweet, drugging kisses until there was nothing else except for Jasper.

My omega.

Hana pushed a thick, flexible dildo into him and rolled him onto his back so I could climb on top. I was already dripping wet and shivering by the time I teased my clit with the tip of his cock, sinking down on him and bringing our hips flush. We both shuddered, and it took only a few thrusts for him to come inside me. I kept moving, carrying him from one orgasm to the next as I chased my own pleasure.

I jumped when Hana pushed my hair aside and scraped her teeth against my throat, pausing only briefly when she found the marks Gabe had left on me before adding her own.

"Thank you for staying," she whispered.

Her fingers dipped between my thighs and stroked my clit. My body was already on the edge, her touch pitching me over as I came with a broken cry, my pussy clamping down on Jasper, setting him off again.

Hana maneuvered us around until I was on my back with Jasper buried in me, and she fucked him relentlessly from behind.

Jasper sucked at my throat and I writhed under him. Everything was so warm. The cells of my body felt like they were vibrating with need.

At some point Jasper succumbed to the haze of his heat, his eyes going out of focus and his coherency disappearing. Hana was a powerhouse, pounding into him, fucking me by proxy.

I was half-awake when the curtains parted again and Gabe froze there.

"Nicky...you're here." His voice was like melted chocolate, a growl and a purr coalescing as he descended first to Jasper, licking into his mouth, before leaning down to me, branding himself against my lips.

Jasper's whimpering spurred Gabe onward, and he shed his clothes, climbing into the nest with us, and closed the curtains again to plunge us back into darkness.

The two alphas held Jasper between them, his weight pulling away from me, my pussy aching at the absence of him. The flood of hormones as the haze took him made me dizzy. Hana spun Jasper around and supported him as Gabe buried himself to the hilt. I unsteadily got to my knees, stroking a soft hand down Jasper's back and sucking at his throat. The air was thick with the scent of sex, slick, and chocolate cinnamon, the alpha scents drowning beneath the overwhelming cloud of our omega.

Jasper was passed back-and-forth between the three of us, though too often I had to sit things out and be an observer. The alphas were like machines, their bodies hyper fuelled to take on an omega heat. I might be high as a kite, but I didn't have the muscle power to back it up.

There was no sense of time in the nest, nothing to mark its passage beyond the number of times Jasper had come, but even that I had lost track of.

I rose out of the fog when the curtains around the nest parted and Tony appeared with Billie in his arms. Our beta was passed over to Gabe, and Tony shed his clothes with an impressive efficiency, pulling Jasper into his arms and fucking into him with one smooth motion. I sat back shivering, unable to tear my eyes away from the sight. We plunged back into darkness as Hana whipped the curtains shut and helped Gabe maneuver Billie up against the headboard with some pillows wedged to keep them in place.

Crawling across the nest towards them restored my feeling of balance. We were all where we were supposed to be now. Little flickers sparked in my mind, trying to remind me of something important, but I was too far gone to know what it was. I tucked myself at Billie's side, kissing their cheek softly and snuggling in for a nap.

A hand on my ankle jolted me awake at some point, and I looked back to see Jasper gripping me like a lifeline, his face pushed to the bed, Tony riding him like he was a rebellious stallion that needed to be brought to heel. They had all been beautiful when I'd had the opportunity to play with them, but now they were *wild*. The fire in their eyes sent a little ripple of fear up my spine followed immediately by heat pulsing through my body, an undeniable, unquenchable desire.

I crawled toward Jasper and stretched out, lifting him just enough so that I could devour his mouth. The alphas groaned. Goosebumps rose over my skin, and a moment later my thighs were thrust apart, Hana's fingers plunging between them. I arched off the bed with a helpless cry that Jasper ate up. My hand slipped beneath him to wrap around his cock, and I consumed the sweet, desperate sound that he made, stroking him to completion with the same diligent effort as Hana's rhythm between my legs.

Billie whined from their position against the headboard, and Gabe tore his gaze away from us to attend to our beta. My brain was too deep in mashed-potato-mode to think about how Billie was supposed to participate in their condition.

I came with a sharp cry, bucking against Hana's hand. That only made the neediness worse.

I was lost to the heat until hunger and the desperate need to pee forced me back to the surface. I stumbled out of the nest and used the en suite bathroom, catching sight of myself in the mirror. My hair was a mess, my body flushed and covered in hickeys. Good thing I had nowhere to be.

I snatched an apple on my way out and scarfed it down voraciously. The alphas showed no signs of slowing down. Maybe it was my job to take care of them? I grabbed an armful of water bottles, gasping at the chill against my skin, and carried them back into the nest.

I held the first for Billie and helped them take some sips, before I opened the others one by one and made the alphas drink between their turns with Jasper. I got Jasper in a rare moment that he didn't have a cock in his ass and got some water into him, too.

His eyes were still glassy.

Hana tossed me a tangle of straps and a dildo almost as thick as my forearm. I stared at her helplessly. She crossed the bed and hooked everything up around my hips, sliding the dildo through the ring at the front before she cradled Jasper.

"Your turn, Nicky."

This was new territory for me, and the hormone soup that my brain had become wasn't making a lot of things clear, but I could probably handle this. I just had to mirror-image flip things in my head. Gabe's hand wrapped around the faux-cock and dragged me forward. I braced myself on Jasper's hips and my omega groaned beautifully. Gabe guided me to fit the toy between Jasper's round cheeks, nudging me until my hips met our omega's.

Jasper whimpered and it was the most perfect sound I'd ever heard.

I pulled out part way and snapped my hips forward again, watching it disappear into his body. That was way hotter than it had any right to be. I stared, transfixed, as I did it again, and Jasper clung to Hana as he took every thrust.

I lost myself in the rhythm. My thighs burned, but I kept going, Jasper's cries the only music I needed to keep time. There was a strange sort of power in this. Maybe Jasper would let me wear a strap-on outside of his heat.

A warm hand wrapped around my throat, a body pressing up against my back.

"You fuck him so well, baby girl." Tony groaned in my ear, his locs tickling me as he leaned to kiss along the curve of my shoulder. "Don't stop."

Tony's hips rolled with mine, and it was like he'd lit a fire beneath my skin.

"Do you want me to fuck you while you fuck him?" he asked.

"Yes, *please.*"

Tony pushed me forward with a hand on the back of my neck until I was plastered to Jasper. My alpha's cock nudged my center, teasing with a few shallow thrusts before sinking into me.

"*Fuck.*" I squirmed and rocked my hips, Jasper echoing the sentiment.

Tony pulled me up, the angle keeping me from taking all of him. When he thrust into me, it propelled me deep into Jasper, our omega pressing his hips back into me, and the three of us set a rhythm that stole my breath. The ache in my body was almost too much to bear.

I couldn't come this way, so fucking Jasper like this had become an exquisite torture of edging that held me so close to that bright flame without letting me touch it. Leaning into Tony, I surrendered to the flow and let him carry me through the movements. Jasper's orgasms came in waves. It took so little to set him off in the height of the haze. I kind of wished that I had the same option as Hana, that my body was able to adapt for him, that I could feel the greedy squeeze of him as I fucked him.

We traded off when my legs gave out, Hana disentangling me from the strap-on and burying her face between my thighs. Tony had taken over fucking Jasper, and Gabe shoved pillows around me, so that none of my muscles had to work while Hana devoured me, before cradling Billie so they weren't left out.

My body shivered and strained, her tongue gliding over my clit, until she lifted her head and dragged my hips closer, slipping her clit-cock into me with one smooth motion. It was a little slimmer and shorter than the cocks of the other alphas, but Hana fucked with a ferocity that dropkicked me into my next orgasm.

Jasper angled himself over me and kissed me until I was light-headed, his fingers sliding down to tease my clit. Having Jasper so close dulled my exhaustion and tempered the ache in my muscles. I pulled him closer and fastened my lips on his throat, sucking a hickey onto his scent gland. He was like a shot of espresso to my brain, relief pouring into my blood.

I came again with a strangled cry and dug my nails into Jasper's skin as he and Hana ruined me. Jasper followed me over the edge, and I slid free of Hana, flipping him over and pulling him away from Tony so I could climb onto his lap, sinking onto his waiting cock, rocking us both to another completion as my eager fingers worked between my thighs.

The next time I opened my eyes I was curled up next to Billie. Every inch of me felt thoroughly exhausted.

"She lives," Billie said with a quiet laugh.

"Barely. How are you feeling?"

"A little better. Not enough to get my world rocked, but less nauseated."

I kissed their cheek. "Good."

"Make sure you're taking care of your basic body needs. Our stuff doesn't slow down like the alphas and omegas."

I blinked at them, not quite comprehending.

"Get some water and food, use the bathroom, and then come back here for another nap," they clarified.

I glanced over at the others who were currently engaged in a fourway. My pussy wanted to be a part of that, but absolutely nothing else had the energy to engage. I shuffled out of the nest and completed my tasks, returning with a bottle of water and a protein bar. Cuddling up next to Billie, I consumed them both slowly, my eyelids feeling like they weighed a million pounds.

"Enjoying the show, Books?" Billie asked.

"Hard not to." I nibbled my snack while we watched Jasper get tag-teamed. "Wish I was that sturdy."

"I consider us all lucky that I'm *not* that sturdy," said Billie. "If I could get dicked down all day with no consequences or limitations, no one would ever get anything done."

I burst out laughing, only briefly drawing the attention of the alphas. "That is very true."

"I'd make sure that you get at least five of these into you," Billie said, tapping my water bottle.

"I'm going to have to. I feel like a raisin, and I would definitely enjoy being a grape again."

Billie giggled. "On your next journey out, bring back as much as you can carry. Just because everyone else can go at it like jackrabbits for days doesn't mean it's actually good for them. I usually try to shove a few meals into them during the haze. Which is not an easy task, let me tell you. They would all shrivel to beef-cake jerky if not for me."

"I will take up the task until you're feeling better."

"I'm super bummed that I'm laid up for this heat. I was going to have you and I DP Jasper with strap-ons."

I choked at the thought. "That's *possible*?"

"Yep," Billie chirped. "Omegas are very stretchy during their heats. Next time, I guess."

We lapsed into silence. When I had finished eating, I stumbled out of the nest to collect more supplies. I handed things to the alphas in between their turns and managed to steal Jasper to pour half a bottle of water down his throat. My energy didn't last long, and I collapsed against Billie once more, the two of us curling up for a nap.

I fell asleep to the sounds of pleasure and the scent of chocolate and cinnamon infusing every breath.

Chapter Fifty

Jasper

Gabe held me by the throat, a firm hand tangled in my hair as I panted and keened, desperate for his touch. I groaned pitifully. If he kept me on the edge much longer, I was liable to force him down, climb on his cock, and force a knot. Not that I was strong enough to do that, but the idea played in my head on repeat.

"Please. God, please. I need to come before I lose it."

Gabe pulled me closer and chuckled in my ear. "Since you asked so nicely."

His hips jackhammered into me, every thrust stroking him as hard and deep as my body could take. The slap of skin on skin echoed within the confines of the nest.

Tony appeared from my peripheral vision and settled himself comfortably in front of me on his knees, his hand closing on the back of my neck so that the two of them created a collar with their fingers. His other fist wrapped around my cock and gave a firm tug that stole my breath as Gabe's hips snapped forward, burying himself deep. Both alphas shifted their hands at the same time and sank their teeth into my throat, one on each side. I came with a scream that had Nicky's doe eyes widening.

Gabe's knot swelled inside of me. The exquisite stretch and burn of him demanding space in my body set me off as surely as the rhythm Tony had set on my cock.

My vision blacked out.

Twinned sets of teeth sank into both of my wrists, laying claiming bites on my scent glands that kicked me over the finish line again, pleasure so sharp I couldn't even draw the breath to scream this time.

When I resurfaced, I was still bucking and writhing in their grip. The pressure of Gabe seated deep in me kept me on the edge. Warm lips wrapped around my cock and plunged it into the sweet heat of an eager mouth. Out of the corner of my eyes, I could see Hana and Billie at my wrists, which meant that it was Nicky and her magnificent tongue that sucked me straight into another orgasm. The pleasure was like a ratchet wheel, cranking up each time as my pack worked as a unit.

"Please," I begged.

"I thought you *wanted* to come, omega." Gabe nuzzled my ear and nipped my earlobe.

I squirmed, caught in exquisite agony as the pack pulled too many sensations from me. The heat made me resilient, able to withstand more than I thought possible every time I went through this with them. I always wanted more as much as I wanted a break to recover.

I flexed my hips, trying to get a little bit deeper into Nicky's mouth, but that tugged against Gabe's knot. I groaned, back to panting and losing all capability to form actual words. Usually, getting a claiming bite on one scent gland was enough to kick me over the edge, but four at once threatened to shut down my brain. Packless omegas would never know that bright, delicious pain that

411

seared down to the bone and branded the feel of those bites into their soul.

I wanted Nicky to bite me, too.

I wanted her to claim me, but the others would have to hold me down, or I would claim her in return and cement a bond that she wasn't ready for. Tony kissed the thought out of my head, and I drowned in the taste of him.

Gabe rocked his hips, and I lost it again. This early into the heat, most alphas didn't knot because of an omega's insatiable demand, but with a pack on hand, they could do with me as they pleased.

And boy, did they please.

They eased me down to the bed, and Gabe took the full weight of me, pinning my arms with his and tangling our ankles like he was a human St. Andrew's cross.

Nicky gave me a wicked grin as she straddled my waist and settled down. Hana slid behind her, fondling Nicky's breasts as if this were my own personal peep show.

"Should we test your training out?" Hana asked her.

Nicky moaned beautifully. "Yes, please."

"Good girl," Hana purred. "If you can take me, then you're one step closer to taking the others."

Tony passed her a bottle of lube, and I held my breath. I wouldn't be able to see what was happening next, but I was eager to feel it. Hana pushed Nicky forward, and she took the opportunity to tangle our tongues and kiss me breathless. She gasped into my mouth and whined as Hana worked her body with a slow rolling flex of hips. I ate up her sounds and felt the first perfect breach as Hana's temp cock slid into Nicky's ass and brushed along mine through the thin barrier inside of her.

Hana moved gently with her, but from the way that Nicky wiggled, I could tell that we were both eager for a little more force.

Tony inched up behind Hana. "Have room for me, beautiful?"

"Always."

She paused long enough for Tony to sink into her, the groan of pleasure rippling down the line of us.

"No fair," complained Billie. "I don't care that I'm dizzy, I want in on this."

Billie crawled over, and, balancing against the headboard, they lowered their pussy right to my mouth. I flicked their clit with my tongue, tasting the light, spicy flavor of them, and moaned against their skin as the movement between Nicky, Hana, and Tony picked up, the three of them finding a rhythm, punctuating every thrust with delicious groans and moans and cursing. Billie's thighs shook around my ears, and I did my best to focus on their pleasure as Gabe pressed up into me and Nicky's hot cunt squeezed me. I shuddered, another blissful, but tamer orgasm rippling through me.

"Perfect omega," Gabe murmured in my ear. "Taking everything your pack wants to give you. You feel so good gripping my cock like that."

Our betas toppled one by one, Nicky coming first, and I grunted, sucking hard at Billie's clit, as they rode my face to chase the last dregs of their pleasure. Hana's cry echoed next, followed by Tony.

I lost track of everyone as my own orgasms rebounded, the pack sliding free of one another and settling around me, except for Nicky who stayed right where I wanted her. She leaned forward and kissed me again, whispering my name and licking at my ear, the syllables coming out breathy.

"Bite me," I begged. "Please. I want you to claim me."

Nicky's mouth slid down immediately, sucking at my scent gland. I craned towards her throat on instinct, sinking my teeth in. I struggled against Gabe's hold, desperate to curl around her, but he held me tightly. When Nicky bit down, I screamed against her skin, my hips flexing between her cunt and Gabe's cock, savoring the burn from tugging on his knot.

"Fuck," his curse echoed in my ear.

I waited for the comforting warmth of a fresh bond, but it didn't come, and I was too hazy to dig into why.

Nicky's tongue swept over my tender skin, and when she raised her head again, it was only far enough to reach my mouth, her hips carrying me through another rise.

Every cell in my body was a live wire.

Nicky kissed me softly one more time before she lifted herself off of me with glassy eyes, slinking down my body until she kneeled between Gabe's and my legs. I squirmed, instincts spreading my thighs further as she leaned in, lips brushing over the crease, her teeth sinking into the scent gland there. Searing heat, pleasure, and pain sang through me, my awareness of Nicky bursting like starlight in the pitch black.

I glanced over, seeing the bright red on Nicky's lips as she sat up again, her eyes impossibly wide. She whimpered, bringing her fingertips to her mouth, gaze flicking between my face and the bite she'd left on me.

A bond bite.

None of the others seemed to notice or grasp what it meant. But I knew.

She was mine now.

Gabe relinquished his hold on me, and we rolled to the side so we could cuddle until his knot went down. I gathered Nicky close and licked over the bite I'd left, savoring every perfect sound she made.

She'd come back for me. My perfect, beautiful beta.

Mine.

Chapter Fifty-One
Nicky

The haze was over and I was *exhausted*. Even with sleeping as much as I could and stuffing my face on snacks at every opportunity, it wasn't enough to offset everything I'd put my poor corporeal form through.

Everyone was fast asleep. I crawled my way free of the nest and stumbled to the bathroom. The mirror showed me a hot mess. My body looked like someone had chucked me into a giant tumble dryer, leaving me bruised, sweaty, and haggard. I leaned on the counter when my legs started to shake from the effort of holding myself upright. A bright red bite sat on my throat. I traced my fingers over it, trying to remember exactly when that had happened, but the entirety of the heat haze blended into one amorphous blob in my brain. The bite didn't hurt, which was odd considering how much the rest of me did, but maybe claiming bites weren't painful and I just had no experience with them?

Sinking down, I leaned back against the cupboards, trying to wrangle my thoughts. It was so hard to think when I was the human equivalent of a raisin. I crawled into the kitchenette and sat on the floor chugging a water bottle before I shoveled some pasta salad into my mouth to start refueling my body.

Roscoe was screaming outside of the door.

"I'm coming, baby."

I crawled to the door, out of breath by the time I arrived, and greeted the little tortie. Roscoe aggressively headbutted me, swirling and purring like a buzzsaw as he restocked his love supplies. I walked downstairs on unsteady legs to get him some food and fresh water. My head ached from dehydration, and my muscles burned, but I was the only one who was really fit to be managing things that involved leaving the nest. The alphas were still in the last phases of their rut, and Billie was still on bedrest, so it was all up to me.

I clicked on the lights as I went and shivered as I hit the main floor. Why was it so cold down here? Maybe I was too used to the warmth of the nest. I fed Roscoe first and chugged a glass of water, wandering to check my phone in my purse that I had discarded in the entryway.

Holy shit.

Sixty-seven missed calls and almost forty-nine text messages awaited me.

Oh fuck. I'd been here for three days according to the date on my phone.

The messages were split between Sidney and Allie, my parents, Luca, my boss, and Miranda. I phoned Sidney first, not bothering to check my voicemail yet.

"Nick, thank god. I've been trying to get a hold of you for days. Are you okay?"

"I'm so sorry. I'm at the pack house for Jasper's heat. I hadn't fully intended to stay. I should've let you know, but I left my phone downstairs when I brought over their groceries."

Sidney sighed. "I'm just glad you're all right. Have you heard about the library yet?"

That didn't bode well...

"What about the library?"

"Fire department was called down there yesterday. The whole facility is shut down."

"What?! What happened?"

"Suspected arson from what I've heard, but they haven't named any suspects."

"Oh shit! Is everyone okay?"

"I'm not sure. I only know what the newspapers have been saying. Have you talked to your boss yet?"

"No, not yet. You're the first one I called. Can you let everyone else know that I'm okay and that I'll be in touch when Jasper's heat is over?"

"Yeah I can do that," Sidney replied. "How's the heat going?"

"I feel like I've been climbing mountains." I laughed quietly. "Everything hurts, but I'm glad I ended up being here for him."

"Good. Take it easy when this is all over. I'll let you get caught up with your boss and get back to your pack. Love you."

"Love you, too."

I sent a quick text to Miranda to update her so she wouldn't keep worrying.

I dialed Patricia next and hit her voicemail. "Hey Patricia, it's Nicky. I'm so, so sorry that I haven't been in contact. I totally understand if I'm fired over all of this, but I swear it wasn't on purpose."

I gave her a quick rundown on how I had ended up in my situation and hung up, hoping that I'd still have a job at the end of all of this, but with the library in the state that it was, who knew if we had any jobs to go back to. Losing my little sanctuary would devastate me, and my stomach heaved at the thought.

If Alphonse had done this to get back at me...

I shook my head and set my phone aside. I hadn't had enough rest to sit through all of the messages that awaited me. I left out some extra dry food for Roscoe and filled him up a fresh bowl of water. Poor little thing had been a bit neglected during all of this. At least Spud was with Sidney and Allie. He'd have been screaming outside Jasper's door the entire time if he'd been here too.

My skin started to itch being out of the nest, so I gave Roscoe one final pat and made my way back to the stairs.

"Nice whorehouse you've gotten for yourself. Do you pay for the luxury here with sex?"

I spun in place and froze, my heart pounding, panic buzzing in my ears.

Alphonse stepped out of the dining room.

"What the fuck?" I crossed my arms over my bare chest, wishing I'd grabbed a robe to come down here. "What do you want?"

"I thought I've been very clear about that. And don't bother covering up. It's nothing I haven't seen." He sighed, his voice unnervingly soft. "Nicky, be reasonable. I know that you love me. You waited for me to come back until this pack brainwashed you. If you would come with me, we could talk: clear your head from their influence."

My skin crawled.

"How did you find me?"

Alphonse shrugged. "You showed me right where you were. I followed you from the grocery store. One of my friends works there and told me when you came in, though it took a while to figure out how to bypass the security for the community. They should really invest in a better alarm system for their home. I've been waiting for you to come down so we could go together."

My brain tried to process what was happening, but I was tired and hungry and dehydrated. Of course he decided to show up when I was at my worst, when I didn't even have a stitch of clothing on. One instinct from childhood burrowed to the surface—call 911 in an emergency—and I tapped 911 on my phone, hitting the call button. I couldn't speak to them without alerting him, but maybe they would get here in time?

"To think you were right next door to my own mother all this

418

time." His body became rigid. "She'd been talking about you, calling you Kiki for some fucking reason. I didn't realize it was you. I could have saved you from these people sooner if I had."

"So you *did* break into my apartment? Why?"

I heard a quiet voice from my phone and turned down the volume so Alphonse wouldn't notice.

"I had to be *sure* that it was you. Your lock wasn't very secure. You had pictures everywhere, and that confirmed it. I'll admit I got a little out of hand in there, but you have to understand how much you've hurt me with your behaviour, Nicky. What was I supposed to do when everything I offered you was rejected so you could degrade yourself for these people? You're not well. You need to get some space from them."

"Get out," I snapped, panic making my voice squeaky.

He tutted. "That's not very welcoming."

"It wasn't supposed to be, jackass."

Alphonse stepped towards me, and I backtracked into the living room, hitting my ass on the couch and bringing myself to a stop.

Okay, maybe I shouldn't have gotten quite that snappy.

"I don't know whether to be proud or furious that my instincts about you were right. You've been spreading your legs for a whole pack. I heard you in there. Moaning like a fucking whore. You used to be so *good*, Nicky. A shame."

He set a gun on the kitchen table and looked at me pointedly.

Fuck.

"What do you *want*?" Panic climbed up to lodge in my throat. I couldn't stop shaking. I only hoped I was far enough away that he wasn't able to see it.

"I want you to fall into line. Or, at least, that's what I wanted before you went and ruined yourself. You used to be so *agreeable*, Nicky. What happened?"

"I found people who give a shit about me, that's what. We're not together, Alphonse. We haven't been together for years! I don't understand why you even care about what I do with my life."

I swallowed my distressed whine, eyes flicking between Alphonse and the gun. If I screamed, would the pack even hear me? How *could* I scream without knowing what he might do when they came down the stairs unprepared, just as I'd been to see him?

None of Hana's lessons had included what to do in this type of situation.

"Because you're *mine*, you ungrateful bitch. That doesn't change because you got it in your head that you weren't. You belong to *me*. Come here," he ordered. "We're leaving."

"Where are we going?"

Getting closer was the last thing I wanted to do—but I really didn't want to get shot either. I didn't trust him to be rational. Maybe I could delay him, distract him, until someone noticed I was gone for too long or the police arrived. Hopefully, they were actually on the way.

"Away. I don't fucking know, Nicky. You had cops all over my fucking house, so I can't take you there. I've been couch surfing with college buddies since you pulled that bullshit. I have friends all over the country. We'll find somewhere."

I squeezed my phone to anchor myself.

That seemed to draw Alphonse's attention to it for the first time. "Drop it."

I set it on the hardwood so the microphone wouldn't be muffled.

I took a step towards him. Then another. I didn't really have a plan, but I had to do something.

"Now, you're going to get on your knees and apologize for debasing yourself. For *ruining* your body when you were supposed to take care of it so I could enjoy it."

Nausea churned in my gut, and I rooted to the spot. "Please don't do this."

"Move," he snapped.

Alphonse picked up the gun, and my eyes flickered instead to the withering bouquet of roses on the kitchen table. I kept my steps as steady as possible, one foot in front of the other, even

420

though it felt like I was walking up to the gallows. I stopped and fisted my hands to hide their shaking, bracing myself on the table. He seemed almost amused.

"Did they use you too hard, little whore? You'll have so much repenting to do when we're finally together, without these people standing in our way."

I made a big show of leaning on the table, breathing heavily and letting myself shake so he wouldn't view me as a threat. Hopefully, all the work Hana had put into training me meant that I was actually strong enough to pull this off...

Alphonse reached for me, and I snapped my hand out, my fingers catching the edge of the vase, and I brought it straight onto his face with all the force I could muster. Alphonse bellowed as water, glass, and flowers struck him. He dropped the gun and it went off, a bullet whizzing past me and embedding itself in the wall. I scrambled to grab it and took off.

I had almost reached the stairs when he barrelled into my back and we came crashing to the hardwood. My whole body erupted with pain, and I screamed at the impact. Alphonse flipped me over, slapping me across the face so hard I saw stars. I threw the gun as hard as I could, cracking one of the living room windows, and I screamed as loud as possible until his hand clamped down over my mouth, pressing my lips against my teeth so that I tasted blood.

"Shut the fuck up or I'll go find that gun, walk upstairs, and kill every single one of this fucking pack that's brainwashed you against me."

It was getting hard to breathe, and panic pounded through my body, demanding I do *something*.

I grabbed at his face, raking my nails over his skin and shoving my thumbs into his eyes until he shrieked and threw me to the side. His weight crushed me, his knee pressing into my spine until I couldn't draw a breath.

Footsteps thundered down the stairs.

Alphonse's weight disappeared, and I looked over to hazily see Hana grab a fistful of his hair and throw him away from me. She

421

barreled straight into him, giving him no chance to steady himself. More footsteps followed, and Tony dropped to my side, gathering me into his arms.

The alphas wouldn't be feeling as worn down as I was, but this was like a fresh fighter being pit against an opponent who had already gone a dozen rounds.

Alphonse got a good hit in, punching Hana when she turned back to check on us. I'd never seen her take a hit before. She stumbled back, one hand covering the side of her face. A hit like that would've probably knocked me out cold. I struggled out of Tony's arms, trying to get to her, and the moment Alphonse reached for me, Tony swept up behind me, his fist bashing out Alphonse's two front teeth.

"What did I tell you about coming for my beta?" Tony growled.

Alphonse let out a string of curses and cupped his now-bleeding face. Hana pulled me aside, and checked me over, her eyes still glassy from the last edges of the rut. She took in my battered body, her growl rising, and her sharp mint scent taking on a burnt edge as the fury rose in her. I shied away from the intensity.

I turned back to the fight as Tony hit the ground, Alphonse holding a handful of his locs with his leg rearing back to deliver a kick. Hana tackled him, and they both crashed to the floor. She drove him face first into the floor by his hair, and his shout was cut off with the impact. Hana struck again and blood splattered over me. Her growl vibrated down to my bones.

Alphonse wasn't moving anymore.

I struggled over to them, stepping over Tony to throw myself at her. "Hana, stop."

She growled and turned her attention to me, gathering me into her arms and breathing deeply up my throat as I burst into wrenching, ugly sobs.

Hana cradled me tenderly. "*Mine.*"

She shook in my embrace, taking deep, gulping breaths to

bring herself back to a properly lucid state to deal with the situation.

"Are you hurt?" she asked.

"I'll be okay," I told her. She didn't need to know right now how much pain I was in.

Alphonse groaned, and there was a flood of relief that I wasn't sitting next to a dead body, that I hadn't just watched my alpha commit a murder to protect me. Hana set me aside and wrenched Alphonse's arm behind his back.

"Tony, see if there's any rope or handcuffs in the drawer under the couch," she said.

He moved unsteadily but followed her order, returning with a pair of pink, fuzzy handcuffs that seemed almost too comical for the situation. Hana locked them onto each of Alphonse's wrists and sat back to survey the damage.

She rubbed her forehead. "God, the rut is making it so hard to think. Have you called the police?"

"I dialed them earlier. The call should still be going," I replied.

Tony leaned against my back, wrapping his arms around my waist, breathing me in as if to assure himself I was real.

"Where's your phone now? Are they close?" he asked.

"By the couch, I think. I don't know how long until they get here." I found my phone where I'd left it and stumbled back into his arms, letting both of my alphas cradle me.

"Hello?" I said into the phone, turning the volume back up.

"Thank goodness!" The operator sounded so relieved. "Everything has been recorded, and the police are about two minutes out. Are you safe at the moment?"

"Yeah, we managed to fight back."

"Can you give me the complete address?"

I had no idea what the full address was off the top of my head, so I put the phone on speaker for Hana to relay the information.

"Can you tell me what happened tonight?"

"Home invasion during an omega heat," I said. "We managed to fend off the guy who'd broken in, but he's hurt, and so am I."

I stayed on the line with the operator and detailed the injuries as best I could—trying to keep my voice from breaking—until flashing lights appeared through the windows.

I fetched one of the blankets from the couch nest and wrapped it around myself, tossing one to Hana and Tony as well before I opened the door. The reality of the situation faded in and out as I answered their questions and they took Alphonse into custody. Paramedics arrived shortly after the police.

They had almost the entire altercation recorded by the operator, and they'd caught him trespassing with a weapon. With any luck, he'd be locked away for the rest of his fucking life. The pack was going to press charges, and the laws were extremely strict when it came to anyone endangering an omega in heat.

Hana had gone upstairs at one point to let the rest of the pack know. The haze was over, but everyone was exhausted, and no one was quite in the right state of mind to handle what had gone down. I answered the officer's questions while the group of us were cuddled on the couch nest. Jasper plastered himself to me.

Safe.

I never wanted to leave this spot.

"Can we take you to the hospital, Ms. Marino?" one of the paramedics asked.

Every instinct kicked into gear, and I burrowed further into the pack's embrace. "Can I go later?"

"We'd prefer you go now, but you can decline transport. Since you say that you didn't hit your head and nothing appears to be broken, you should be all right to delay seeking medical attention. Though, I don't anticipate your next few days being very comfortable."

That was already in my future anyway with the toll the heat had taken. I would deal with the pain if it meant staying near my pack.

Alphonse groaned. He mumbled something, the words obscured by his missing teeth and swollen face. I vaguely caught *press charges*, or at least that's what I thought he might have said. It seemed likely given the context.

One of the officers near him laughed. "Good luck with that, buddy."

The paramedics took Alphonse away, the police having replaced the fuzzy handcuffs with standard issue, cuffing him to the gurney.

We waited on the couch nest while they began their sweep of the pack house.

"God, Nicky," said Gabe, nuzzling my cheek. "I'm so fucking sorry. I should have been there. I should have—"

"You were keeping Jasper and Billie safe," I insisted. "They're your pack and they needed you."

Gabe started to growl and swallowed it down. "*You're* my pack, too." He nudged Tony aside to settle next to me, and I breathed in the sharp bitterness of his tea scent that slowly mellowed the longer he held me.

Jasper turned red-rimmed eyes to me. "It was *my* fault Gabe couldn't help you. We were knotted, and...if I wasn't in heat, you wouldn't have gotten hurt."

"Jasper, no." I pulled him into my arms. "*Alphonse* is the reason I got hurt, not you."

"You're the one who sent me to check," said Hana to Jasper, turning next to me. "He was freaking out, and no one could figure out why. He said you needed us."

As the adrenaline faded, a fresh wave of exhaustion claimed me, and the pack let me nap until the police had finished their work. They had collected the gun and found the original window Alphonse had broken in through in the dining room. It took them a couple of hours to finish their investigation. It was cut-and-dried from my perspective, but they wanted to be thorough.

Jasper whined next to me, and his scent spiked, his whole body shivering. The alphas shifted restlessly.

"Nicky," Jasper gasped. "I can't stay down here."

I kissed him softly. "Go upstairs. Take everyone with you. I can finish up here." I didn't want the pack to leave me, and Jasper leaving, in particular, made me queasy, but he couldn't have a flare-up in front of the police.

"You can't stay down here alone," said Jasper, shuddering.

"I'll stay with her and clean up when they're done," said Hana. "Go. We'll be there soon."

Most of the pack retreated back upstairs, leaving only Hana with me on the empty main floor. The police finally finished their sweep and deemed the property safe enough.

Downstairs was still a mess. Hana had me wait in the couch nest while she swept up the glass and wiped up the lingering blood and water from the floor. I wanted to help, but even without moving I was in too much pain to manage. Hana taped up a garbage bag over the broken window in the dining room and deemed things as good as they were going to get, finally turning her attention back to me.

Her eyes were clear by this point. "What do you need?"

"A shower hotter than a volcano, to start with."

Hana directed me to the main floor bathroom.

"Close your eyes. I don't want you to see the blood." She patiently soaped me down under the blistering spray. "I'm proud of you."

I shivered. "Why?"

"Well, unless someone else was down here, I can only assume it was you that fought. That *you* were the one who hit him with the flower vase and disarmed him before I got there."

My tears started up again, and I sobbed until my throat was raw. Hana held me throughout.

"I was so scared," I finally managed, voice cracking.

"I know. I heard the gunshot. I wasn't sure what it was at first with the haze clouding me, but then Jasper lost it, and I took off with my heart in my throat."

Hana hugged me fiercely.

"Thank you for saving me," I murmured.

"I just came in at the end. I have no doubt that you would've been able to save yourself, but I'm glad I got the chance to be there." She lifted my chin and kissed me softly. "My brave girl."

I plastered myself against her. "I don't want to ruin the heat. Should I stay down here?"

426

"*No.*" Hana grabbed my face with both hands. "Your presence ruins nothing. If you're nearby, then we can comfort you and take care of Jasper and Billie at the same time. Don't isolate yourself. If you truly want to stay down here, then I'll stay with you, but if you're doing it for any reason besides wanting to for yourself, then I'm going to have to insist you come back upstairs."

I nodded slowly, too tired to argue when I didn't *really* want to be alone. "Okay, I'll go back."

She took me straight into Jasper's bathroom and got the bath running for me to soak my aching muscles. Billie came to join me, with some assistance from Gabe, and the two of us sat in the warm water. Hana brought me a water bottle and some painkillers along with a bowl of stew she warmed in the microwave. Being in Jasper's presence pulled her instincts to the surface again. She was drawn back to him, and the others took turns checking on me while I snuggled in Billie's arms.

"That asshole is lucky Hana didn't one-hit kill him," Billie said. "Threatening a pack member while an alpha's in rut is wildly stupid."

I tucked closer. "I'm not a pack member though."

Billie snorted. "I'm pretty sure if we took a vote on that, you'd be proven wrong."

"But... No one has *said*."

"Gabe said downstairs, and I'm saying right now. Girl, we gave you your own bedroom here. Granted, I know that's not words, but I personally thought it spoke pretty loud. I don't wanna know what life is like without you. I want you to be part of our pack and stay with us, love us. Because I'm pretty fucking sure that I love you, and I don't care how early it is into our relationship, I'm saying it."

I shivered and sucked in a breath. "I'm pretty sure that I love you, too."

My tears made another appearance over the declaration from this bright, beautiful beta who had laid their eyes on me and given me everything I had now. Billie caught me in a smooth kiss, and I let them distract me from the terrible happenings of the day, sinking into the affection and the reality their words brought forth.

"You could ask any of them, and I know they would say the same," Billie said. "I'm sorry that we weren't louder about it. Once that lot is fully back in their right mind, I'd probably have to duct tape their mouths shut to keep them from telling you. Do you want all that, Books? To be with us?"

"It feels scary to say yes," I confessed. "I want to, but I think I need to let everything settle a bit. I don't want all the amazing and terrible to be muddled up in this clusterfuck of a day."

"I can respect that. For now, let us take care of you, okay?"

"Okay," I agreed.

"Good." Billie kissed my cheek. "Now take your medicine and eat your food."

Chapter Fifty-Two
Hana

Holding Nicky made me feel better. Unfortunately, it made everyone *else* feel better, too, so I had to wait my turn while they cuddled her in the nest. As the heat had faded to a manageable level, the reality of what had happened hit the pack hard.

Nicky had been below our feet, fighting for her life.

We had promised to keep her safe, and we had failed.

"Do you think they'll let him free?" Nicky asked quietly.

"No fucking way," said Billie. "The laws are super strict around omega heats. He totally fucked himself by choosing to come at you during Jasper's. They're definitely going to throw the book at that asshole."

Intellectually, I knew that we weren't at fault for what had happened, but it didn't make the acceptance of it any easier. It wasn't often that I felt helpless, and I was *not* a fan of it. Now, I had to grapple with the idea that, if we hadn't noticed in time, Nicky might be dead right now. I had told her that I was sure she could have saved herself, but she'd been pinned when I'd gotten down there, and it wasn't a position that was easy to get out of for anyone, let alone a newbie. A couple of extra minutes and she could've passed out, been kidnapped, or killed, or...

I sucked back a sniffle.

Reaching over, I stole her from Gabe, curling myself around her, and burying my face at her throat, breathing in the delicate scent of old books and nutmeg.

"Will Hana and Tony get in trouble for hurting him?" Nicky asked.

"Also no fucking way," answered Billie. "Alphas in rut protecting their pack are pretty much absolved from anything they do in self-defense. Even if they'd committed murder, there's no court that would convict them when *he* broke into *our* house during a heat."

I had never known that level of fear and rage before. If Alphonse didn't actually get locked away forever, then I would kill him myself the moment he was free. It was only Nicky's intervention that had stopped me from killing him to begin with. If all three of us alphas had descended upon him in a full rut, Alphonse would've never survived.

I was still on the fence as to whether that would've been better or not.

I wanted him to suffer, but I also wanted Nicky to feel safe in the knowledge that he could never hurt her again.

Nicky squeaked in my arms, and I loosened my grip. "Sorry."

"It's okay," she murmured, closing her eyes and snuggling deeper. "I don't mind being squished, I just need to be able to breathe."

"Question," said Billie after we all settled back into silence.

"What?" I asked, lifting my head.

"Is anyone else going to comment on the bond bite situation?"

I had noticed the bite on Nicky's throat and assumed it was a claiming bite. "What are we supposed to comment on?"

Billie pried Jasper's thigh open, revealing a matching bite.

"*Jasper!*" I gasped. "When?"

Nicky was bonded. To my omega. Did she even know?

I glanced down at her, and she opened sleepy eyes. "What're we talking about now?"

I wasn't quite sure if her finding out would be good or bad. She hadn't even intended to be part of the heat, and now she was walking away with a permanent bond. I knew that alphas and omegas had a compulsion to complete bondings, but I hadn't thought that was something betas dealt with. I vaguely recalled her biting his throat, which wouldn't have mattered since Billie and Tony had already claimed those spots. She'd have had to go out of her way to complete the bond. Maybe it was on purpose?

"Nicky," Tony said her name softly, settling in by her head to stroke her hair. "You and Jasper bonded during the heat."

She went rigid in my arms. "But... When? How? I don't..."

Jasper wriggled towards her, and her body relaxed, like a sigh released, the moment his hands were on her. I still remembered the effects of a fresh bond. It got quieter over time, but early on it was vibrant, and the craving that came with it was only quenchable by the person you'd bonded with.

Our omega nuzzled the bite he'd left on her throat, and Nicky's eyes closed slowly.

"Are you mad?" Jasper asked quietly.

Nicky shook her head, fingers lacing through his hair.

Until Jasper's heat was over, any one of us could bond her, but now that the haze had passed we were in our right minds, and I couldn't imagine pushing her for that. I wanted her to choose us, and I could be plenty patient about that, even though she and Jasper had obviously chosen each other during the haze.

I thought about asking what she'd like us to do, but a bond was permanent. There was nothing to be done if she didn't want it.

Nicky sat up, her fingers tracing over the bite on her throat.

We all watched her expectantly. "It feels nice," she said quietly, "but I need to process. And sleep. I feel like I've been hit by a truck."

Jasper and I sandwiched her gently between us. His purr lulled her to sleep almost instantly.

"Jasper," I whispered. "Do you remember bonding her?"

He shook his head. "Just snippets. I want to feel bad, but I love it. I forgot what a new bond feels like. I already knew that she was mine, what my instincts were telling me, but now she really is, and I'm just happy about that."

I buried my face against Nicky's throat, paying closer attention this time, taking in the subtle overlay of Jasper's chocolate and cinnamon with Nicky's nutmeg and vanillin.

Gabe took over caretaker duty, getting a meal prepared in the kitchenette and forcing food on those of us that were awake. I chewed on a croissant, trying not to get crumbs all over Nicky while she napped, but I was only mildly successful. Jasper licked the crumbs off her skin and left tiny kisses that had Nicky sighing in her sleep.

Tony and Gabe helped Jasper through his next flare-up, and I kept watch over Nicky, cuddling her softly. She woke after a couple of hours, agitated and restless until Jasper curled around her. I envied him that ability. Nicky responded well to all of us, but it wasn't the same as having that extra connection.

"Do you want to have your family over when the heat is done?" I asked.

"I'd love that," Nicky said, turning over in Jasper's arms.

"I think you should meet some of our family, too," I said. "If you'd be comfortable with that."

"Yes, please. I want to meet the people important to all of you."

"Mine won't be coming," said Billie, tone more than a little bitter.

"My parents are in Seattle, so they don't visit much," I said. "My brother lives around here. I can invite him over."

"I'll invite my moms," Jasper offered. "I want them to get to know you, Nicky."

"I'd love to meet your moms, Jasper. And Hana's brother!" Nicky turned to the other alphas. "What about you two?"

"My parents are out of the country right now, but my aunt and her bondmates would definitely come if they're near town," replied Tony. "I can give them a heads-up and see if they're traveling our direction."

"My parents are more phone call people," said Gabe, "but I'll put it out there for them. I'd like for our families to know about you, especially now that you're bonded to Jasper."

Nicky tensed, like she'd forgotten that fact again, and Jasper was there to soothe her, making her melt once more. "I want to meet everyone," she said slowly. "It's nerve-wracking as hell, but it feels like an important step."

She laced our fingers together and kissed the back of my hand.

The rest of us didn't have family involvement anywhere near to the same level that Nicky did, and having the Marinos around more often would be a change. I was mostly okay with that, though. They were important to Nicky, and while I wouldn't be comfortable with it immediately, I would try for her.

Jasper started to get squirmy, his sweet scent spiking. Tony took over, laying out behind Jasper and fucking into our omega's ass. Nicky's scent spiked, too. One thing heats were good for was dispelling stress. The temptation to let myself sink back under the full influence of Jasper's heat hormones was like a neon sign in my brain demanding my attention. Instead, I turned to Nicky and caught her upturned mouth in a kiss.

I'd been so focused on her that I hadn't fully acknowledged how much Alphonse had emotionally fucked me up. Our home wasn't safe. I had almost been too late to save Nicky, and I would never forgive him for making any of us feel unsafe here.

Nothing like a brush with death to make you crave feeling alive again.

I drank in the taste of her, needing the distraction. Nicky

wiggled against me, hips seeking, until she hissed and came to a standstill. "Ow! Sorry. Everything is still really tender."

"You don't have to apologize, Nicky. If you want to rest…"

"But I *don't* want to. If I let my mind get too quiet, it goes places I don't like. I know I'll need to get real help with that, but right now I don't want to think. I just want to feel safe with you."

"I'm proud of you. It's hard to come to terms and admit when we need help." I looked down at her, at the sweet, beautiful beta that had snared me down to the soul. Her eyes were wide, her cheeks flushed, her skin coated with the lightest sheen of sweat and her body trembled under my scrutiny. "I can be gentle if you want to play."

Nicky nodded, shivering harder. "Please."

I captured her mouth again and threaded my fingers through her hair, cupping her head softly. Her lips were eager against mine. I kissed her until her whine broke through and she was up to the point of begging, her fingers kneading me.

"Hana, please."

I shifted her around and settled her in Billie's lap, our other beta arranging a pillow for Nicky and stroking her hair. Gabe turned his focus onto her as well, and Nicky tipped her head back for Gabe to lay his palm over her throat.

A growl burned in my chest. She was too perfect.

Nicky's hips flexed, a silent request for me to give her a little more focused attention. Our omega gave a sharp cry, and I lifted my gaze briefly to watch him come. My sweet boy shuddered as Tony slid out of him, and Jasper immediately scooted closer, settling himself between Billie's leg and Nicky's body, fastening his lips over her nipple.

Her breath came in sharp pants, and she groaned beautifully as she buried her fingers in Jasper's hair, arching up against his mouth. The mattress dipped on the other side, and I turned to see Tony stretching out on Nicky's other side, his head pillowed by Billie's thigh as he lifted the swell of Nicky's breast to his mouth.

But then her breathing shifted, and a burnt sugar bitterness laced her scent.

"Wait," she gasped. "Red." She burst into tears as we all backed away to give her space. "I'm sorry. I'm sorry. I thought I wanted, I just, I don't—"

"Nicky, it's okay," I crooned, taking her hand in mine to kiss the back of it. "Take a breath for me."

She obeyed, though it was shallow and stuttering. It broke my heart.

"Can I touch you?" Jasper asked. Nicky nodded, and our omega lay at her side, draping his arm over her waist. "What do you need, my love?"

"I don't know. There's too many things crammed into my head." She sniffled. "I just wanted to feel okay for a little while."

Billie stroked Nicky's hair. "Would you like a pack bath? We can turn on the jets, get you some more water and painkillers. Unlimited snuggles."

Nicky craned her neck to look up at Billie. "That sounds really nice. I'm not enjoying how much my body hurts right now."

There wasn't anything I could offer for that. She had injuries on top of the wear and tear from the heat, and it would take time before anything else was particularly useful to combat it. Once she stopped being quite so tender, I could work with her on some easy stretching and massage so her muscles didn't lock up, but I would also bow to whatever the hospital said when we finally got her there.

Gabe leaned down and kissed Nicky's forehead. "I'll get the water running."

Tony got her a fresh dose of painkillers and a bottle of water as well as a cookie so she wasn't consuming them on a totally empty stomach. "Here you go, baby girl. Do you need help?"

"Just with sitting up," she murmured. Tony took her hand and pulled while I supported her back. She winced and whimpered the whole way up and gratefully took her medicine, scarfing down the cookie immediately afterward.

Alphonse was fucking lucky he was in police custody because

435

every time she showed an ounce of pain, it made me want to snap his bones like a twig.

"Good girl," I whispered against her skin, kissing her cheek. "We're going to take care of you."

Nicky leaned into me. "I don't like feeling this way."

"I know, sweetheart." I kissed her hair. "I think I'll join you in getting that professional help once the heat is over."

"I'll shore up the security in the house too," said Gabe as he returned. "I know it won't undo anything, but hopefully it'll help everyone feel safer going forward. Do you want to come pick out a bubble bath, Nicky?"

"Okay."

We surrendered Nicky to Gabe, and I snuggled myself between Tony, Billie, and Jasper. "Things are a mess."

"They are," agreed Tony, "but we've weathered things this bad before. We can manage anything together. Nicky knows that we love h—"

"Actually, she doesn't."

We all turned to Billie.

"What?" I asked.

"She knows that we like hanging out and that we like fucking her. But if you don't explicitly tell her something, she's not going to assume. She and I already talked about it. All the actions and behaviors are great, but Nicky needs the words. Just so y'all are aware."

I stewed on Billie's revelation. "I'll tell her soon. I don't want to overwhelm her."

"I already told her I loved her, so up to you if and when you feel like doing the same." Billie's eyes gleamed. "Does that mean you have some feelings to confess?"

I felt every eye on me, and didn't like that one bit. "I'm going to go help them with the bath."

Leaving Jasper, Billie, and Tony on the bed, I poked my head into the bathroom where Nicky was cuddled in Gabe's arms next to the bath. I approached slowly, making sure to put myself in her line of sight before I enveloped her from the other side.

"Ready to soak?" I asked.

"My fingers are going to be perma-pruney from how many times I've been in the water lately. But, yeah, I am."

Gabe and I helped her into the water. She sank into the peach-scented foam, and we climbed in after her, the others joining us a moment later. Tony tied up his locs and assisted Billie in tying their own hair into a bun, then helped them climb into the water. Jasper took over primary Nicky cuddles, but I tucked in on her other side, lacing our fingers together beneath the foam.

"Baby girl," said Tony. "Are you up to having a conversation, or would you rather wait until you're feeling better?"

Nicky squeezed my hand. "Can we wait a little bit?"

"Of course."

"It's nothing bad," I told her, hoping it would soothe her anxieties.

"Oh," she said quietly. "I'd still like to wait, if that's okay? Good or bad, I need more rest before I can handle complex thoughts."

I settled in, relieved to have this small reprieve. It didn't take long for Nicky to fall asleep, propped between Jasper and I.

"Do we have a plan?" Gabe asked quietly.

"I definitely don't," I replied.

But I would have to think of something. She was too important to let things slide. We needed to make it clear how important she was to our pack so she didn't get any ideas in her head that we didn't love her as much as we all loved each other.

Chapter Fifty-Three
Tony

"Holy shit."

"What is it?" Billie asked.

"Councillor Harvey went completely unhinged in my voicemail."

I had ignored my phone during the heat. Everyone knew not to bother me while on heat leave. Harvey *knew* I was away from work for Jasper's heat, and apparently she had taken the opportunity to go absolutely hogwild.

I went back to the beginning of the messages and put them on speaker so my encroaching pack could hear the vitriol she had spewed at me.

"How dare you? Reporting me to the mayor for embezzlement when I've spent the last twenty years in service of this community? You've

got a lot of audacity, Agani. I'm going to ruin you for this. We'll see how long your career lasts with me as an enemy."

"I won't say the words that I want to you because, quite frankly, they are too crass to belong in my mouth. You're a twisted snake. A stalker. I can't believe you wasted your time being so focused on me that you would dig back through two decades of records!"

"If I had known that you were as morally corrupt as all of those night workers at that facility, I never would've given you those measures to edit. You're just like the rest of them."

"Enjoy the fruits of your labor. If I can't save people because of your intervention, then I'll find another way. Consider yourself fired."

The words in her last message slugged me in the gut. Maybe I didn't *love* my job, but it was mine, and I felt like it was valuable. Billie had always been insistent that none of us had to work if we didn't want to, but that alpha compulsion to provide had kept me firmly employed. Now that had been ripped out from under me.

"Wow. What the fuck? What the hell does she mean about saving people?" Billie asked

"Oh my god." Nicky clapped her hand over her mouth. "You don't think she's one that set fire to the facility? I thought maybe it might've been Alphonse, but she had some kind of vendetta against it, didn't she?"

The air froze in my throat. Had Harvey torched Nicky's precious library because of me? The idea of it made me nauseated.

"Uh, yeah, she did," I agreed. "I never thought she would go that far."

"Send the voicemails to the lawyer," Billie said. "Add it to the case."

"My poor library." Nicky sniffled and slid into my arms. "Can she really fire you? Does she have that power?"

"If the others don't vouch for me, then absolutely." I sighed. Fucking Harvey.

"Would this be a good time to tell people my idea?" Billie asked.

The pack turned towards them.

"Okay, so, it's all still in the concept phase, but if you all think it's a good idea, then I'll move forward with a business plan." Billie took a deep breath. "I want to open a new facility, privately funded by me, so that we don't have to bow to public opinion on things the way a publicly funded facility would."

"What kind of facility?" Hana asked.

"Multi-use. Like the one where we met Nicky. We could have another library, a gym where Hana could teach fitness classes, maybe a second location of *Go with the Dough* for Jasper to expand, some freelancer rental spaces, art classes. All kinds of things! Whatever the community needs, we could see about setting it up."

"That's...surprisingly thoughtful," said Gabe. "I think it's a great idea if you can get the business side managed. Might help to burn off some of your unlimited energy."

I dragged my sour thoughts away from Harvey. Billie needed my attention, and that was a decent distraction. "I love the idea of freelancer workspaces. A lot of them are so expensive for anyone starting out, and it would be nice to have something that takes true affordability into account without denying people resources."

Billie bounced in place. "Yes! And we could have a library of things where people can rent equipment and stuff that's too expensive for them to buy, but they might only need short term."

"Do you think I could handle two locations?" Jasper asked.

"Two might be a stretch," I said. "But you've said for ages that Yan and Rita are management material. You could always hand over some of the reins to them and set up a second location."

"That's true," he said. "They're a good team. And I'd be able to take Luca on as an apprentice, show them how to build up the business from the ground up."

"*My* Luca?" Nicky asked, perking up.

"Yeah. We briefly talked about it the last time your family was here, and I told him we would pick the topic back up after my heat, when I've had time to sort through some things."

"I love that!" Nicky wiggled happily in my arms. "I was kind of hoping you two would become friends."

I kissed her cheek. "The Marino clan is integrating."

There was little that I wanted more than for Nicky to feel like our pack was home. Jasper and Luca becoming friends, and potentially master and apprentice, would go a long way to her feeling like we accepted every part of her and that her family, that was so important to her, was always welcome.

"I should get in touch with the police, and probably the mayor, about the messages Harvey left," I said. "Wish me luck."

"Good luck," Nicky stood on her toes to kiss my cheek. "I've got a million calls and messages to catch up on, so we'll both be having the time of our lives."

I retreated to my office, contacting the lawyer first and getting copies of the voicemails onto my computer to send them as part of the investigation. Harvey's network was wide, and she'd been in politics for the last twenty years, long enough to build herself some allies that could help her skate under the radar or make things very difficult for us.

Once my first task was complete, I placed a call to Mayor Carlisle's office.

"You've reached the office of Mayor Carlisle. I'm not available at this time. Please leave your name, number, and a brief message, and I'll get back to you as soon as possible. If this is in regards to a matter that is handled by the City Council, please contact us via e—"

I hung up. "Well that's useless." I called the administration line instead, in case the mayor was just out of her office.

"This is Katrina speaking at City Council offices, how may I direct your call?"

"Hey Katrina, it's Tony Agani. I was trying to get through to Mayor Carlisle. Do you know if she's in the office today?"

"Oh, heavens no, she took a leave of absence a few days ago. Something about a family emergency. I'm not sure when she'll be back. If it's urgent, Councillor Timmons is covering for her in the meantime."

"No, that's okay. Thanks for your time. Have a good day."

That poked some serious holes in my desired theory that the mayor wasn't involved. It could be coincidence, but the timing was wildly suspicious. I had no way of knowing if the background investigation against Harvey had actually started. Maybe Carlisle had run straight to Harvey after my meeting with her. Or maybe she had kept the knowledge to herself, potentially wanting a rival out of the way. Frustration burned in my gut. I wanted answers, but I had no idea how to get them.

A knock at my door drew my attention from my phone. "Come in."

Billie's head popped through when it opened. "I heard you get quiet and thought you might be done."

"For the moment," I replied. "Did you need something?"

"I wanted to make sure that you're not super stressed." Billie scampered across my office and parked their butt on my desk. "Any luck?"

"Not really, but maybe in time." I pinched the bridge of my nose to stem my rising headache.

"Do you want me to give you some special attention to de-stress you?"

Billie edged my chair back with their toes and slid off my desk to their knees.

"You just finished the main recovery for a concussion. I'm not letting you give me a blow job at my desk. How many times have you banged your head doing that?"

"If you held my head that wouldn't happen," they teased. "I'd offer you a shoulder massage instead, but your chair is too tall for me to work around. Short person discrimination."

"Maybe it's a sign from the universe that you should rest."

"The chair may be too tall, but the desk is the perfect size for me to climb under it." Billie braced a hand to each of my chair arms and rose up with wide blue eyes gleaming with mischief. "Kiss me for good luck so I don't concuss myself again."

I could only chuckle, wrapping my hand around the back of their neck and leaning down to capture their mouth. "You shouldn't tempt me like this. You're supposed to take it easy."

"That's why I'm offering this instead of asking you to rattle a headboard with me." They grinned cheekily. "If you don't want me, I'll go."

"That's unfair," I said. "I always want you."

"Then take care of me while I take care of you."

I sighed in defeat. "Okay, but if you start to feel dizzy again, you have to stop. No pushing through that."

"Agreed."

I kissed them slowly, breathing deep, searching for any notes of distress in their scent. My beta wasn't always great at taking care of themselves. They got far too restless and tried to get back into things before they should, but they also tended to kick up a fuss if we got too strict about it. The best we could do was make sure they were safe while they pushed their limits.

I sat back as Billie eagerly undid the front of my pants. "When I'm back to one-hundred-percent you have to take me on a date."

"Pick the time and place, and I'll be your chauffeur. Anywhere you want to go."

"Well, if I'm picking, then we're going to the beach. I can photograph some cute birds and dip my toes in the ocean."

I caught them in another kiss while they freed my cock from its confinement, teasingly stroking to bring it up to full attention. I barely had time to suck in a breath before Billie pulled away and dipped down, wrapping warm lips around the tip. Hissing, I set my hands on the back of their head, cradling as they sank down as much as they could manage and pulled back, my hands cushioning so they didn't hit their head against the desk. Billie wiggled us around until they were tucked fully under my desk, lips and tongue sweeping up my shaft, hands gripping what they couldn't take.

"Do your work," Billie said. "I like when you struggle to focus while I do this."

"Wicked little tease." I opened a project from one of the Councillors. My thoughts were like a dropped box of ping-pong balls, bouncing and scattering as Billie worked me over.

A knock at the door had me tensing, but it wasn't something the pack hadn't walked in on before.

"Come in," I said, proud of myself for keeping my voice from breaking as Billie swallowed me down again.

Nicky slipped inside and I held my breath. She wasn't the one I was expecting, and she had definitely *not* walked in on this before.

"Hey," she said. "I wanted to talk to you about the mentorship program, if you have time. I just got off the phone with Miranda, and I was hoping to move forward with it at another facility while the library and everything is under repairs."

"Yeah, of cour—"

My breath cut off, the back of my hands hitting the top of the desk from Billie's movement, their giggling sneaking out. Nicky's gaze flickered to the desk and back to me.

"Is Billie..."

Billie lifted their head from my cock with an audible pop and nudged my chair away to look at Nicky over the edge of the desk. "Yep."

Nicky's cheeks flared pink. "Not what I came up here for, but I dig it. Room for one more?"

I stared at her, surprise freezing me in place.

Billie looked up at me, pawing at my thigh. "Answer the lady."

Their words prompted me.

"By all means, if that's something you're into," I replied.

"Something I'm into? You mean getting on my knees for someone who not only helped save my life, but has also done everything possible since we met to make sure that I felt loved and safe?"

444

"Yeah," I swallowed hard, my throat dry, "that."

She crossed the short distance with confident steps and leaned down to kiss me, lacing her fingers behind my neck.

"You don't have to repay me for any of that."

Nicky let her forehead rest against mine, moving slowly to kiss me again, then pressed her lips to my throat, nuzzling my scent gland and breathing deeply.

"Maybe I want to," she whispered, nipping my ear. "Maybe I want to spend as long as you'll have me making sure that *you* feel loved and safe, too. Oh my god; okay, I wasn't intending to get sentimental, but I might have some big feelings that are sneaking out."

"Nothing wrong with that, baby girl. I've got a few of those big feelings myself."

"Yeah?" She kissed me, slow and deep, and my heart beat my ribs like a hammer. "Because I'm pretty sure that I love you."

"Good, because loving you is something I'm absolutely sure about."

Billie pawed at our legs. "Not to ruin this beautiful moment that's bringing a lot of dreams to fruition, but do you want to take over, Books? Or, do you want to tag team?" Billie asked.

Nicky reached out, stroking Billie's cheek, our beta leaning into her touch. "Well, you and Jasper already tag teamed me this way in the limo. I think I should get a turn on the other side of it."

Nicky's eyes glinted as she dropped down next to Billie. I liked this new, sexually confident Nicky. I liked her even better when she licked up the length of me and put the tip into her mouth while maintaining eye contact. Billie immediately set back to work. I threaded my fingers through their hair, holding the two of them without guiding, letting them do as they please. Breaths came sharp and fast.

Two mouths and four hands touching me wasn't a rarity with the pack, but familiarity did nothing to dampen the sensations. Having Nicky on her knees for me for the first time added a special edge to the experience, and I settled all of my attention into it. Billie might enjoy it when I tried to work through it, but I wanted my focus on Nicky right now.

My alpha purr rumbled between gasps and groans. I squeezed too hard, pulling Nicky's hair as she pushed the tip of my cock to the back of her throat.

She moaned and sat up, her eyes beautifully bright. "A little harder."

"Yeah?"

Nicky bit her bottom lip, and, when I got myself a firmer handful of her hair, I was rewarded with her full body shiver.

I watched her face carefully, guiding her onto my cock slow enough to give her plenty of time to prepare or call off the play. She stuck her tongue out when she got close enough, and I eased her down until her nails dug into my thighs. I let her rise under her own power and pressed her back down, forming a steady rhythm between the two of us.

"You know, I wasn't intending to get myself off when I came up here," said Billie, "but how the hell am I supposed to skip it when this is my view?"

Billie slipped one hand into their pants and wrapped the other firmly around the base of my cock, helping Nicky along with her task.

My breathing stuttered. "Fuck. You two are dangerous."

Nicky took me deeper and rose off with a little cough, expression furrowing for only a moment before she initiated her own descent again.

"Damn, Books. Anyone ever told you that you look exceptionally pretty with a cock in your mouth?"

Nicky snorted and lifted her head sharply, laughing too hard to continue. Her giggles were as exquisite as the tongue she'd had wrapped around me.

"You can't say things like that when I'm occupied!"

"My commentary can't be stopped."

Nicky laughed again. "You're a menace."

She captured Billie's menace of a mouth, and I was treated to the view of them making out as they stacked their fists, continuing to stroke me. My body slowly tensed, pleasure coiling tightly.

My shifted breathing and string of quiet curses gave me away. Nicky broke away from Billie and took me in once more. I needed all of my willpower to not choke her by bucking into her mouth. She swallowed me with ease, and I struggled to watch, briefly giving in to the urge to squeeze my eyes shut and pant through the swell of sensation.

Nicky showed no sign of stopping once I had emptied myself down her throat. The overstimulation had me curling away, her mouth chasing me until I pulled her off by the hair, enamoured with her grin when she looked up at me.

"You've been spending too much time with Hana," I said, chuckling.

"You mean you *don't* want me to keep sucking your cock until there's nothing else in the world you can think of and you beg me to stop because it's just too much?" Nicky rapidly blinked her eyes, the picture of innocence.

"Jesus Christ." I sucked in a sharp breath.

Billie cackled next to us. "Books is going to wreck us all if we let her keep hanging out with Hana."

"It's *your* fault," she told Billie. "You're the one who started me on this path of carnal revelations."

Billie nodded solemnly. "I accept full responsibility for this delightful path change in your life."

Nicky caught me off guard with one more quick lick before she climbed straight into my lap and kissed me until my brain turned to mush.

"Now about the mentorship program..."

I laughed hard, full bellied and loud. "You have to give me a few minutes to let my brain reassemble itself."

"Not to worry," she said, kissing the tip of my nose. "I can be patient."

Chapter Fifty-Four
Nicky

"We should head back," Hana said.

Hana had taken me on a walk—a flat one—to work off my nervous energy before everyone arrived. She'd been remarkably indulgent about my swinging our joined hands together. I couldn't help it. I had told two of the pack that I loved them, and I was trying to come around to telling the others, which meant my anxiety translated into fidgeting.

"What if they all hate me?" I asked.

"We've only invited the family members who are most supportive of our situation in general. And honestly, I couldn't give a flying fuck what any of them think. What matters is that *we* want you here. But in any case, my brother will probably love you, and Jasper's moms definitely will. Tony's family is protective, but they open up quickly."

"How do you know your brother will love me?"

She pulled us to a stop and yanked me close. "Because I've decided that *I* love you, and that's the only thing Koji has ever cared about with my partners."

My breath caught in my throat. Hana loved *me*.

"You know, I'd been planning on telling you that first," I said.

"Is that so, little beta?" Hana purred.

"It might be. I've sat with a lot of feelings lately, and I know for certain that what I feel for you and the rest of the pack is bigger and better than anything I felt for anyone else I've been with. So yes, it *is* so."

Hana kissed me until my brain scrambled, right out in the open, under the bright sunshine. It only felt safe enough to do so because of Alphonse's impending trial and the fact that he was handcuffed to his hospital bed, still recovering from Hana and Tony defending me.

"Are you telling the whole pack the good news?" Hana asked.

"Billie and Tony already know," I said. "Billie confessed first."

Hana snorted. "They mentioned that, and I'm not remotely surprised they were the first to confess."

"I still have to talk to Jasper and Gabe."

"Well, I'm glad it's coming up. You've been through a lot in a short time, and I know that can speed things up for people. Don't be afraid to slow down if you need to."

"Nothing with this pack has *ever* gone slow," I said, getting our walk going again. "I don't mind though. Feels like I lived my whole life in slow mode. I think I needed things to kick into gear to bring me to where I was supposed to be."

Hana kissed my hand and didn't say a word as I started up swinging them again.

"As long as you're happy," she said.

"Pretty sure I've never been happier. I know there's a lot of stuff to still figure out, a lot of conversations that need to happen, but I think I finally feel like I belong." My breath hitched, all my emotions sneaking out through the net of anxiety that had contained them under the nervous panicky buzz. "Dammit I was *not* supposed to start crying on this walk."

449

Hana stopped us again and leaned down a bit, pressing my nose to her throat so I could breathe in the bright, earthy mint scent of her. Her purr kicked on, and the sweet rhythmic sound of it untangled my knots of stress.

"You *do* belong," she said. "I was the most hesitant, and I'm saying that. Never doubt that this pack adores you."

I huffed her like paint, minty matcha invigorating me until I had pushed the tears back down. "Sorry, I don't know why I'm so emotional today."

"Confessing your feelings is a pretty emotional thing, to be fair. If I were a different person, I would probably cry right along with you."

We finished up our walk back to the pack house, and already there was a car I didn't recognize in the driveway.

"Oh god, I'm not ready. Who's here?"

"I'm pretty sure that car belongs to Jasper's moms."

"And they're nice, right?" I squeezed Hana's hand to reassure myself.

"Very nice. They've been really supportive of the pack. I don't think they'll ever complain about more people being interested in loving their son."

"That's so sweet."

"Come on inside now. If by chance anyone today is rude to you, I'm not going to let it slide. The family members we all still talk to are well aware of our boundaries and the treatment of other pack members."

I nodded along and nervously chewed my lip. Hana cupped my face with both hands and pulled my lip from between my teeth with her thumb.

"Excuse you. That lip is for *me* to bite. Your job is to take care of it until I get to it again."

I giggled helplessly, excited butterflies turning over in my stomach. "Yes, *ma'am*."

Hana's eyes glinted. "Get inside or I'm going to detour you to the garage and do unspeakable things to you in there."

"That's not a lot of motivation, but I suppose it would be rude to keep Jasper's moms waiting."

I opened the main door, and the entire pack turned to us as well as a statuesque woman with a red pixie cut and another about my height with red curls down past her shoulders, thick green-framed glasses perched on her button nose. They were both too cute for words.

The tallest of the pair swept towards me, arms open. "You must be Nicky."

She pulled me into a bone-crushing hug and kissed each of my cheeks.

"Yep, that's me."

"It's so nice to finally meet you. I'm Beryl, and this," she said, gesturing to the other redheaded woman, "is my wife, Opal. Jasper's told us all about you."

"Oh my god! I just realized you all have rock names! That's so cute."

Beryl stepped back with a laugh. "Yes, Opal and I met at a gathering of local redheads back in the day and bonded over both having gemstone names. Obviously, we had to share that with our son. He hasn't decided yet if he's going to share it with his future children, too."

"Mom!" Jasper's face turned red up to the tips of his ears, blending in with his hair.

"Well, I think it's an adorable tradition, whatever Jasper decides," I declared.

"Do you want children, Nicky?" Beryl asked.

Jasper practically leapt over the kitchen table to get to me and wedged himself between his mother and me. "Mom, for the love of god!"

I giggled as Jasper wrapped me in his embrace and covered both of my ears.

Opal had trotted after Jasper and stole me out of his grasp to hug me herself. "Don't mind her dear."

"That's rude, Opal. You're lucky you're cute," Beryl said, a smirk turning her lips.

451

"Come on, you know the rule about flirting in front of me," said Jasper, stealing me back from Opal.

In retaliation his moms' delivered about a dozen very loud kisses all over one another's cheeks, much to my delight.

Beryl stared me down again. "I do think we should be allowed to know our son's new bondmate's feelings on family, though."

"Oh." I shrank under her scrutiny, nestling against Jasper. "Um, well, I had a stretch of not great relationships, so it was never something I let myself seriously consider, but I think a pack baby would be the sweetest. I'd love any child that came into this house, no matter which of the pack were the parents."

That seemed to satisfy Beryl, and Jasper nuzzled my cheek.

The front door swung open, and I froze, my heart leaping into my throat at the sudden intrusion. Hana put herself bodily between Jasper and I and the door. I stared at the black silk of Hana's hair and the tension of her shoulders, the burnt edge of her scent invading my nose. She was *scared*.

"Koji!" snapped Hana. "You're supposed to knock like a civilized human being."

I recognized the name and peeked around her, looping my arm through Hana's.

Koji sauntered in, his black hair spiked into a faux hawk, his denim jacket covered in patches and pins, and his smile a mile wide. "I only knock when I don't know for sure whether you're occupied with the pack or not. Presumably, if you're having guests over, you'll be fully clothed."

Hana rolled her eyes but held open her arms for Koji to slide in for a hug. She was a solid foot taller than him, and I felt a little bit like a giant when he turned to me.

"Glad to see my sister's taste hasn't gone downhill in her old age."

It was a sweet enough sentiment, considering I was still recovering from all of the chaos that had happened.

Hana flipped him the bird playfully. "Don't be a dick. Nicky's older than me."

"I'm never a dick," Koji said. "I'm pure delight."

I snickered. "I'm going to agree on the delight part."

"Don't encourage him." Hana smushed down his faux hawk, and Koji tried to play bite her hand.

"Introduce me properly," Koji demanded.

Hana sighed and pulled me closer. "Koji, this is Nicky. Nicky, this is Koji, my little brother who is also a punk-ass bitch."

Koji snorted. "Only the first of those three descriptors *actually* applies. You doing okay since the break in?"

"Um, more or less. I'm doing physiotherapy for a little while that Hana's helping me with, and I met my psychologist for the first time this morning. She seems really nice."

"Props." Koji grinned. "Healing is hard work, no matter what kind of it you're doing. You like your therapist?" he asked Hana.

"So far, so good," Hana replied. She'd met hers this morning too. We'd managed to find two that worked in the same building and seemed to suit our needs, so we'd gone together.

Some motorcycles roared up to the house, and we all turned the front door.

"That'll be my clan," said Tony.

He opened the door for them, and a group of four tromped in wearing their leathers and heavy boots. Tony was pulled immediately into a raucous group hug.

When they had all finished joyfully greeting one another, he turned back to me. "Nicky, this is my auntie Angelica and her pack."

Another pack!

Angelica was taller than Hana with a rainbow of box braids and a little gap between her front teeth that somehow made her smile even brighter. Tony went down the line, introducing the rest of the pack: Kendra, a plump blonde omega, Jonas, a beta with neat locs hanging to his shoulders, and Shawn, a pale, willowy alpha that rivalled Angelica for height.

Angelica thrust out her hand for me to shake, with a warm grin. "Good to meet you, Nicky. It's a shame that you have to wait to meet Antonio's parents until they get back from Costa Rica, but we all collectively raised him, so I'd say we count enough."

"Yeah, absolutely! I'm happy to meet anyone that loves my pack."

Tony sidled up next to me. "Baby girl, I think that's the first time you've called us *your* pack to anyone."

My cheeks burst into flame.

"Are you calling out your girl, kid?" Jonas asked. "Pack declaration is a big deal. I kind of assumed she was already a formal member."

"She's pack in all ways, except government documents," said Tony.

"They're treating you well?" Kendra asked.

"They're perfect," I replied, looking softly at Tony. "I couldn't ask for a better pack."

Kendra playfully punched Tony in the arm. "Always a continued relief that we raised this one right. In the summer we'll have you lot over for a barbecue. Maybe hit the highways on the bikes."

"Yeah, I would love that! Gabe took me on his bike, and it was great." I turned to Tony again. "Can you take me out, too?"

"Anything you want, baby girl."

"Good. We appreciate a lady that loves to ride," said Angelica, with a wink. "There's a standing invitation, but we'll plan something more specific once the weather warms up."

Gabe and Billie had finished arranging all the food on the kitchen island and along the bar. Billie hopped their way between us and Angelica's pack, accepting a group hug in the crowd around them.

"How are you holding up, little beta?" Jonas asked, setting their hand on Billie's head. "Over your stint at the hospital?"

"Yep! Right as rain. Come grab some snacks with me."

We were still waiting on my friends and family, and already we had a crowd of a dozen. Koji followed me around, asking me questions about being a librarian as we munched on countless trays of food the pack had prepared. Roscoe made his rounds through all of the guests, collecting attention until he was all petted out, and flopped down in a sunbeam.

The doorbell rang, announcing the arrival of my guests. My parents came first, followed by Luca, Sidney, Allie, Meg, and Luna. I figured it would be easy to sneak some friends onto the list when we were already hosting so many. They passed me between them for fierce hugs, each reassuring themselves of my safety now that they were here in person.

Allie handed me a cat carrier, and I looked through the netting at my sweet little boy. "Hey Spuddy! Were you good for auntie and uncle? You glad to be back home with mommy?"

"We had some quality sleepovers while you were busy," said Allie. "But he definitely missed you."

Once the door was secured, I set down the carrier and set Spud free, stealing some cuddles for myself before I carried him over to Roscoe. They headbutted each other and took off running like two floofy bats out of hell.

Luna stepped up to me. "Damn girl. Your pack is swanky. If you ever need anyone to house-sit, hit me up."

I laughed. "I'll let them know you're available if we need someone."

"Did someone say house-sitting?" Billie asked, popping up behind me. "Because I think after all that we've been through, our pack deserves a little vacation. Throw a dart at the map and go where the wind takes us."

Ordinarily, I would say that I needed to work, but after finally hearing back from my boss, I was on unpaid suspension until the library was ready again. They couldn't fire me for taking a heat leave, but I was still on the shit list for doing it with no warning. I was trying not to think about it all too hard.

"Nicola." Mom poked my arm. "You have to introduce us to everyone. How am I supposed to converse without a proper introduction?"

"Don't you worry, Mama Marino," Billie said. "Let me take you around."

Mom looked at me with wide eyes.

"Billie knows everyone a lot better than I do," I said. "They're the perfect person to help you get to know everyone."

Mom relented and let Billie hook their arm through hers and take her to meet all of the guests.

"You look like you're doing well Nick," Sidney said as he dropped an arm over my shoulder.

I leaned into him, surveying my pack and our loved ones. "I am. I'm excited for the future."

Allie snuggled into my other side. "I'm really happy for you, Nicky. Do you think you'll get bonded to them?"

Sidney ruffled his wife's hair. "That's probably not a conversation to have in front of two dozen people."

Bonded.

I liked the idea of being stuck with my pack. Bonding was very permanent, but that didn't scare me much. I could be part of the pack without being bonded to everyone else right this second. There was no rush. During one of Jasper's future heats, we could make it happen.

"That's a future Nicky situation," I said, "but I would like to one day."

I introduced Meg and Luna to my pack. Luna took an immediate liking to Jasper and hung out with him and Luca while they chatted about the bakery. Meg gravitated toward Hana and Koji. It settled a lot of questions and worries for me to see the pack welcome my own and to finally meet some of the people dearest to the ones I loved. I retreated into the kitchen to snuggle into Gabe's side. He and Billie were the only ones without their own guests today.

"You okay?" I asked Gabe.

"Yeah. I'm used to the crowds, and I love everyone's family."

"Do you wish that you had someone here?"

"Nah, my parents *hate* crowds. It's better for everyone that they're not here. I'll take you to meet them someday soon if you'd like."

"Yes, please. I want to meet everyone important to you."

Gabe kissed my forehead, and I cuddled closer. Billie joined us after getting my parents into a conversation with Angelica's pack. Each of us wrapped an arm around Billie, and I nuzzled their hair.

Our beta had no one to invite. They had told me early on that they didn't begrudge anyone having a positive relationship with their family, but I had to assume that it was probably difficult for them, in any case.

"Love you," I said and kissed their hair.

Billie squeezed my arm. "Love you too, Books."

I leaned up to kiss Gabe's cheek and breathed in the rich scent of tea. "Love *you*, too."

Gabe stroked my hair. "Didn't know you were ready for that yet, or I'd have told you the night I got you on my bike."

"I'm a little slow on the uptake sometimes, but I get there eventually."

He chuckled, and I lifted my head for a quick kiss.

"I love you, too, Nicky."

Before dating the pack, I had never said '*I love you*' to anyone that I dated. I loved a lot of people in my life, but it was still surreal to find multiple partners that made me want to say it. I felt safe, treasured. I wanted to spend the rest of my life making sure they all felt the same.

"Nicky!"

I turned to see Luca waving me over.

"I'm being summoned," I said. "I'll be back, and if I get stolen, you can come reclaim me."

I slid away from Gabe and Billie, venturing over to where Luca, Luna, and Jasper were clustered together, sipping mimosas on the couch nest.

"What's up, babes?" I asked, sliding in to cuddle against Jasper's side.

"We're talking more about the second location of the bakery," said Jasper.

"We having an omega party over here?" Koji asked, hopping over the back of the couch nest to land next to Luca.

"Not quite," I said. "Just bakery chat, and we're missing Allie, Kendra, and Opal to make it a proper omega party."

"Oh yeah, I forgot you had a bakery," Koji said to Jasper. "Did Hana ever show you my cookie designs?"

"No, I don't think so," said Jasper.

Koji fussed with his phone and turned the screen toward Jasper and I. There was a whole series of photos of cookies that were basically artwork: a plethora of whimsical designs in a rainbow of colors, geometric shapes, and replicas of famous paintings.

"Holy shit, these are great!" Jasper snatched up the phone and scrolled through them, zooming in to get a better look.

"Have you ever thought about offering custom cookie designs at your bakery?" Koji asked.

"These are well beyond what I personally have the patience for, not to mention they require artistic skill none of my staff possesses. It's a little fussier than I would usually consider, but I love the idea. Are you asking because you want to work at the bakery?"

Koji shrugged. "I was thinking it would be cool. I sell the cookies on the side sometimes. It might be nice to get involved in some other baking. Do you do cookies at all?"

"Not at the moment, but I can't see them not being popular if we expanded the menu. My current location isn't set up to display stuff like this, but we could look into it for a second location if all the Billie stuff works out."

"Cool." Koji grinned. "Hit me up when it's moving forward. Are all the rest of you working at the bakery?"

"None of them at the moment," said Jasper. "Luca and I are talking about him apprenticing in the future. He'll have to do all the food safety classes and whatnot on his own, though when it comes to the actual baking I think that anyone can be taught."

The group of us sat together until the mimosas ran dry, and by then I was starting to feel a little claustrophobic with how many people were around me.

"Do you want me to take you outside for some air?" Jasper asked.

"Please." I smiled and nuzzled his cheek, wondering if he'd sensed my need for a break through the bond. "That would be lovely."

We excused ourselves from our guests with promises to return shortly.

My omega and I walked hand-in-hand down the stairs from the main level deck to the backyard below. He paused hesitantly in front of the greenhouse, and I couldn't help but wonder if he was remembering the last time we had been in there together. That wouldn't do. Jasper shouldn't have uncomfortable memories associated with his home. I had enough of those because of Alphonse, and I didn't want Jasper to have them because of me.

I pulled him inside and shut the door behind us, enveloping us in the thick scent of earth and plants and the warm heat of the little conservatory.

"Since we're here, I wanted to talk to you about something important," I said.

Jasper swallowed hard. "A good or bad important?"

"Good, I promise," I said, taking his hand to assure him. "First, I want to officially apologize for making you feel like I rejected you about your heat. I'm not going to apologize for doing what I thought was right for myself at the time, but I'm so sorry that it hurt you. I never want to do that again."

"Now that my brain is less of a hormone soup, I completely understand why you didn't feel like you could be here. I'm glad you came back, though."

"Me too." I burrowed into his arms and listened to the frantic thump of his heart. "This pack is so important to me. *You* are so important to me. I'm going to keep working on my self-confidence, and I'm going to do whatever I can to make every single member of this pack feel as incredible as you've all made me feel."

His arms tightened around me, and his sweet chocolate cinnamon scent overpowered the plants, tinging my every breath. He moved us over to the round couch in the middle of the conservatory, and I snuggled as close as I could get short of straddling his lap.

"I hate that I wasn't there when Alphonse broke in," Jasper said, voice cracking. "I want to be able to protect you."

"You *do* protect me. You don't have to fight someone to do

that. You protect me by making me feel safe and loved, and you've done that right from the start. Jasper—"

"Nicky—"

"I love you," we chorused.

The two of us burst into relieved laughter.

"You said the magic words," Jasper chuckled. "Now you're stuck with me."

"I was already stuck with you because of the surprise bond, but I can't think of anyone better to be stuck with."

"I'm really sorry about that, by the way. I know you weren't ready for something that big."

I had thought about it a lot since, and I needed him to understand. "I finished what you started, and whether or not I thought I wasn't ready at the time doesn't change the fact that I love being bonded to you. Maybe by the next heat I'll be ready to bond the others, but in the meantime, I like having this one special thing between us."

"Thank god for Billie going balls to the wall when they met you. We're so fucking lucky to have you, Nicky. I'm going to bake Billie some brownies to thank them for their unrelenting thirst."

I collapsed into laughter and snared him in a kiss and drank him in until I was breathless and needy, perfectly ready to climb on top of him right there in the greenhouse.

"Nicky, if we fuck out here, everyone's going to know. And I usually wouldn't mind, but my moms are here. I know that they know I have sex, but I don't want them to *know*, you know?"

I giggled helplessly. "Extremely fair. I'm not such a fan of my parents knowing, either."

Jasper and I went for a walk around the gated community until we had both calmed down enough to go back inside without arousing suspicion.

Chapter Fifty-Five
Nicky

I was bordering on hoarse from talking so much by the time all of our guests left for the day, but the energy from the greenhouse had sat at a low simmer in the background for me.

"Is it cool if I pick out some stuff from the playroom for tonight?" I asked.

The pack scents burst as one, and I breathed in all those gorgeous coffee shop and bakery smells. They had been so gentle with me since the break-in, and I was finally feeling well enough, in body and spirit, to dive back into how incredible they could make me feel.

"Pick out whatever you'd like," said Hana. "Do you need any help?"

"Nope. I think I'm okay. I'll grab anything that looks interesting, and then I'll leave it up to you to figure out what we do with what I gather."

Hana nodded. "Which room do you want to play in, and who do you want involved?"

"Maybe the gym? I liked the mirrors last time. And if everyone's up for it, I thought we could make it a whole pack affair."

I scampered away before the scent of them made me too needy and slipped downstairs.

The playroom was equally as intimidating as the last time I had been there, but there was more curiosity mixed in on this occasion.

I bee-lined for the wall full of colorful toys. I wasn't one-hundred-percent sure how the whole strap-on situation worked, but I definitely wanted Hana to fuck me with one. I picked out a fairly thick purple dildo with intriguing ridges down the length of it. Setting it atop one of the sharply angled ramps in the middle of the room, I went in search of some more items.

There was a set of hooks along a wall that held a series of poles, each of them with two or four cuffs attached. I picked out what looked like a fairly simple one with two cuffs at each end and grabbed another set of fuzzy wrist cuffs like Hana had used on me, adding them to the pile in the middle of the room. I grabbed a few bundles of rope, too. I wasn't entirely sure what we would do with them, but I figured: if they were here, then the pack knew how to use them.

A good portion of the stock they had were things that I had never seen before, let alone gotten experience with. Maybe in time I would get to try everything that was here.

I looked down at the pile I had acquired. If I needed other things to supplement to make them work, then I would let the pack pick those.

When I opened the door, I found Hana and Gabe wiping down the mats together. Both of their gazes locked on me.

"Find what you're looking for?" Hana asked.

"I think so?"

"Bring it out." She patted the mats. "Let's see what we can arrange for you."

I retreated and gathered up my treasures, pushing one of the ramps with my toes until I'd gotten it all out of the room, and Gabe grabbed the ramp for me, transporting it to the mats.

I laid everything out and Hana whistled. "Someone's feeling adventurous today."

"You guys have so much cool stuff. How was I supposed to pick?"

Hana cupped my cheeks and kissed me until I got squirmy in her grasp.

"I can think of quite a few things we can do with your little collection here. Now the question is: do you want it all focused on you, or would you like to have a little competition?"

The question sent a little thrill down my spine. "What kind of competition?"

"Beta versus beta. We can set you and Billie up the same and see which one of you beauties lasts the longest."

I shivered and squeezed my thighs together. "Competition sounds fun."

"Brave girl." Hana purred. "Let me grab a few more items to balance things out, then we'll go get the pack."

"Should I strip and kneel again?"

Heat flashed so hot in her eyes that I almost went down to my knees.

"Princesses don't strip themselves. We're going to peel off every bit of clothing for you, and you're going to watch it happen."

I swallowed hard.

"You wait right here. Gabe, go get the others."

Gabe kissed me before he left, eager hands kneading my butt cheeks until he finally pulled himself away and headed upstairs.

I stood there on the mats, flushed and needy, as I waited for everyone to return.

The energy shifted the moment the pack came into view. It lit a fire in my belly, and my breath came quicker.

Hana laid out two ramps, exchanging the one I had chosen

for one that had a gap in the center where my hips would go. I wasn't entirely sure what the gap was for, but I trusted her judgement. She also fetched doubles of most of the other items for Billie. Tony closed up the curtains, blocking us from the outside world, and Jasper dimmed the lights to half power.

Billie bounced over to me and stole a kiss. "Do you think you can outlast me, Books?"

"Nope." I laughed. "But I'm very interested in seeing how close I can get."

"Nicky, are you fine with the entire pack fucking you?" Hana asked.

"More than," I replied.

"Good." Hana pressed herself against my back and wrapped her arms around my waist. "This will be similar to when you played with Gabe and I—lots of attention, and you're going to get overwhelmed, but you can stop if you need to. Tell me your colors."

"Red to stop, yellow to slow down or readjust, green is good," I recited.

Hana laid a wet kiss on my throat. "Good girl."

I let out an embarrassing squeak at her words. She and Gabe took a place on either side of me while Jasper and Tony flanked Billie.

I was kissed by each in turn before Hana and Gabe set about stripping me down. Mouths and hands worshiped my skin as they first lifted my shirt off. Gabe slid to his knees in front of me. Perfect hazel eyes stared back at me.

Hana unhooked my bra, tossing it to the side, and Gabe sucked one of my nipples into his mouth, drawing a strangled cry from between my lips. I stared into the mirrors and saw Tony in the same position in front of Billie, Jasper peeling down their pants. Hana removed my own, and I stepped out of them when she tapped my ankles.

When she rose up again, she caught my gaze in the mirrors and bit down on the curve of my neck, hard enough to make me jump, but not so much to break the skin. Her fingers wandered and buried themselves under my panties, in between my already slick folds.

I wriggled in their grasp, panting and desperate though we had barely gotten started. They stripped off the last of my clothing and left me naked in front of the mirrors, Billie standing close enough to touch and equally naked. I took their hand, my eyes wandering over their pale skin.

Hana and Tony stepped away to grab the ropes from what I had selected. Billie and I stretched out our arms and spread our legs for the alphas to create an elaborate harness around our torsos, including strapping what I could only assume was a vibrating wand to our fronts, exactly where the bulb would meet our clits.

I shivered through the whole ordeal with nipples perked, pussy aching, and goosebumps covering every inch of me. Hana and Gabe checked over the entire apparatus to make sure nothing was too tight and did a brief test run, turning on the wand so that it buzzed against my clit and had a surprised curse leaping out of my mouth.

"Down on the ramp, princess," Hana ordered.

I kneeled carefully and glanced over to see Billie getting similarly situated. The gap in the ramp that I had questioned before fit the wand perfectly so it didn't dig into my body.

Gabe took my hands and wrapped each wrist in one of the fur-lined leather cuffs, linking them together and hooking one of the additional rope bundles to pin my arms out in front of me. He flipped up a bit of the floor, revealing the 'O' top of a heavy duty screw that he wove the rope through to secure me. Behind me, Hana locked the thick cuffs at the ends of the pole I'd chosen just above my knees.

"Have you ever used a spreader bar, princess?"

I shook my head.

"The one that you picked is telescopic. It will go further apart, but it'll lock in place if you try to bring your legs together again. Are you comfortable right now? Anything need to be adjusted?"

"I'm good. Green and ready to go," I replied.

I glanced over to see Billie similarly trussed up. Their blue eyes were luminous when they looked over at me with a cheeky grin.

Hana hooked herself up with a strap-on, adding the ridged purple dildo I had selected. "We'll start slow, one person each, to make sure our betas are warmed up, and then it's a free-for-all."

"Is there a prize for whoever lasts the longest?" Billie asked.

"Mostly bragging rights," said Hana. "Did you want me to go out and have a custom trophy made?"

Billie and I both giggled. I could imagine having a trophy like that in my room and the looks I would get from family when they visited.

"Everyone ready?" Hana asked.

"Ready!" Billie and I chorused. I could see the rest of the pack nod in the mirrors.

Hana fetched a couple of bottles of lube from the playroom, tossing one to Tony, and used her own to drip the lube directly onto my spread pussy, rubbing some onto the dildo.

She reached between my thighs and turned on the wand that had me immediately gasping, and arching. Hana palmed both of my ass cheeks, nudging my center with the tip of the dildo. My pussy flexed around it automatically. The buzz of the wand was already turning me into a mess, and I breathed through the sensation, willing my body to relax and welcome Hana. Each ridge that pressed inside was exquisite, an easy stretch, and unique enough that I felt every inch enter me.

I came from the wand before Hana had even finished warming me up, gasping and pulling on my cuffs as my body rode the wave of pleasure that was unrelenting from the buzz against my clit.

Hana's movements grew more fluid. I buried my face against the ramp and did my best to keep breathing. Billie's panting cries and Tony's groans as he fucked into them were a delectable soundtrack that only made it more difficult to keep control of myself.

I was going to lose this competition so fast.

Hana had gotten me to fourteen orgasms when she and I had played with Gabe. I wanted to match that at least.

Jasper and Hana traded places. I looked to the mirrors so I could see his face as he sank into me and my pussy squeezed him sharply as the wand forced another orgasm out of me. Jasper's movement stuttered, his fingers digging into my hips.

"Holy shit, Nicky," Jasper gasped. "So fucking perfect. You feel like a goddamn dream."

He began to fuck me as my pussy's grip eased off, and the slap of skin on skin joined the symphony of pleasure.

It was a good thing I was tied down. I had nowhere to go, and my only option was to take the sensations offered. Jasper rode me to his own completion, bucking so hard against me that I squeaked with every impact, the wand dragging me over another peak, my pussy squeezing hard as Jasper emptied himself into me with a breathy moan.

Tony took up his place behind me as Jasper stepped aside, and I groaned pitifully at the initial emptiness that was quickly replaced by Tony's cock, which stretched me open with the most perfect burn. He moved slowly to let me adjust.

I whined desperately, craving more while being unsure that I could even handle it.

I held onto the ropes in front of me like they were my only lifeline and rocked my hips back against Tony.

"Baby girl, you paint the prettiest picture right now. Let's see how deep you can take me."

I whined again, wriggling enough that the spreader bar inched wider and snapped into its new length.

Tony gathered up a handful of my hair to lift my face so he could watch it in the mirrors as he rocked his cock into the depths of my pussy.

"You're getting better, baby girl. I bet by Jasper's next heat you'll be able to take a knot."

The thought of it set a rush of excitement through my body, and my pussy spasmed around him, the wand carrying me away once again.

"Fuck." Tony gasped. "I can't wait to knot you. You're going to ruin me when the day comes."

"Yes, alpha."

Tony growled, goosebumps rising freshly on my skin at the sound.

He let my hair go, and I collapsed, panting back down to the ramp. Tony kept right on fucking me, forcing me through another pair of orgasms before finally sliding free. Gabe replaced him a moment later, but instead of a cock sliding into me it was three thick fingers that curled perfectly inside me, and had me thrashing against the swell of sensation.

The spreader bar clicked again, holding me a little bit wider.

It was all wonderfully, perfectly, *achingly* too much.

I couldn't catch my breath.

Every cell in my body hummed an overwhelming melody.

Gabe removed his fingers, replacing them with his cock, sliding as deep as my body would allow. He pinned me down further by the back of my neck, and I cried out, cock and wand breaking me one more time.

I'd stopped keeping track of how many times I had come. It was too hard to think. Gabe leaned over me, the warmth of his body trapping me even more.

"Fuck, princess. I feel like this pussy gets better every time you let me in."

I was bordering on hyperventilating beneath him. Dizziness swept over me, and I was a few seconds away from tapping out.

"Breathe for me," he ordered, slowing his thrusts. "Breathe with the pace."

I struggled to obey, inhaling as he drove deep and exhaling as he pulled free. The dizziness abated in increments, and I held my breath as I came again, Gabe nestling somehow deeper until his hips touched mine.

"Good girl." He growled in my ear. "One more, then you can have a break."

I shuddered and squirmed, throat dry from panting and pussy impossibly wet as he fucked me over the edge one more time. I screamed myself hoarse and buried my face against the ramp, babbling incoherently.

"Wand off?" Gabe asked. I nodded frantically, my nerves shot.

The buzzing disappeared almost instantly and all the tension melted out of my body at once. I glanced up at the mirror to see Hana behind us.

Gabe nuzzled my cheek. "Color?"

"Yellow? But don't move."

Hana inched around and kneeled by my head, gentle hand stroking my hair. "Are you up to some wax play to wind down?"

My brain flashbacked to when Tony had used the wax on me in my apartment. "Yes, please."

Hana disappeared into the playroom and returned with a plastic box of paraffin candles in a rainbow of colors as well as a small ramp. She lined the candles up on the floor and got a half dozen of them burning.

"Why so many?" I asked.

"Just to speed things along. We can use a little bit from all of them. Plus, more colors are fun."

Billie called for a break to see what we were up to.

The first droplets of hot wax hitting my skin anchored me, easing me down from the bright, vibrant high of being fucked six ways to Sunday by my pack.

"Color?" Hana asked.

"Green."

She nodded and tilted the candle again, sprinkling droplets of green wax over me. Red and yellow followed, then blue and white, painting my skin in her perfect canvas.

I wasn't sure what made it relaxing. I gasped and arched each time, but even so, the little pinpricks of heat were oddly peaceful.

Jasper undid the rope on my cuffs and removed the spreader bar so Gabe could roll me over and they could paint the front of me with wax instead. I mourned the loss of Gabe's cock for only a few seconds before he slipped back between my thighs.

Jasper leaned down and, cradling my face, kissed me until I couldn't remember any taste except for him. My omega dipped

469

wicked fingers to tease my clit with slow circles, supplementing the easy pace Gabe had set. My breathing degraded to panting and whining, my body already primed and hovering on the edge.

"Will you come for me, Nicky?" Jasper asked, bracing his hand on the cuffs that bound my wrists over my head.

I nodded frantically, his fingers coaxing me up at the sharp peak of pleasure. "Jasper, please."

Hana tipped more wax, decorating both my body and Jasper's arm as Gabe's pace picked up and Jasper followed, the two of them ruining me together. My pussy clamped down on Gabe, making his every movement felt twofold until his hips met mine again. I listened to his gorgeous moans as he lost himself too and Billie's perfect cries as Tony fucked them up to the edge and over.

I was half asleep and floating on a cloud by the time they had finished with me. They removed the wax from my skin carefully, and I let the pack manhandle me into the showers next to the gym. They washed me up with a tenderness that had tears slipping over my cheeks. I wasn't sure how they could tell when my face was already wet from the shower, but they cuddled me tighter all the same.

Our next stop was the hot tub. They carried Billie and I into the frothing water, and I was nestled onto Gabe's lap, Hana leaning against my back with her arm around my waist. Jasper sat on Gabe's other side, holding Billie's and my legs across his, and Tony held the rest of Billie securely.

"You beat your record, princess," Hana said.

I lifted my drowsy head and angled myself to kiss her before I spoke. "Did I?"

"Yep. I counted for you. You made it up to sixteen."

"Good job, Books!" Billie said. "I have no idea what I got to."

"Fifteen," Tony supplied. "If I didn't miss any. One less orgasm, but you outlasted for time."

"Snacks?" I asked, tucking my face against the curve of Gabe's throat to breathe in his sugary tea scent.

His chuckle sounded infinitely loud in my ear.

"What kind would you like?" Gabe asked. "There's still some left over from the party."

"Leftovers are for breakfast," said Billie. "We need special post-sex snackies."

"Tony pancakes?" I asked.

"We could go slightly fancier and make them Tony waffles," he offered.

"I'm happy with anything you put in my mouth."

Billie cackled.

I was too worn out to blush.

After we had stayed in the water long enough for my stomach to start growling, we rinsed off the chlorine, and I was carted upstairs.

"We should have a kitchen nest so that I can snuggle in while food is happening," I suggested.

"Don't tempt me into more construction," said Billie. "Cuz I'll do it."

Tony and Jasper got rolling on our waffles, and Hana fetched Billie and I packages of gummy bears from the pantry and a glass of water each to tide us over. I ate my confection and drank my water while standing in the kitchen, plastered to Gabe, Billie against my back, as we watched the food come to fruition.

Hana whipped us up an apple pie topping for the waffles, and by the time I was done with my treat, enough food had been made so we could sit down together at the kitchen table and stuff our faces.

"Can we all sleep in my room tonight?" I asked.

"Of course," said Hana. "Why don't you pick us out a movie to watch so you don't ruin your sleep schedule?"

After I was all waffled up, I flipped through the streaming options and picked out an action adventure romance about an omega spy.

Despite my best efforts, I ended up falling asleep on Hana and woke only to make the trek up to my bedroom. We piled into my bed, Spud and Roscoe joining us as soon as we were settled, and curled up under the plethora of blankets.

I was still a little in awe of how full and wonderful my life had become, and I owed it all to my late night library job, the one my mom had insisted would keep me from happiness. Joke's on her, because I found the perfect love with this pack.

A bunch of night owls.

Just like me.

Bonus Chapter

*A note before you move onto the bonus chapter. There will be a pregnancy plot line in book 2. If that's not your thing, stop reading now and let the story stand on its own (minus the unresolved Councillor plotline). The bonus chapter will introduce a separate conflict to be resolved in the rest of book 2, and I don't want you stuck with a cliffhanger if the contents of the next book aren't to your taste <3

Content Warnings for Part Two:

Police (intense interactions between a POC and police, home search, questioning, misgendering, arrests, corruption, improper procedure, violence), pregnancy (and eventual birth), mpreg, gun violence, threat to pregnant people, kidnapping, premature labor, parental abuse and manipulation towards their adult child (both current and references to past issues), transphobia (deliberate misgendering and deadnaming that is challenged on page), needles for medical injections, discussion of fertility issues, and scenes in a hospital.

Please be aware the police CW is present in the bonus chapter.

Chapter One
November
Nicky

I cuddled against Jasper's side while he stirred a giant pot of marinara for our eventual dinner of chicken parmigiana. We were only a few days out from the end of his heat, and while he and the alphas had bounced back quickly, I was a little slower on the recovery front. Hana helped me with physio a couple of times a day, and there was no shortage of cuddles and care while I physically healed. Emotionally, things were...slightly less optimal. My therapist was great, and I'd been to her twice now, but I had a lot of baggage to work through between my own self-esteem issues and the abuse Alphonse had put me through. It felt good to have taken the step, though. I wanted to be the very best version of myself for my pack.

Jasper kissed my forehead, soft affection flowing through our bond, before lifting the spoon so I could taste test the sauce. I darted out my tongue to sample some.

"Hmm, needs a few more red pepper flakes, I think."

Jasper took his own taste and nodded decisively, red curls bobbing with the movement. "You're absolutely correct."

I tucked my face against his throat, breathing in his chocolate cinnamon scent. It didn't quite mesh with the deliciousness of the bubbling marinara, but I was ready to consume them both.

Billie popped up in my peripheral vision and wiggled their way between Jasper and me. "My attention stores are running low."

I giggled and kissed their temple, tucking their purple curls behind their ear before squeezing them until they squeaked.

"Taste, please," Billie said, popping open their mouth like a baby bird.

I sprinkled in more red pepper flakes, and Jasper gave it a stir before letting Billie test it out.

"Fuck yeah. That's perfecto."

Knocking pounded on the door, and the three of us turned towards it. Tension radiated through me so fiercely my head instantly ached, muscles going taut as my shoulders leapt up to my ears. The alphas looked up from where they were lounging on the couch nest, and Gabe hopped over the back of it, the first one on the way to the door. Visitors we didn't know about were exceptionally rare, considering the pack house was in a gated community with security at the entry gate.

Gabe opened our front door, and I held my breath as three men came into view wearing jeans and jackets with police badges hanging from chains around their necks. All three were average in every way, and I wouldn't have been able to pick them out of a crowd. Billie slipped away from us and moved to Gabe's side.

"We're here to speak with Antonio Agani," one of them said. "Can we come inside?"

Hana and Tony were up off the couch nest in an instant.

"Nope," Billie snapped. "I'm the property owner, and I don't give you permission to enter. If you need to talk to anyone here, it can be off premises and with a lawyer present."

Tony came into the kitchen to stand with us, putting his body between us and the police, while Hana moved to flank Gabe. Jasper flicked off the stove, all our attention focusing on the trio at our door.

The officers frowned. "We're going to have to insist. Antonio Agani is a person of interest in an arson case, and we have a warrant to search the property. Please step aside."

I held my breath, latching onto Tony's arm as Gabe pulled Billie out of the way. Our beta was instantly on their phone, calling who I could only assume was a lawyer. Everyone around me was stiff as a board.

Hana pulled out her phone from her pocket and held it up to the officers. "I'll escort you and record your search."

Billie ended their call and glared at the officers, raising their phone. "Phones out, cameras on."

Jasper and Gabe did the same. I'd left mine upstairs in my room, and Tony seemed frozen in place.

"Badge numbers, names, and precinct numbers, please," Billie asked sharply. "Our lawyer is en route. I'm going to need to see a copy of that warrant as well."

The middle officer rolled his eyes. "My name is Detective Jensen. This is Detective Brown and Officer Rosenberg." He gestured to the men at his sides. They didn't look happy about it, but they did state the information Billie asked for.

"There are only five registered members of this pack," Detective Jensen stated. "Which of you is the guest here?"

Hana growled when I started to raise my hand, and I tucked it back out of sight.

"You said you were here for a search," said Gabe, "so search. Questions aren't part of that."

Officer Rosenberg stepped towards the kitchen. "I need to take note of the IDs of everyone in the premises at this time. Is there anyone else here right now?"

"Just our two cats," said Gabe.

The officer nodded. "The detectives will be doing the search. If everyone could grab their ID for me, I'll record them."

"Mine is upstairs," I squeaked. "I left my purse in my room."

"Jensen and Brown can take you up," Officer Rosenberg told me.

I stepped away from Jasper and Tony, trying not to shake as numbness crept into my fingertips and my chest locked up. Hana was next to me a moment later, wrapping her arm around my waist.

"We'll all go up together," Hana said. "Jasper and Tony can stay with Rosenberg, and the rest of us will go with the detectives."

I trudged up the stairs at Hana's side as if I were climbing up to the gallows. Billie and Hana never once strayed in keeping their phone cameras trained on the detectives. They started in my room. It made me queasy to watch them dig through my shelves and drawers, so I took my purse and retreated downstairs. I fished my ID out of my wallet and handed it to Officer Rosenberg.

His eyebrows climbed up his forehead as he read it. "Ms. Marino, you've been difficult to track down."

I blinked. "Why would you need to track me down?"

"Because you're also a person of interest in this case."

I stared at him, completely uncomprehending. They thought I had burned down my library? My *sanctuary*? It was such an absurd idea that I would have laughed if my anxiety hadn't shot through the roof at his words. Panic turned in my gut, and I took a deep breath to quell the swell of nausea.

"*What?!*" Jasper snapped.

"You called out of work the day before the fire and went completely MIA. That's not the behavior of an innocent person."

"That's because she was here for my heat," insisted Jasper.

Tony's hand clamped down on Jasper's arm. "Don't say anything until Billie's lawyer gets here."

The irony of the situation wasn't lost on me. They had originally told me there was nothing they could do about Alphonse stalking me and breaking into my apartment because the evidence was circumstantial, and now they had shown up at our door telling me I was part of an investigation because I happened to not be at work the day of the fire. At least they had *that* on me. I couldn't even imagine what they had cobbled together in their minds to link Tony to the fire.

Tony ushered me over, and I burrowed into his arms. "Take a deep breath for me. We all know you were here. You have nothing to worry about, baby girl."

"Why do they think you did something?"

"Your guess is as good as mine."

Knowing both he and I were innocent did absolutely nothing to help my anxiety. Two men were rooting around our home, trying to prove the opposite. The minutes stretched on into eternity as we waited for them to finish the search. An hour later they finally returned to the main floor with a container of something in a plastic evidence bag.

"I want to state *again* that this is absolute bullshit!" Billie yelled behind the cops. "I am literally an artist with an in-home studio. Of course I have fucking paint thinner in there. What the fuck does this have to do with the fire?"

"Ma'am—"

"Not a ma'am," Billie hissed.

"Regardless, paint thinner is an accelerant—"

"So is fucking *hairspray*. And nail polish remover. And fucking *alcohol*. You're gonna arrest someone because we have a bottle of scotch in the cupboard or we paint our nails? My lawyer is going to rip y'all a new one."

The pack coalesced around Tony and me in a protective circle.

"Let's hurry the sweep up," Detective Jensen ordered. "Marino, Agani, you're with us. The rest of you step away."

Jasper hesitated in front of me. The world narrowed down to pinpoints, panic clawing its way up my body. I'd never gotten in trouble growing up. I'd lived to please authority as a child, and now that the police were looking at me like I'd done something terrible, it made me want to throw up. I clung harder to Tony. What if we couldn't prove we'd done nothing? I'd only just gotten my pack, and now they were trying to tear us apart.

"Books!" Billie patted my cheek, and I shifted my gaze to them. "You're both innocent, and I've got a lot of money and some kickass lawyers to prove it. I'm putting the full weight of my name and fortune behind both of you."

Gabe's hands turned my face to him, his thumbs wiping away tears I hadn't realized were streaking down my cheeks. "Nicky, it's all going to be okay. We'll get the evidence we need. Billie's lawyer is already on her way, and we'll meet you at the station, okay? Don't say a word until you see us again."

Jasper and Hana murmured similar assurances to Tony, but their words faded in and out, all of my energy focused on not sinking to the floor.

"I said *step away*." Detective Jensen planted his feet, crossing his arms. "If you all don't back off in the next three seconds, we're going to cuff them."

Tony's arm wrapped around my waist, and I curled my fingers into his shirt as the pack reluctantly moved away from us.

Detective Brown, who hadn't said a word while in my presence, patted the cuffs hanging from his belt. "You two, come with me. Jensen and Rosenberg will finish the sweep once you're secured."

My feet felt like blocks of cement as we followed him out to the cruiser and climbed into the back seat. Tony sat stiffly next to me. I couldn't stop the escape of a sob as Detective Brown slammed the car door and returned to the pack house.

"What now?" I whispered.

"We wait." Tony took my hand, and I snuggled up to his side. "Billie is going to go feral over this and their lawyer is top notch. We just have to hope they can find a way to prove we were at the pack house the entire time."

"And if they can't?"

Tony laid his palm on the back of my neck and kissed my forehead. "Don't think about that, baby girl."

Detective Brown offered a smile that made me uneasy, a sharp gleam in his gaze.

I sucked in a sharp breath, pushing down the swell of nausea at his words. I wanted to believe that the pack could protect us, but...what if they couldn't?

Acknowledgments

Thank you as always to Vera Valentine for being my literary rock, listening to me flail about this story, and reading over it with me as I wrote. You're the bestest bookspouse and you deserve the world <3

Thank you to everyone who loved my story in the early days: my patrons (Lindsay and Kylee <3), and my beta reader team (Sienna, Kristen, Kai, Cassie, Kayleigh, Poppy, Devon, Mylan, Jen, and Kylee). Y'all ROCK! This book is better because of you and I am infinitely grateful for you loving my story.

Thank you to Kristen, not only for being an awesome friend and for loving my stories, but for stepping up to help me proofread.

And, finally, thank you to all my readers. I couldn't do this without you <3

Also By Sierra
Omegaverse

Nicky and the Night Owls: Part Two

Sidney & Allie

Luca & Luna

A Perfect Pack Christmas: A Nicky and the Night Owls Novella

Conference Confidential

Heat Play Love

First Heat

First Heat: Second Chances

First Heat: Tying The Knot

Contemporary

Salacious Salvation

Playtime with Professor

Paranormal

Into The Depths

Want to connect? Find Sierra here:

Website and Newsletter Sign Up: sierracassidyauthor.com

Twitter: @SierraCassidyXO

Instagram: @sierracassidyauthor

Tiktok: @sierracassidyauthor

Facebook Group: Sierra Cassidy's Sinners